JOA

# Flames
# On the Hill

# Flames
# On the Hill

*Angela O'Neill*

PIATKUS

First published in Great Britain in 1993 by
Judy Piatkus (Publishers) Ltd of
5 Windmill Street, London W1

**The moral right of the author
has been asserted**

*A catalogue record for this book is available
from the British Library*

ISBN 0 7499 0177 2

Phototypeset in 11/12pt Compugraphic Times by
Action Typesetting Limited, Gloucester
Printed and bound in Great Britain by
Biddles Ltd, Guildford & King's Lynn

For Derek

# Author's Note

The historical background of this story is the period of Landlordism in Ireland. In 1879 Michael Davitt founded the Land League. Charles Stewart Parnell became its President. The league was formed to carry on the campaign against the landlords, but it was not until the Wyndham Land Purchase Act of 1903 that a Bill was passed which finally ended their power in Ireland.

It was the custom to light a bonfire on the hill to call the attention of the people. When the flames burnt low it was a signal that a meeting was to be held at the parochial house hall. When the flames burnt sky high, it was a sign of rejoicing.

## Bibliography

*History of Landlordism in Donegal* by Frances O'Gallagher
*The Course of Irish History* by Moody & Martin
*Victorian England* by W.J. Reader
*A Century of the Scottish People* T.C. Smout
*A Short Story of the Irish History* by Seumas MacManus
*Mevagh* by Leslie Lucas
*The Life and Times of Winston Churchill* by Malcolm Thomas
*Maud Gonne* by Nancy Cardozo
*The Rat Pit* By Patrick MacGill
*Daughters of Erin* by Elizsbeth Coxhead
*A Servant of the Queen* by Maud Gonne MacBride

Rent. Who speaks of the rent?

We Irish, who till the soil

Are ever ready to pay the tribute your laws
impose:

You, the conquering race, have portioned
to each his toil,

We, the conquered, bring the ransom due
to our woes.

WILFRID SCAWEN BLUNT (1840–1922)

# Chapter One

'Is it true, Sean,' Tom Logue the school master asked, 'that Parnell, a member of the English Parliament, is to be made President of this Land League we hear so much about?'

''Tis right enough,' Sean O'Neill replied wearily. Over the past few days he had been travelling on horseback from Lisdare to Slievegar, breaking the journey in Dilford to see his lawyer. He had been anxious to attend this parish meeting, then to get home to his wife who was expecting their first child.

'And when do you think that all the grand ideas that this Land League proposes will reach our wee part of Ireland?'

Before Sean could reply, Skin-the-goat Duffy, as he was called, shouted out: 'Wid ye tell me for the love of God, why the son of a Protestant landowner should fight beside a Fenian like Michael Davitt?'

Sean smiled. 'Well, it seems that Parnell has an American mother.'

'Sean ... ' Father Gibson hurried into the hall. 'I've just heard word that your wife is near her time. Perhaps you had better hasten home now.'

Startled, he jumped quickly to his feet, knocking back the chair he was sitting on. 'Father, the child's not due for weeks yet.'

'Ah, well,' the priest said confused, 'it may not be the right way of the story. Someone called by the house and told my housekeeper. That's where I got it from.'

Sean dashed out of the hall and mounted his horse again.

The wind which had been blowing steadily all evening had increased. He took a short cut across Duffy's land, not caring for the first time in his life that he was abusing another farmer's crops. The westerly wind began to whip at his face, making the horse toss its head sideways and slowing their progress. We'd have done better in the shelter of the roadway he thought, tugging at the reins and changing their direction.

They galloped across Togher Glen to a low white-stoned wall which reminded him of a batch of well-floured baps on the pantry shelf. Out on the highway again, the fury of the gale battled with the trees which on a fine night made friendly gestures to travellers on the lonely Togher road. He spoke comfortingly to his horse but the words were shredded by the cutting wind and rain. When they reached the bridge of Cresslow the force of the elements came roaring down the river and buffeted them across the road. Sean tightened his grip on the reins, fearing that they would both land in the river below. Then without warning, the animal went down on its forelegs; the reins were wrenched from his hands and he went flying towards the wall.

Sean flung out his arms and gripped the edge of the rough stones. Below the swirling water tugged at his legs as he fought for a firmer hold on the wall. Afterwards he wondered how long he had been dangling in that precarious position before he was able to haul himself to safety. The animal, which had quickly righted itself, did not desert him.

With great care he led the horse off the bridge. A mounting sense of urgency made him ignore the friendly glow from a friend's farm, where he could have changed his breeches and enjoyed a warming drink while his exhausted horse was cared for. Even so, he began to consider the priest's words again. Perhaps a man of the roads had called at Garton, and hearing that the mistress was expecting assumed it was immediate. That was the way tales got round the countryside. The travelling men liked to bring a bit of gossip in return for a bite to eat. Hadn't Theresa herself assured him before he left that she was in the best of health? And anyway, she said, it wouldn't be the first baby that Biddy Coll had brought into the world, if such an emergency arose.

2

The lighted windows of Garton shone out in the night. A hurricane lamp had been placed at the end of the drive and another outside the stable door. When Sean rode into the yard, Paddy, one of the farmhands, came running from the kitchen. Without a word he took hold of the reins as his master slipped off the animal's back.

He was accustomed to seeing his wife or Biddy Coll, the housekeeper, sitting at the spinning wheel at this time of the evening. A roaring fire filled the hearth; above it hung an iron kettle which spat furiously into the flames. He moved the crane hurriedly, not bothering to lift the kettle off the crook. Just as he made for the inner door, Biddy came through it with tears streaming down her face.

'Willie's gone across the fields for the priest, Mr O'Neill.' He stared at her. 'Yer wife ... she's passed away. 'Twas before her time and the doctor wasn't at home.' The woman wrung her hands in despair. 'I've helped to bring many's a child into the world but ...' She sobbed incoherently as Sean tore up the stairs, the sound of his feet ringing out protestingly on the wood.

At two o'clock the following morning Biddy Coll and the two farmhands were still sitting around the fire drinking tea. The practical and distressing task of laying out the body of her dead mistress and attending to the child had kept the housekeeper busy. The little one in the cradle was her main concern now.

'Under God, what's to be done wi' the child?' she cried.

''Tis a fearful problem right enough,' Paddy said, which was all he ever offered when any kind of emergency arose at Garton.

'What about Grace Boyce o'er in Iskaglen?' Willie said thoughtfully. 'She lost a wee thing a few days ago.'

'You say?' Biddy's eyes brightened. 'That might be the answer. Willie, take yerself there in the morning and ask the woman if she'll nurse Sean O'Neill's child?'

'Ah, Jayus, Biddy, sure I'd be lost for words on such a matter. If the wind is down I'll take yerself o'er in the trap.You spake to her. Widden ye ask the master afore makin' such a move?'

3

'He's past caring. Is it a clean house?'
'None better.'

It was Sean O'Neill who went to Iskaglen peninsula the following morning and returned with Grace Boyce, accompanied by her two daughters. Grace's husband was agreeable about managing on his own. Indeed, he had not much say in the matter for the white-faced master of Garton was determined that this was the way things should be arranged.

The woman and her two children were settled in an upstairs room containing a large comfortable bed, a pink washbasin and jug, and a wooden cradle that had been in the house for over a hundred years. Grace felt that she had landed in the lap of luxury; the sheets were pure linen and there was an abundance of food. Also, the ache in her heart was eased as well as the pain in her bound breasts when she took Rosha O'Neill into her arms.

Nellie, the eldest girl, helped with the baby and made herself useful in the kitchen when she came home from school.

'Can I come and work here when I leave school?' she kept asking Biddy Coll.

And every time the question was raised, Biddy assured her laughingly, 'I'll have a word wi' the master.'

Bridie, at three years old, never left her mother's side. She played with baby Rosha but hated the demanding wee thing who claimed all her mother's attention. Her sister Nellie, who used to pet her, had no time for her now either.

Rosha O'Neill thrived over the next few months and brought a smile back to her father's face. When she was weaned, Biddy Coll put the cradle in the kitchen where Sean's daughter had the constant attention of the entire household.

Seven years later, Biddy kept her word and Nellie Boyce was hired to work at Garton.

# Chapter Two

'Rosha O'Neill, get out of the corn this minute or I'll skelp ye!' Nellie Boyce shouted.

'I'll race you to the shore, Nellie.'

'Ah, get out, pet. 'Tis plundering its goodness ye are, and it all ready for cuttin'. Sweet heaven, there's the men wi' the scythes. *Get out!* They'll be tellin' Biddy Coll I let you run wild and I'll lose me place.'

The thought of Garton without Nellie was unimaginable. Though Rosha had been reminded often enough by Biddy that *she* was the one who had pulled her into the world ten years ago, before her dear mammy crept out of it to a better place, it was Nellie Boyce she loved. As she grew older, Rosha realised that the housekeeper's words were unfortunate because they had built up a vague resentment towards her dead mother. There was a feeling that she had deliberately crept out of the world to a better place.

'Hurry now,' Nellie urged, 'for Biddy wants a basketful of winkles for supper. Here, take the wee can and get to work.'

She tied the straps of Rosha's pinny, tightened the blue bow on her long dark hair, then catching up her own red flannel skirt the servant girl skipped across the seaweed, her sturdy boots landing confidently on the rocks.

Slievegar Bay was practically landlocked. Across the bay was the peninsula of Iskaglen where small stone-bound fields reached down to the shore. Beyond, were smooth green glens and low hills shaded blue in the late-afternoon sun. The dark woods that fell to the shore near where Nellie and

Rosha worked, marked the boundary between Sir Thomas Catalong's estate and Sean O'Neill's land.

Rosha watched as Nellie worked the hinges of two scallops together, trying to prise them open to search for the precious pearl that would signal untold wealth for her and enable her to buy passages to America for herself and family.

'Ye'd have better luck with oysters,' Biddy Coll said tartly every time she caught her at it. 'And aren't ye the lucky one to have a good place in the house of O'Neill, one of the few men around here who owns his own land?'

'What are you doing?'

The unexpected voice made Rosha start and trip over her can which was half-full of shellfish. A boy dressed in a fine tweed jacket and knickerbockers was looking at her curiously.

'Picking winkles for supper.'

A tall woman in a dark grey bombazine gown with a toque to match emerged from the trees. Fascinated, Rosha studied the frizzy hair that fell below the brim. Nellie told her once that fashionable ladies were known to glue those curls to their foreheads. The woman called to the boy in a foreign accent. He shrugged.

'In a minute, mam'selle.' The French woman looked disapprovingly at Nellie and Rosha, then turned and walked away.

'What is your name?' the boy asked.

The imperious tone annoyed her. It was as if he felt he had a right to know. Or maybe it was his strange accent that made the question sound like a command. 'Rosha O'Neill. What's yours?' She guessed who he was. It might cut him down to size if she pretended not to.

'Edmund Catalong. I live at Merifield, around the other side of the bay.' He smiled with an unexpected shyness. 'People here call it a castle but it's only an ordinary manor house. My father and I have just returned from England.'

Nellie's head turned sharply and a flash of alarm crossed her face. Lowering her skirt, she scrambled up to the boat lying on the shingle, snatched her shawl and called, 'C'mon, Rosha, we'll go along the shore.' Before they could move away, a man emerged from the path running from the woods.

'Go home, Edmund,' he said irritably, 'Madamoiselle is waiting for you.' Nellie bobbed a curtsey, picked up her bucket and grabbed Rosha's hand.

'Ah, I see you've been stealing some of my shellfish, young woman,' Sir Thomas Catalong said.

'Stealing, sir?' she retorted indignantly, forgetting for a moment that she was addressing her betters. 'I think by right the shore and the water in the bay belong to neither God nor man.'

'You are mistaken,' he said easily, 'I own all the mineral rights on this shore.'

Nellie recalled the incident the men were discussing the other night when they came to ceildhe at Garton, something about a farmer removing the skin of a dead horse washed up on the beach. When Sir Thomas Catalong heard about it he demanded the skin, declaring that anything cast up by the sea belonged to him. And sure her own father, when he was alive, dared not snare a hare or rabbit even though they were destroying his crops. Poor crops meant no money in the house, though nevertheless the rent would be demanded without mercy while not even a piece of bog-fir could be taken out of the bog to help the household finances. Oul Tom Cat claimed the lot.

Anger gave her rein to her tongue. 'Sure I won't deprive ye of yer rights, sir, but I've been pickin' on this shore since I came to work at Garton.'

Thomas Catalong stepped back quickly as Nellie went to tip the contents of her bucket at his feet. A light came to his eyes at such a defiant gesture from one of the lower orders. She glanced at the handsome, dissolute face close to her own and the black eyes with the devil looking out of them. Sweet Christ deliver me, she prayed.

'I would like to offer you work at Merifield, my dear,' he said smoothly.

'Thanks, yer honour, but I'm well settled with Mr O'Neill at Garton,' she replied hurriedly, the colour heightening her round cheecks.

Rosha, who had moved a little distance away, realised that

7

something was wrong. She ran across and tugged at Nellie's skirt just as Sir Thomas asked, 'What is your name?' He turned impatiently. 'Run off child.'

Nellie, thankful for the interruption, bobbed a quick curtsey, picked up her bucket and, clasping her charge's hand, hurried away.

'Wait, Nellie, 'til I get my can.' Before Nellie could stop her, Rosha ran down to the rock. She found Edmund Catalong sitting behind it picking up the winkles which had spilt from the can. He looked up, his straight light brown hair falling across his brow.

'Has he gone,' he asked.

'Are you meaning your father?'

'I am.'

'I think he's frightened Nellie,' Rosha said severely. 'I don't think I like your father.'

Edmund tossed another winkle into the can and, handing it to her, said, 'I don't like him either.'

The kitchen at Garton House was large with a wide fireplace. A built-in dresser stacked with blue and white crockery filled one wall; next to it was a door that led to the room where Paddy and Willie slept. When young Mrs O'Neill came as a bride to Garton in 1875 with a fine dowry, including a servant girl, she soon realised that her husband was not going to change the tradition of the house. It had always been a place where neighbours came to ceildhe. An accomplished craftswoman, who expected her servants to occupy themselves in the evening with needlework, she talked Sean into opening up the fireplace in the dining-room where he could enjoy the company of his friends without the prattle of the womenfolk. Biddy knew very well what was behind her dead mistress' suggestion. The dear soul couldn't stomach the oul clay pipes, not to mention the spittin' in the hearth.

With the door between the two rooms left ajar, Biddy was able to hear what was going on in the parish without setting a foot outside the house. I'm well set-up for life, she often thought contentedly, looking around the stone-flagged kitchen where shanks of ham and bunches of herbs hung from the black beams, Mistress of Garton and no oul husband to bother her. Not run off her feet either, with Nellie to give a hand.

Biddy raised her head from the churn when the servant girl came into the kitchen with Rosha skipping at her heels.

'Careful, pet,' she said when Rosha took the plunger from her, 'the butter's nearly ready.' They pulled up the lid and peered down at the rich creamy crust. 'Nellie,' Biddy called, 'bring o'er the crock.' Turning, she caught the expression on the girl's face. 'What's the matter?'

Nellie gave a warning nod in Rosha's direction. Disturbed by her unusual pallor and agitated expression, the house-keeper said hastily, 'Be off, Rosha, and see if you can find me a few fresh eggs.'

'Oh, Mrs Coll,' Nellie cried, 'a terrible thing's happened to me.' She explained about Sir Thomas Catalong approaching her on the shore.

'Musha, he'll be after you,' the older woman said tact-lessly. 'Anyone that catches that man's fancy ...'

'I told him I was Sean O'Neill's servant and didin need a position at the castle. D'ye think that'll be an end of it?'

With feverish movements Biddy Coll washed and salted the butter, then beat it into shape with a pair of ridged platters. 'Be off home wi' ye at once and warn yer mother. 'Tis the wise thing to do.'

'Sure, Biddy, the oul devil canna *make* me go to work at the castle. Mr O'Neill wid stand by me.'

'Bless ye, child, I know the master is the only man in Slievegar and Iskaglen able to stan' up t'him, but doesn't Catalong own the house ye live in and the bit o' land? If ye refuse to go he'll evict yer family like many's a wan.'

'Sweet God, I wish the flames of hell wid claim him soon.'

'Hush! There's Rosha.'

The two servants began to converse swiftly in Irish, then Nellie took her shawl from the nail behind the door and wrapped it around her shoulders.

'I'll tell the master it's time to visit yer mam,' the housekeeper said. 'We'll not disturb him wi' the true story ... not yet. O'Neill is a fierce man when aroused

9

and might take the law into his own hands, God protect us.'

Rosha took the basketful of eggs down to the pantry. Why had Nellie slipped away home in such a panic? No one had called at the house to leave a message.

'Go and get a needle to help me with the winkles,' Mrs Coll said tersely, worried that Catalong might waylay Nellie on the way home.

Rosha hated this task because the winkles reminded her of worms. Quietly, without protesting, because Biddy suddenly seemed old and tired, she went over to the window where the big velvet pincushion hung and chose a needle to probe through the shells.

Nellie Boyce tore across the field to the road. Looking carefully in all directions, she jumped off the hedge and crossed to the next field which led to the shore. Here the bay narrowed to a stream which was crossed by a wooden footbridge. Before she was the owner of a fine pair of boots, Nellie had always paddled across in her bare feet to reach her home in Iskaglen. She ran up through the glen, not stopping as was her custom to drink from the little stream and breathe in the sparkling clear air. People living on the peninsula swore that the air was better here than across the bay.

Within a mile of home, she saw her sister Bridie driving their two cattle in the direction of the hamlet where they lived. 'Bridie . . .' she called.

The young girl turned round, leapt into the air with delight and raced down the hill towards her. 'What are you doin' atal? Sure 'tis no time since you were home.' The sisters hugged each other, linked arms and walked towards the hill. Bridie was tall and slender with fine bones, not like Nellie who was stoutly built. Both had heavy dark eyebrows. Of the two, Nellie's hair was darker, almost black, whereas her sister's was a rich dark brown.

'How's Mam?'

'She's well, thank God. How's Miss spoilt Rosha O'Neill?'

'Ye shouldn't talk of m'master's daughter like that,' Nellie told her.

10

Bridie's eyes danced mischievously. 'Sure we're milk-sisters.' She raised her grey homespun skirt to her knees, leapt over a large stone, then danced around excitedly. 'Why are you back so soon again? Is it a fella? Have ye been asked for?'

'Fella? Who'd want to marry me without a ha'penny to my name?' Bridie's face fell at the sound of her sister's voice, 'Then ye've been dismissed. Where's yer bundle?'

'M'darlin, 'tis neither of them things. I just want to see Mam about somethin'. Come on, let's get the cattle home.'

The sound of horses coming around the bend in the road made Nellie grip her sister's arm in alarm. They were not farm horses whose feet struck the road with a heavy ring; the movement had the sound of the highly bred steeds owned by the gentry. There was nowhere to run and hide. She and Bridie were on the face of the hill, and the low stone wall would not conceal them.

'That'll be Sir Thomas Catalong and his agent,' Bridie said excitedly. 'I'll be able to get a good peep at them from here. Mam's forever makin' me hide when we hear them on the road.'

Fear tightened Nellie's grip on Bridie's arm. What was she going to do?

'Och,' she tutted, 'the lace on m'boot has come undone again.' She bent down quickly as the two men passed by. Pray God he wouldn't recognise her. The sound of Catalong's voice rang out discordantly through the mellow evening.

The horses stopped. Desperately Nellie tugged at the lace. Out of the tail of her eye she saw to her horror that Bridie was curtseying and smiling in her warm open-faced way. The expression on Sir Thomas' face as he stared at Bridie changed her feeling of alarm into one of sheer panic. No longer concerned about herself, she jumped to her feet and put a protective arm around her young sister's shoulder. Catalong looked surprised, then indifferent, at Nellie's sudden appearance. His eyes crept over the younger girl again and he smiled.

The agent who had accompanied him cantered discreetly

on down the road, well used to his master's enthusiasm where young women were concerned. Nellie grabbed Bridie's hand and raced around the foot of the hill out of sight, as far away from their home as possible. He mustn't find out where they lived. She kept to the difficult parts of the land where a man on horseback might hesitate to take his valuable animal.

'What are you doin' atal, Nellie?' her sister complained. 'The cattle will be through that fine fence his honour put up and ye know what that means. They'll be taken from us and put in the compound.'

Her sister raced on.

'Nellie Boyce, ye haven't a wit o' sense. Will ye stop it now?'

Nellie slowed down and in the shelter of a boreen threw herself on the ground, panting. 'Whist, will ye!' She wound up her long hair which had come undone.

'Ah, Nellie, listen to me.' There was the sound of tears in Bridie's voice. 'Mam said Sir Thomas had been considerate to her, fixing up the oul hen house after daddy died.'

'When he took away one of our fields.'

'But he's allowing us free grazing on the hill for the cattle. Arrah, ye'll have us in great trouble this day.'

Nellie looked at her fourteen-year-old sister and said severely, 'You just keep out o'sight of them castle folk. Come on now, home to Mam.'

'Yer a crabbit oul thing.'

When they arrived back at the hamlet, Blackie the dog was easing their two cows into the yard. 'Aren't ye the wee dote?' Bridie cried, flinging her arms around the collie. ''Tis up on yer own ye'll go the morrow to herd the cattle.' She ran into the house forgetting her sister's strange behaviour. 'Look who's here, Mam.'

Grace Boyce scraped a scone of bread on to the iron pan, made a cross on the surface with the back of the knife, then lowering the iron hook, eased the crane over the glowing peat. 'It's yerself, Mrs Donovan,' she said, thinking it was their neighbour.

''Tis me, Mam,' Nellie said quietly.

Grace swung round, alarm racing across her face.

'Ah, musha, ye haven't lost yer place?'

12

'Indeed no, Mam. The housekeeper gave me special permission to come home and see ye.'

'Isin she the privileged wan?' Bridie cried gaily, filling two mugs with buttermilk from the brown crock.

'I must speak to ye alone,' Nellie whispered urgently to her mother.

'Away and start the milkin', Bridie love,' Mrs Boyce told her younger daughter. 'We haven't a drop o'milk to make yer sister a sup of tay.'

'Sure there's buttermilk to take the thirst off her. It must be the thirst that made her carry on like a wild billy goat on the hill.'

'I'd sooner have tea, Bridie,' Nellie said gently.

'Ay, well . . .' She took the milking can down from the dresser and, swinging it, went out the door.

Nellie drew her mother towards the settle. 'Mam, a terrible thing's happened. I met Sir Thomas Catalong on the shore and he asked me to go and work at the castle.'

'Sweet God protect us,' Mrs Boyce cried in alarm.

'Mam, 'tis worse, much worse. Bridie and me were on the hill a while ago when he and his agent were passin'. It wasn't me he was lookin' at or showin' any interest in now, 'twas Bridie — and her all smiles, the way she is with everyone.'

The blood drained from her mother's face. She threw the apron over her head with a cry of despair. 'Mam . . .' Nellie touched her arm.

'She's only thirteen,' her mother whispered.

'Nearly fourteen. The age Mrs Donovan's daughter was when he took her into service at the castle. Remember she was only fifteen when her baby was born?'

Grace Byoce lifted her head and looked around her home. The dresser with its shining bowls and plates. Her dead husband's special drinking mug with its wee shelf on the rim to protect his moustache. The strong tables and chairs he had made after they were wed, and the curtained box-bed in the corner where generations of Boyces had lain, loved and birthed. The cosy loft under the roof where the children slept. Every detail of her tiny home projected itself vividly as her heart turned in anguish, knowing she would have to leave

13

it sooner than sacrifice one of her daughters to that man. How many lives had he wrecked when a young girl caught his fancy? Them that defied him were evicted. She had been so happy when Nellie got the place in Mr O'Neill's farm. Her master was a good man. He would protect Nellie. But wee Bridie ... it was unthinkable. A sweet innocent child full of goodness. She rung her hands in despair.

'Mam, listen, didin ye tell me Rory and Eileen Donavan were goin' to the hirin' fair in Lisdare?'

'Aye.' She looked sharply at her daughter. 'Yer not thinkin' ...'

'If we could get Bridie into a good place away from here, he widden be able to touch her. She'd be earning a few pounds. God willing, maybe the three of us will find a way of getting to 'merica yet.'

'Arrah, love, dreams give me no heart. How can I send that child to the hirin'?'

'Mam,' Nellie said severely, 'just because she's the youngest you keep thinkin' she's still a child. Sure wasin meself over at Garton just after my fourteenth birthday? If she goes to the fair with Rory he'll keep an eye on her. Rory Donavan is a good steady lad. Mam, we *must* move quickly.'

'All right, child,' Grace said wearily, age suddenly climbing on to her shoulders and making an old woman of her at forty. 'Go yerself to the Donavans and tell them the situation. I'll help Bridie with the milkin'.'

The three Donavans were sitting around a creel of spuds. A bowl of dippity, milk with a seasoning of salt and pepper, was on a stool. Each mouthful they ate was dipped into the bowl. The Donavans' cottage was exactly like the Boyces'. One room, thatched with straw and a tiny window with a pane of glass. Mr Donavan was over in Scotland for the potato picking. It had been a bad year over there, Mrs Donavan told her neighbour, and her husband had indicated that he was probably staying on to pick up a bit of money doing other jobs until the next year's crop was ready. Her mam had said as far as she knew there had not been another word from across the water since that news reached them. Poor Mrs Donavan was wonderin' if her husband had got lost. Intentionally, Mam added, knowing the likes of *that* character. Nellie hoped her mother was wrong for they were a nice family and there was grief enough with the eldest daughter being misused by oul Tom Cat.

'There's great trouble on us,' Nellie annouced. 'I think that oul buck Catalong has got his eye on Bridie. No more than a look, mind ye.' Her eyes flashed in anger. 'They say that's how it starts.'

Mrs Donavan crossed herself. 'Heaven protect her. We know what that sorrow is in this house. That's why Rory's takin' Eileen here off to the hirin' in Lisdare. They're setting out tomorrow. Their unfortunate sister got a good place last year and is now settled wi' a good mistress.'

'That would be just right for Bridie, Mrs Donavan. A kind house.'

Rory, a strongly built lad of seventeen, with red hair and a freckled face, said, 'Nellie, she can come wi' me and Eileen. I'll look after her and see she's well placed. We're startin' out for the fair tomorrow, as Mam says. An uncle of ours at Dilford will bed us for the night, so it'll be an aisy journey.'

Mrs Boyce and Bridie came through the door as though they were visiting a wake. Bridie looked subdued and confused. She didn't want to leave her mother who had tried to explain the tyranny at the castle, and the possibility of her having to go there and work.

Mam must have spoken out to Bridie about the worst thing that could happen to a girl, Nellie thought. I hope she made a good job of it for Bridie is so innocent, so trusting. She'd be happy in a convent if we had the money and the knowledge to know how to get her there.

Rory saw the look of unease on Nellie's face while their mothers decided what to pack for the long journey. 'Don't fret, Nellie,' he said. 'I'll see that yer sister is well placed. With God's help she might get a situation wi' us.'

'That wid be grand, Rory.' They walked to the door and for a while stood there in silence watching the sun sinking behind the hills. Rays slanted down across the glen, burnishing the land and firing the streams that tumbled through the gorse and heather. Curlews called their sad note

15

while the shepherd boy on the hill played his flute. Johnny down the lane scraped a jig on his fiddle, accompanied by his mother who beat out time on the old tin tub that hung on the wall below the thatched roof.

Nellie was comforted by the familiar sights and sounds of her childhood, until another brought an expression of fear: a horse galloping in the direction of the hamlet. She turned in alarm to Rory. He crossed the yard to the midden and stood in the shelter of a fuchsia.

''Tis Catalong's bailiff. I know by the cut o' him. Come inside quickly and we'll shut the door.' When the heavy bolt was shot into place the women, understanding the urgency, began to get into a panic. 'Now listen,' he said sternly, 'we'll need to use a bit of cunnin' or all's lost. When he finds yer cottage empty, Mrs Boyce, he'll come down here searchin'. You girls git up to the loft and don' make a sound. Mam, you and Mrs Boyce shift into the bed and pull the curtain across. If we keep dead quiet he'll maybe think we've gone to the chapel. He's not likely to go up there.' The creel of uneaten potatoes and the stools were pushed out of sight. 'Here he comes, not a minute to lose.'

The two women scuttled into the bed. Giggling, as though it were a game, the girls scrambled up to the loft with Nellie after them. '*Shut up!*' she snapped, pushing them to the far side against the wall. She was trembling. It hadn't taken the castle long to find out where she and Bridie lived.

Rory clenched his hands in helpless anger when the door was banged. The sound filled each one of them with terror. A miasma of fear filled the cottage. Even simple-minded Eileen realised that silence was imperative. He shut his eyes and pressed his head hard against the wall, hurting it to ease the rage that tore through him. Sir Thomas Catalong wasn't wasting any time. Likely he'd sent his bailiff to demand that Bridie return with him to work at the castle, the way it had happened with his own sister. One day, he swore, I'll get even with that unjust man.

A shadow fell across the tiny window. Now he's trying to peer in, Rory realised. There was a soft sound of the two women praying in the bed, whispering the rosary to ease their fear. When the horse was heard to move away

16

from the yard, Rory called out: 'Stay where ye are. I'm goin' outside to make sure he's taken himself off. If he hangs around, we're lost.' He returned after a while and pushed the bolt across the door again. 'He's on the hill. Now listen, 'tis tonight we leave. If we wait til morn it'll maybe too late.'

Grace Boyce sat on the edge of the bed weeping quietly while Mrs Donavan lay on the quilt behind her finishing the rosary.

'Hush, Mam.' Nellie put an arm around her mother. 'Sure maybe 'tis off to 'mercia we'll be goin' soon, where there's work a plenty and no landlord to throw folk out of their homes or havin' his way wi' young girls.' Maybe, she thought, Mr O'Neill would lend them the money for the fare, the way he'd helped other folk in a state of desperation.

Rory's head shot up, startled. 'Ah, don' be talkin' that way, Nellie Boyce. His honour's days are numbered. When I come back after the hirin' a bit will be put aside. Pistols cost money.'

His mother leap out of bed like a fox before the hounds, her piety dissolving in a blaze of anger. 'Don' dare say such a wicked thing, my son. D'ye think I wan to see ye strung up on the gallows at Lisdare jail?'

He smiled to ease her anxiety. 'Mam, sure I'm only gassin'. I'll wait 'til I'm an oul man wi' grey hairs.'

I wonder, Nellie thought, looking at Rory with new eyes. He turned and caught her intent gaze. She blushed and dropped her eyes. He reddened too, then began to speak briskly. 'Now it wid be best if Bridie stayed here – just in case. Go and get her bundle together, Mrs Boyce, and a bit of food.'

'I've baked a scone,' Grace told him, drying her eyes and letting her mind turn to practical things. 'Big enough to last the three of ye for days.'

'I'll fill it wi' salt herrings,' Mrs Donavan said. 'Tin Lizzie got a barrel in yesterday.'

This was the name given to the owner of the tin hut that Sir Thomas Catalong had built on to Lizzie McGinley's cottage for her to start a shop. One of the rare gestures he had made towards the people, and it had aroused suspicion. They all considered Lizzie thoughtfully and failed to see how the ugly, bad-tempered string of a woman could please a man who had a weakness for young fresh-faced girls.

'We'll not starve or thirst for there's many a stream along the way,' said Rory confidently.

Bridie, now that the shock of her sudden home leaving had settled, began to feel excited. They were going to travel over the hill, keeping well away from the roads. What sights she'd see! Her letters to Mam wid be full of them if she could get the words together.

After the three young people left, Nellie drew Mrs Donavan aside and asked her to keep her mother company for a few days. 'She's petted Bridie for fourteen years and it'll be hard on her to be parted.'

'Arrah, Nellie, isn't it meself that knows all about the heavy heart? We're goin' down to the burn to do our sheets and blankets before the weather breaks. And maybe next day we'll take to the hills with the donkeys and bring home a bit o' peat.'

# Chapter Three

The morning following the departure of Bridie and the two Donavans, Nellie set out for Slievegar. It was a busy time at Garton with all the extra hands for the harvest to be fed. Grace Boyce and Mrs Donavan took a load of washing down to the burn. The two women were trampling a pair of blankets in the soapy water when Sir Thomas' bailiff came along on horseback. He approached quietly, keeping the horse to the grassy verge.

Before he could open his mouth, Mrs Donavan said in Gaelic: ''Tis a fine day, sir. If yer needin' a refreshing drink there's a wee well over there by the stone wall wi' a mug in attendance.' She began to hum a little song to keep time with her feet.

'Speak in English,' he said surlily. 'I don't understand you.'

'Praise be to God, Mrs Boyce, 'tis just as I expected, the big guldering ape hasin the Gaelic. He's come for a purpose. Now ye can put in a word to guide me when the questions come, in case I make a slip.' She looked at the bailiff and said humbly, 'Sorry, sir, I was offerin' ye refreshments then tellin' my neighbour to go aisy wi' her big feet for aren't them me best blankets under the weight o' them?'

He turned to Grace. 'Are you Mrs Boyce?'

Grace clutched her skirt and bobbed. 'I am, sir, and not too aisy wi' the English tongue for 'twas never spoken in the house of m'father.'

'Your younger daughter ... she's off the school register in a week's time. I believe?'

'God be praised.'

'She'll be ready for work then. There's a place for her at Merifield Manor.'

'Dear me,' Grace Boyce said regretfully, the fear of yesterday touching her again. But they had been expecting this visit. 'If only I'd known. And she gone this very day to seek a situation.'

'Musha, don't overdo it,' Mrs Donavan hissed. 'Remember what Rory told ye.'

'What's she going on about?' he asked angrily.

Grace tapped her forehead. 'She's got it for a habit, sir. Always talkin' to hersel'. The head's gone a bit.'

'Where did your daughter go? There's little enough employment for servant girls in these parts.'

'Away down towards Ballymore.'

'You let a young girl of her age go off like that?' he asked suspiciously.

'Careful now, he's trying to trap ye, the big hairy brute. He's the one who does all the castle's dirty work. The evicting. Pulls the roofs off the cabins and lights his pipe wi' the straw.'

'Ah, no, sir, in the company of Mrs Donavan's son and daughter. Wi' the pinch of winter on its way we'll be needin' their wages.'

'Why did they go that way? Lisdare would have been a better direction.'

'The boy had a promise of employment from someone. The girls are travelling wi' hope. Good day to ye, sir, and God bless yer journey.'

Mrs Donavan bowed her head meekly and muttered, 'The devil accompany you, and may ye fall into a pig midden and break your black neck.'

'What's she saying now?' he asked suspiciously as he mounted his horse.

'Ach, 'tis the praying she's at now, sir.'

When the bailiff was a long way off, the two women skipped out of the water and rolled on the mossy bank, helpless with laughter. Grace Boyce wiped her eyes and thought, Ah, after all I did the right thing by me little daughter, even though the ache is raw in m'heart.

Before Rory and the two girls left Dilford, where they had spent the night, his uncle gave them a penny each. 'That'll get ye a night's lodging at the Red Barn between here and Lisdare. It's a farm that stands on the hill, can't be missed. There's three more pennies,' his uncle went on, 'The mistress of the house will provide a bowl of milk for breakfast if ye pay yer way. If not, 'tis a clout ye'll get on the ear. Ah,' the elderly man said sadly, 'the folk wi' money are the hard ones. Only God and the poor help the poor. Farewell now, and may the Virgin keep an eye on ye.'

Outside Dilford, Bridie and Eileen took off their boots and put them in their bundles to save wear. Rory tied the laces and slung his boots round his neck. He carried a strong stick in one hand, in case a rabbit or any other nourishing creature crossed their path; he needed his other hand to help the girls to clamber over awkward hedges. They were keeping off the roads, just in case. In his pack he had a tin with a lid. The evenings were chilly; a drop of hot water, with wild mint, made a warming drink beside the fire.

It was a good journey. The girls, particularly his sister, were a bit of an encumbrance right enough. Poor Eileen had always been a trial. Imagine relieving hersel' on a bed of nettles and then whining because her backside got stung! Wasin Bridie the bright wee thing, plonking her on a bed of dock-leaves to soothe the stings? She's a grand girl entirely, Rory thought. Full of life. Dancing along, brimming with joy, when by a hair's breadth she'd missed a terrible fate.

All three were feeling footsore and weary when Bridie called out excitedly, 'There's the Red Barn, Rory. On yonder hill. See the trees waving a welcome?'

'A welcome as long as we've pennies in our pockets. The mistress there is a turncoat. Changed her coat wi' marriage. It's soured her nature.'

'You say? Whatever was she atal? Not ...' Bridie's eyes rolled in horror ' ... not a Catholic turned Protestant?'

'Be God, I widden rightly know, but I honour her for showin' such strength of nature and followin' her heart.'

'Maybe 'twas money she was followin',' Bridied said mischievously.

As they approached the barn, Rory's heart sank at the

crowd around the entrance. The bad potato season in Scotland had sent them all home again looking for work. The turncoat mistress was not to be seen, only a serving girl who told them the barn was full, but they were welcome to shake down in the byre with the cattle. Rory and the three girls looked into the barn and saw with great envy the fresh-smelling straw strewn across the floor: those who had arrived early were lying exhausted on the ground.

'Could you not find a bit of space?' he pleaded. 'For meself I want nothing, but the girshas here are bone tired. We've been journeyin' for two days. I canna lower them to the company of cattle.'

The servant girl looked at the strong young man. To another she would have said, 'There's better than youse wans have slept in a byre'. But he did not look away embarrassed from her cruel hare-lip, like others. His eyes were laid on hers with a kindly pleading expression. 'Ah, sure, there's a wee end down there at the back if ye don' mind squeezin' in.' She pushed away his hand. 'An' don' be givin' me money either. There's enough within the house to pave the place wi' gold.'

'God bless you, lass,' Rory said warmly.

Bridie and Eileen followed him to the far end of the barn. No sooner were they seated when someone began to play 'The Rose of Tralee'. Soon everyone was shaking the sleep from their eyes and joining in. 'The pale moon was rising above the green mountain ...'

A yell came from a big fellow further along the floor who had been fast asleep. 'Will ye shut yeer gobs and let a man get his rest?' he shouted.

'We're enjoying ourselves, yer honour,' a scraggy wee man with a nose as sharp as a slate protested cheekily.

The big man scrambled to his feet, picked up Wee Scraggy as though he were a fistful of chaff and let him drop back on the floor again. There was silence until the young man next to Rory and the girls said fearfully: 'Begob, if it isin Mad Billy himself, that's in it. Last year he was in the mad house. Christ, I'm gettin' out o'here. The least thing sets him off. He could murder a body.'

Bridie went pale and Eileen began to whimper. 'Let's go

Rory,' she pleaded. 'Maybe it's losin' his head, he is. He musta killed that wee scrap o'er there because there's not a move in him atal.'

'Och, let's go, Rory,' Eileen moaned, scratching herself furiously.

'What are them wans girnin about?' Mad Billy yelled again. 'Is a man not to get his sleep the night?'

Rory rose quickly to his feet and caught the girls' hands. 'Sorry, sir, me sister wants to relieve herself. We'll take our bundles and settle down near the door so as not to disturb ye when we come back.'

Big Billy grunted and said gruffly. 'The call of nature has to be answered. No need to lose yeer places.'

Bridie looked closely at him, then at their neighbour who was gradually spreading himself out until he had covered the space that all three of them had occupied.

Outside the door, she said, 'Rory, that fella next to us was coddin'. He just wanted our places.' She began to jump around delightedly, 'Ah, isin it just grand to get out in the fresh air again?'

'Aye,' said Rory worriedly, 'but we need a good night's rest. There's an early start and a long journey ahead of us tomorrow.'

The three of them went on down the road, Eileen clinging to her brother's arm, complaining away. 'Rory,' Bridie clutched his other arm excitedly, 'just lay yer eyes on that field. As if all the gold in heaven were poured over it.'

He laughed. 'And a few mice as well, alannah.' He went through the gap and picked up a stook of corn. 'Down under the hedge the pair of ye go.' He arranged the corn on the ground then took another stook and covered them with it. 'If you girls are hungry, there's a bread and cheese tree sheltering us.'

The girls munched away for a while on the red berries from the hawthorn tree, then fell asleep. Rory lay looking up at the sky, a great velvet canopy studded with points of light. How he longed for the knowledge to know what it was all about. Sometimes he had dreams about roaming through the world, seeking learning, seeing other places. He shrugged. Seventeen years old and all he had to look forward

23

to was getting himself hired at a fair to bring home some money to Mam. His father had had dreams too. By the look of it, Rory thought grimly, he's away off to do something about them. Not a word for months. A bad sign. Still . . . his heart beat fast when he thought of Nellie and the look they had exchanged; a look of surprise then joy as if they had just met instead of knowing each other all their lives, even going to school together. It was a terrible thing that he was a year younger than herself. Maybe now that they were grown up, it wouldn't make much difference.

Dawn broke across the sky, casting an apricot glow into the grey shadows of the night. Rory shook the girls gently. 'Let's put the sheaves of corn back again and get up to the farm before the others stir.'

They went down to the stream at the edge of the field, splashed cold water on their faces, then tied their bundles and hurried up the road. The servant girl was in the dairy surrounded by crocks of milk. Her face lit up when she saw Rory. With a brisk little movement she filled three blue and white bowls to the brim with rich milk.

''Tis the skimmed I'm supposed to be servin' the barn-lodgers,' she lisped. 'Wid ye like a piece of oatmeal bread to put down wi' it?'

'Don' be gettin' yerself into trouble now,' Rory said, embarrassed by her attention.

Bridie and his sister looked at him in wide-eyed desperation, frightened he was going to refuse the offer. They tried not to look at the girl because of her hare-lip. Rory had warned them not to stare. The warning was for Bridie. His sister would do that anyway.

The servant girl broke the bread into three pieces, guided by the cross indented on its surface. A piece for Bridie and Eileen; two for Rory. Aware that she could get into trouble over her generous action, they ate greedily, dipping the bread into the milk to soften it.

'Where're ye'll goin'?' she asked curiously.

When Rory told her, she said sadly, 'What a great life youse 'ave, travellin' the roads. And the hirin' fair? Widden I just give me right hand for such a chance. Me mammy hired me out here as a skivvy, 'cause she said who'd want

24

to look at the likes o'me all day long? Ah, sorrow me, livin' up the lane there and this is as far as I'll ever go.'

Bridie felt pity for the girl. 'I like you fine and yer kind,' she told her shyly. The sound of feet came across the yard.

'We'd better be on our way now,' Rory urged. 'Finish up yer milk quickly.' He put out his hand and touched the girl's shoulder. 'I like ye well and won't forget such kindness.'

'Ye'll be comin' back again?' she said eagerly.

'Aye, one day. What's yer name now?'

'Maggie.'

Rory and the girls avoided the other travellers who went along the roads, often bare-footed and singing. Bridie felt that the three of them might be missing out on a bit of fun until something happened which made her realise how wise Rory was to be cautious. The high hedges were gradually falling away. Soon there would be only stone-bound fields between them and the road. Rory looked at the hill on the right covered in patches of scrub and long-stemmed heather with shreds of silvery mist steaming down. It would add hours to their journey if they climbed up and over to the other side. Still, it would be safer.

Just then he heard the sound of wheels and a horse pounding along at a steady pace. The boys and girls on the road stopped singing. He drew Bridie and Eileen into a slough where their bare feet sank into soft brown mud. His sister whimpered at the expression of fear on her brother's face.

'Hush.' He put his arm around her as a conveyance stopped and Catalong's bailiff began questioning the travellers.

No, they had not seen anyone. 'Sure, sir,' one lad informed him, 'everyone going to hiring fairs travel together for the company and sport.'

The castle men will climb that hill to get a good sight of the countryside, Rory thought. Just then he smelt peat smoke. 'Come on,' he whispered to the girls, 'follow me.'

The door of the little cabin was wide open. Sitting in one corner was an old woman smoking a clay pipe; in the other corner a sow suckling several piglets. He spoke swiftly in Irish, explaining how they were being hunted by the castle men.

'God curse them,' she muttered and pointed her pipe at a low doorway. 'Hide in there. Silence will hold my tongue.'

Perspiration broke out on Rory's face. If they see the cabin, he thought, it's here they'll come. And pushing up the top of a settle-bed, he got Bridie inside. He and Eileen squeezed under the wooden bed built into the corner.

When the old woman heard footsteps approaching she prodded the sow viciously with her stick; the animal staggered to its feet, leaving its young squealing around her. The bailiff and his man glanced in, then backed away from the angry swine. The woman watched them as they climbed the hill and then returned to their side-car which set out in the direction of the castle.

That night Rory and the girls slept under a hedge. It was cold and uncomfortable and all they had to eat for breakfast was a turnip which they had picked in a field. The morning was fine. Dew lay like fine lace on the leaves of the trees and beaded the grass with a shower of diamonds. ''Tis a jewel of a day,' Rory said contentedly as they made their way to the river to have a good wash.

Near Lisdare, they put on their boots and walked through the silent streets of the town where their feet echoed like those of an alien army.

'We're far too early,' he said peering at the clock on the top of the town hall.'

'Is there time to see St Columba's church?' Eileen asked. 'The master at school told us if ever we went near the place to be sure and visit it.'

And I wish to God that's where the pair of you were at this moment, instead of trudging along to a market place to be hired, Rory thought angrily. But there was nothing they could do about the stranglehold of poverty and this humiliating system of employment. Eviction hung over their heads like that terrible sword Master Logue had talked about at school one day. Rory would love to work on his own land but someone had to earn money. It was a sad joke the landlord played on them; if you made a sturdy fence or roofed an outhouse, an increase in rent was likely to be demanded. Neglect the place and you were in worse trouble.

They made their way to the market place where booths were being set up with farm produce, livestock and second-hand clothing. There were medical quacks, itinerant musicians, ballad singers and trick-o-the-loop men. Hawkers, pedlars and jugglers, all tearing around. In the centre area a group of young men and women were gathered for the hiring. Subdued, they no longer jested with one another. Rory, with the two girls by his side, took up a position. Bridie and Eileen looked scared as the crowd of farmers scrutinized them thoughtfully. The farmers were impatient to pick a strong worker and get back to their farms.

Rory explained to Bridie how important it was for him to find a place that would take his sister as well as himself. Bridie, her eyes beginning to show signs of anxiety, said, 'Och, don' ye be worried about me, Rory. Sure I know poor Eileen isin all there and needs an eye kept on her.'

'I'll do my best to keep ye wi' me too.'

'Come on now,' a burly farmer bawled impatiently, 'scatter out, will ye, and let's see how yeer set up and what mettle's in ye. *You*! The big fella wi' the red hair. Do a walk for me.'

Rory walked up and down. The man followed behind studying the shape and strength of the youth's body. 'What wages d'ye want from me, young fella?'

'Two pounds, ten shillings, sir.'

'Get out! Yeer meat will be dear on me. Two pounds, a full belly and a warm bed in the farm loft.'

'I'm worth more than that, sir, beggin' yer pardon.'

The man paused thoughtfully. Red head was a strapping lad. Do the work of two men. 'Right,' he barked. 'I'll take ye at yeer price.' He held out his hand to seal the bargain. Rory drew back.

'There's my sister, sir. She's a fine worker. Strong as an ox. I won't take a place without her. I swore to m'mother. And the other wee girl, a neighbour's daughter ... I'm responsible for her too. I suppose you ...'

27

'Bejays, he's brought the whole family wi' him,' someone joked nearby.

The farmer's mouth fell wide open as though he were a mute. Then he gave a roar of anger. 'Wimin on me farm? Bedamned if I will! Isin a wife cross enough to take a man to an early grave wi'out payin' for another two heifers? Lazy good for nothing wimin.'

Rory took Eileen's arm and walked away a little distance, his face crimson with embarrassment. He realised now that his sister was going to be a big obstacle to his getting employment; to include Bridie as well was disastrous. Several more offers came, but no one wanted Eileen. They had eyes in their heads and could see that she was wanting. Feeling really worried, Rory accepted the fact that his chances were dwindling. Impatiently he looked at Bridie. She was not setting herself out to be noticed.

Terrified, and embarrassed by the staring crowds who regarded the hiring as great sport, Bridie hung back almost out of sight. Forgetting his own problems for the moment, Rory steeled himself, and catching her arm roughly, drew her right out in front of the crowd.

'Dosin anyone want a fine strappin' girl for milkin' the cows?' he shouted angrily.

Bridie dropped her head and blushed painfully. Rory felt as though a knife was being twisted in his breast. God, he thought, we have to sell ourselves like farm stock. Animals have the advantage though, they don't have to speak up for themselves.

A woman dressed in the clothes of an upper servant came over to them. 'Lift your head, girl,' she ordered.

Bridie, realising how desperate Rory was to get her placed, smiled eagerly and gave a little curtsey. The woman asked some questions to which Rory gave all the answers.

'Hasn't she got a tongue in her head, boy?'

Frightened that things were not going well, Bridie looked anxiously at the woman. To her surprise she saw a smile in the other's eyes and kindliness around her mouth. 'I have indeed a tongue, ma'am. I'm a strong girl as he's tole ye. Helpin' me mither to run the farm, digging potatoes, herding and milking the cows. I can even clean out the byres. Ach, sure, me mither says I'm a great hand around the house altogether.'

The woman's smile deepened. ''Tis an indoor servant I'm lookin' for, dear. Are you fit for that?'

Before Bridie could give another glowing account of her capabilities, Rory said quietly, 'Ma'am, Bridie comes from a good home. Her mother put her in my charge. Where wid ye be comin' from now?'

'From Horton House in Glenlag. I'm housekeeper there.'

Delighted, Rory said happily, 'Sure I know the estate well, ma'am. I delivered trees there from the last farm I worked on.'

He was so relieved to get Bridie placed in such a good situation that he forgot for a moment the problem he had with his sister. He carried Bridie's bundle to the pony-trap where Mrs O'Sullivan's husband, Barney, was waiting. 'Keep up yer heart, alannah, and God go wi' ye,' he said in farewell.

The three young people waved to each other until they were out of sight, then Rory caught his sister's hand and they made their way back to the rabble on the other side of the market place. Nearly all the boys and girls had been hired. He looked at the spectators standing around waiting for someone to entertain them. There was pity in the women's eyes for they realised that the fine-looking young man would not stand much chance to hire himself, encumbered with a sister who was not all there.

A low-set man with broad shoulders edged his way forward. 'What price d'ye put on yerself, lad?'

Rory told him, then added quickly. 'My sister ...'

'I wasin lookin' for a lass but no doubt the wife will find a use for a pair of extra hands. Take yer bundles and follow me.' They turned right from the market place and went down a steep street. 'That's me,' Rory's new master said, pointing to a signboard, 'Bill McGowen, Pawnbroker.'

Bewildered Rory looked around him when they went inside. There were rows of clothes hanging on long iron poles suspended from two walls. Each item of clothing had a white label on it with a name, date and number. 'This is the missis' department.' He ran his hand across the clothes.

'Widden think there was money in them oul duds, wid ye?' He winked. 'I do a line in second-hand jewellery as well.'

'Mr McGowen, what do ye want me to do?' Rory asked in bewilderment.

'I'll tell 'ee, lad. I've got a wee bit of land outside the town, cattle and a few sheep. That's what I want ye to do, work out there.'

'Yeh poor weans,' his wife said warmly, 'must be bone weary and starvin'. Them rabble days in the markets are terrible. Still, if there wasn't a half-yearly hiring fair, what would the likes of ye do? Now sit down the pair of ye and fill yer stomachs with that good pork stew. What's yer names?'

'Rory and Eileen.'

'Grand names.'

'Thank ye, Mrs McGowan, 'tis a grand spread,' Rory said clumsily.

'Thank ye, missis, 'tis a grand spread,' Eileen repeated, remembering her brother's warning to watch the way he did things and not show them up.

'A parrot, begob!' Mr McGowan joked good-naturedly.

Bridie felt very strange sitting in the trap beside her employer. She had never travelled in one before. Along the way, farmers saluted them and the O'Sullivans called 'Good-day to ye' in return. The young girl echoed their greeting, not sure what to do. Shyness was killing her; once she found her tongue she'd be all right. Her employer was dressed in a fine black skirt with a short cape to match. Bridie's eyes grew wide in wonder watching the little bonnet perched on her employer's head. Every time a greeting was made, Mrs O'Sullivan gave a little nod which set her bonnet in motion. After a brisk little tap it settled down into the thick hair like a dog snuggling into a rug. There was something quare about it, Bridie thought uncomfortably.

Nora O'Sullivan decided that she and Barney were the luckiest servants on earth since they had found the good position at Horton. No mistress or master to bow and scrape to and now this wee girl to give them a hand. True, Barney could do with some help on the land. She

30

was supposed to be assisting him, but the agent had warned her that the house must be well cared for as the owner might light on them at any time. Fires had to be kept burning in some of the rooms because of the valuable furniture and pictures. Nora knew all about good things. Her late mistress who had gone to live in foreign parts had valuable possessions too. She had given Nora a pile of grand clothes and bonnets before leaving. The bonnets were a size too big, right enough ...

'Ma'am,' Bridie said hesitantly, ashamed of her forwardness but becoming increasingly alarmed in case something unpleasant was about to make an appearance from under the rim of her employer's bonnet, 'wid there be somethin' unknown to ye resting under ye bonnet? 'Tis known for mice to seek comfort where there's warmth.'

Her employer gave a shriek of laughter. 'No, child, it belonged to a large member of the gentry. Her head was a sight to remember. 'Tis sizes too big and resting on me bun with a piece of elastic in loose control.'

Bridie gave a sigh of relief. 'I'll fix it for ye, ma'am, for I'm a great hand at the sewing, m'mither says.'

'She'll be missing you.'

'Och, she will so, especially wi' the milkin'. She says our cows like me but the minute *she* touches the tiddies, the oul devils goes dry. Now isn't that a quare thing?'

Another shriek of laughter came from her mistress. 'Did you hear thon, Barney?'

'I did so. A character, begob. She'll be the best of company.'

Nora reached over and touched Bridie's arm. 'You're a nice wee thing. We'll get on fine.'

Bridie, who had never worn a pair of boots for so long in her life, felt their hardness rubbing against her skin. She couldn't bear to glance down at the great clumsy things on her feet.

'Are the boots hurting ye, child?' her companion asked, knowing well the sort of poverty-stricken homes hired girls came from. The boots probably belonged to another member of her family.

'Their ugliness is hurting me the worst, ma'am.'

31

The woman smiled. 'Soon be in Glenlag. You can take them off and rest your feet then.'

When they rounded the coast and faced west, the sun sinking into the sea stained the water a deep red and spread a pink glow across the land.

'Isin it beautiful?' Bridie said in a whisper, amazed at the expanse of the ocean.

Horton House loomed darkly out of the night. Barney removed the lamp from the pony-trap and opened the back door which led straight into the kitchen.

'Stir the fire, Barney, before ye put the pony to rest,' his wife told him. 'I don't want ash on m'best clothes.'

Soon the kettle began to boil under his attention. Bridie's bedroom was off the kitchen. It was a small room with a tiny window set high in the wall.

'This one,' she was told, 'has always been occupied by the youngest servant girl for early rising so as to get the fire going, then the porridge on the boil for the breakfast. If you feel lonely down here, dear, come upstairs to another room and I won't say a word against it.'

'Thank ye, ma'am,' Bridie said shyly. 'Sure I'll be fine, and if yerselves don' mind I'll be able to sit beside that gran' fireplace in the evenings and get on wi' m'crocheting.'

'The three of us will do that, child, for it's the only comfortable place in this big house. So ye crochet?'

'Every spare minute I've got, ma'am. Mam says it's an aisy way to earn some money, doing something that gives ye pleasure.'

Dear help them, Mrs O'Sullivan thought. The travelling dealers pay them very little for their hours of eye straining work which they then sell to the gentry for a good profit.

After the best meal that Bridie had ever eaten in her life, cold roast meat and potatoes that had been cooking all day in hot ash, she went to bed and lay between linen sheets. For the first time in three days she began to feel homesick and thought of the coarse bleached flour bags ridged with seems that covered her bed in the loft at home in Iskaglen. And she thought of Rosha O'Neill, pampered by Nellie, not knowing what it was like to leave her own hearth to earn a penny.

# Chapter Four

Rosha loved harvest time. Stooks of corn stood around like gossiping women, the richness of its smell mingling with the scent of wild flowers and herbs that grew between the stalks. She stood for a moment watching the harvesters shearing with their reaping hooks; curved steel blades with teeth that were sharpened by the blacksmith's hammer and chisel on the anvil. The slashed corn fell back on their left arm, then each sheaf was tied and stooked. Afterwards the stacks would be built, thatched and tied with ropes of straw. In the evening, all the young people came and played tig, racing around the stacks.

Edmund Catalong watched the girl from behind one of his father's rowing boats. He remembered last year how a crowd of them had played a noisy game under the harvest moon while the older ones went down to the crossroads and danced to the fiddler's tunes. Edmund would have like to take part in their games. If he approached, the boys tipped their caps respectfully, while the girls turned away blushing furiously. If only they knew how lonely his life was in the big dark house. There were parts where he was not allowed to enter, particularly the kitchen and servants' quarters. All the servants were elderly. The young girls who sometimes came to work at the manor usually disappeared after a few months. Worst of all was his father whom he actively disliked. Thank goodness he would soon be going away to school again.

Rosha sat down at the shore end of the field and chewed a piece of corn. She was different from the others, he thought.

As he went to move out of his hiding place, his foot slipped on a piece of seaweed and he fell with a clatter on the stones, banging his head. Looking sheepish, he scrambled up and came over.

'Sit down,' she invited. 'Did you hurt yourself?' She made a space for him on the little grassy mound, but to her amazement he planted himself without looking on the sharp stump of the cut corn. Springing up again, he muttered, 'Oh, damn!'

'What a silly thing to do. Now you're sore at both ends.'

They burst out laughing. At that moment a yell came from the top of the field and a loud ringing noise that scattered the birds on the trees. Nellie Boyce appeared carrying a big can of tea with a necklace of tin mugs strung around her neck. In the other hand was a basket piled with thick slices of scone bread made with fistfuls of dried fruit and thickly buttered. 'Come here at once, Rosha,' she shouted.

'You're going?' he said disappointed.

'You come too.' Realising that this was going to annoy Nellie, Rosha marched defiantly up the field, Edmund following uncertainly.

'Yer not to talk to that Catalong boy,' Nellie said angrily.

'Can you spare another mug?'

'No,' the servant girl snapped, filling one with hot sweet tea. 'Share that.' She pushed two pieces of bread at them.

The harvesters were all grouped together around a stack of corn. When Rosha and Edmund passed, their conversation stopped and they dropped their heads in silence. The two young people went on down towards the end of the field again. Rosha handed Edmund a slice of bread and the mug of tea. He shook his head. 'You must drink first,' he said politely, sinking his teeth into the freshly made bread.

They threw bits to the big white seagulls who swooped down and gobbled it up. A heron flew across from the peninsula and perched on a rock close by. Grey and graceful, it ignored the voracious seagulls and gazed intently at the water.

'Right. Have you finished?' Nellie stood over them like

an avenging angel. 'Yer wanted up at the house. Visitors. Better git up there quickly.'

Rosha sprang to her feet. She loved visitors. They always brought presents. Edmund brushed crumbs off his grey tweed breeches and moved away awkwardly. 'Thank you for the tea.'

'See you tomorrow,' Rosha called as she skipped up the field.

You will not, Nellie vowed to herself. Edmund watched them go out of sight. He did not believe the servant girl that there were visitors at Garton House. His English tutor, Mr Moss, who had a house in the grounds, said frequently, 'Have a care with the Irish, young man. Polite to your face but they smoulder, boy . . . smoulder. Your Grandfather was well liked by these people. But your father — ah, well . . . great responsibilities were placed on him by inheriting this estate. He cannot forget the terrible poverty that existed during the famine. Now he has introduced new techniques. All these new ways will surely make a difference to the people, if such a disaster should strike again.'

'Mr Moss, why were the people so hungry during the famine when so much corn and grain is grown in this country?' Edmund had asked.

His tutor took out a snuff box, tapped and opened it then pressed the spicy powder to his nose. 'Now,' he said without replying, 'let me see your English exercise.'

That evening the games had already begun when Rosha ran down to the meadow. They were playing Bat. The bat was made of plaited straw, thick at one end, narrowing to where it was held in the hand. One of the boys or girls chased the others through the stacks; whoever was tigged with the bat took over the chasing. Once again Edmund watched from the shore, his eyes following Rosha's movements. Her cherry-coloured frock looked warm and glowing in the moonlight. He noticed how skilful she was at evading the chaser and how purposefully the boys went after her.

Aware that he was watching, Rosha became gayer, shouting and laughing because his presence heightened her enjoyment of the harvest game; then, feeling bored, she outdistanced her pursuer and hid behind a stack near

35

the shore. Edmund climbed into a boat and began paring a piece of cane with his knife. He tied string to both ends, picked up a shorter cane with an arrow-head then stood up and aimed it across the bay. Rosha thought he looked like the figure of the Lonely Hunter that hung in the parlour at Garton.

'Isin that powerful?' Jamsie Hudie called to Charley the blacksmith's son. 'Wid ye think now the likes o'him had it in him?'

'Aye,' Charley agreed. ''Tis a wonder he didin send it in our direction for the gentry think we're no better than the sport they chase in the fields.'

Another arrow-cane shot gracefully across the bay. 'C'mon, Charley lad,' Jamsie said, running towards the shore. 'Let's put an end to his sport.'

Rosha tore after them and they turned expectantly towards her. 'You're just jealous because he's doing something clever instead of playing a silly game,' she blurted out.

'Jay,' Famsie muttered, 'yeh better not hang around, missie, when the likes o'them bucks are in the vicinity.'

'What are you talking about?' she snapped.

'At him, Charley. We'll wet his dandy wee suit. You gup the field, Rosha O'Neill.' He winked. 'We'll just have a wee chat wi' his lordship.'

Alarmed, Rosha looked at the two thick-limbed boys in their ragged trousers and torn shirts. Edmund heard the crunch of footsteps and growl of threatening voices coming towards him. He fixed another cane in position. Mr Moss had often warned him to be careful after daylight, not to stray far from the grounds. His father was a strict landlord, he said. The people were resentful.

When Jamsie crept up to the boat, Edmund was ready for him. He moved aside just as his attacker brought down a heavy hand. Jamsie stumbled forward. His weight tipped the boat, sending him reeling into the water.

'Run, Edmund!' Rosha shouted. She couldn't believe her eyes when he turned to face the two angry youths. All three fell on the pebbled beach. Flailing arms and legs made it difficult to see who was getting the worst of it.

A figure shot passed Rosha and jumped straight into the

battle. 'Oh, aye, two big brave gasairs, ye are,' Nellie yelled. 'Ye'll not be so brave the morrow when O'Neill hears of this.' She kicked Jamsie Hudie's backside hard and yanked at Charlie's hair until he cried out in pain. 'Fine to be earning a wage but not another casual day's work will you git at Garton, as God's me witness.'

The two youths slunk away. Edmund jumped to his feet, blood trickling down his face. He was furious, not at his attackers but at Nellie. 'I don't need Rosha's nursemaid to defend me.' He walked over and plunged his head into the bay then pulled out a handkerchief and dried his face.

'Of all the ungrateful ... Well, young sir,' Nellie said, 'I'll let them kill ye next time, for all I care.'

Edmund strode into the woods without a backwards glance. There was a flash of admiration in Nellie's eyes. 'He's a tough one, begod.' She tugged at Rosha's arm. 'But don't let me see you talkin' to that boy again.'

Her voice lacked its usual ring of authority.

A bitter little wind stole unexpectedly across the bay and cooled the flush of anger on Rosha's face. *Rosha's nursemaid ...*

A few days later Rosha followed Willie and Paddy into the castle grounds. The farmhands had felled a tree on the previous night, sawn it in half and hid it under bracken. Every time there was an eviction in the community they cut down one of Catalong's trees and fuelled the fires of Garton. The woods edging on O'Neill's estate were dense and it was easy to dodge the castle bailiff. Paddy took the lighter end of the tree while Willie, younger and stronger, hauled the heavier load on his shoulder.

A whiplash fell across Paddy's shoulder, knocking him to the ground. 'You thieving damned scoundrel. Get the other one,' Catalong shouted, but Willie was racing away like the wind with the bailiff at his heels. The whip fell again, cutting across Paddy's face and forehead.

'Jayus, yer honour, yer killin' me.'

Rosha, who had wandered off, heard his cry and tore back through the woods. 'Stop it!' she screamed at Catalong when she saw Paddy lying on the ground. Picking up a stone, she threw it at his back.

Catalong swung around angrily, saw his son and the look of contempt on the boy's face. Furious, he strode away. Paddy stumbled down the path to the edge of the woods. Nellie, her eyes standing in her head, was in the meadow.

'Mary and Joseph, what was goin' on in there? Paddy, come over to the stream quick 'til I clean ye up afore O'Neill sees the state yer in.'

'Rosha, don't go yet,' Edmund said quietly, 'let's finish Paddy's job. Take the other end of this tree.' They carried the two piece out to the lawn and placed them under the hedge.

Nellie and Paddy stared disbelievingly at the tyrant's son helping to steal from his father's land. A light sprang to Nellie's eyes. 'Begod, Paddy, he's got the makings of a man.'

Sean O'Neill, wondering what the commotion was about, looked out of the window. The tide was high, he noticed, lapping the shelf of land that lay below the field and sloped to the shore. When the tide went out, a bountiful supply of seaweed would be left behind, waiting to be carted away for fertilizing the land. Gone were the days when horses and carts trundled along the shore-road returning with wrack piled high on sturdy little carts, all brightly painted in blue and red. He missed the sight of them and the laughter of the men and women. Now the men came stealthily by night with strong sticks in their hands, ready to beat the bully of a bailiff should he attempt to stop them. Sir Thomas Catalong's bailiff was only brave and threatening in daylight when he and his helpers pulled the roofs off poor tenants' cottages. He was less willing to serve his master at nightfall.

'Mr O'Neill,' the housekeeper called, 'the minister is needin' a word wi' ye,'

'Come in, Mr Stewart. Come in, sir. You're welcome to my house.' Sean held out his hand to the minister. 'Sit down and make yourself comfortable while I pour a drink.' He smiled warmly at the man who lifted the tail of his clerical jacket and sat on the edge of the settle. 'You're always the first one, Mr Stewart, to come and pay the quarterly rent for the field I let you for grazing.'

'Mr O'Neill,' the cleric dropped his head, 'to my great shame I've come empty handed this time.'

Sean looked embarrassed. 'Forgive me, sir, I feel as though I've put my hand in your pocket. You're welcome any time.' What the devil is wrong with the man? Sean wondered, pouring two glasses of whiskey.

'Just a drop for me, Mr O'Neill. I've no head for drink, and at the moment I need my senses about me.'

'Mrs Coll,' Sean called, 'bring some tea.'

The housekeeper spread a white damask cloth on the oak table, then laid it with freshly made oat bread, a dish of butter and slices of boiled fruit cake. Her dead mistress's pink and gold rimmed porcelain made a pool of warm colour on the cloth. Only the best for the men of God, she thought, never mind what church they preach in. She poured the tea, set the pot on the copper pot-stand by the fire, then went out of the room leaving the door ajar. There was something up wi' the wee minister. She must get to the bottom of it.

'Sit up to the table, sir,' Sean urged, 'and clear your head with a cup of tea to follow the medicine.'

'Aye, the best medicine in the world, taken with caution.' The minister took a sip of tea. 'A terrible thing has befallen me, Mr O'Neill,' he said in a low voice.

'You say? I haven't heard a word.'

'You're the first to know. Sir Thomas' agent came to see me last week.'

Sean's head turned quickly. 'And?'

'As you know, I've been carrying out extensive improvements on my property, or the one I rent from the big house. The agent has informed me that my rent was going to be raised to what I consider an unreasonable sum and beyond my pocket at the present time. I haven't been able to meet the increase, Mr O'Neill. An eviction order was served on me this very day.'

'Catalong can't get away with that sort of thing any more,' Sean said angrily. 'Haven't you seen the Land League poster up in Dilford?'

The minister shook his head a little impatiently, then said

gloomily, 'I failed to look closely at the new agreement Sir Thomas presented me with some time ago. According to the wording, I am lawfully bound to pay and there's nothing I can do about it.'

'Dear God, to do that to a man of the cloth.'

'My dear friend, there are worse off than me,' he said sadly. 'At least I am always assured of an income from my church, little though it may be. A widow with her two children belonging to your own church was evicted last week. Her husband, before he died, spent £100 in improving his farm. Because she was behind with her rent, Catalong took over her property without compensation.'

The frown deepened on Sean's forehead. He moved restlessly about the room. In other parishes the Land League had branches; the people were following their advice and taking action.

'Mr O'Neill, I am a minister of God's Church and I must obey the law of the land. It's just that with more time I could have improved my financial position.'

'This is dreadful. What about the widow? What is her name and where does she dwell at the moment?'

'Maria Flaherty. A man named Dan Murphy has given her a little cabin to tide her over.'

'I know the place. About your own predicament, I'll tell you what I'll do to help, Mr Stewart. I'll give you a bit of land to build yourself a house. Your family will need a roof o'er their heads before the winter sets in.'

The minister blew his nose to cover his emotion. 'You're a good man, Mr O'Neill, but I haven't the money to pay for the land you offer. I owe Sir Thomas a quarter's rent. I wouldn't care to take on the responsibility of another debt at the moment.'

'You needn't be in my debt, sir. You can repay me, indeed do me a great favour, if you would tutor my daughter.' Sean had not intended to be so forthright, but suddenly he saw the answer to a problem which had been bothering him for some time.

'Teach your daughter?' There was a sound of alarm in the minister's voice. What a task, he thought, trying to teach O'Neill's spoilt daughter.

'She's not getting much learning at the moment. I don't want the girl to grow up unlearned and ignorant to be at the mercy of the landed gentry who consider it their right to whip up a girleen's skirt ... forgive me for being so blunt in your presence, sir. The blaggards take our land and shame our daughters. Who knows how long I've got on this earth? I must leave my child well equipped for life.'

Mr Stewart was taken aback by Sean O'Neill's suggestion and his coarse words. 'The school, isn't she attending?'

'Thomas Catalong is responsible for the running of it, as you know. He's forbidden books to be taken home for the children's homework. Says there should be no studying at home because they ought to be helping their parents on the farm. So, Mr Stewart, if you would supplement the teaching, I'd be grateful.'

'It's little enough to do in repayment for your kindness,' the minister said slowly, despite his unwilling thoughts.

When the clergyman left the house, Sean called his daughter. 'Rosha, come with me to visit a Widow Flaherty who has been evicted by Catalong. Patrick Murphy's father has let her live in that wee cabin near the farm.'

'Are you frightened of her?' Rosha asked mischievously.

They laughed as they cut across the field. But after a few minutes in the tiny dwelling, which despite its outside appearance was as well set up as its mistress, Rosha had misgivings; especially when she noticed the look of admiration on her father's face and the graceful pose of the attractive woman sitting by the spinning wheel. Rosha would have been more alarmed if she knew what was going through Widow Flaherty's head. My, the woman thought, I can see that Sean O'Neill admires me. I would be in clover if I could hook him. A little smile played across her face. Mistress of Garton ...

Uneasy at her father's glowing expression, Rosha rose abruptly to her feet. 'Daddy,' she said, glancing at the large saucepan of water simmering by the hearth, 'I think we have disturbed Mrs Flaherty when she was about to prepare a meal.'

The widow raised her eyes. 'That is my weapon in case Sir Thomas Catalong or his bailiff dare put a foot across my door.' Sean looked shocked. 'How else', she said gently, fondling a piece of sheep's wool, 'can a lone widow with a child protect herself?'

Rosha parted from her father who was going on to see Dan Murphy. Before he turned away he asked: 'Do you like Patrick Murphy?'

Surprised, she replied: 'He's all right, I suppose.' Later she was to remember those words and regret them.


Sir Thomas Catalong was riding down a path in the woods when he saw a young girl ahead of him. By heavens, he thought, that fool of a bailiff ... young Bridie Boyce did not go away to service after all. He urged his horse to a quick trot. When Rosha turned around he realised that this was a younger girl, in fact O'Neill of Garton's daughter.

'Good afternoon,' he said pleasantly.

Anger darkened Rosha's eyes. 'You struck our farmhand,' she said accusingly.

He smiled. 'The man was stealing my wood. I seem to remember that you struck me with a stone. What a spirited young miss you are!' As he spoke, Catalong swung his leg off the animal's back, his eyes never leaving Rosha's face.

She was alarmed by his expression but tried not to show it. 'Good day,' she murmured, and turned blindly towards the trees, then blundered on into the undergrowth where briars and branches snatched at her clothes. She heard the horse moving slowly on the path.

'Miss O'Neill, where are you? Come out and I'll escort you through the woods.' He was trying to make his way in among the trees now.

Rosha, in a dark tunnel of undergrowth, lay flat on the ground with her face pressed into the earth. She crawled slowly forward until she saw a stone wall a little way ahead. Frightened to appear in the open she listened for the sound of a horse; it came from some distance off. Cautiously she rose to her feet and crossed a yard to a back door which was partly open. Then she realised where she was − at the back of Merifield Manor. Voices came from a far off kitchen, and at that moment a young maid appeared carrying a basket.

'Why, it's Miss O'Neill from Garton ...'

'Is Edmund Catalong around anywhere?'

'The young master's in Dilford,' she said, looking curiously at the state of Rosha's clothes.

'I got lost in the woods.'

'Come wi' me. I pass Garton on the way home.'

Rosha was overwhelmed with relief. As though the girl could read her thoughts, she said: 'I know a path to get away from this place. No danger of meeting anyone.'

'Under God, where were you?' Nellie asked in a scolding voice when Rosha arrived home. To her astonishment, the girl began to cry. 'Musha, what ails you?' she asked in alarm, having never seen her charge cry before; spoilt, with every wish granted, there had been no need for tears.

Upstairs, while Rosha washed and put on clean clothes, she told the servant girl what had happened.

'Holy virgin, save us from that devil.' Then, bluntly and fully, Nellie told her all the facts of life, adding that was why Rory Donavan had taken his sister and Bridie away to the hiring fair.

'Does Bridie know all this?' Rosha asked, pale and horrified.

'I pray to God m'mam made a good job of telling her.'

# Chapter Five

Bridie ran excitedly up the main staircase of Horton House to the big bedroom at the top of the stairs. The place seemed familiar now because she cleaned this room once a week. Mrs O'Sullivan had shown her how to dust the worn curtains and bed-hangings, carefully explaining about the old but valuable pink brocade.

'You must improve yourself, child,' she said. 'Never know when or where Opportunity will hand out a token.'

After that, Bridie listened carefully to everything the housekeeper told her, determined to improve herself. A welcome opportunity came that morning when Mrs O'Sullivan tried on her best boots and found they were setting her corns on fire.

'You'd better have them, dear, and don't say a word to Himself for they'd fetch a fair penny from the pedlar.'

'But he'll see them on me, ma'am, when I go to Mass.' Bridie knew the boots fitted her because she often sneaked into them when she was cleaning her mistress's room.

'Deal a bit of notice he'll take. Himself isn't all that bright. I'm the one who got us well placed in life. Twice.'

In the room with the pink brocade curtains was a cheval-mirror. Bridie lifted her skirt and pirouetted around admiring the boots from every angle. They had dear wee black buttons down each side with tiny steel tips set in the centre. Like a string of stars, she thought, as they twinkled in the glass.

When she went downstairs to change into her hobnailed boots, the housekeeper said, 'They were made for the feet of a lady, child — my last mistress — so don't offend them by entering quarters that would belittle their previous existence.'

Bridie blushed, realising that the housekeeper was referring to the byre, which Bridie preferred to use for the call of nature, instead of the wee house down the rose garden, which had a good view but splinters in the seat.

'I'll wear them to Mass on Sundays, Mrs O'Sullivan, when we leave by the front door. Sure they'll never know that they've come down in the world!'

When Barney came in and heard their laughter, he wondered how he and his wife had existed by themselves in this great barrack of a house. The lack of company in such a lonely part of the country was lamentable. They would have been welcomed to ceildhe at the farms down the glen but the agent's orders were that the place must never be deserted at nightfall. There was unrest in the country and the gentry were scared of the Fenians. Begod, so was Barney himself!

One afternoon Bridie was ironing bed linen on the kitchen table when there was the sound of a cart drawing into the yard.

'Who can that be?' the housekeeper wondered. The packman and pedlars either came on foot or on horseback. Nora O'Sullivan peeped out of the window and said in surprise, 'It's your friends, dear. Go on out and bring them in for a bite and sup.'

Bridie placed the flat iron on the hearth beside the other one which was heating and ran out to the yard, leaping around in her old joyful way because she had slipped out of her boots. Rory jumped down off the cart and held out his hand awkwardly, not used to this new Bridie, with her hair neatly rolled, and dressed in a cream blouse and dark green skirt under a white pinny. Only her dancing feet were familiar, except that they were no longer bare but covered in black woollen stockings.

She ignored his proffered hand and hugged him and Eileen. He smiled broadly. Bridie hadn't changed a bit.

Eileen did not respond to this warm greeting. ''Tis a wile big place, isin it?' she said fearfully, glancing up at the house as though it were about to attack.

'Come and greet my mistress. She welcomes ye.'

45

Rory saluted the housekeeper shyly. 'I had business for my master in this locality, ma'am.'

'Bridie will be pleased to see her friends. Now get the ironing out of the way, child, and lay the table. But first put on your boots.'

It was a rebuke. Bridie coloured. She was not allowed to take off her boots during the day or to be seen in the bare feet. When the visitors had eaten, she took them down to the shore. The two young people chatted away about home which Rory had recently visited. He was to be allowed home again in the spring, he said, to sow the crops. Eileen, who had run down to the beach, called, 'There's pretty shells here.'

'How's she gettin' on, Rory?'

'Her mistress talks away to her as if she had the same sense in her head as the rest of us.'

'Maybe that'll be the curing of her. She must work hard for that's a terrible pair of hands on her body.'

'Aye, there's a lot of rough floors to be scrubbed and my sister's an expert at it, the mistress says.'

'Wouldn't I pay the same compliment if someone scrubbed my floors!'

Rory laughed and glanced at Bridie's hands. 'I'm sure ye do yer share, though they're not showing much sign of toil.'

'I rub them with a liquid Mrs O'Sullivan makes from wild flowers. Rory, ye know, Mrs O'Sullivan's goin' to make me fit to be a lady's maid one day.'

'Sure yer showing signs already. Don't change too much, Bridie — yer just right.'

Eileen ran up the shore. 'Rory, did ye tell Bridie the way I slapped the dog's lug when he ate the wee birdie?'

'And ye nearly slapped mine as well!'

'Ah, yer coddin!' His sister ran off again, her face shining with pride.

'Did ye see Nellie when you were home?'

'I did,' he replied, turning his face away to hide the rising colour.

'Are you courtin' her?' she asked mischievously.

'I am.' Rory recalled the journey he had made across to Slievegar. The dance at the crossroads, the stealing into the hedge and kissing. Nellie surprised him by her forwardness and himself getting into a hell of a fire and her whispering in a desperate voice, "If only it weren't a sin." Then, "If only I weren't frightened to get into trouble." And Rory, fighting his nature too because he realised it would not take too much persuasion to make Nellie change her mind, wished she had not put words to her thoughts. It was taking things too fast, too soon.

A few days after the Donavans called, Bridie came in from the byre after the early morning milking and found to her surprise that the O'Sullivans were in a state of great agitation. Mrs O'Sullivan had a letter in her hand. Bridie took the milk down to the dairy, poured it into a crock, then washed and scalded the can. She felt uneasy about the strange atmosphere in the kitchen.

'Come here, Bridie.' The sharp tone of her mistress' voice sent her scurrying up to the kitchen again. 'We've had a letter from the agent and he's agreeable that your six months' employment should be extended.'

'That's grand, Mrs O'Sullivan.'

'Now that the six months is nearly up you'd better take your wages and go home to see your mother.' The housekeeper made brisk little movements with her hands. 'So, as himself is goin' across the hill today to Lisdare, it would be a chance for you to get a lift that far. Barney'll put you aboard the mail coach leaving at two o'clock for Iskaglen. Thank goodness we won't be so cut off when the coach starts coming down this way.'

'*Today*?'

'Don't gawp, child, that's what I said. Now dress in your best clothes and I'll be getting a bit of food and drink together. Barney will be in Lisdare to meet you again on Friday, so be on the road in good time to catch the coach.' Mrs O'Sullivan saw the expressions racing across the girl's face — surprise, joy and bewilderment. Bridie was the daughter she had longed for. She must look after her well and protect her from the terrible danger that could threaten her in this house.

The older woman wanted to embrace the young girl before she stepped into the trap, but suddenly remembered

47

the words of her last mistress: 'Always live up to your station in life. Don't be too familiar with lower servants.' But I've made a good job of her, Mrs O'Sullivan thought with satisfaction, remembering how Bridie had looked in the old shawl and hobnailed boots.

''Tis a grand day, Barney, isn't it?' Bridie said excitedly, enjoying sitting in the pony trap in her fine new clothes. She always called him by his christian name because he wouldn't answer to any other. He grunted. She tried again. 'A dear wee robin has settled itself on the trap door, Barney. I think I'll give it a crumb to eat.'

'Hould yer hand or the cheeky wee bugger will make a mess on us,' he growled.

Ingidnant colour flooded Bridie's cheeks. Yer an oul cross bugger yerself, she thought. She loved robins. The one she fed every day at Horton often hopped into the kitchen, not a bit scared. Her little friend, she called it. Her hand crept into the basket, separated the linen cloth covering the food and crumbled a piece of bread which she scattered on the seat opposite. The little bird pecked at it happily. She put out her tongue at Barney's back. It might be her robin.

Rosha and Bridie met on the doorstep of Boyce's cottage at Iskaglen. Bridie was furious when she saw her. Why did *she* have to come today? Spoiling the lovely surprised expression on her mother's face when she saw Bridie's new clothes. Now her attention would be divided between them. When they walked inside, the kitchen was empty and the fire burning low.

'Where is she atal?' Bridie murmured, disappointed. 'Maybe with Mrs Donavan. You stay here, Rosha, and I'll find her.'

Rosha was startled by Bridie's appearance. The shoulder cape and the bonnet she wore looked like the rig old Biddy Coll wore to Mass on Sundays. Bridie Boyce's obvious displeasure at seeing her, combined with the unsuitable clothes, made the girl seem threatening and unfriendly. She never liked me, Rosha thought.

When Bridie reached the door of Donavan's cottage, she was annoyed to find Rosha O'Neill at her heels. Trust her to have her own way, spoilt brat. But there was mam rushing towards her with an expression of surprise and joy.

'Bridie, love, sure I wasn't expecting ye. Ah, alannah, what fine clothes. Like a lady, ye are. Och, is that wee Rosha as well?' As Grace looked at the two girls she thought they could be sisters; the lovely eyes with high cheekbones, and the same colouring. She hugged Bridie and kissed Rosha on the cheek.

A smothered cry from Mrs Donavan sitting by the hearth drew their attention. The woman's head was bent in an expression of despair.

'What ails Mrs Donavan, Mam?'

'She's been evicted, and her not all that far behind wi' the rent. Other neighbours and the Protestant minister have already left Iskaglen.'

'Mam ...' Bridie tugged at her mother's skirt. 'I've got me wages. Couldn't ye give her that and Rory will pay us back.'

'No!' Rosha said quickly. 'My father says all evictions must be resisted. Wait, Mrs Donavan, I'll go home and tell him. He'll know what to do.'

'Child, there isn't time,' Grace Boyce told her. 'The bailiff and his men are comin' early tomorrow mornin'.'

Rosha ran out of the door. Bridie and her mother followed. A pony, which Bridie hadn't noticed before, was standing over by the hedge feeding on the grass. Before their startled gaze, Rosha whipped up her skirt and flung her leg across the animal's back. White frilled drawers came down below the knee of her black stockings. She's a sight but it doesn't bother her, Bridie thought enviously. She's so sure of herself.

Glancing over her shoulder, Rosha called out, 'Don't tell Nellie. I'm not allowed to ride this way.'

'Ah, child, what if ye meet the holy father?' Grace was very concerned about Rosha's immodest appearance.

'I'll jump off and whip my skirt down.'

'Her father bought the pony for her birthday,' Grace told Bridie. 'I pray to God she doesn't break her neck on it. Come in and I'll make some tea and we'll have yer news. I'm feared there's goin' to be terrible trouble in Iskaglen tomorrow.'

*

49

At Garton, a line of white sheets in the orchard billowed like sails in the wind. The grass in its new growth was brightly patterned with daisies and buttercups. Further down the orchard, tight buds clustered on the branches of the apple trees. It was a mild spring which had brought early lambing and all around the hills men were busy attending to their sheep. Rosha ran up to her father. 'Daddy, do you know what's happened?'

'Dammit to hell,' Sean swore when he heard what his daughter had to say. 'So Catalong's back and using new tactics, curse him. Why didn't Grace Boyce let me know? She's got more sense in her head than the neighbour. Surely Rory explained to them what action to take if such a situation arose?'

'I think word had just come from the castle, Daddy. Mrs Donavan is in a dreadful state. She can't stop crying.'

'Willie ... Paddy,' Sean shouted. 'One of you get up to the hill top and alert the countryside for a meeting this evening.'

Rosha caught his arm. 'Let me go and light the fire. I know what to do.'

'Good girl. Off you go then. Everything's at hand. Here, take these dry matches. Stay with it until one of the men can take over.'

Rosha made her way up through the pass to the summit of Crockmar. She loved hill walking and often took this path searching for wild flowers. The heather and moss were beginning to lose their dingy grey appearance and show a pale green colour. Now the winds of winter had changed to a soft spring breeze which made walking a pleasure. She removed the stones from the hollow on the hillside where the fire equipment was hidden.

When the first leaf of flame shot up, Rosha had a feeling of excitement, aware that the fire would affect the lives of the entire countryside that evening. She looked down below where the farmers were turning over the rich black earth or sowing seeds. The figures stopped when they saw the flames on the hill and waved their arms. Rosha waved back. Through the trees by the bay she could see the outline of Merifield Manor. Somehow it was difficult to associate Edmund with that place and the man who owned it.

Though two meetings had previously taken place in the parochial hall, the castle landlord still outwitted the people, seemingly by just keeping on the right side of the law. There were people who starved themselves to scrape the money together to pay secretly to the landlord the excess rents which were contrary to the Land League's rules. Sean realised that he would have to be twice as smart this time. Catalong was now bringing in extra bailiffs and emergency men. The constabulary were always at hand to clear the way. Canon McFadden of Gweedore had opposed the landlords in that area by showing an organised resistance and Sean was planning to follow his example. The Canon's action had aroused great interest and prompted questions in the British Parliament.

Over in England, the man in the street, though not completely understanding the situation in Ireland, was asking questions too. Letters were steadily flowing across the Atlantic to Irish immigrants in America and stirring feelings that had lain dormant during the immigrants' struggle to establish themselves in the new land.

It was still night with moonlight flitting through the clouds when a crowd of men wearing cloth caps plodded along the roads towards the parochial hall. There was no sound of talk or laughter, only the loud ringing of their hobnailed boots. The force of men gave each other courage: they might be the next to face eviction.

Patrick Murphy was running across Togher Glen to catch up with the men when he noticed a light near the old ruined cottage. His father said no one would live there because the place was haunted by a murdered redcoat. Patrick thought it was unlikely that a ghost, especially a redcoat, would carry a lighted lantern at this time of night! He crept closer to the old building and froze in consternation when he saw a group of constables bending over a map. They extinguished the lamp and turned in the direction of the road. He moved away and sped in the direction of the men going to the meeting. Panting, he caught up with them.

'Get off the road and scatter out. A group of constabulary have arrived from Lisdare.'

'Is that you, son?' Dan Murphy hissed. 'Git home to yer books.'

'No, Father,' Patrick said determinedly, 'I'm going to hear O'Neill.'

The hall was jam-packed, with the door firmly bolted. Sean O'Neill placed a chair in the middle of the crowd, stood on it and told them what had happened. 'My friends, I know why the castle landlord is moving so fast. Apart from rumour, I have studied the area where recent evictions have taken place. The ground in the peninsula of Iskaglen is very fertile. Catalong has come to the realisation that sheep farming is a profitable concern. He wants your land – the land that is yours by right and for which you have been paying a rent, an increasing rent that is beyond most of your pockets.'

There was a howl of rage. He held up his hand. 'Whatever action we take must be within the limit of the law. Tomorrow morning early, at six o'clock, I want every man here to gather around Donavan's cottage in Iskaglen. You must *not* carry any weapons. Mrs Donavan is on her own. All the children are away from home working.'

'She's no longer on her own, Mr O'Neill,' Rory called from the back of the hall. 'I've just come back to see to the crops.'

'I'm very glad to see you, lad.'

Dan Murphy came up, caught Sean's arm and whispered: 'There's a Judas in the company.'

'A Judas?'

'A member of the constabulary.'

'No! Thank God we're speaking in Gaelic.'

'This one is a Gaelic speaker. He's been sent deliberately. Someone's just warned me. He knows every bliddy word that was said. A stranger in these parts.'

'Well ...' Sean was troubled for a moment, then threw his head back defiantly. 'All right. So, we'd better be well prepared in the morning.'

Next morning Rosha slipped out of bed when a pale sun

52

was breaking through the grey haze over in the east. She splashed cold water on her face, dressed warmly and crept downstairs to the kitchen. Nellie was stirring the big black-bellied porridge pot, while the two farmhands slunk reluctantly from their room to the rain barrel outside the kitchen door where they washed themselves.

Sean came into the kitchen, his heavy twill trousers pushed into high leather boots. 'Rosha, what are you doing up?'

'I want to go to Iskaglen to keep Grace and Mrs Donavan company.'

'No need,' Nellie snapped, furious because the master wouldn't let herself go. 'Isin our Bridie there? And Rory came home last night.'

'When the men come back later, Nellie, you can go and see your mother.'

The girl swung round with the dripping porridge stick in her hand; it splattered the cat which spit and fled. 'Oh, can I, Mr O'Neill?' Her plump cheeks flushed a becoming pink and her eyes sparkled at the thought of seeing Rory Donavan again. The last time he came home they'd had a great tussle in the hay and she'd had to save herself by saying a prayer. Out loud. That cooled him!

'Daddy?'

'No, Rosha. It's no place for women, especially young girls.'

She stamped her foot in anger. 'No place for women? And what do you call Grace and Mrs Donavan and Bridie Boyce?'

Sean shook his head impatiently. He liked quietness in the morning. 'If you promise to stay up in Grace's house, you can ride on my horse. Now eat up your breakfast.'

The anxious expression on Sean's face lightened when he crossed the stream to Iskaglen and saw floods of men approaching from all directions towards the hamlet. What a sad lonely place the glen was now, he thought, remembering the time when it was bright with children's laughter. What a bloody nerve of Catalong to fence in part of the hill! Surely the hills belonged to the people since time began? Catalong should remember the fate that had met other men of his kind. Damn his arrogance.

Bridie was at the door when Rosha slipped off her father's horse. 'What brings you here, Rosha?' Bridie asked as the two girls walked into the house.

'Keeping you company.'

'I don' need company. I'm goin' down to Donavan's now. You stay here.' Bridie pulled her mother's old shawl from the peg on the wall, wrapped it around her shoulders and went out slamming the door without another word.

Sean was heartened to see the crowds of men surging around Donavan's cottage, as though some invincible force was driving them on. They parted to let him ride through. On the doorstep he held up his hand and spoke. 'A council of war, my friends! We'll defend this house to the last. Agreed?' There was a shout of assent.

It was decided that Dan Murphy, Rory and the two women would barricade themselves inside. Supplies of wood were pushed through the door by willing hands. While the two men built a barricade, Grace and Mrs Donavan cooked a huge pot of porridge for defending the cottage. They had not long to wait for the attack. Fifty armed members of the constabulary marched down the road, accompanied by the Resident Magistrate and Catalong's agent, Captain Hurl; also the bailiffs and a medical officer. The senior policeman pleaded with Sean to withdraw his men and avoid bloodshed.

'I must tell you, sir,' he said in a loud voice, 'that Donavans have lived in this cottage for over one hundred years. Sir Thomas Catalong has demanded an immediate rise in rent and has not given sufficient time for Mrs Donavan to find ways of procuring it. Apart from that, the increase is totally unjust. I beg you, take your men away and allow this case to be considered.'

'We have to do our duty, sir,' the officer said.

'Inspector,' Catalong's bailiff called impatiently, 'get your men to clear a way. I want to make an entry.'

The solid mass of farmers was pushed roughly aside. After banging on the door, the bailiff went round to the back of the cottage. The far gable, close to the trees, was undefended. He went at it with a crowbar, striking at the foundation of the building. Inside, Rory placed a ladder against the gable and

54

quietly made a hole through the thatched roof, above where the man was working. He climbed down again and carried up a boulder which he dropped on the unsuspecting bailiff, who crumpled in a heap and was immediately carried away to receive attention from the doctor. Dan Murphy swiftly blocked up the hole again.

Sean was beginning to lose control of his men who were arming themselves with stones which Bridie was carrying from a little quarry nearby. Rosha, who had ignored Bridie's suggestion, wrapped an old egg-shawl around her head and sneaked down the road where she helped with the stone gathering.

'Dirtying yer hands, are ye?' Bridie said, though she was glad of Rosha's help.

'Where will they attack next?' Rory asked Dan Murphy.

'Begob, it's hard to know, Rory. If I wis them I'd have a good poke at the door.' Just then, the sound of splintering wood was heard. Dan removed some pieces of the barrier while Rory hurried to the pot of thin porridge bubbling on the hearth.

'Let me have the pleasure,' Grace said quietly, dipping a can into the pot.

There was a banging, then the bailiff called through the hole which he had just made.

'Open up in the name of the Queen, afore one of ye is harmed,' he shouted threateningly.

'Open yer mouth wide!' Grace called, and flung the contents of the can into his face.

Rory and Dan quickly made good the broken barrier, unconcerned by the squeals of pain outside.

'By the power of God, one's comin' down the roof,' Mrs Donavan cried hysterically, grabbing her rosary beads.

By the power of the devil, Grace thought, but it was a saying her friend had. Poor soul, she was losing her nerve entirely. Dan Murphy pulled a long, sharp bog-spear from behind one of the beams supporting the roof and, standing on the table, thrust it through the thatch. Another shout of pain came from outside. We'll make them very angry, Grace thought, pouring water from the kettle into the saucepan of porridge to keep it thin in case she needed to use it again.

55

The mood was growing ugly, on the side of the pro-
testers – and of the law. Sean had trouble restraining
the men who were throwing stones at the constables. Two
bailiffs injured and the house still uncaptured, he thought
with satisfaction.

Impatiently, the officer in charge called on the Resident
Magistrate to read the Riot Act, passed by the British
Parliament to suppress riots and disturbances in Ireland.
The Magistrate produced a copy, cleared his throat and
read out loud: 'Our Sovereign Lady the Queen chargeth and
commandeth immediately all persons assembled to disperse
themselves, and peacefully to depart to their habitations or
to their lawful business, upon the pains contained in the Act
made in the twenty-seventh year of the reign of King George
the Third to prevent tumultuous risings and assemblies. God
save the Queen.'

An uneasy silence grew when the constabulary lined up,
loaded and pointed their rifles at the men surrounding the
cottage. My God, what am I going to do? Sean wondered,
now seriously worried. This is how Catalong and his like
are getting away with their evictions. I'll have to order them
out of the cottage immediately or there'll be bloodshed. I'm
afraid I can't stop this eviction.

At that moment, something happened which shattered
everyone and gave Sean time to think of a possible course of
action. Two policemen walked from the ranks, unloaded their
guns and placed them at the feet of their senior officer. With
tears in his eyes the older one said, 'We will not be responsible
for firing on our down-trodden countrymen, sir.'

While the two constables were being seized and arrested,
Sean took advantage of the commotion the followed. He
hurried across to Patrick who was urging the two girls to get
away up the road and told him what he had in mind. Patrick
followed him eagerly to the back gable. The girls came too.

'Rory, Dan,' Sean called in, 'unblock the hole the bailiff
made ... quickly!'

When all the loose bricks were pulled out, he said,
'Listen, Patrick's coming in. When he's hidden himself
in the loft, you're to open the door immediately and give
yourselves up.'

But Patrick wasn't able to get through the hole. 'I'll do it,' Bridie offered eagerly. Sean groaned when he saw that she was going to have exactly the same problem. The hole simply wasn't big enough.

'All's lost,' he said, defeated. Before he could say another word, Rosha was wriggling through the broken stonework.

Inside, Rory pushed her up into the loft and gave hasty instructions while Sean waited helplessly on the other side of the wall, terrified in case his daughter got injured. He tried not to think that a minute ago he'd been quite prepared to let one of the other young people go instead.

Rory, Dan Murphy and the two women were in the hands of the constables when Sean walked around to the front of the cottage again. Three bailiffs went inside, extinguished the fire in the hearth, threw out the Donavans' bits of furniture and nailed up the window and door, then read the eviction order.

But the eviction order was made invalid because someone was in the cottage and the fire was lit.

Captain Hurl, the castle agent, suddenly became aware of the odd atmosphere and the expressions on the rebellious faces. 'There's something going on here,' he said hurriedly to the Magistrate and senior policeman. At the moment a flow of smoke came from the chimney. A loud deafening cheer broke from all Sean's men and, as the smoke wafted across their heads, they felt as blessed as if they were in church and incense flowing from the thurible.

Inside the cottage, Rosha was tearing fistfuls of straw out of the mattress in which she had concealed herself in the loft and piling it on the fire. She had been over-generous with the can of oil that came out of the cupboard in the dresser and nearly caught her skirt alight. She prayed hard that her father's plan would work. The roar of the flames, dancing merrily up the chimney, seemed to be telling her that they had won.

The agent was furious and tried to bluff himself out of the situation, though he felt uneasy in the presence of the Constabulary. He was aware that he and Catalong had often used the instrument of the law to suit their own purposes. This time, unfortunately, they were up against Sean O'Neill.

57

'Captain Hurl,' Sean said curtly, 'take your bailiffs away from here at once.'

The man hesitated, wondering if there was some way he could still carry out the eviction. Catalong will be furious, he thought.

'It is illegal to try and execute a decree that has already taken place,' Sean reminded him sharply.

'That's right, Captain Hurl,' the police inspector said reluctantly. 'Fresh proceedings will have to be taken out, but it is disgraceful how these people got round the eviction in this shabby manner.'

'Shabby?' Sean gave a harsh laugh. 'I could use a stronger word for the eviction of a poor lonely woman. Sir, remove your people at once.'

'Two bailiffs have been injured. These two men were responsible and are under arrest,' the inspector told him. 'A charge will also be brought against the women.'

Bridie hurried over to him. 'Sir, wid ye be kind enough to allow me to take me mam and Mrs Donavan over to the shed to relieve themselves?'

She got a curt nod of approval and with eyes cast down modestly the three women walked slowly across the yard. Inside the shed, Bridie jammed the door with a wooden post. 'Don't sit down,' she hissed as Mrs Donavan whipped up her skirt. She pushed them through the broken stonework on the back wall which led into the undergrowth outside. The three of them took to their heels and didn't stop running until they were across the burn and safely inside Garton with Nellie.

# Chapter Six

Lying in her comfortable bed at Horton House, Bridie Boyce had a feeling of guilt when she found herself comparing this bedroom with the loft at home. While she was away, Mrs O'Sullivan had made new curtains for the window and covered the floor with a woollen rug. When the housekeeper and her husband retired at night, Bridie always opened her bedroom door and enjoyed the warmth from the fire in the hearth which Barney banked up with peat before going to bed. In the morning, all that was left was a fine silver ash covering the glowing wood-cinders. Soon the fire was kindled again and the kettle on the boil for breakfast. By the time the O'Sullivans came downstairs, the porridge was bubbling, the table laid, and the egg-saucepan simmering expectantly for the freshly laid eggs Bridie collected from the hen house.

Her visit to Iskaglen had not been the pleasant event she had anticipated. Bridie couldn't get over Rosha O'Neill hiding herself in the straw mattress up in the loft to stop the eviction or make it invalid. Though willing at the time, she herself would have been terrified: the bailiffs were known to be ruthless. Rory and Dan Murphy had been thrown into prison for a month while Mam and Mrs Donavan were discharged on bail. The little escape plan cheered up their hearts then, but they didn't get away with it for long.

Though their neighbour returned to her cottage when it was habitable, Mr O'Neill warned that the problem would crop up again: Catalong was determined to clear the glen. The Boyces' cottage was safe for the time being because the ground close to it was covered with the bones of ancient rock and scree. When the second notice of eviction was served on Mrs Donavan, the bailiff found to his delight that she was away from home. A nephew's wedding had taken her to Dilford where she had stayed, not the two days that Grace Boyce had expected, but several. On her return to Iskaglen Mrs Donavan found all her property stacked in the byre and a new tenant in possession of her home. The baker gave her a lift back to Dilford and carried the news on to Rory in prison at Lisdare.

Grace, who had taken the cow in with her own and fed the fowls, was helpless to do a thing. She missed her neighbour and took to singing to keep herself company. When the band started down the road, outside the fiddler's house, she sat out on the hedge and joined in. The new tenant in Donavans' was an employee of the castle who came under the Land League strict order of boycotting – a harsh rule that forbade Grace Boyce to make any contact with these people. The man was surly-looking and his wife, who crept along the hedges like a shadow, looked as though she was silently apologising for her existence. These strangers in their midst were completely isolated in the small community. Tin Lizzie was not allowed to serve them with goods, nor the blacksmith to shoe their horses. Grace raged silently at the landlord who had created such an unhappy situation. But a total boycott was the reprisal for an unjust eviction and God help anyone who broke that rule. She felt pity for the new neighbours and wondered if they existed on air. Their cow had disappeared overnight and their hens were suffering from a strange sickness.

One day when her husband was at work the little hedge-wife, as Grace called her, took to the road and headed for her parents' home, some thirty miles away. When the husband followed in pursuit, Grace flew over to Garton and returned in the trap with Sean and Rosha. But action to reclaim the cottage was lost for the bailiff and his men moved in immediately and razed the little building to the ground. Grace couldn't believe her eyes. All the fun she had there. Now it no longer existed. Just a pile of stones left.

A few weeks later Rosha was in the field with the horses

when she saw Rory Donavan crossing the stream. He moved purposefully, cap pulled down to his eyes, long arms swinging by his side. There was something odd about him as if the time in prison had sent back an older, harder youth from the one she knew. When he returned to Iskaglen and saw the demolition of his home, tears came to his eyes and anger filled his heart. Everything he had dreamed about had gone: the land he had worked hard to keep going, the crops he had sown earlier on, all dug into the ground by a stranger's hand. 'Curse ye to hell, Catalong,' he swore.

Grace Boyce, who had been spreading sheets over the fuchsia bushes on the high ground behind her house, saw Rory staring down at the ruins of his old home. Never had she beheld such a look of despair about another living creature. Tossing the sheet from her she ran over the rough ground to the road.

'C'mon, lad, there's always a place for ye under my roof. Sure 'tis no wonder ye've a grievin' heart.' She did not know what words of comfort to offer him.

He was quiet, almost sullen as he ate the meal she prepared. 'Ye'd have called at Dilford ... how's yer mam?'

'Settled wi' the uncle. She never wants to see this place again.' Grace winced. After another long silence he rose, pulled the cap down on his forehead again and went to the door. 'Thanks for the meal, Mrs Boyce. I'll get my land back one day.'

'Faith, ye wil, lad. Times will change. 'Tis a terrible thing surely when we canna be sure of the seat by our hearth.'

Rory made the mistake of climbing over the gates of Merifield Manor and drawing attention to his presence. At that moment, Sir Thomas Catalong and his agent were crossing the parkland near the house.

'I don't like the look of him, Sir Thomas,' Captain Hurl said anxiously.

'Nor I. Get the men.'

Recklessly, Rory broke into a run when he saw Catalong walking on his own towards the manor. It was as well the agent with the bailiff and one of his men reached their employer first for Rory felt murderous. The two castle servants sprang on him and, twisting his arms behind his back, pushed and dragged him down to the gate where they swung him over like a bag of chaff out on to the rough stone road where he lay stunned and bleeding. Rory was soon on his feet again. He picked up a handful of large stones lying by the hedge and flung them after the bailiff who caught one on his neck. Outraged, the man held up his blackthorn stick and said threateningly, 'If I catch you near this estate again, Donavan, I'll use my pistol.'

'By God, I'll be back and don' ye forget it!'

When Rosha saw Rory coming down the road again, she galloped to the hedge and called: 'Have you been to see Nellie? Your face ... it's all cut.'

Reluctantly he looked towards the hedge but not directly at her. 'That's a fine animal ye've got there.'

'Rory, your face is all bleeding.'

'Aye, so.' He dabbed at it hurriedly and took the road towards Dilford.

Rosha shrugged, slipped off the animal's back, and slapping it affectionately, ran down to the shore road. Something attracted her attention over by the bay. It was an arrow gliding towards the water then plunging down. She immediately forgot about Rory Donavan and sped across the shingle, the skirt whipping about her legs and hair flying in the breeze.

When Edmund saw her coming he waved his hand. She paused at the sight of a woman sitting on the grass, near where he was standing. This casual, relaxed attitude in a member of the gentry surprised her. Shyly, Rosha approached them.

'Aunt Madeline, this is the friend whom I told you about.'

'Hello, Rosha. I am so pleased Edmund has found a friend here.'

'My father doesn't know,' he informed her quickly. 'Nor does Rosha's.'

Madeline Allenby smoothed her dark blue checked skirt and straightened the short matching jacket. 'I'll keep your secret, my dears. Now I must be getting back to the manor.' She smiled at Rosha and walked away, thinking, My brother-in-law would be furious if he knew his son was associating with one of the locals. Why doesn't he bring his next-door neighbour's children, the Meckins, over here at holiday time? She suspected the reason and a disapproving frown crossed her face. Other children might show a curiosity which was forbidden to his son.

'I like your aunt, Edmund.'

'She's my mother's sister. Their father, my grandfather, used to own this estate. Mama inherited it, then it became my father's. Or ...' he paused ' ... my aunt said one day that it was settled on my father. I don't really understand. Come, I want to show you something.'

They went down to the water's edge. 'Take off your shoes, Rosha, or can you jump? We're going over to the little island.

She lifted her skirt and jumped across the muddy ground, missing the water by inches. 'Nellie says this tiny island was a piece of earth that fell off God's spade when he was setting Ireland down between the Atlantic and the Irish Sea.' Edmund laughed.

The thin emaciated trees at the water's edge gradually grew upright and strong towards the centre where she discovered he was building a tree house. The old tree's strong out-spreading branches were at a convenient height from the ground. The house was floored with odd bits of boards roughly slatted together, and now he was trying to weave lengths of cane to make sound walls. She showed him how the men did it at Garton. They worked away, chatting and munching sweets from the poke she had bought that morning from Tin Lizzie's shop.

'Why are you making a tree-house here, Edmund, instead of out in the woods?' she asked, remembering the times when water sneaked up on the island.

'Because here I can get away from ... everyone.'

That's not what he meant to say, Rosha thought.

'You're the only one who knows about it,' he told her, and added mischievously, 'That fierce Nellie won't be able to find you here. You know,' he said with a sudden frown, 'I thought my father was going to be injured today.'

'What happened?'

'A youth jumped the gates and was about to attack him when the agent went for help.'

'Rory Donavan,' Roshas said flatly, her happy mood slipping away.

'Donavan? Who is he?'

'Nellie's boyfriend. Your father got the bailiff to pull down his mother's cottage, right down to the ground so that the Donavans wouldn't be able to live in it again.'

Edmund's hand tightened on the piece of cane he was working on. She noticed his look of shame. ''Tis not the first time,' she said severely, anger beginning to build up against him too, as if he shared his father's guilt. Her anger increased. Now it was directed at herself for wanting to play with the boy from the castle, the son of the man who put fear in to the faces of the people and had frightened her the other day. She rose abruptly, dusted the knees of her black stockings and said shortly, 'I must go.'

'Rosha ...'

'Yes?'

He didn't turn to look at her; his eyes were far away on the hills behind Iskaglen. 'When I'm older ...' He turned then, saw the unfriendly expression on the girl's face and added quickly, 'When I inherit this estate one day, everything will be changed.'

She bent her head and said quietly, 'I'm glad you told me that, Edmund.'

Patrick Murphy could not believe his good luck about sharing lessons with Rosha O'Neill. He loved his books and resented the times his father had kept him home from school to help on the farm. There must be something behind this arrangement to make his father strike the bargain ... something powerful. Rosha was beginning to resent Patrick. He was too possessive of her, she thought. Nellie praised him, her father encouraged him. Such a good young fellow, they said, throwing resentful glances at Rosha who felt hampered by his presence, and made guilty by his acts of kindness. She did admire the way he grappled with the terrible arithmetic problems set by Mr Stewart. She had to work them out repeatedly on her jotter, their dullness battering at her reluctant brain. English was different. Rosha loved the language, preferring it to Irish which the servants spoke all the time when they were together. Her attitude angered Patrick who was a brilliant Irish scholar, excelling himself in his historical knowledge of their country.

And all the time Nellie Boyce watched them, thinking, Why is Sean O'Neill trying to make a match between this pair?

Indignant, one day, because her father had suggested Patrick should do his homework at Garton in future, Rosha ran down to the shore and began to pelt seagulls sitting on an old coracle. When she turned her head, Edmund was standing some distance away about to fire an arrow. Ashamed by her childish outburst, she hurried across to him and said quickly to cover her embarrassment: 'There's a wood pigeon. Quick! Kill it before it gets away.'

He lowered his arms. 'Why should I kill it? Perhaps it has a family waiting in the woods. It would be cruel.'

'Cruel? My father shoots birds and we eat them. Sometimes there are dozens of tiny birds covering our kitchen floor. And doesn't your own father take people out shooting on the hills? Nellie says they should leave them for the poor people to catch, to fill their stomachs, instead of sporting themselves.' Rosha clapped a hand across her mouth at the indiscretion.

Edmund lowered his arms and said quietly: 'Nellie's right. My father and his friends bring back bagfuls. One day I found a pit in the grounds full of dead birds. Some of them were quite warm. Come on, you try.' He put his hands on her shoulders to steady her arms and looking directly at her said: 'He wanted me to go to Scotland with the Meckins. I wanted to stay in Slievegar, because of you.'

Rosha felt the colour rising in her face and her heart skip a beat.

'Has he returned yet from Lisdare?' she asked quickly to cover her confusion.

'Back tomorrow, I'm afraid. Come to the island in the afternoon and we'll work on the tree house.'

Rosha waited a long time the following day but Edmund did not turn up. Disappointed, she left the little island and was about to walk up the field to Garton when she heard him calling.

'Sorry, Rosha, we had visitors at the house. I'm afraid I've come to say goodbye. Father is sending me on ahead of him to spend a few days with his cousin in Lisdare. Would you like to have my bow and arrow? I wouldn't be allowed to use it at my prep school.'

She swallowed and turned her head away in case he saw the tears starting in her eyes. 'You'll come back?'

'Next spring. I'm spending Christmas with Aunt Madeline.' There was a note of excitement in his voice now as though he couldn't wait to get away from Slievegar.

He'll soon forget about me, she thought, feeling miserable. Then he turned and said in a quieter voice: 'Look after our tree house, won't you? We'll finish it when I get back again.' Edmund noticed the unshed tears in her eyes and added gently, 'Rosha, I'll always come back, you know. Always.'

The next morning she was awakened by the terrible sound of pigs squealing out in the shed. Once she had witnessed the killing ritual and the memory never left her. A red river of blood had flowed out through the shed door to the midden where it seeped away into the dung and straw. Patrick said the first pig was all right but the others knew what was coming.

When she was eating breakfast, Nellie called from the pantry: 'There's Neddie the boy, wid ye pour him a bowl of tea? He's come for the pig killing.'

Poor Neddie, Rosha thought. An old man's face with a body that never grew. He came in and hopped up on the chair.

'Nellie, I hear yer courtin'.'

'And who wid I be courtin' unless yerself makes an offer?'

He looked down at his disfigured body. 'Arrah, isn't meself wishes the good fairies had taken a hand at the birthing. I'd be after ye a'right. The fiddler's comin' to the crossroads t'night, Nellie. I'll walk ye down.'

'I'll walk m'self down.'

66

'I'm only suggesting it out of the kindness of me heart 'cause I've heard the oul sow walks after the killing.'

'Haven't we enough two-legged ghosts going around this country wi'out encouring the pigs to come out of the other world as well?' Nellie said impatiently, piling an armful of peat on the fire.

Rosha laughed as she handed him the bowl of tea. 'Neddie, how would anyone know the sow was dead? It could be a live one that ran out of the sty.'

'B'jabbers, that's the holy terror of it. Dosin the ghost of a sow walk on its two front legs and the road aflame wi' blood!' A sudden change came over his mood. 'If I was you, Nellie Boyce, and young Rosha, I'd be feared of more than ghosts in these parts. One day there'll be blood on the road but it won't be pig's,' he added ominously.

Rosha found herself going pale at the threat in Neddie's voice. This unexpected side to his character disturbed her. Previously she had seen only the dwarf's sunny nature that endeared him to everyone.

When the morning lessons with the minister and Patrick had ended, Nellie said quietly to Rosha, because Sean O'Neill would not approve: 'The men are going to the hill this afternoon. Wid ye give me a hand up in the half-acre, weeding and thining the carrots?'

Rosha, missing Edmund's company, was glad to have something to do. Also it was a job she enjoyed because the movement of her fingers aroused the scent in the tiny wild flowers growing among the fragile plants.

They had been working quietly for about half-hour in the warm sunshine when there was the sound of someone running on the other side of the hedge, then a voice.

'So this is where you disappeared to ...'

'Christ,' Nellie whispered, 'aul Tom Cat.'

'Let me go, yer honour, m'mither is ailing and needs help wi' the childer.'

Rosha recognised the girl's voice. It was the castle servant who walked home with her the day Edmund's father had alarmed her. Nellie threw down her weeding fork and scrambled through a hole in the hedge. Rosha followed cautiously. Catalong, with a gun slung across his shoulders, was advancing on the young girl who looked terrified. As she backed further into the hedge, he placed his gun on the ground.

'Let her go,' Nellie shouted at him.

When he turned his head, the girl ran away and Catalong's lascivious expression quickly changed to one of outrage. Then, just as suddenly, he smiled and grabbed Nellie's arm. Rosha, who was standing behind a bush, feared that Nellie was going to be subjected to the fate she had spared the young girl, and in desperation ran forward and picked up the gun.

'Put it down,' he said pleasantly, not showing any sign of fear at her wavering hands. Dragging Nellie with him, he approached slowly.

'Rosha,' Nellie said, terrified of Tom Cat and alarmed by the unsteady movement of the gun, 'put it on the ground, love, and go down to Garton and tell the men to come up here.'

'But ...' Rosha began, then bit her lip for they both knew that the men had left for the hills.

The figure that swung from one of the trees by the hedge seemed like a giant insect: arms held out like claws, short powerful legs drawn back. Catalong never knew what had descended and felled him to the ground or who had delivered the severe blow to his head that completely stunned him. Nellie, rolling away from the onslaught, caught Rosha's hand and they ran as fast as they could to Garton.

When they reached the house, Rosha gasped, 'Remember, Nellie, how we laughed when Neddie told us that he had worked in a travelling fair with wild animals?'

'Begod, he's caught one to day anyway! Blessed Virgin, weren't we lucky Neddie didn't go to the hill, too? Hush! There's Biddy Coll.'

# Chapter Seven

Crossing the burn, Grace Boyce noticed how the hills had bronzed with the dying season. Coppery-red leaves fluttered down on the green grass in their last moment of glory before they shrivelled away and died. As she stood there for a second under the wide blue sky, a shaft of sunlight split through the glen from the west and for one minute the land glowed in a final burst of light. In the distance, she saw her cottage, washed in the pale pink glow.

The peace of the land ahead was beautiful but the quietness tugged at her heart. Gone were the happy voices of children, the call of the shepherds' flutes: slowly and surely the landlord had cleared the glen. Grace stumbled and peered into the distance. Under God, what was that queer sight around her cottage? Like hundreds of geese with crows sitting on their heads! Then the sound of bleating came to her ears. Shocked, she realised that the black-faced sheep from Scotland had arrived in Iskaglen to take over the land.

Sir Thomas Catalong's fence ended a few feet from her cottage. Grace put her head over and looked at the alien sheep. They stared back curiously. Begod, she thought, they look brighter than the Irish ones, and began to laugh. She was sitting by the fire sewing when the half-door was pushed open and in came a big burly man with a bush of red hair and beard.

'Will ye mash m'tay, wifey?' he demanded.

Frightened, Grace jumped to her feet and said indignantly: 'I'm a widda wimin and don't allow men in m'house.' Then she saw his skin colouring with embarrassment and noticed the sorry state of him. He wore a pair of ragged tartan trousers. Over a torn jumper was a sleeveless leather jacket nearly in shreds. 'If yer asking for tay, I can't afford it.'

He held out a black tin with used tea leaves lying at the bottom. She took it from him and poured in water from the kettle singing on the hearth. 'Are you the shepherd?'

'Aye.'

'Where are ye staying?'

'Doon the road in a bittie of a cottage.'

'Is there a roof on it?'

'Aye, but nae door and the fire went oot.'

She took a piece of candle, lit it and put it in a tin. 'Take it steady now and keep yer fire going.'

'A'right, mam.'

God help him, a harmless lump of a lad, far from home. 'Wait ...' She poured milk in a can and broke off a piece of scone cooling by the window. He flushed at her generosity, dropped his head and walked out without a word of thanks. 'The lord save us,' she said to the cottage, 'as if we hadn't enough eejits in Ireland.'

An hour later Grace heard voices outside. It was Bridie and Rory Donavan. Overjoyed, she ran to the door and drew back the bolt.

''Tis yerself, Bridie and Rory. What a surprise!'

'I see you've got neighbours, Mrs Boyce,' Rory said. 'O'Neill was right, that's why they've cleared the glen. Ah, well,' he murmured peaceably when Grace was expecting him to rage, for a right hot-head he was becoming, 'perhaps we'll let the castle folk pay us back a bit of what they owe us.' He took a penknife from his pocket, sharpened it on the hearthstone, then picking up a sack from beside the dresser, went out.

Bridie hugged her mother. 'Rory's on the road wi' the horse and cart, selling things for his master. He called at Horton and the housekeeper said it would be convenient if I came home for a few days.'

'How are things at Horton, love?' Grace asked, hanging a pot of vegetable broth over the fire to heat for their supper.

'The housekeeper is still at the same aul carry on, sending me away from the house at a minute's notice and her in a state of nerves in case I dally. One day I'll get to the bottom of it.'

Grace felt uneasy about this strange behaviour of the housekeeper at Horton. There was something frightening the woman and it had to do with Bridie. What could be happening that the girl was not allowed to witness?

Rory did not return to the cottage for nearly an hour. Then he came in, flung a heavy sack on the floor, opened it and handed Grace a leg of mutton. 'It'll fit in your big iron pot, Mrs Boyce.'

'Mary and Joseph, Rory Donavan! Ye never slayed one of them sheep?'

'I did. Entrails and fur buried feet deep. The burn's washed away all signs of Catalong's generosity!'

Bridie began to laugh, then found herself considering Rory with admiration. He was so determined about things once he made up his mind.

''Tis stealing, Rory Donavan,' Grace said disapprovingly.

'And what do you think Catalong has been doing to us for years? Our homes ... our land. The right of tenants is gaining momentum. Catalong and his like days are numbered,' he said triumphantly. Rory touched her arm gently. 'When did you last have a taste of meat in yer mouth?' He grinned. 'There'll be a fine smell going up many's a chimney t'night! Bridie, make sure you bury the bone well.'

When her daughter left again, Grace felt very lonely. The shepherd had moved all the sheep away up the hill and not a sight of him had she seen since. Thank goodness the fiddler and his aul mother were still down the road. Cheered by the thought, she took her needlework and a pile of sacks outside to sit by the hedge. The clouds had lifted from the hills and the sun was gradually making an appearance. As she sat there working away on her piece of lace, Grace became poignantly aware once again of the silence creeping through the glen. At this end of the peninsula there was only herself and the musicians down the way. Over the last few

71

years all the cottages had been emptied and wiped from the face of the earth.

The scraping notes of the fiddle came up the road, lifting her heart. The music was so welcome, and wasn't it nice of the oul mother and son to compliment Grace on her singing that time? Happy now, she continued with her work, waiting expectantly for the mother to beat out the time on the wash tub. Fifteen minutes passed, and all that could be heard was the scraping of the bow on the strings. Ach, he'll be all right in a minute, she thought, when the oul mother gives him a bit of encouragement. But the dreary tuneless sound went on and on.

'Under God, what's the matter wi' him?' she muttered impatiently. Tossing her work aside she sprang off the hedge and hurried down the road, averting her eyes from the place where the Donavans had lived.

The fiddler was sitting outside the door, staring into space, the instrument dangling from his hands. 'Where's yer mam?' she called.

'Gone to the workhouse.'

'*Workhouse*?' The word knocked Grace speechless for a moment.

'She took ill. His honour sent someone to make arrangements. I'll be shifting mesel' too for they're needin' the bit of land.'

'Don't you *dare* leave!' she shrieked at him in shock. 'Get over to Garton at once and see Mr O'Neill.' Her voice dropped. 'Or have ye been offered a passage to America?'

'Divil a passage. The cousin is livin' just outside Dilford and he's takin' me in. I'll work on the farm for me keep.'

'You should have come and told me about yer mother,' Grace said in a quieter voice. 'I'd have looked after her.'

'Ah, well, a body dosin want to bother neighbours. It was sudden ... the illness.' His face brightened. 'Sure I'll be near the workhouse and able to visit her.'

As he spoke, a cart and horse trundled up the road. Grace stood back while the driver and the musician piled all his belongings into it and drove away.

Rosha and her father cantered to the top of the hill where

72

they stopped and rested their hoses. A mist of rain was falling far out across the Atlantic Ocean, screening the rays of sunlight which were beginning to break through in a hazy orange glow. Rosha was thinking about Edmund and wondering what his school in England was like, while Sean was thinking of his father, Thomas Catalong, who was silent in his demands these days, because like other landlords in Donegal, he had taken himself off to England until the spring. Suddenly, Sean sat forward on his horse. The figures of a woman and little boy were walking along the riverbank down below.

'Rosha,' he said hurriedly, 'will you light the fire? There's a meeting in the hall tonight.'

Dismayed, she watched him galloping down to join Mrs Flaherty. Yesterday she had overheard a conversation between Nellie and Mrs Coll in the kitchen which made her angry. 'Begod,' Nellie said, 'Widda Flaherty will hook him yet. The master is desperate for a woman, and not gettin' far wi'her from the looks of it. Still taking his cold plunges across the bay to cool his passion.'

'Nellie Boyce, stop that loose talk in my kitchen.'

'Aye, and by the grace of God it'll remain yer kitchen. If that bitch puts a foot across the door, we're done for ...'

That evening in the hall, when Sean O'Neill told the meeting that they must studiously ignore British law if any of them was called to the Petty Sessions Court in Lisdare, Skin-the-goat Duffy shouted: "Tis a'right for you, O'Neill. Ye own yer own land while the likes of us are beholden on the big house.'

'Wid ye listen to O'Neill?' Patrick Murphy's father shouted

'Aye, Murphy, and yer in the same comfortable boat. Fine to talk about the Land League removing landlordism from the country but ...'

'Don't forget what Michael Davitt said,' Sean interrupted abruptly, 'landlordism has worked the deadliest wrong to our country. That it caused famines, bloodshed, national impoverishment and degradation.'

'Christ, man, I haven't time to think about what Davitt

73

said. My weans are hungry and I owe you money for the field ye let me. And what about Parnell, another great man ye talked about. Fine example he is!'

Poor Parnell, Sean thought, his affair with Mrs O'Shea, the wife of a member of the Irish parliament, had grievously stained his moral record and damned him in the eyes of everyone, including Gladstone and all the churches. Now Gladstone threatened to cease working for Irish Home Rule. Adultery, he thought grimly, was an unforgiveable sin when it became public knowledge. God forgive me, Sean thought, I could commit a like sin myself if I got half a chance with that cool beauty who drives me halfway to hell and across the icy cold bay every day. Well, he had committed himself now and invited her to Garton on Sunday. He could wait no longer for a woman in his bed. He was still a young man and living the life of a monk.

Rosha's eyes blazed with anger and hurt when Nellie told her about the widow's visit. 'I don't believe you,' she said unreasonably, for over the past few days she could see the excited, happy look on her father's face.

'Believe it or not,' Nellie said bluntly, 'he's havin' her and the wee boy over the morrow for tea. Poor Mrs Coll is frightened she'll have to go.'

'Go where? This is her home.'

'If he weds the widda things will change at Garton, I'm telling ye,' Nellie said crossly.

Rosha glanced at Biddy and saw that she had shrunk into herself, like the old women who were condemned to the workhouse after evictions. She put her arm around the housekeeper. 'Don't worry, Biddy. Daddy would never let that happen.'

'Ah, alannah, there'll be no room for three wimin in this kitchen. And where wid an oul body like me find employment?'

'Jayus,' Nellie said with an unusual viciousness, 'I could slit that bitch's throat!'

On the Saturday, dark clouds moved across the sky heralding a storm. Soon a splatter of light raindrops was falling against the kitchen window and clinging to the freshly cleaned glass like children unsure of their next movement;

74

then, overtaken by the next swarm, they rushed on. The wind rose and pitched into the activity too. Showers swept through the open window, spraying the newly baked scones of bread standing cooling in their floury coats.

'Paddy,' Mrs Coll screamed rushing into the kitchen, 'get hould of them scones and shut the window quick!'

''Tis a fearful problem when the weather turns sour,' he mumbled.

'Any eejit could see it comin',' she scolded. Her mild soft voice had been rising to a pitch of hysteria throughout the day.

'Only an eejit wid clean windows afore a storm,' he said slyly.

'Aye, quick wi' yer tongue, aren't ye? Just see how quick ye are wi' the bisom. Go after any cobwebs that are hangin' around the rooms and make sure the chamber pots are hid under the beds. This minute!'

The widda will get rid of him when she settles in, Biddy Coll thought.

Maria Flaherty sat back on the seat of the trap, pleased that so many people were on the road to see her driving out with Sean O'Neill. That would set tongues wagging! He *must* speak today.

'Rosha, take that sulky look off yer face. Yer father and the widda's arrived. Biddy, she looks like gentry. Wid ye think the likes of her came out of thon poor wee cabin?'

'She's seen better days, dear. Sure it looks serious. I'd be as well to pack me things. No place for two mistresses in this kitchen and I'll not go back to being a skivvy, for that's how she'd treat me.'

Maria Flaherty was taken aback when Sean O'Neill stopped the trap at the back door. She had been looking forward to sweeping through the impressive front entrance. To Sean's dismay, the servants slouched around the doorway and his daughter looked sullen.

'Mother of God,' Nellie whispered in alarm, 'we forgot to put on our white pinnies.'

'Deel a hate I care, we're not entertaining gentry.'

Holding on to Maria's son Ruairi's hand, Rosha followed

75

her father and the tall elegant widow around the house. She saw the woman's eyebrows rising in disapproval and surprise at the shabby rooms, tarnished copper and silver.

'Och, they're rough and ready,' Sean said. 'But,' he added hurriedly, 'it's a happy house,' as if that excused the slovenliness of his servants. 'Rosha, take the little fellow down to the kitchen while I show Mrs Flaherty the other rooms.'

Maria smiled thoughtfully and Rosha wondered if the woman was thinking, there'll be changes around here. The wide wooden stairs led to three bedrooms; and on the floor above, the attic rooms where the housekeeper and Nellie slept. Sean's bedroom was large and chilly and Maria noticed how cobwebs netted the hearth and wound skeins around the rusty iron bars. He put his arm about her waist and led her towards the bed, feeling disappointed by her frowns of disapproval. Frustrated, and yearning for more warmth from this woman whom he desired with increasing passion, he began to kiss her then undo the button at the top of her blouse. He would marry her soon, now that his mind was made up.

Maria wound her arms around his neck, disturbing the movement of his fingers and making it quite impossible for him to undo the second pearl button on her blouse. She had never embraced him so closely. His heart rose in delight. Now she was murmuring against his cheek, gently and softly. 'Sean, dear, was there a purpose in your bringing me here today?'

'God dammit, woman, isn't it obvious?'

'You haven't spoken,' she said slowly, with contrived shyness.

'I want to wed you soon ... very soon.'

Sean's lovemaking was becoming more insistent. Maria's hair was in a state of disorder. So was her sensibility. It was not the place nor the time, she thought. Really, she had expected better of Sean O'Neill.

'What d'ye think's goin' on up there, Mrs Coll?' Nellie asked.

'They're in his bedroom,' Rosha said drily.

'Put a pig on horseback,' Biddy added spitefully. 'She'll be telling him about the grand new curtains she'll be wanting.'

Nellie thought differently. The master was a hot-blooded man. If she hadn't been a poor servant girl and he a good Catholic master ... she'd seen him looking at her at times.

'Sean,' Maria said, drawing away from his ardent embrace, 'I will marry you any time you like. At our age there's no point in waiting.'

She sat up quickly and began to gather her disordered hair into a neat roll. He caught her around the waist again and pulled her down against the bedcover. Like a loose woman, she thought disapprovingly.

Maria gave a little laugh and said tentatively, 'Sean, there's more to marriage than bed, you know. I would like you to know that I'm not too fond of that.'

She felt safe now. He had spoken. Not before time, after courting her for a couple of years. Considering her poor circumstances, the proposal should have come sooner.

Sean's body tensed and he suddenly felt as if he had taken a plunge into the bay. 'And what about love, Maria?' he asked in a strained voice. 'Surely it leads to marriage and ...'

'Oh, yes,' she agreed quickly. 'I know, but ...' A little laugh and her eyes swept over the bed. 'Some men think of nothing else. I'm sure you're not like that, Sean?'

And when had he spoken of love? Oh, aye, she'd heard a great deal about Parnell's love for Mrs O'Shea ... what a brazen hussy that O'Shea woman was, living so openly in sin. Full of compassion for *their* predicament, Sean was, while herself to whom he was paying attention lived in a lowly cabin, and all he could offer was a grab and a kiss.

Sean was struck by her unfortunate choice of words. There was a certain lack of delicacy that he found distasteful in a woman. Maria knew by his expression that she had spoken too bluntly. Still, if his thoughts were always on bed, she'd be breeding like the gypsies!

When they went downstairs again, a great spread was laid on the table: a platter of cold meats, pickled beetroot with scallions, three kinds of scone bread − plain, oatmeal and one heavy with fruit. Also fadge, jelly and cream.

Rosha, with the face of a saint welcoming martyrdom, came through from the kitchen holding the hand of Maria's son. The child, Ruairi, had not opened his mouth once since his mother left him in her charge. Nellie wondered if he was all there.

'Your son has been a good boy.' Rosha repeated the words that Nellie had put into her mouth.

'The best boy in the world,' his mother added, sitting him down at the table. Maria's eyes flitted around the room again. A few pieces of quality furniture but the absence of beeswax was evident. I'll soon do something about that she thought. Nellie came in, placed the teapot by the hearth, gave a little bob and scuttled out again. Rosha bent her head and clapped a hand across her mouth to stifle a sudden urge to giggle at Nellie's unfamiliar behaviour.

Sean did not keep his promise to visit Maria on the following day or for some time afterwards. One of the horses developed a fever and there was a complicated calfing. All this went on for two weeks while his only thought was for his livestock. Maria was a sensible woman. She would understand, he told himself. When the horse which was in foal died, he suffered a heavy financial loss. There had been many heavy expenses in recent months. Now there was the consideration of further education for Rosha. The minister had advised a young ladies' establishment in Dilford where she could continue her studies.

Maria was furious at Sean's indifferent behaviour. Perhaps he'd had second thoughts about the proposal? she thought anxiously. When Patrick Murphy's mother died suddenly, Maria went up to the farm and offered to help Dan with the children. Previously she had been no further than the kitchen. She was surprised to find how well furnished and comfortable the house was. Of course Murphy's farm was known to be prosperous. Late one evening when she had brought a potion to one of the Murphy children, Dan walked back down the road with her.

'Mrs Flaherty,' he made himself bold enough to say, 'Sean O'Neill is taking his time getting you to the altar, isn't he? You told me he asked for yer hand a time back an' he hasn't been near ye since.'

'Will I ever get to the altar, Dan?' she said with an honesty that surprised herself. Suddenly her fear that O'Neill had changed his mind — she remembered his expression when she showed her disgust over the bed — exploded in a rush of anger. 'He's arrogant, Dan. If I was somebody, I'd put him in his place.'

He stopped and touched her arm. 'Mrs Flaherty, that rough wee cabin is not good enough for you, and winter's on the way. I was going to ask you to be my housekeeper,' Dan Murphy stammered and flushed crimson, 'but folk might blacken yer name. I know ye have no feeling for me, lass, but I'll always respect the distance ye put between us. Woman, dear, wid ye wed me? I've got plenty of money and land. Ye can have more than your share.'

Surprised out of her life, Maria was silent for a while, then she held out her hand. 'I accept your offer, Dan, if you're prepared to accept my ways.' She had always considered the man rather uncouth but since his wife's death he had become gentle and quiet. Maria was quite certain she would be able to keep him that way.

It was Skin-the-goat Duffy who told Sean the news when he came to pay his rent for the field. Rosha, who was working with her father in the room, had to lower her eyes to hide her look of relief.

'Ah, man,' Duffy said consolingly, 'to marry once is a necessity. Twice could be a luxury or a damnation. I widden like to put me chance on Widda Flaherty!'

Sean went on writing the man's account. 'Thank you for telling me.' What an unsatisfactory year this has been, he thought bitterly. The Home Rule being vetoed in the House of Lords after a third reading and now his hopes for some personal happiness snatched away under his nose by Dan Murphy. At that moment he forgot about his unsuccessful attempts to try and woo the widow, or the fact that she had offered no promise of warmth when the ring was on her finger.

Bridie Boyce, who was whitewashing the byre over at Horton, looked up in surprise when Rory Donavan drove into the yard. 'I have a message from yer mam, Bridie,' he said. 'Is yer mistress about?'

'No, she and Barney have gone to the shop.'

'Good. Your mother told me to call in and tell you that the widda Flaherty, who married Dan Murphy, is lookin' for another servant girl and she's put in a word for you. I must tell ye that Nellie's not pleased at the idea for she doesn't like the widda.'

Bridie put the brush down and wiped her hands. 'But, Rory, even if I wanted to leave Horton, I'd have to serve out m'time here. I couldn't just leave like that.'

'Ah, well, Bridie,' he said, walking across to the house with her, 'there's something about this place that's upsetting her. I can't get to the bottom of it. Are ye still happy here?'

'I am, but it's so isolated and I get lonely at times. The priest has stopped the dances.' Her face brightened and she laughed. 'Sure one of these days I might meet a fella and that'll make a difference.'

'How are ye going to meet a fella if there's no opportunity? Somebody should ask the priest that!'

When Rory drove away again, after Bridie had given him a good feed, he thought, Grace Boyce is anxious about something to do with Horton. Strange, for she's a sensible woman. It must be some vague fear, caused by loneliness since his lordship cleared the glen. Sure Bridie couldn't be in a safer house, thank God.

# Chapter Eight

The following summer Rosha and Edmund made several plans. They were not to know that this would be the last day they would spend together for a very long time. All the afternoon they worked on the tree house. Its seclusion was perfect. Sometimes they heard Nellie on the shore calling and Edmund's tutor, Mr Moss, raising his genteel voice in search of his pupil.

'Edmund,' Rosha said, breaking their silence, 'do you know what I'd like now? A stick of Peggy's Leg.' The soft cinnamon-flavoured rock, which had always been her favourite sweet, was unknown to Edmund until she made him taste it.

'If there's no one around the shore,' he suggested, 'let's take the boat and go by the short cut.'

There was not a soul to be seen across the miles of pale golden sand and pebbled beaches. The only movement came from the small white puffy clouds sailing across the clear blue sky. Down by the bridge they pulled the boat up under the crab apple tree which grew in an unwieldy way from the hedge, sending long shoots towards the water as if seeking a reflection of the pinkish-white blossom.

'Do you know what you remind me of?' Edmund said unexpectedly. 'I think the people here call it a wild rose, except it should be vivid ... red, not pink.'

Rosha laughed, trying to hide her pleasure at the strange unexpected compliment. Edmund didn't laugh. He put out his hand and caressed her face, then drew her close and kissed her. After a moment he raised his head and said her name. She wanted him to kiss her again and rested her head against his shoulder.

'Wait,' he said, his lips touching her hair, 'until we get back to our tree house.'

Delighted at the thought of being alone in their secret place, she said impulsively, 'I must tell Nellie what you called me.'

As though her words had touched their freedom, he said quickly, 'Don't tell her anything. Servants are not to be trusted.'

She frowned. 'Nellie is my friend. She talks to me about things ... about Rory who works in Lisdare and whom she rarely sees these days.'

'That's the chap who injured our bailiff.'

'Just think, she was about my age when she came to work at Garton.'

'That's the difference you fail to see, Rosha. At fourteen Nellie had to work for a living, but you're going to do something better. You are different but Nellie will never change.'

A sudden anger made her flare. 'And *why* did she have to leave home and work at fourteen? Because your father claimed most of their land and *her* father had to go to work in Scotland on the rough potato fields.'

Edmund looked embarrassed. 'Rosha, don't let's quarrel.'

'He died there, and my father had to send money to bring him home to be buried.'

'Rosha, I'm merely trying to point out how a way of life can affect some people. Forget it ... it was silly of me to express myself in that way. The system is exactly the same in England,' he added flatly, and walked on. Then suddenly he turned back and smiled. 'You are maddening. Come on, race you to the shop.' Laughing, they tore through the fields disturbing the cows drowsing in the afternoon sunshine.

Rosha made a habit of ignoring Tin Lizzie's custom of having only one customer down in the shop while the others waited their turn in the kitchen. Like a Confessional, she always thought. The fierce gabble, as Edmund called it, stopped immediately when they walked in. The black-shawled women with baskets of eggs by their

82

feet welcomed them with pleasure and a little awe. After a few words in English they broke into Gaelic with gesturing hands. 'What beauty in the pair of them. Does Sean O'Neill know the company his daughter's keepin'? The son of that father couldn't be good.'

Another added quickly, 'The boy has inherited the kindness and manners of the one who bore him. A lovely lady.'

The woman in the next chair said sadly, 'Poor critter, she put a cross on her back the day she wed.'

The two young people went from the kitchen through a passage to the shop, passing firkins of paraffin oil and sacks of meal. Hobnailed boots, ling fish and thick seamen's socks hung from the ceiling, pair by pair. Also some ropes of tobacco that was cut and sold by the ounce.

When they entered the kitchen again Edmund paused for a second. Sitting apart from the others was another customer who had not been there when they came in: it was the housekeeper from Merifield Manor. He didn't like her. Sometimes she showed a strange familiarity and he had noticed, when there were no visitors staying at the manor, how she and his father went out walking through the grounds in the evening.

Late that afternoon, Edmund was told by one of the maids to go to the study. When he walked into the room his father rose quickly from the chair behind the desk, lifted his arm and slashed Edmund across the face with a metal ruler. 'How dare you keep such undesirable company? I hear you've been running around with O'Neill of Garton's daughter. So that's where you go when Mr Moss has been looking for you.'

Edmund felt blood trickling down his face. He didn't brush it away. His father hated the sight of blood; he let others draw it in his name.

'I will horsewhip you if you go near that girl again. Do you hear?'

'The O'Neills descend from a noble family, sir,' he said stubbornly, repeating what his tutor had told him one day.

It was the worst possible thing he could have said. Thomas Catalong was aware that he could not make the same claim.

'Get out of my sight,' he snarled. 'Just remember, it is an accepted fact that we don't mix with those people. They are barbarians.'

When Edmund turned to go, the voice behind him ordered: 'Wait! Get your bags packed. You can accompany me back to London tomorrow.'

Edmund thought of Rosha coming to the tree house on the following day and finding him absent. Bitterly disappointed, he clenched his hands tightly in protest. There was nothing he could do about it. He must try and leave a note somehow.

On the way down the drive from Merifield Manor next morning, Thomas Catalong said to his son: 'Apparently you've done well at Harrow in the papers for the preliminary Army examination. There has not been time to discuss this matter, with guests in the house.'

'Father, I don't really want to go into the army.'

'What else is there for you here in the bogs, eh? Make up your mind to get through the entrance examination to Sandhurst.'

Edmund turned his head as the carriage passed Garton. Nellie, who was in the drive, gave an impulsive wave when she saw him. He returned the salute and smiled.

'Who are you greeting?' his father asked tetchily.

'The maid at Garton.'

'That trollop.'

Rosha did not tell Nellie what Edmund had called her. To utter the words might expose the wonderful feeling in her heart to Nellie's unpredictable moods. She might scold or, worse, sully it with coarse laughter. Or even ask awkward questions.

'Where are you goin'?' Nellie called as Rosha hurried through the kitchen the following day. 'Come and give me a hand. Stand on that chair, love, and hang up this shank of ham, will ye?'

Clutching the heavy shank in its thick covering of muslin, Rosha pushed it on the heavy iron hook that jutted from a beam.

'Saw the castle coach goin' off this morning,' Nellie remarked. 'Good riddance to oul Tom Cat for a while.

84

Now we can walk without lookin' o'er our shoulders.'

'Piles of luggage?'

'Aye, he and the boy's.'

'Edmund wasn't in the coach too?' Rosha asked in dismay.

'Off to school again and don't pretend not to know. Or have ye fallen out?'

Praise be to God he's out o' the way for a while, Nellie thought. If Sean O'Neill knew the pair of them were running around together, he'd kill me.

'He's nice, Nellie,' Rosha said, blinking back tears of disappointment.

'Aye, I think he is, pet, but he's got bad blood. Soon ye'll be off to that grand place of education in Dilford and be forgettin' all about him.'

Rosha left the house and made her way through a path in the woods where trees linked overhead and gave shelter from the rain. A steady downpour began to strike the cold grey motionless water in the bay as she approached the shore; it came on faster, giving a sense of immediacy as though the clouds were anxious to unload their burden. She pulled off her stockings and stuffed them into her boots which she placed in a sheltered spot. Why had Edmund left so suddenly? Surely he would not go away like that without leaving a note? Not after yesterday when he had kissed her so fiercely in the tree house that a plank gave way under their weight.

She beat her way through the dripping branches into the centre of the little island, then stopped dead. Confronting her was the burly figure of the bailiff. Above him in the oak, the tree house which she and Edmund had so diligently worked on for so long had completely disappeared. All around lay the evidence that it had ever existed. The bailiff put his hand out and caught her wrist.

'So, O'Neill's daughter.'

Frightened, she lifted her foot and landed a kick on his thigh, then fled.

It was the disappointment over a friend's wedding in Slievegar that made Bridie angry when the housekeeper would not give

85

her a definite date to go home. It had something to do with that letter ... All the years she had been working at Horton the arrival of a letter still send the housekeeper hopping around like a hen disturbed in the nest. Furious, Bridie banged the milk cans in the dairy. She was going to miss all the fun. When did she last have a bit of fun, stuck out here in the wilderness? How am I ever goin' to meet a fella? she wondered, struck with terror at the thought of ending up an old maid.

In the byre, her hand on the cow's tits became hard and insensitive as the warm stream of milk filled the pail. The animal, uncomfortable and missing her friendly chatter, turned its head.

'Be still,' she snapped.

It gave a protesting sound and slapped its tail. Bridie grabbed the other tit to hasten the job and pulled them simultaneously. The cow, not used to this hasty treatment, lifted its foot and sent the full pail of milk frothing over the dung on the floor. Tears filled her eyes. Maybe she should write to her mother and find out if the widda Flaherty — or Mrs Murphy now — would keep the place for her. Life was getting harder at Horton; she was expected to dig potatoes and pit them, as well as thin turnips, beet, and every other dratted thing that needed thining. And there was the housework, with not a minute to get on wi' her lace.

Mrs O'Sullivan could see the young girl's discontent and prepared a good tea. Afterwards, she came back to the kitchen bearing a new smoothing-iron which she placed before her with a triumphant flourish.

'What do you think of that now?'

The iron was large and hollow with a little shutter which could be lifted up to insert a stone that heated in the heart of the fire. The wonder of it restored Bridie's good humour straight away. No more smuts on the white linen from the flat iron. She couldn't wait to start on the next batch. An opportunity to use the iron did not occur until later because she was told to get herself home in the morning. When Bridie was down in the dairy souring the milk pans she heard the housekeeper saying to Barney: 'So he's in Lisdare ... The agent must have found out about that land across the way going cheaply and they'll be coming to see it before he crosses the water to England.'

Mrs O'Sullivan immediately packed a bag of provisions for Bridie's mother, including a ham and some dried fish. She took it gratefully but knew that her mother was not doing so badly since the sheep arrived in the glen. Every time Rory Donavan returned, he slit the throat of another animal and gave her a generous portion. She would be glad to see her mother for there was a rumour that Catalong was bringing in another shepherd, an older man with more experience who would need a place to live. Mam's cottage was the only one left. Apparently the number of the sheep were decreasing rapidly, caused by the change of climate in the Donegal hills as well as Rory's depredation. Mam said the young shepherd was getting too friendly with the boys who were filling him with poteen down in the shebeen, but the same shepherd was not above selling the odd sheep to eke out the small wage the castle paid him.

Next morning Bridie was taking the short cut across a field to catch the coach at the hotel when she saw a farmer working his plough horses down through it. She knew it would be unlucky to cross their path and too long to wait until the team turned again. She decided to go across the bog-moor instead. Slipping off her boots and stockings she placed her feet on the bright green grass of the bog – a smile on its face and death in its belly, Mam always said. Cautiously she made her way over to the hedge where there was a little stream.

The man standing behind a clump of trees in the corner of the field watched the girl intently when she pulled up her skirt and washed her feet and ankles; then he noticed how she kept glancing down at Horton where the agent and housekeeper were standing outside talking, and how quickly she pulled out of sight when Mrs O'Sullivan glanced in this direction. Suddenly he recognized her. It was the young Boyce girl from the peninsula. Sir Thomas Catalong slapped the cane against his boot and laughed. So this was where she'd disappeared to!

On the morning that Rosha was leaving for Dilford to attend

the Miss Houstons' Establishment for young ladies, Nellie began to sob. Rosha hugged and kissed her cheek. 'Things could be worse, Nellie. What about that widda with her foot in the door?'

Nellie blew her nose. 'Aye, right enough it could be far worse and ye'll be back for Christmas. Thank God Biddy Coll's novena worked. She finished it on the day yer father was jilted.'

'Maybe you stuck a few pins in a bit of wax!'

Nellie caught her hand. 'You'll be good, won' ye?'

'What else can I be in that grey Houstons' Establishment? I'll be locked up.'

'Begod, they'll not keep ye in if there's a window in the house.' Nellie wiped away a tear. 'Now, pet, ye know what I told ye the other day, when yer womanhood trials began? About boys –'

'Nellie,' Rosha said quietly, 'I'm in love with Edmund Catalong and he's nowhere near Dilford. He's studying at a place called Harrow in England.'

The tears chilled on Nellie's cheeks at the note in the girl's voice. She tried to laugh. 'Och, go away wi' ye. Sure you'll be marrying Patrick Murphy in a few years' time.' An obstinate look came over Rosha's face. 'Don't you be thinking about that castle boy,' she scolded. 'If he comes back he'll behave like all the other gentry and stick to his own kind. You won't be good enough for him, love. Anyway, he's a Protestant.'

Rosha thought of the girl, Alice Meckin, daughter of an earl and Edmund's next-door neighbour in London. He often spoke about her. Please God don't let him forget about me, she prayed.

# Chapter Nine

Though Bridie felt rested after the few days at home, a feeling of discontent lingered, as though time was passing too quickly and her life was never going to change. She was worried about her mother having to leave the cottage.

When she and her mother went across to Slievegar to visit Garton, Nellie was not in a good mood. She scolded about her employer giving too much away. The bills were lamentable and her wages slow in coming.

'And what about Patrick?' Bridie asked, trying to change the subject.

'The sooner that Rosha weds him the better,' she told them. 'We could do wi' another man on the land. He and Rory Donavan are as thick as thieves, away in the hills sometimes wi' a secret society, and the priest from the altar promising such activities everlasting punishment.'

When Nellie went down to the pantry to get some milk for the tea, Grace whispered to Bridie, ''Tis Rory's the trouble wi' her. He'll never wed her, I fear, love. There's something not right between the pair of them.'

With her thoughts of the home-visit to keep her company, Bridie poked the fire and placed two irons in its heart. When they were white hot she carefully eased one into the cavity on the new iron. Setting it on the stand to heat through, she went out to the orchard to bring in the dry washing.

The sound of a vehicle approaching the cottage was always an event. Now that Rory was travelling the roads selling for his master, there was always the possibility that it might be him. She drew back in surprise when a sidecar came into the yard, driven by a gentleman. Upstairs in the house, Barney was helping his wife to hang a pair of heavy curtains on a window. 'Now what are ye goin' to do, woman? His honour has just arrived.'

'Yer seeing things, Barney O'Sullivan. Wasn't he here only last week?'

'Begod, it looks as though I'm seein' him again and from the look of him he's going to stay.'

One glance out of the window sent the housekeeper into a state of sheer panic. Sir Thomas Catalong with a portmanteau in his hand. 'Bridie ... she's in the orchard. Slip out the other way, Barney. Be quick. Send her up the hill to the dressmaker.'

'Too late. She's talking t'him this moment.'

'Get down, ye silly man, and escort him into the drawing-room. And nod to Bridie to get up the hill.'

For the first time in their long married life, Barney O'Sullivan blazed with anger. 'Will ye have some sense in yer head? What's he goin' to think o'that? Is it out in the road ye want the pair of us? The girl ... the girl. That's all ye ever think about.' He lifted his hand as if to strike her. *His* life wasin going to be disrupted by a slip of a girl.

Bridie came shyly into the yard with an armful of linen. The man was still standing there looking about him. He turned when he heard her footsteps. She curtsied, not able to believe her eyes. It was Sir Thomas Catalong. He smiled and Bridie remembered well that rugged, handsome face from years ago.

'Well, young lady, you're far from home, aren't you?'

She felt honoured that he remembered her. His friendliness and the way he looked at her were flattering. It lifted Bridie's spirits and eased her shyness. 'I am, sir, and very happy at Horton.'

'How long have you been working here?'

'A good many years. I came when I was fourteen.'

He frowned. 'You've not been about on my previous visits.'

'That is so, sir, because we do a lot of business at the huckster shop. I take quantities of butter and eggs in exchange for other goods and, sometimes poultry. As you can see from the account books,' she added smartly.

Thomas Catalong was always getting glowing reports from Captain Hurl about this Godforsaken estate. Still, there was good shooting in this part of the country and, he smiled to himself, an attractive servant.

Mrs O'Sullivan came fluttering out of the house with Barney at her heels. Bridie had never seen her so put-out. She curtsied, 'Good day, sir.'

'Mrs O'Sullivan, I've decided to spend a day or two here to survey the estate while my lawyer in Lisdare is attending to some business. Barney, have you got the guns in good condition?

'I have, yer honour.'

Before Sir Thomas walked away with the housekeeper, he turned and smiled at Bridie. What a bit of news to tell Mam, she thought excitedly. The castle owned Horton. What had her mother said all those years ago? Catalong was a cruel, bad man and if Bridie didin leave immediately she would have to go and work at the castle? Maybe now that he was getting old there was a change in his nature?

Lunch was served in the dining-room. Bridie helped the housekeeper to carry dishes in and out. When Mrs O'Sullivan turned from the table, Sir Thomas smiled at the girl. She felt herself liking him ... such a friendly man. What a pair of hands on him. Never had she seen such clean nails.

After two days, Bridie decided that Sir Thomas Catalong was a perfect gentleman. The polite way he treated herself and she just a serving girl. She couldn't understand why the housekeeper was so tense and sour these days. On the third morning he turned from the window while they were clearing the table and said: 'Mrs O'Sullivan, I would like to visit your local shop which serves my estate so well. Bridie can accompany me, as I am unknown to them.'

'Very well, sir. I'll get Barney to bring the trap around.'

'On such a fine day I would prefer to walk. The girl can show me the way.'

The housekeeper became agitated. 'Would you like me to accompany you too, sir?'

He tipped ash off his cigar out the window. 'Surely not

necessary?' His tone left her in no doubt that he did not want her company. 'If you'd be so kind, Mrs O'Sullivan, to provide some refreshments.'

Mrs O'Sullivan's thoughts were in an uproar. After all these years ... such bad luck. She'd always had a letter from the agent when one or both were coming to Horton. Before Sir Thomas and Bridie left the house she found an opportunity to whisper, 'For the love of God, keep to the roads, dear. None of your short cuts.'

Bridie couldn't believe her good luck. A hard morning's work in the field had been planned by Barney, now he would have to get on with it by himself. She felt very privileged and proud to have been asked by Sir Thomas to accompany him to the shop. Wait till Mam heard about this. Her mother was so in awe of the castle folk that she would nearly curtsey to their shadow! Even the bailiff got a friendly nod from her these days. Poor Mam was frightened to get on the wrong side of the castle, frightened to lose her home.

'No matter what ye say, Barney O'Sullivan, I'm getting the girl home to her mother. She can spend the night wi' the dressmaker.'

'After she's babbled about just coming back from there? Woman, ye'll have us out on the road if all the things we've been hearing are true. That one's a friendly, cheeky wee miss, but plenty of sense,' Barney consoled her. 'He'll not have his way wi' her as he's done wi' many others.'

Mrs O'Sullivan could not explain to her thick-headed husband about the change that had come over Bridie recently. The new iron had brought back a bit of her old sparkle. What a queer life when a young girl of nineteen had to have her heart lifted with a smoothing-iron instead of a fella. Rory Donavan, when he came, always cheered her, but he was older and promised to her sister. I'll take her to my bed the night and send Barney downstairs to sleep, just in case. That's what I'll do, she thought and immediately felt better.

At the turn in the road, Thomas Catalong stopped. 'Surely, Bridie, there must be a shorter and pleasanter way to the shop?'

'Indeed, sir, but wid ye not be frightened of dirtying yer boots?'

'You can have the pleasure of cleaning them this evening,' he said flirtatiously.

Bridie gave a peal of laughter as they crossed into the heathland. The manners in him. Taking her arm at every wee mound then holding on, in case, he said, she might injure herself. God look to his wit! Wasin she skippin' o'er this land at least once a week? The protective hand on her arm was nice though and the way he took the basket from her. It wasin every day a girl of her station was led across the moor like a lady.

'Have you a boyfriend, Bridie?' he asked.

'A boyfriend? Bless you, sir, I'm only allowed out in the evenings as far as the byre.' Catalong laughed. 'There used to be dances in some of the cottages,' she told him, 'until the priest put a stop to it. Mrs O'Sullivan used to let me go if I was accompanied by the dressmaker. An oul maid and likely to stay that way. Och, the barn dances were the best.'

'Why?'

'Because the barns were always whitewashed for the dance and the floors swept.' She giggled mischievously. 'No chairs for the oul folk to sit around in and watch every move.'

'So the boys were able to lure you outside?' His finger touched the faded blue cotton of her frock, caressing her arm gently. She didn't draw away. If they were not willing that caress sent them scurrying off. Catalong began to breath quickly, excitedly.

Bridie skipped across the moorland stream. 'Careful of yer boots here, sir. Och, look, now you've splashed yer boots. Take them off and I'll give them a rub.'

'Could we not find a place for a little refreshment, then I'll take them off? I'm beginning to feel weary of this rough ground.'

Obediently she looked around the wild landscape.

'Over there, my dear, in among the rocks and gorse,' he suggested.

It was not a place Bridie would have chosen, but she followed him and laid out the contents of the basket: a chicken pie, cake, and one linen napkin with the cutlery. He sat down and held out his foot. Laughing up at him she removed the boots. What a delightful little minx, he

93

thought. I think she knows what she's about ... If she's not so willing, I know how to persuade her. Catalong took out a flask. 'Have a refreshing drink first, my dear.'

'I don' know that I should ...'

'It's just a simple wine. Possibly like the one you make at home.' He unscrewed the top and poured two generous measures.

Some home-made wine, Bridie thought, taking a sip, and laughed. It was delicious, heavy with a strange richness. Thirsty, she drank it down quickly. He refilled the glass again. She shook her head, then didn't know what to do with the glass because she wanted to cut the chicken pie. It wouldn't balance on the glass so she drank it up quickly.

Bridie cut a large slice of pie, leaving a tiny piece for herself. He immediately cut half of his portion and placed it on her plate. A sigh of contentment passed her lips. The kindness of him. I'm not keepin' me place, she scolded herself after a while, and began to giggle, no longer caring. Forgetting her manners, she ate the pie in her fingers and laughed again when the birds gathered for their share.

'I love the dear wee robins,' she told him, battling to keep her eyes open.

'You're a dear little robin,' he said softly, moving closer. 'I think I'm falling in love with you.' He stroked her hair and her face. 'What a luscious mouth. I must kiss it.' His mouth covered hers in a way she had never been kissed before.

Through the muddled sensation in her head, Bridie had a feeling of alarm. He shouldn't have kissed her ... not like that. His hands began to roam around her body.

'No, sir! 'Tis not right, sir.' Her eyes flashed.

He drew away. She was not going to be easy after all. 'Bridie, I suppose you know that your mother will soon be leaving her cottage? Captain Hurl says that part of Iskaglen peninsula must be completely cleared.'

She blinked uncertainly. 'Is it for sure, sir? Oh, sir, can you not stop it? Mam loves her wee home, not even minding the loneliness when all the neighbours had to move away.'

His arm went around her waist and pulled her close. 'I will do everything I can to prevent it, but you must be nice

94

to me. Come on, lie down. You like me stroking your hair, don't you?'

Dismayed, not knowing what to do, Bridie tried to move away but her head was reeling and her feet unsteady when she tried to stand. He laid her down on the ground. She shut her eyes. Please let him go away 'til I have a wee rest ...

'To hell with it! She's not going to sleep on me,' he muttered impatiently, and shook her. 'Bridie,' he said hurriedly, 'I promise, if we're friends, your mother can spend the rest of her days in that cottage.' Impatient now, his hands were fumbling with her skirt, touching her legs and pulling at her drawers. She tried to battle against his strength. Finally his weight pinned her to the ground.

The birds screamed and fled to safety at the disturbance on the moor. Bridie cried out once in pain, then, wide awake and sober, endured his hateful attention with the realisation that this was her fate – this violation of her body by the man who promised not to throw her mother out on the road. When he rolled away, she fled to the stream and was violently sick. Afterwards she cleansed her body.

It was obvious to Bridie when she returned to Horton that the O'Sullivans were having a row. 'I want him to sleep down here the night and you come to my room,' the housekeeper told Bridie as Barney stamped out of the kitchen.

When Bridie did not reply, Mrs O'Sullivan said with a frightened look at the girl's pale face, 'You kept to the road?' Her silence made the housekeepr cry out in fright: 'Sweet Jesus, he's used you.'

Suddenly, before Bridie's eyes, the housekeeper began to carry on like one of the old women evicted from their homes in Iskaglen. She wrung her hands and in a voice without dignity said, 'I dare not interfere now, child. 'Tis too late. If I take you upstairs to my room he'll know what I'm about – me and Barney wid be out on the road by mornin'.

'It's all right, Mrs O'Sullivan, I understand,' Bridie said dully. 'He filled me wi' some kind of wine and threatened to take over my mother's cottage. He promised not to touch her if ...'

Mrs O'Sullivan turned like a mad woman and raced out of the cottage to the orchard where she went around the hedges pulling out bits and pieces of wild flowers. Back in the kitchen she put them in a saucepan, poured boiling water over the plants and left them simmering by the hearth. 'I'm goin' to help you, dear. T'will stop you getting in trouble.'

In a detached sort of way, Bridie watched her. Trouble? I'm in great trouble she thought. I'm in so much trouble I want to die.

As she drank a mugful of the bitter-tasting concoction, Mrs O'Sullivan said: 'Did your mother not warn you about men? I thought you would understand, coming from the same part of the country as Sir Thomas Catalong. That's why I always sent you away. I didn't even want the agent to see you.'

Bridie paused for a moment, remembering how her mother used to stop Nellie from saying things. Sex was a sin and you didin talk about sin.

'When I was fourteen, Mrs O'Sullivan, my mother told me I had to get away to service because Catalong might want me to work at the castle. He was a hard, cruel master and likely to beat me, she said.'

'Was that all?' the housekeeper shouted incredulously. 'The stupid, silly woman to send a young girl out in the world without that knowledge.' She shook her head in confusion. 'I'm sorry, dear ...'

'I was young for me age,' Bridie told her, taking no offence for she could see now how wrong her mother had been. She remembered Nellie trying to find out if Mam had mentioned the worst thing that could happen to a young girl. 'She didin want such things to reach my ears. You see, Mrs O'Sullivan, this place is so far from Merifield Manor. Not even Rory knew it belonged to the castle.'

'No, because Sir Thomas inherited it from an old aunt some years ago. That's why Barney and me found it so rundown.'

I was so flattered, Bridie thought with bitterness. A silly, childish girl. And I was worried about Mam losing the cottage.

Pale and silent, she helped Mrs O'Sullivan to prepare supper and began to make plans.

When the first milking pail went across to the byre it contained a large hunk of bread with a lump of cold bacon. Wrapped in a piece of an old pillowcase was a roll of lace. She tossed her shawl casually on top of these things and knotted a few pence in her handkerchief which she hid in the leg of her drawers.

Bridie placed everything in the space between the top of the stone wall and the roof of the byre, then carried on with the milking. Later, when the O'Sullivans were locking the door and attending to the fire, she filled the iron kettle as usual. It was early for them to retire but they knew what their master would expect. With scarcely a word or glance they hurried from the kitchen. Guilt had frozen their tongues and the eyes in their heads. Bridie felt betrayed and very alone. Now, more than ever, she was determined to disappear into the night.

Just as she was slipping back the bolt on the door, the inner one opened and Thomas Catalong walked into the kitchen.

# Chapter Ten

Rosha came to the startling realisation, after only two weeks at the private school, that her lessons with the Reverend Stewart far exceeded the standard set by the Houstons; though she began to understand why the minister had recommended the place to her father. The Miss Houstons were middle-aged ladies who wore long black knitted jackets over cream blouses and brown skirts. Miss Bossy (as the pupils called her) was a large woman with a thundering voice. She taught all the basic subjects while his sister took music, needlework, drawing and The World. The latter subject, conducted during needlework, riveted Rosha's attention. Apart from England, she had very little knowledge of other countries. Geography had thrown some light on their existence but Miss Edith, in an interesting and humorous way, had opened up the vast mysterious continent of Europe.

For some time Rosha wondered why Edith did not take history and geography instead of her sister who, she felt, was very over-worked. Eventually it was explained by one of the pupils that Edith was not trained to teach anything. Bossy was suspect regarding her educational qualifications but, as all the pupils were fourteen years old and over, restrictions on that point seemed to be vague. It was a young ladies' establishment and no one was expected to achieve any great heights in the academic world.

When the Gaelic League was founded that year by Douglas Hyde, the daily routine was completely disrupted. An assistant was taken on the staff to teach the pupils Irish step-dancing; Miss Edith and Bossy taught lessons in Gaelic or tried to improve the knowledge of those who had not grown up in Irish-speaking communities. Though the sisters were known to be what was called The Old English, whose ancestors settled in Ireland hundreds of years back, they seemed totally committed to, as Edith put it, the kindling of a new fire in the ashes of dying nationalism. It was, she said, the duty of every pupil to ignore foreign influences in the country and cultivate the Irish language and ideals.

One day, bored with all the dancing and gabbling in Irish, Rosha discovered a way of getting out of the house unobserved. Not through the window that Nellie had predicted, but a low-set door in one of the store rooms. She pulled back a bolt and stepped out into the vegetable garden which led to the orchard; here she climbed up the wall and jumped down to the other side.

In the centre of an uncultivated piece of land a young lad was leading a horse around in a wide circle. It was pulling a pole with an attachment which the boy told her was a pug-mill. Rosha understood when she looked across the field and saw Sweeney the Potter digging out clay with a long shovel. On her next escapade she made her way around to the other side of the main street in Dilford, crossed over and went down a lane to where the potter's yard was situated.

Wasn't it the good luck, she thought afterwards, that her father knew the man and she was able to go right into the work-shed and have yarn with him? Every time she appeared over the next few weeks the potter made her welcome. They chatted away while his hands moved in a steady rhythmic movement, beating clay, shaping and raising objects on the hand-turned wheel which the boy worked.

'Is he learning his trade?' she asked Mr Sweeney one day, when the boy left the shed.

'Divil a bit o'it. He's not all in it, poor lad. More's the pity for the wife and meself were not blessed with children.'

On Saturday afternoons the young ladies were allowed out − 'on their honour' − to go shopping in town. Rosha always made her way to the potter's yard where she spent her time helping Mr Sweeney. Soon he was allowing her to knead bits of clay while he talked about his craft; at other times they worked in contended silence.

'Mr Sweeney,' she said one day, 'would you consider taking me on as an assistant when I finish school? I could dig the clay and ...'

He scratched his head and laughed. 'Wasn't I thinking ye had a notion of me, and begod it's the pots yer after all the time!' He put a handle on a chamber pot which was one of an order for the workhouse. 'Aye, lass, I think you've got it in ye but what is Sean O'Neill going to say about the matter?'

When Rosha went home for Christmas she told her father about her interest in pottery. 'Mr Sweeney says I can lodge with him and his wife when the time comes.'

Sean pared a piece of tobacco, rubbed it in his hands then pressed it into the bowl of his pipe and lit it. 'A potter? And what happens when you learn the craft?'

'I'll make pots ... I've got all sorts of ideas. I just want to *do* something,' she insisted.

Sean did not understand. What more did a girl want to do other than care for the home, help in the dairy, knit, sew, and have a family? 'The potter's a poor man. You'd soon get fed up making crocks and pots.'

'I've got ideas,' she repeated stubbornly. One day in the Houstons' library she had found a beautiful book. The unusual colour combination and exquisite design of ceramic objects in it had fired her imagination.

'Well, finish your education with the Miss Houstons and if you're still of the same mind in a few years time, I'll have a word with the potter. The Miss Houstons are accomplished ladies, my dear. A bit of polish will do you no harm.' Rosha's face fell. On a more encouraging note, he continued, 'There's plenty of clay on Dan Murphy's land. No doubt Patrick will be pleased to bring you supplies if you want to play around with it when you're at home.'

'I'll get it myself,' she said shortly. Patrick! Her father couldn't open his mouth without bringing him into the conversation.

'In the meantime, stick to your books.' By next year she'll

have got over the idea, he thought contentedly. A potter? The nonsense of it.

Several days after Christmas Rosha was awakened by the sound of shouts and screams. Her room was filled with light as a shower of crimson sparks and tongues of flames shot into the night, lighting up the windows of Garton. She jumped out of bed and fell over her bag already packed for returning to school in the morning. Everyone in the house was running down the landing to the stairs. 'It's the new storing shed, the barn,' they shouted. 'My God, the wind's drawing it towards the house ...'

Sean and Willie raced to the stables to free the terrified animals, while Mrs Coll and Nellie drove the cows to the field. Rosha ran to the pig sty to help Paddy get the pigs out. Paddy was not to be seen. She picked up a stick and beat out the reluctant swine. As she tore up the yards again the cries of terrified animals were rending the night in a cacophany of fear.

'Where's Paddy?' she called. No one answered.

'Oh, my God, he must have been caught up in the barn,' she sobbed. It was now a raging inferno. Neighbours, carrying armfuls of empty buckets were pouring in from every side. Dan Murphy, Patrick and his brother were the first to arrive. Nellie shouted, 'Rosha, get the milk pails from the dairy.'

When Rosha turned she blundered into someone.

'Ah, Jayus, 'tis a fearful problem ...'

'Paddy!' Overjoyed she flung her arms around him and smelt the strong brew sold at the shebeen; the power of it made her stagger back. 'Come on, help me get the milk pails.'

A chain of men and women worked from the pond, stream and well, to douse the flames before they devoured the house as well as the outhouses. But it was hopeless; all the essential winter stores for the household and animals were completely destroyed. Hours later, when the fire was extinguished, weary men and women crowded into the kitchen for refreshments. Sean O'Neill stood apart, his face ashen. Dan Murphy picked up two mugs of tea and went over to him.

'Sean,' he said, 'I can let ye have everything you need

101

to keep you goin' until spring. There's plenty of seasoned wood up there to start you building again.'

Moved, Sean gripped his hand in silence. It was the first time they had met and spoken since Dan married Maria Flaherty. Hours later, when the smouldering skeletons of the outhouses stood gaunt against the grey dawn sky, the lamps went out at Garton. How did the fire start? everyone asked, but no one had an answer.

In the morning Nellie carried a can of water into Rosha's room. 'Time ye were up,' she said gruffly, pouring water into the basin. Her eyes were red-rimmed from smoke.

'Is my father awake yet?'

'Long ago, and down sorting out his affairs.'

'I'm not going away today,' Rosha told her.

'Well, that's where yer goin', like it or not. Isin it a blessin' the fire didin lick around to the coach house? At least there's a conveyance left t'us. Trap and cart were spared. If mice hadin taken up residence in the oul black coach it wid do a turn too.'

'Nellie, what started the fire?'

'D'ye think I know? There hasin been a bit of luck in this house since that widda set foot in it.' She threw all the bedclothes over a chair.

'Don't be silly.'

Nellie marched out of the room and returned with an armful of snow white bed-linen, fragrant with the scent of lavender that hung in bags from the shelves in the hot-press. 'Another thing,' she went on, 'Murphy's farm is thriving since she took over the reins. Patrick says she does the books and has her hand on the purse. The sooner that lad gets to Garton the better.'

Rosha always ignored these remarks which she noticed were becoming increasingly frequent. 'Nellie, imagine waking up and finding Dan Murphy beside you in the bed.'

'That's a pleasure the widda has deprived hersel' of, I hear. I widden have oul Dan if the Pope in Rome came and begged me on his knees ... Oh my God,' she wailed, 'what a disaster to fall on us!'

'Nellie, listen, I don't want to go away today. Just look at that sight outside. I should be staying at home, helping.' Tears stabbed Rosha's eyes. Her poor father.

Nellie threw down the pillow she was about to put on the bed, came over and put an arm around her. 'Don' fret, asthore. Sure once the men get building ... '

'Just think what it's going to cost.'

There was no sign of her father when Rosha went downstairs. In the room, all his account books were spread across the table and she noticed how her father had been working out figures on a piece of paper. An envelope addressed to Miss Edith Houston was propped up beside his tobacco jar. Rosha had taken the school bill home with her before Christmas; her father had commented then on how lax the ladies were. 'The bill should have been set out at the beginning of term,' he said. Lax in every way, she thought, apart from Gaelic culture. Though Miss Edith's talks had opened up exciting subjects which encouraged Rosha to read more, their enthusiasm for the ideals of the Gaelic League were now given priority. Also, one of the older pupils told her that Edith's knowledge was limited and the talks became repetitive.

'Paddy,' Rosha said impatiently as the trap approached Dilford, 'go around by the potter's?'

'B'jabers, Rosha, I'm in a wile hurry to get back,' he said impatiently.

'It's wild important. Turn here,' she told him.

Her sudden appearance surprised the elderly man. 'Good morning, Mr Sweeney. A terrible thing happened at Garton. We had a fire.'

'You say? Bad?'

'Yes, very bad. Mr Sweeney, do you remember we discussed about me coming here to work one day?'

'Aye, in a few years' time if I'm still around.'

'I'd like to start straight away ... today. How much would it cost to learn my trade and lodge in the house?'

The potter never stopped his work for anything or anyone, but now he touched the young lad's shoulder to stop the wheel and gave Rosha his full attention. 'Does your father know?' he asked, startled.

'He does,' she told him untruthfully.

He scratched his head in embarrassment at the thought

of having to discuss money. 'Ach, a bit to the wife for your board ... I'll want nothing else.' Mr Sweeney had always hoped that one day someone would ask what this young girl suggested. Now he scarcely knew how to handle it. He wiped his hands nervously. 'I'll have a word with the wife.'

Rosha waited anxiously. Paddy was sitting up in the trap fast asleep, his head on his chest. The potter's wife came hurrying out with flour on her hands. Her face was pink with pleasure.

'It'll be grand to have you, Miss O'Neill. The best room's all ready. Come and see it.' A large double bed took up all the space in the tiny room but the window pictured a view of a distant range of hills with a lough sparkling nearby.

'It's lovely, Mrs Sweeney. I'll get Paddy to take up my trunk.'

Paddy was speechless with shock. 'Ah, Jayus, Rosha ...'

The next part may not be so easy, she thought, when the trap drew up outside the Houstons' school. Miss Edith was the boss, thank goodness. Bossy would ask questions.

'Oh, my dear, a fire? How dreadful. You say your father has suffered a great financial loss? And the potter is anxious to get an assistant to train in his craft?'

Edith bit her lip, battling with this impossible situation of a girl leaving in the middle of term. Rosha could see she was weighing up this fact against her burning interest in the campaign of the Gaelic League for the preservation of Irish culture.

'He has no children, Miss Houston.'

'Still, you're young to be throwing up your studies to take on this work. Your father was so anxious for you to spend a few years with us. I'm surprised he's ...'

'The fire,' Rosha said quickly.

'Dear me, yes.'

'He'll be writing to you.' Rosha took out the envelope from her velvet pouch, handed it to Miss Edith and began praying. She desperately needed some of that money back to pay the potter's wife but realised she wasn't entitled to any of it. Her father had made an agreement which she was breaking.

'Well, now.' Miss Edith shook the gold coins on the table, moved them about and began to work out elaborate sums on a piece of paper. Rosha's face was flushed with guilt. She couldn't bear to think of her father's reaction to this. 'In the circumstance, I think I should return some of this money.'

Rosha danced all the way to the potter's yard. She felt incredibly happy and free, until the destruction of the fire loomed in her mind again. At least she was doing something positive to help her father, though he may not approve of it at first. She would write him a long letter this evening explaining as best she could.

Sean O'Neill couldn't believe his eyes when the letter arrived from Rosha. He was furious. 'How dare she make such a serious decision without my consent?' he shouted at Mrs Coll as though she were responsible in some way. 'Nellie, here at once!'

She tripped over a can of buttermilk in her haste to answer his call; the stream ran after her out of the dairy.

'Did you know what the girl was up to?' he shouted.

'As God's my honour, Mr O'Neill. What's she done?'

'Paid off Miss Houston with half the money the woman was entitled to, then goes and boards with the potter and his wife so that she can play around with bits of clay.'

It was as well for Rosha that Dan Murphy and his two sons came into the yard at that moment with the first load of wood to start building, for Sean was about to jump on his horse and journey to Dilford. 'I'll leave Patrick wi' ye, Sean – a pair of extra hands.'

'I'm more than grateful, Dan. I'll settle with you later.'

'Don' mention it Sean ... don' mention it. We'll settle between ourselves when the work is done. A load of hay will be down in the afternoon.'

When the men left the kitchen, Nellie slipped into the room and read the letter Rosha had written. 'Wid ye believe it, Mrs Coll? The cheeky wee article.' Her eyes were shining with pride and admiration.

''Tis a good skelping that girsha needs,' Mrs Coll grunted, fed up with the mess on the kitchen floor since the fire. All the extra work was killing her.

105

# Chapter Eleven

Grace Boyce was churning when the knock came on the door. It sounded too polite for the shepherd.

'May I come in?' Edmund Catalong called and pushed open the half-door.

Surprised, Grace said: 'Yer welcome, sir.' She scarcely recognised the tall handsome young man that Rosha O'Neill used to play with years ago.

Edmund apologised for calling. 'Thirst drove me to your door, Mrs Boyce,' he laughed. 'I'm fishing down below the house.'

'Yer more than welcome, sir.' She liked this young man with the sensitive features and friendly smile. 'Ye'll have a cup of tay, sir?'

'Well, actually, I was thinking of a drink of cold water.'

'As ye like now.' When Grace handed him a glass of spring water she noticed that his eyes were fastened on a piece of pottery standing on the mantelpiece, which she knew was out of place in her humble home. It was a small vase made in coils and painted in delicate colours of green and gold. 'Isin it lovely? Rosha ... Rosha O'Neill made that. She's a great hand at the pottery making.'

His expression altered. 'Rosha? I haven't seen her for a long time. Where is she? I thought I might have met Nellie to enquire.'

'Ah, ye didin know? She took herself off to Dilford to learn about pottery ... no, I'm not telling the right way of the story. Her father sent her to a grand school in Dilford and didin she think the expense was too great? About the time of the fire at Garton, it was, and she went to the potter to learn the trade.' Edmund threw back his head and laughed. 'Och, Rosha's a holy terror! Mr O'Neill wasn't pleased about it. Now he wants her wed and settled soon.'

'Surely she's too young?' Edmund spoke quickly, almost protestingly.

'Wasin her mother and meself wed at the same age? A lucky girl she is for there's a fine young man waiting for her hand.' A trap coming into the yard made Grace glance out at the window. 'Well, if it isin herself ...'

Rosha took the reins from Paddy. 'Are we near enough to the door of the shed to get the bag of potatoes in? Hello, Grace, what about coming back with us to Garton? Paddy can get you home later in the evening?'

'Ah, Jayus, Rosha,' Paddy grumbled.

Edmund came out of the cottage and stood at the door looking at her. Rosha turned her head and saw him. She paused for a moment, then flinging the reins to Paddy, jumped off the trap. 'Edmund!' He took two long strides across to meet her. They stood for a moment, just starting at each other, then began to laugh.

'How tall you've grown,' she said breathlessly.

'And you.' She's beautiful, he thought, staring at her. So beautiful.

Grace drew inside again, feeling troubled at the way the two young people were looking at each other. No longer children; young adults becoming aware. Thank goodness Rosha was at Dilford most of the time now. Off tomorrow, praise God. Rosha and Edmund were talking eagerly about what they were doing and laughed about times past. Grumbling, Paddy dragged the sack carelessly across the yard. He didn't see the piece of iron jutting out of the ground until it pierced the bottom and held it fast.

'Wid youse wans give me a hand,' he called irritably.

'Oh dear,' Rosha exclaimed as Paddy jerked at the bag and split its bottom. They ran over as loose potatoes raced towards the midden. Laughing, they tried to stop them with their feet. She went into the shed and found an old bath. The three of them pushed the sack into it and dumped the

107

contents inside the door. Paddy rubbed his dirty hands on his trousers while the two young people dipped theirs in the duck pond.

'Go on in and have some tea, Paddy,' Rosha rold him. 'Sure you've worn yourself out.' As he shuffled off, she said, 'That's the laziest man on God's earth.'

'When can I see you again?' Edmund asked. ''Fraid we're far too old to play on the shore!'

'I'm going back to Dilford on Monday,' she said slowly.

'I have to be in Dilford on that day,' he told her untruthfully, and they both smiled.

On Monday morning Rosha asked Mrs Sweeney if she could have some sandwiches as she wouldn't be home for midday dinner. A friend of hers was coming into town, she told her. The potter's wife cut thick slices of beef and bread while Rosha washed a bunch of scallions and filled a bag with apples.

'You'll be dry. Bring her back for a cup of tea or a glass of my apple wine,' Mrs Sweeney offered.

'It's all right,' Rosha said quickly, realising that her friendship with the son of Sir Thomas Catalong might give offence; also bewilder the woman for it was well known that O'Neill and Catalong disliked each other.

Edmund came early and instead of waiting outside, strolled in. Rosha was in the yard trimming wicks on the lanterns that were used in the pottery during the night. She shrugged. Ah, well, I'd better introduce him to Mr Sweeney, she decided.

The potter gave a sharp glance at the young man with the stamp of his class in manner, speech and clothes. Nevertheless, he greeted him courteously though aware that Rosha may have tried to deceive them about the true nature of her friend. He apologised for not shaking hands as he was busy working on a truncated cone of clay on the wheel. Fascinated, Edmund watched as the potter's fingers penetrated the lump of clay, then the quick order to the lad who helped him: 'Slower, boy!' And the wheel moved at a different speed as the pot began to take shape.

Rosha touched Edmund's arm. 'Would you like to see

108

around?' She took him into the drying shed and explained how the pots had to be turned regularly in a free circulation of air. He asked questions and she tried to explain all the work involved in the pottery. 'Sometimes when the night is frosty Mr Sweeney comes down and lights the brazier because frost shatters unfired pots.'

'In the middle of the night?'

'When there's a firing we all take turns 'til morning. Mrs Sweeney doesn't work here but she understands everything that's going on.'

'What an extraordinary thing for you to become involved in, Rosha. Where will all this lead to?' he asked.

'I would like to start a pottery at Garton one day. The work here is coarse ware, like those tall crocks over there for storing buttermilk and the wider vessels for cream.' She ignored the row of large white chamber pots. 'What I'd like to do is work on fine ware, make objects with colour and ...'

'Ceramics, porcelain?'

'Yes. Of course I must convince my father that I'm capable of doing something that will eventually produce an income, because the initial outlay will need quite a bit of capital.'

'Have you no plans for marriage, children and helping to run a farm?' he asked lightly.

Rosha turned away abruptly. 'Everyone has those sorts of plans for me,' she muttered bleakly, remembering what Nellie had said at the weekend when Rosha remarked how Patrick always seemed to be around Garton. 'Sure he'll be here one of these days for good, and well ye know it.'

When they left for the river with the picnic basket, Edmund said: 'I had planned to take you to the hotel for a meal.'

'You wouldn't like it there, Edmund. It's terrible food they serve. It'll be nicer by the river.'

'Why don't we hide in the woods?' he suggested half-jokingly.

She didn't reply until they were by the water. 'You know why we can't be seen together. If our fathers knew it could be awkward.'

He touched her arm and she turned towards him. 'Rosha,

109

when I came back again to Slievegar, I looked everywhere for you.'

'Why did you leave so suddenly that time?'

'The woman who was called the housekeeper saw us in the shop together.'

'I went to the island and found the bailiff pulling down the tree house.'

'He was ordered to.'

'That man's good at pulling down houses, especially when people are living in them.'

'It was the letter I left for you that the bailiff found and gave to my father.'

And that's why I went back to the island, she remembered. 'What did you say in the letter?'

'I ... I can't remember.' Then with a smile, 'Something foolish.'

They ate their lunch and sent bits sailing down the river. Afterwards they went into the woods and found a spring-well by a little mossy bank covered with clusters of wild violets. When they had drank their fill of the sparkling cold water, Rosha asked: 'Edmund, what do you do when you're in London?'

'Visit my aunt and our next-door neighbours, Roger and Alice Meckin.' He stopped abruptly, not wanting to talk about London or anything else.

'Is she nice, Alice Meckin? I've never met an English girl.'

'Alice? Yes, she is.'

They sat quietly on the bank, listening to the rustling sounds in the woods. After a while she said reluctantly, 'I must go.'

He took a watch from his breast pocket. 'Yes, I'm afraid so.'

'I won't see you again. You've got to leave this week, haven't you?'

'Ah, I forgot to mention it, I'm not going until next week. I told my father this morning.'

'He didn't mind?'

'I have gone up in his estimation. Though I still don't shoot, I love fishing which I do better than him. Also, I

110

did well in my entrance examination to Sandhurst. Roger Meckin, Alice's brother, failed twice and has been sent to an army coach. My father is much impressed. So, Rosha, I have gained a little respect and am allowed to make a few decisions for myself. Can I meet you after work?'

'All right. It's a fairly, quiet week in the pottery.' Where can we go unseen in this small town? she wondered. People will talk.

'The fishing is very good on the river. I've decided to spend a week at the hotel.' He smiled. 'With parental consent! By the way, Rosha, the food there is also good. We own the place!'

Laughing, they piled everything into the basket and hurried along the path. Just as they went to cut up under the bridge to the road, Miss Edith Houston made her way down.

'Why, Rosha, I was planning to call and invite you to our musical evenings. My dear, we have such fun. Poetry readings and music. And your friend, he must come too. Why,' she exclaimed in surprise, 'it's Sir Thomas Catalong's son, isn't it?' Edith was delighted. She could scarcely believe it. This young couple together. What an exciting possibility for the future if they could make a match.

There was a noticeable chill in the Sweeneys' manner when Rosha returned that afternoon. At tea they were full of questions. How long had she known the son of Sir Thomas Catalong? The potter looked strict and his wife worried. Catalong was feared and not respected. There were some dreadful stories about the man. Rosha was aware that these kind people judged Edmund by his father, little knowing that he was completely different. She answered their questions casually then, after a while said excitedly: 'Oh, Mrs Sweeney, I met Miss Edith Houston this afternoon and she has invited me to their home. They're holding musical evenings this week and as we are not so busy here, I accepted the invitation.'

This seemed to please the potter's wife. The Miss Houstons were considered to be gentry in Dilford, as were all Anglo-Irish families in the county. It was an honour to have their lodger and assistant invited to their home.

When Rosha followed Edith upstairs to their drawing-room

that evening, she discovered that Edmund was already there and had been given a seat right at the back of the room on a Georgian settee which held just two people. A young man read some poetry. Next came a duet sung by a middle-aged man and Edith, who was dressed in a long emerald-green satin gown. The firelight and lamps threw a gentle glow over the room, softening the faces of the aged and unattractive. Edith's sister, Bossy, who played the harp, seemed diminished by the beauty and power of the instrument; the shadows claimed her and only the movement of her fingers, which appeared magically white and slim, seemed alive. Another duet was sung by two younger people. It was poignantly sad and accompanied by the voice of the harp gave no hope to the longing of an Irish emigrant far from his country. Its sadness could not affect Rosha because Edmund slipped his arm around her waist and drew her close.

After refreshments were served people began to drift away to their homes. Rosha remembered the old orchard where she had made her escape in the time when she attended the Houstons' school. They went down between the apple and the pear trees until they found a log to sit on, where they talked quietly until Edmund bent down and picked a bunch of white daisies which he arranged around the hem of her blue gown. Laughing, they held hands, and he kissed her.

Every evening after that they sought the shelter of an apple tree where, with their increasing love, they began to talk about a future together. Rosha shut her mind to the problems that could bring. Edmund ignored his troublesome thoughts, too, and told her about a little property on the other side of Donegal which his father might be prepared to let him manage.

'It's rather isolated, Rosha, but there's good fishing and shooting over there. Not all that far from Lisdare where you could go shopping.'

'Edmund,' she said one evening, 'my father expects me to marry Parick Murphy.'

'How can he decide who you should marry?' he protested, though aware that marriages were frequently arranged in this country. He held her close, overwhelmed by the love he felt for her, yet protective because the passion in Rosha's nature was combined with a complete innocence. She had no idea the effect their lovemaking had on him.

Miss Edith's evenings continued, though not so frequently. Edith, delighted with the young lovers, and understanding their problem, had suggested they used the parlour to be on their own any evening they wished. Two nights before Edmund had to leave for England, they were in the orchard. Playfully he pulled all the pins out of her hair and pressed his face against the long dark strands. Rosha was trying to smother her laughter at his recklessness when a sound reached her ears.

'Edmund,' she whispered alarmed, 'there's someone over there watching us.'

'Surely not Miss Edith?'

'No, she wouldn't do a thing like that. Let's go.' She rolled up her hair quickly and stuck the pins in anyhow. It might be the maid, she was thinking, when the figure of Bossy moved furtively through the trees in the direction of the house. How many times had she stood there watching them? Rosha wondered, and felt her happiness touched by something unpleasant.

The following evening was their last together. They decided to go for a walk in the woods where no one would see them. With arms entwined they strolled down through the overgrown paths. Honeysuckle and the pungent smell of wild flowers and herbs filled the air. From some secretive place came the call of a corncrake. When they came to the little grassy mound where they had sat before, Edmund said: 'Sit down, Rosha, I want to give you something.' He took a box out of his pocket, opened it and handed her a ring with a small opal stone.

She held it up and saw a vivid lustre as though the specks of colour were burning inside the stone. 'It's beautiful.'

He smiled at her look of pleasure. 'Wear it.'

'Nellie will ask questions.'

'Hide it somewhere then. Keep it safely.'

She pushed it on her finger and he put his arm around her. They slipped down on the mossy ground and lay back, gazing up at the moon fleeting busily through the clouds. In the orchard they had always stood modestly under the apple tree, but here they were in a different world; free and wild like the plants and wildlife around them. Edmund kissed her with an unbearable feeling of loss. He dreaded the weeks and months ahead when he could no longer see her. His increasing feeling made him cautious and after a while he said with an abruptness that startled her: 'Rosha, I think we should go now.'

'Oh, no, Edmund,' she protested, 'it's early yet.'

'It's not that. I'm thinking of you ...'

With unconscious abandonment she pulled him closer. It was then that he forgot his feeling of protective caution and crushing her down into the bed of violets, began to make love to her as the night grew darker and the woods silent.

Afterwards they dabbled their toes in the cool water by the river and spoke in whispers, as though the trees might be listeners. Rosha prayed that the Sweeneys would have taken themselves off to bed by the time she returned. Edmund felt that the fulfilment of his love for Rosha had become a responsibility, though not a burden. He was quite determined to marry her and defy all the conventions of his Anglo-Irish upbringing.

'Rosha, when we get married I'll build you a pottery at Horton, the estate I was telling you about. I'll take you to see Belleek where they make very fine porcelain. That will give you some ideas.'

'Horton? Did you say Horton?'

'Yes. Why?'

'The name has a familiar ring. Perhaps I've heard about it before from Nellie.'

'It's a long way from here.' He touched her face. 'Are you all right? I shouldn't have done that.'

'Don't say that Edmund ... not now.'

'I must write to you when I'm away. I must know how you are. You can write to my aunt's address in London. Oh —' he paused ' — she's planning to go abroad again.'

'Edmund, you can't send me letters. Nellie reads everything that comes into the house.'

'Grace, she wouldn't do that?'

Rosha shook her head. 'That's no good either. She might be curious and worry if letters came to me secretly. I saw how

114

she looked that day when we were in the yard together.'

The Sweeneys were not at all happy about Rosha. The potter noticed how unwilling the girl had been recently to take on evening work, whereas before he couldn't stop her. His wife waited up, determined to talk to her. She was an observant woman; she noticed how carefully Rosha dressed before going out these evenings. There were quiet moods; other times a sparkle of hidden joy. It was fine if she was courting a lad, but the person she was keeping company with was most unsuitable. Nothing could come of it other than trouble. Alarmed by the girl's lateness, Mrs Sweeney went off to bed and listened for her footsteps. Finally, she heard voices, looked out of the window and saw down below the evidence of the unsuitable courtship at her very gate.

It was the potter who told Rosha in the morning that he was cutting down on the work with a view to retiring. He had taught her all he knew, he said, and wished her well when she set up her own pottery at Slievegar. Rosha was shattered by her sudden dismissal, then thought what a lonely place Dilford would be when Edmund was no longer there. Now she would have to persuade her father to start a pottery at Garton. Edmund said she should have a wheel that could be worked by foot instead of being dependent on another person's action.

Nellie was not in when she arrived home but quiet voices came from the room next to the kitchen. She opened the door and found her father talking earnestly to three men whom she did not know.

'The landlords are growing very anxious since the last Land Act was passed,' he was saying.

'Small remedial measures to keep the Irish quiet,' one added. 'The landlords in this part of Ireland will push harder before it all ends for, my friends, the end is in sight at last. Sean, they've been getting away with too much in this area. Catalong has feathered his nest well here. I think you should call another meeting for the reason we've been discussing.'

Sean turned, about to reply, and saw Rosha standing there. 'Ah, Rosha, my dear, you've come home for the weekend. Gentlemen, my daughter.'

She smiled at the men and went quickly out of the room again, sorry now that she had bothered to disturb them. Upstairs in the bedroom, she took Edmund's ring from her bag and slipped it on her finger to admire the changing colours in the small but beautiful stone.

'Rosha ...' The door opened and Nellie came barging in. 'Someone told me ye had arrived back.' She frowned. 'What's that on yer finger?' Before Rosha could hide it, Nellie pounced across the floor. 'Where'd ye get that funny wee ring in the name of God?'

'I picked it up in the shop ... the old one in Dilford.'

Nellie saw the rich glow of gold and frowned; it reminded her of the ones the master kept in the desk belonging to his dead wife. To her annoyance, guilty colour stained Rosha's cheeks. Before she could put the ring away, Nellie pounced again and picked up the leather case with the name and address of a London jeweller embossed on the lid. Alarmed, she looked at the girl's revealing expression. There was talk at Tin Lizzie's the other day about the young master at the castle spending a lot of time fishing over in Dilford.

'Did ye see Edmund Catalong o'er by Dilford?' she asked abruptly.

'Yes,' Rosha said, putting the ring back in its case and casually throwing it into the drawer as if it were of no importance. 'We met a few times at a musical evening.' She then proceeded to tell Nellie about the pottery and the end of her apprenticeship.

For the first time in her life, Nellie kept a still tongue. Rosha's manner made her feel very alarmed. She had seen young Catalong riding past Garton one day and had thought then that he would take the heart away from any girl. A fine figure he was and a lovely easy manner when he greeted her on the road. Such a handsome face on him — and there's Rosha pretending he didin' matter! The sooner she's wed to Patrick Murphy the better.

Rosha realised that Nellie was suspicious. It was the first time they had not been close, telling each other everything. She might have told her more if the secret she shared with Edmund had not been so serious. Nellie would blame Edmund when Rosha knew it was just as much her fault.

116

After the men left the house she went in and talked to her father. He took out some papers dealing with the land on the estate because, he said, the last time he had spoken to the potter he had seemed very impressed with her work.

'We mustn't waste your skills, my dear. There's no reason why you shouldn't start up here in a small way. We built on an extra building after the fire. You could use that and the old barn.' He took a map from the pile of papers and pointed. 'That piece of land there, Rosha, near Togher Glen. A man wants to buy it. I can do without it and it'll bring in a bit of extra money.'

'You've always been reluctant to sell any land, Father.'

'Times have changed and Garton has plenty of land. Rosha ...' he hesitated. 'There's something I want to say.'

'Yes?'

'I'm hoping that you and Patrick will make a match of it. The boy is not happy with his stepmother, and to be honest, I could do with him here to help me. Paddy's useless. Willie's a good worker but I need someone responsible because apart from everything else, I'm not getting any younger. Also, I have taken on certain responsibilities in the community.'

Rosha wished she could tell him about Edmund but they had both agreed that they would approach their parents at the same time. They must wait for a few years until they were older and thought responsible enough to make such serious decisions, he said.

'I'm not in love with Patrick.'

'Give it time, my dear. You like him well enough, don't you? It would be a good match for you.' Sean looked at her hopefully but she made no reply. 'Rosha, as he's coming here to live and your children will inherit Garton, there'll be no question of a dowry involved. Dan and I have discussed it and agreed on the matter. Unless,' he added in a harsh voice, 'Dan Murphy's wife sees a way around it.'

She bent her head to hide the anger in her eyes. How could such a kind, loving father try to make a decision that would affect her entire life and happiness? One day, she thought obstinately, I will make him realise how impossible it is. She was about to say that he mustn't build his hopes on such a plan for her future and that it wasn't fair, when Mrs Coll called them to the kitchen for tea.

Rosha was slipping into bed when she heard an alarming noise out on the road. She rushed to the window and saw, when the moon slid from behind a cloud, a company of soldiers in bright red uniforms running along at a brisk trot. Others were on horseback.

Nellie burst into the room. 'Mary and Joseph ... dragoons!' Biddy Coll came hurrying after her. 'Oh, Mrs Coll,' Nellie wailed, 'they're after O'Neill and him up at the parochial house at a meeting. The Constabulary will be comin' in the opposite direction from Lisdare and himself in the middle like a mouse between two cats.'

'What's to be done?' The older woman wrung her hands helplessly. 'I didn't know there was a meetin' this evenin'. There was no fire on the hill.'

''Twas a secret meeting. News went around by word of mouth ... Rosha O'Neill, what are ye doin'?'

Rosha was pulling on her underclothes. Ignoring Nellie, she ran down to her father's room, dragged a pair of his breeches and a guernsey out of the cupboard and put them on. Without a word she tore downstairs and out of the house.

'Rosha,' Nellie yelled, 'what are ye up to wi' the countryside red wi' soldiers?'

Paddy appeared at the barn door as she ran past. She snatched the cap off his head. ''Tis wile dirty,' he called after her as she ran into the stable, piling her long hair under the rim. She dragged the horse from its comfortable stall.

'Troth, ye look just like a gasair,' Paddy called after her as she mounted and rode speedily out of the yard.

Rosha felt incredibly free riding across the countryside in her father's breeches and Paddy's smelly old cap. If she were not so worried about her father this would have been an enjoyable ride. The animal, sensing her urgency, pounded along at a steady pace, scattering daisies and buttercups that freckled the path across Togher Glen. She urged the horse on, anxious to get off the glen in case she should be seen from the road that was now within sight.

Near the stretch of land belonging to the church, she saw to her dismay that Nellie was right: a consignment of constables were approaching from the direction of Dilford. She moved in among the trees as the soldiers surrounded the church building. Uncertain and frightened, she stayed where she was and began to pray.

In the hall, Sean looked around at the assembled men; it had been hard work getting them together without lighting the fire on the hill. It was of the utmost importance that this meeting should be held without the knowledge of the authorities. He was surprised to see Patrick on his own. Sean beckoned to the youth. 'Where's your father, lad?'

Shades of discomfort crossed Patrick's face. 'He's not coming this evening, Mr O'Neill.' Before he could stop himself or give the excuse that had been suggested before he left home, Patrick said with bitterness, '*She* stopped him.'

Why should Maria do that? Sean wondered. He cast his eyes around the hall for Judas, as they called him. There was no sign of the man. Good. Their plan of secrecy had succeeded. 'Patrick, will you take a look outside for the officials coming to speak at the meeting?'

Patrick pushed his way through the throng of men around the building and climbed up on the hedge. He stood transfixed for a moment, not able to believe the sight that met his eyes. He jumped from the hedge and fled inside again, shouting, 'Mr O'Neill, the Constabulary and the Dragoons are coming. Will you try and get away, for God's sake?' Others surged into the hall in confusion.

'Quiet everyone,' Sean shouted. 'Stand quiet. We must hear what business they're about. It'll be me they're coming for.' The men shouted for him to get out the back window quick. 'No, I'm not running away,' he said firmly, and turned to Patrick. 'Whatever happens, Pat, get over to Garton ... see Rosha. Help them there if I'm ...' he paused ' ... away from home for a while.'

Patrick swallowed with emotion. 'I give ye my word, Mr O'Neill. For the love of God, why don't ye make a run for it?'

'Good lad.' He touched the boy's shoulder and walked to the door of the hall where he was met by an inspector

119

who informed him that a warrant had been issued for his arrest. He was taken immediately under a heavy escort to Lisdare jail.

Rosha was spared the sight of her father being taken prisoner for just as she went to make her way on foot towards the hill, a figure came galloping in her direction. She ran out and waved her hands. For the first time in her life she felt deeply relieved to see Patrick Murphy. She stared at him wordlessly, her eyes wide with fear. He slipped off the animal's back, put his arm around her and explained what had happened up at the hall.

'Patrick, what will they do to him?' He felt her trembling and drew her closer, protectively.

'They'll grant him bail surely. You and I and Willie will drive up to Lisdare tomorrow morning. We'll take some things to him ... just in case.' Patrick didn't really know what would happen to O'Neill. The Constabulary were in an ugly mood, angry about the meeting. Why in God's name did they send the Dragoons as well? Were they expecting trouble? Everyone had listened to O'Neill and left quietly.

Rosha looked at the strong young man whom she had resented all her life and felt thankful that he was beside her now. He seemed to have grown more mature since he and Rory Donavan had become friendly.

'Get up on your horse, Rosha. We'd better get away from here.'

'If this meeting was supposed to be held in secret, Patrick, why did they come? I mean, how did they know to come?'

His mouth tightened in anger. 'Because someone informed the authorities.' Now he knew why his stepmother wouldn't let that fool of a father of his go to the meeting. It was her doing. What was his father turning into anyway since that woman came to the house? She had taken over entirely. And her dislike of O'Neill was venomous.

Nellie rushed out of the house when she heard them coming. 'Rosha O'Neill, if it wasin for the size of ye, I'd put ye across my knee. Imagine goin' to that meeting all dressed up as a lad! Look at the cut of ye. Come in, Patrick Murphy, the tea's just wet.' Rosha and Patrick glanced at each other; there was a note of hysteria in Nellie's voice. 'Willie got back a while ago', she shouted at them as if they were both stone deaf. 'He says they've taken the master. Ah, blessed virgin, what will become of him?'

'You'll have him home the morrow, Nellie,' Patrick said firmly, sitting at the table before a bowl of tea and thick slices of scone bread.

Nellie ran down to the men's bedroom, banged on the door and shouted: 'Put yer britches on again, Willie Doherty, an' come on out. Patrick says the master will be home t'morrow.'

Rosha went over and sat beside Patrick. 'Shall we make an early start in the morning?'

Willie, with his hair standing on end, tightened the belt of his trousers and muttered, 'Leave it to me and Patrick, Rosha. 'Twill be no place for a girl.'

She placed her cup on the table and looked at him. 'I'm going to find out what's happening to my father.'

Usually undemonstrative, Willie stabbed the table with his finger. 'You stay at home now. The master won't like it one bit if ye turn up there. The military followed the Constabulary to Lisdare. They're expecting trouble.'

'Yer not to go to Lisdare and that's an end of it,' Nellie said in her snapping voice.

Rosha jumped to her feet, her eyes sparkling with anger. 'In my father's absence, *I'll* make the decisions here. Don't dare tell me what to do.'

There was surprised silence. They all stared at her. 'All right, Rosha,' Patrick said, 'we'll set off early in the morning so.' He felt an uncontrollable rage growing against his stepmother. He would never have suspected if he hadn't heard her warning his father not to go to the meeting because there was going to be trouble.

Willie and Patrick were eating their breakfast next morning when Rosha came downstairs. Patrick had spent the night at Garton, sleeping on the spare bed in Willie's room. It had rained earlier on but now the sky was clearing. Paddy, who was out in the yard getting the pony and trap ready, came in and stamped his dirty feet all over the floor. For once neither Nellie nor Mrs Coll scolded him.

121

'Put a good bit of food together, Nellie,' Patrick suggested. 'Lisdare prison is not known for its hospitality.'

By the time they were ready to leave, the soft swirling mist on the hills was lifting and the sun striking light into everything it touched. It fell on the overhanging branches in the drive and rimmed the leaves with silver. Muddy pools of water were touched with gold and needles of light darted through the pond to the hedges which glittered with a magical luminosity.

About a mile along the road Rosha looked towards the hill road and saw several horses and carts coming down. They were loaded with men. 'Patrick, look, where are they going?'

'Making for Lisdare. They're going to crowd the town out in a protest. They can't throw everyone into prison.'

His words silenced her. She knew her father was popular because of his work for tenants' rights. Still, it was unusual for poor farmers to take a day away from their farms. 'Was all this organised?'

'It was. Rory is stirring the people in Lisdare. Your father has held meetings there. He won't be forgotten.'

'Protesting might do more harm if they're considering letting him out on bail.'

'Rosha ...' Patrick's brown eyes were troubled. 'I don't think they'll let him go so easily. They've been waiting for this chance to get him. For others in the same situation, it's been a charge of taking part in a criminal conspiracy.'

Crowds teemed along the roads, some travelling in traps or carts, others on foot. Rory met them outside the town. 'I knew you would be on the way,' he said climbing into the trap. 'Willie, up the next lane. It leads to the farm belonging to my employer. We'll go into the town on foot because the place is crowded out.'

The four of them took a short-cut into the centre of Lisdare. The three from Slievegar were unprepared for the sight that met their eyes. Hundreds of people crowded around the prison, singing. Dragoons paraded the streets, also a force of Constabulary with batons drawn. Rosha's feeling of anxiety increased; she was convinced the people's reaction would antagonise the authorities. First, she must

122

find the lawyer, Mr Duggan, and visit her father in jail.

She was allowed only a few minutes inside the prison. Sean was pleased to see her and get the things she had brought him. 'I'm feeling quite well, my dear,' he said, 'but you must return to Slievegar straight away. There'll be trouble in this town from what the lawyer has told me.'

Later that day they knew the worst. Sean O'Neill had been refused bail.

When the date of his trial was announced, people from all around the countryside travelled through the night to reach Lisdare. Their journey was in vain for the town was declared Proclaimed which meant no assembly of people was allowed to congregate in the streets. Rosha and Patrick stayed with Rory at the farmhouse. Only Rosha was permitted to attend the hearing, accompanied by their lawyer. Sean O'Neill was charged with inciting the people to take part in an unlawful conspiracy by refusing to pay their rents. Other charges were brought against him too.

Judas has done his job well, Sean thought bitterly in court; the man was gifted with an extraordinary imagination. Everything he declared had a grain of truth but perhaps after all his knowledge of Gaelic was not so perfect. Rosha felt distraught at the six months' sentence her father received. Everyone decided that the advocate defending him had not been strong enough.

When Rory and Patrick heard the news they said angrily but determinedly, 'We'll carry on his work.'

In her grief Rosha began to feel burdened with guilt. Thank goodness she hadn't attempted to tell her father about Edmund. He had convinced himself that she was going to marry Patrick. Perhaps that was now giving him some comfort in prison. Rory persuaded them to spend another night at the farm. He and Patrick had things to discuss, he said. Rory was doing well these days, managing the farm and now in charge of a second-hand jewellery shop his employer had opened in Lisdare. Though he missed travelling on the roads, he was pleased to be getting on in life.

Rosha took the opportunity to slip away to the church. She rang the bell in the vestry and went into the confession box. In the darkness of the Confessional, she confessed 'the sin of the flesh'. The priest did not speak for a long time. My sin has shocked him into silence, she thought, and trembled at the magnitude of it.

'How many times has this grievous sin occurred?' he asked at last.

'Once, Father ... in a hurry. I mean, we were parting. It was terrible.'

The priest, young and just out of the seminary, said quickly: 'Avoid bad company at all times,' and gave her absolution followed by penance.

Bad company? What would he say if she told him Edmund was the son of a Protestant landowner? Suddenly Rosha felt overcome with exhaustion and relief. She crept out of the confession box and knelt behind a large pillar where she could hide her burning face.

# Chapter Twelve

It was a night of winter. Heavy rain spat viciously down
the chimney and high winds tore around the old walls of
Horton like demented spirits. Windows rattled and were
battered with onslaughts of broken twigs and hails of
gravel. Trees became uprooted and shrubs bent low in
defeat. In the meadow, canes were lashed to the ground
but with obdurate persistence sprang back again. The three
sitting around the fire clutched their blue and white bowls of
stirabout made with Indian meal which had been sold in the
country since the time of the famine. In the morning it was
the custom to use oats. The two women drew their shawls
tightly around their shoulders as they sipped the hot meal.
On the mantelpiece the oil lamp flickered, sending ghostly
shadows leaping around the walls.

''Tis surely as bad as the night of the Big Wind when I
was a lad,' Barney mused. 'Every clout in the house was
piled on the beds as the devilish wind snarled through the
very stones on the wall.'

''Tis an act of God this house hasn't been blown down,'
his wife commented.

'Begod, His hands must be full t'night holding up walls,'
Barney said blasphemously, and winked at Bridie who felt
a bubble of laughter in her throat.

'May the Lord forgive you for those words, Barney
O'Sullivan. Next time I hope they strangle you. Bridie, I
hope the stone bottles are in the beds,' the housekeeper
said when they finished the rosary.

'This past hour and as hot as they could bear.'

'Good girl. Take yourself off now. Barney, wind the clock and we'll make a start. Ach, 'tis difficult to leave a good fire. The wind is dying down all the same. After all it might be a peaceful night.'

Nora O'Sullivan used to give Bridie a large mug of the bitter herb potion before bedtime, until she realised that a pregnancy was definitely established and nothing, other than some wicked action, could alter the situation.

A banging came on the door which wasn't bolted yet, then someone began to push at it.

'Coming,' Barney called, thinking it was a traveller journeying on the roads. On such a night he would be made doubly welcome. Often they came in winter, were given a bowl of stirabout and offered a bed in the barn. The travellers of the night were always decent men, prepared to do a morning's work to pay for their supper and lodgings.

'Open up,' a voice demanded.

Barney scowled. An order, begob. 'Use yer shoulder to it,' he growled, forgetting the agent's warning about Fenian outrages on big houses.

'Aren't I always telling you to do something about that door in the winter?' his wife scolded. 'If there was a fire we'd never get out.'

'Aye ye would, Mrs O'Sullivan. Ye'd be the first out. Wait till ye get to the pearly gates. Ye'll be knocking St Peter over to get through.'

'Eejit! Bridie, off to bed, dear.'

She was moving down the kitchen when the door burst open. Two men with unbuttoned caps pulled down over their eyes came in. A scarf covered the lower part of their faces. One carried a gun. She thought of the carefully cleaned guns in the room down the hall which Catalong had used for shooting on the moor.

'Over there,' the tall man with the gun ordered when Barney made a move towards the inner door. Bridie was surprised at his bravery but felt somehow that a gun might be more effective in his wife's hands.

'Listen carefully,' the man said. 'All three of you collect your belongings as fast as you can. My friend will accompany you upstairs. Don't attempt to go near the windows. Another

126

man is outside watching the house. Quickly please,' he repeated. 'When you come down get the pony and trap ready. The three of you can drive to the hotel for a night's lodgings.'

Shock had silenced the housekeeper until she found her tongue. 'We're in charge of this house,' she said, and added bravely but foolishly, 'we're not leaving it.'

'There'll soon be no house standing for you to bother about, ma'am. Get upstairs at once for your belongings or else you can leave without them.' He turned to Bridie. 'You the servant girl? Where's your room?' She nodded her head. 'Get ready.'

Bridie bundled everything into a shawl. The lace was still in the piece of pillowcase since the night she tried to run away from Catalong. Depressed, she had not touched the work since. Wrapped up warmly in her outdoor clothes, she left the kitchen with her bundle. Outside in the yard a man was driving the cows to the field behind the byre.

'Are all the pigs out?' she called.

'They're in the field.'

'Yer sure the wee drolyeen is wi' the sow? Would you take a look, mistah?'

He took a step backwards and as he did so, light from the kitchen fell across his head. Despite his disguise Bridie knew who it was. She was about to speak to him, to plead, when Mrs O'Sullivan came out of the house.

The expression on Bridie's face made the housekeeper say sharply, 'Do you know who that man is?'

The eyes under the peak of the cap met Bridie's. 'No, indeed, ma'am. Sure I was just making sure the wee pig was with the rest of the litter.'

'All the animals are safe,' he said. 'They're at the far end of the field.' His voice was as gentle as she remembered, not hard and authoritative like the other man's. But then, Patrick Murphy had always been a gentle boy.

Barney brought the trap around accompanied by the second man who was short and broadly built. Not one word passed his lips. It made him seem ominous; in fact he was dumb from birth.

'What are you going to do with the property?' Mrs

O'Sullivan demanded. The question was unnecessary for the three of them could see the large oil cans lined up by the shed.

'We're sorry that this is necessary,' the soft voice of Patrick said.

'Sorry? Huh! Much good your sorrow will do when the three of us are without a roof o'er our heads. Have ye thought of that?'

'No doubt the owner of this property will reinstate you in his other residence,' the leader replied.

With fear and rage in her voice, Nora O'Sullivan pleaded, 'Won't you allow us to take a few of the good bits out, sir? It's a sin to destroy what's in that house.'

Bridie thought of the cheval-mirror and felt some regret. A few months ago she would have cried at the destruction, now she didn't really care. Sir Thomas Catalong had made the world a black place for her. Objects and things that used to delight her had no importance any more. She just wished he was tied up and burnt with the house.

They were a few miles away from Hoton when the heavens and hills were lit by the flames that consumed it. Grimly, Barney drove on to the hotel with his two silent passengers. There was only one room available. Bridie and Mrs O'Sullivan shared the bed and her husband slept on the floor. The following morning word was sent by the Constabulary to Merifield Manor about the fire. Barney went up to Horton and came back white-faced. 'They made a good job of it,' was all he said. Arrangements had been made with a neighbouring farmer about the animals and poultry until the agent came.

Captain Hurl arrived a day later. Mrs O'Sullivan was never so pleased to see him.

'Oh, sir, what's to become of us? We did our best to stop them.'

'Captain Hurl,' the constable said finally, 'we might as well look for a flea in a mountain. They'll be miles away by now. The country has been alerted. We can do no more.'

When Mrs O'Sullivan told Bridie that they had been offered employment at Merifield, the girl was terrified. Really, she hadn't given the situation much thought. She was tired, sick and frightened, but felt cherished by the woman whom she had worked for all these years and who treated her like a daughter.

'Don't worry, dear, Sir Thomas has gone out of the place 'til spring. By the time he comes back you'll be off to Lisdare for the confinement. The manor is empty for the winter,' she added. How empty she could not have guessed.

'Yer sure, ma'am? What if someone from around about the place is working there and knows me? It'll kill m'mither if she finds out what happened t'me.'

'The possibility has occurred to me, dear. In that case I've another plan. You'll go and work where the confinement will take place. As I told you, the matron is an acquaintance of mine. The child will be taken away and placed in a Children's Home.'

'I never want to see the thing,' Bridie said venomously.

'Now write to your mother, tell her about the disaster at Horton and that you're staying with my sister waiting for a new post. In six months' time you'll be able to visit her again. She'll be none the wiser.'

The driveway leading to Merifield Manor had rhododendron bushes growing along each side. Beyond were parklands where large trees grew and cattled grazed. The manor stood on rising ground which gave it a clear view of the bay out to the Broadwater. It was an unprepossessing grey building with two mounting-stones at the front door. This part of the house was facing south. At the back, the kitchen and other quarters were shadowed by tall trees, which added to the gloomy feeling of the three people in the trap.

Mrs O'Sullivan was expecting some staff to be at the back door to greet her. And where was Captain Hurl to introduce them? Barney opened the door without ceremony and walked into the kitchen. The two women followed. In the bleak interior there was immediate evidence that mice had been the main occupants here for some time. Cold grey ashes, like an old man's beard, clung to a burnt stump of wood. The big stone sink, grimy with ancient grease, had been attracting the mice too. On a long shelf above the sink was a collection of copper pans dull with neglect. The housekeeper flung open the cupboards as a glow of anger spread across her face. To Bridie's horror, tears suddenly filled Mrs O'Sullivan's eyes.

'Now, now, Nora,' Barney said awkwardly patting his wife's shoulder, 'sure you and wee Bridie will have it spick and span in no time.'

Her eyes flashed, dispersing the tears. 'And what will you be doing, Barney O'Sullivan, while me and Bridie try to make this place habitable? Sitting on your backside like the last occupant of this kitchen?'

'Ah, jabers, woman . . .'

The lethargic feeling that had clouded Bridie's days and stilled her laughter suddenly lifted. She threw off her cloak, rolled up her sleeves and pulled an apron out of her bag. 'Don' ye worry, ma'am, the three of us will get it straight — and when that's done we'll have a cup of tea.'

'No wonder the agent was so willing to place us here,' Mrs O'Sullivan snapped. 'Where is he anyway?'

'We're early, Nora.'

A horse galloped into the yard. All three hurried to the door. Captain Hurl called to someone. A sheepish-looking farmhand shuffled out of the barn. Nora O'Sullivan marched over to him.

'Good day, sir. Are there any more servants hiding themselves away in the straw?' Barney rolled his eyes.

The agent jumped off his horse and greeted her. 'I must apologise for the state of the house, Mrs O'Sullivan. The . . . er . . . housekeeper left unexpectedly and it's not easy to get help out here.'

Bridie, who had tried to hide in a dark corner, jumped when something larger than a mouse ran over her foot. The captain looked in her direction. She gave a quick curtsey. He looked again in surprise.

'This is Bridie who assisted me at Horton,' Nora said. 'Do you live on the estate, sir?'

'Yes, I have a house nearby.' Captain Hurl looked at the angry little woman and thought, You're lucky to have another job to go to. 'Come and see the upstairs rooms,' he suggested.

When the other two went upstairs, Bridie said, 'Barney,

put a bit o'life in that fire and I'll fill the big black saucepan with water and start scrubbing.'

'The missis is in a bad way.'

'Can ye blame her after the lovely kitchen at Horton?'

'Forget about Horton,' he said gruffly. ''T'was a wild country over there. Quiet folk live here and it's well populated.'

Aye, Bridie thought, with Patrick Murphy and his friends fighting the landlords wi' a can of oil and a torch in their hands. Begod, if they come round here anytime, I'll welcome them in!

The dark passage from the kitchen led to the dining-hall. Nora O'Sullivan thought it was very poorly furnished. Colourless, apart from an ornate fireplace that could have housed a family. Captain Hurl showed her upstairs where there were several bedrooms. In the ones allotted to themselves, Nora pulled the clothes down on the bed and, as she expected, the linen needed changing. In her present mood she was fit for anything.

'Everyone,' she said crabbedly, 'seems to have left in a hurry, sir.'

'It's difficult to get staff here,' he repeated. 'The two maids who were clearing up have taken themselves off.'

'I'm not surprised. It's not a house for young girls.'

He gave a quick cautious look, then added with the polish of his station, 'We require someone like yourself, Mrs O'Sullivan. Horton was a credit to you and your husband.'

'Captain Hurl, I want to speak to you about the young girl downstairs in the kitchen.' In a few bitter words she told him what had happened to Bridie.

He listened with his head lowered, then spoke with carefully chosen words. 'It is regrettable, Mrs O'Sullivan, but the girl must not remain here when Sir Thomas returns in the spring.'

'Everything is arranged, sir.'

'Thank you for handling the incident so discreetly,' he said and walked away.

*Incident*? Mother of God, give me patience, Nora thought. A young girl's life is ruined and he calls it an incident.

131

Downstairs she found Barney had made a good job of the fire. Bridie was busy scrubbing the sink with soda. 'I won't be long, ma'am. Next I'll do the draining board and then get all the crockery out for a good wash. Widden ye just love a cup of tea? D'ye know, I've got me eye on them pots and pans up there. Wait till ye see the shine I'll put on them. It'll warm your heart.'

Like many childless women, Nora thought pregnancy was an illness. 'Don't overdo it, dear. You mustn't injure yourself.'

'I'm just grand, ma'am.' The sickness had now passed and Bridie felt hungry all the time.

While she scrubbed, the housekeeper inspected the press where the clean linen was kept. She took an armful and made for the back stairs, then stopped. 'Barney, we'll have fires in the bedrooms t'night for there's damp creeping around this house fit to kill.'

'Aye, right, Nora,' Barney said eagerly. Like Bridie, he could not get over the tears of despair in his wife's eyes. ''Tis yerself that knows how to get a place straight, m'dear. I'm about to sweep out this floor afore Bridie scrubs it.'

'What about scrubbing it yourself?' she snapped. 'A good strong dose in the water to kill the germs.'

'Scrub a floor?' he cried indignantly. 'Bugger that,' he murmured under his breath.

Bridie gave a peal of laughter.

It was the worst winter that Rosha could remember, yet every week she and Patrick or Willie made the long journey to Lisdare to see her father. Sometimes they stayed overnight at Rory's employer's farm, which made it easier. They always rose at dawn and ate a good breakfast before they set out. Often the weather was so fierce that they had to give up the idea altogether.

Sean was not neglected in prison. Rory and others living in Lisdare visited him when it was allowed and brought food and comforts. Mrs Coll spent her days knitting endless pairs of socks and guernseys. Though the warders were civil enough and showed no harshness towards their prisoner, the old jail was freezing cold. Rosha worried about her father's health because he seemed to have a constant cough and was sometimes short of breath. He was pleased about the way they were running Garton. At the beginning of the winter Rosha decided to send some of the livestock to market to ease the feeding problem. It was a wise decision for the animals made good prices which built up their capital. All this money she put in the bank.

She longed to see Edmund again but had no idea when he would return. Also, she longed to feel a piece of clay between her hands, though that wish would have to wait. At the moment there were more important things to be done. The servants were annoyed and alarmed when she told them that the entire house had to be decorated, every room whitewashed, curtains mended or remade. This was a new Rosha, bustling with energy and authority.

Grace Boyce left home early to go to Garton to help Rosha make some new curtains. As she was walking along the road, about a half-mile from the shebeen, she saw the figure of a man leaning against the hedge; although he was partly hidden by a hawthorn bush, Grace knew immediately from the old frayed tarten trews that it was the shepherd.

'What are you doin' resting yerself in there at this hour of the morning?' she called, crossing the road. The eyes stared straight at her. She went closer then opened her mouth and began to scream: the shepherd was frozen stiff in the rigour of death. Grace didn't stop running until she reached Garton. Rosha and Nellie were eating their breakfast when she dashed into the kitchen.

'Under God, Mam, what's ailing ye?' Nellie said, jumping from the table.

Grace pushed her out of the way and tore down to the men's room. 'Willie, get up and go for the priest and constable. The shepherd's dead in the hedge. Paddy,' she shouted, 'were you at the shebeen last night? Come on out, I want to speak to you.'

Paddy shuffled up to the kichen, pulling a pair of braces over his shoulders.

'It happened at the shebeen, didn't it?' she demanded.

'Ay, Jayus, Grace, he wodden stop drinking and never

home did he go for a bite. He fell on the floor and they hoisted him into the barn to come round ...'

'And he never breathed again, poor man, and was carted well away from the place so as no blame would fall. isin that it?' she shouted at him.

Paddy dropped his head and muttered, 'We thought he was sleepin' it off in the barn.'

'Grace,' Rosha said quietly, 'I don't think Paddy should repeat that or the constable will round up every man who was in the place. Sir Thomas Catalong will make sure they get the highest penalty.'

'Mam, Rosha's right,' Nellie agreed, 'someone could swing for it.'

'Aye,' Grace murmured wearily and thought, Catalong cleared the glen for his sheep but it was too lonely for the Scottish lad. God help me, now 'tis only me and the sheep in the lonely glen.

'Willie, just speak to the priest,' Rosha advised, 'he'll know how to handle the situation.'

When Nellie got over the shock of the shepherd's death, she turned her mind to the master and Rosha. Nothing, she thought, could be done about Sean O'Neill but something desperate would need to be done about his daughter. Rosha had become very moody and unapproachable. Nellie remembered the ring with the opal stone and the rumours over in Dilford. Almighty God, could anything have happened between the pair of them over there?

'What's the girl up to?' she whispered to Biddy Coll one day, when Rosha shut herself in the room for a couple of hours.

'Wet the tay, take a cup in and leave the door open,' Biddy suggested. Before the tea could draw, Rosha walked out briskly again.

'Is Patrick Murphy around or has he gone home for a change?'

'He's gone home for another load of firewood.'

'Why do we need wood from Murphy's? There's a stack out there.'

'The wind played tricks wi' the rain last night and wet it,' Nellie said.

134

'Paddy!' Rosha yelled through the door of the men's bedroom. Fed up with all the decorating that she expected them to do, they were sitting on the floor playing a sly game of cards. Resentfully, Paddy shuffled into the kitchen.

'Get yourself outside and stack some of that wood in the shed,' she ordered him, then turned to the two women. 'At the rate Maria Murphy's been charging us we'll soon be bankrupt.'

'Wheesht!' Biddy murmured. 'We don't pay for half o' that wood. She's taken a spite to Patrick and he's getting his own back.'

'I don't believe it. Patrick would not be so dishonest as to steal from his father's farm.' Rosha had spent the last hour going through her father's accounts. What had alarmed her most was the large number of bills from Dan Murphy, all neatly made out in Maria's hand. She noticed that if a bill was not paid promptly, another was sent demanding immediate payment. Such a thing was unheard of in Slievegar. Farmers usually bartered their products: money rarely came into it.

At that moment, Patrick drove a loaded cart into the yard. Rosha shot to the door. 'You can take that right back, Patrick Murphy. I don't want to see anything else coming from your farm.'

He let down the back of the cart, tipped the load out against the wall and turned with a guilty smile.

'Have you brought the bill with you?' she demanded. 'Or will you allow us a little time to settle it?'

'Ease your mind on that score, Rosha. It's a present. If I spend my days cutting down trees and chopping wood, then begod I'm entitled to do what I like with part of it.'

'That suits me,' she said promptly, remembering his honesty when she used to steal cakes from the larder. 'Your stepmother has been charging us plenty for everything else.'

Patrick frowned. 'What do ye mean?'

'Come into the room.' They sat down at the table and she laid out all the bills that had arrived from the Murphys since the year of the fire.

'Damn that woman,' he said, embarrassed. 'My father would have charged only half of that for the building wood.'

'Why did Garton need all those loads of feeding stuff?'

'Garton didn't pick up for a time after the fire, then there was a blight on the potatoes and some of the other root vegetables. It affected many of the farms around here.'

'I didn't know that.' Or, she thought guiltily, I just didn't take any interest in what was going on here when I was at the pottery.

'Things got a bit run down because yer father's been away a lot over the past few years working for the tenants' rights. This used to be the most prosperous farm in Slievegar. It'll pick up again.'

'My father promised to sell a piece of land so that I can start a pottery. I find, going through these papers, that he's sold quite a lot of land. Why has he done that Patrick?'

'Rosha, he's been helping people. Look at the homeless on the roads. There's been a great need.'

'And what has your father been contributing towards the people's need?'

'Up to a point we've been helping ...'

'Up to Widda Flaherty's point,' Nellie said, marching in with two mugs of tea.

Rosha rose, waited for Nellie to leave the room, and slammed the door after her.

'Let me take a closer look at the bills,' said Patrick. 'Damn, look what she's charged there.'

She put out her hand and bunched them together. The sight was making her blood boil. 'It'll have to stop, Patrick. There'll have to be some changes around here.'

She walked to the window and looked out. 'There's something I must say.'

'What is it?'

'My father wants us to get married one day, as you probably know. I like you, but I can't promise that because it's not ... the right feeling.'

He came over and stood beside her. 'Well, now, Rosha O'Neill, I don't remember proposing.'

She gave a little laugh at his surprising reply, turned and saw that though a smile was on his lips there was hurt in his eyes. Her hand went out to him. He clasped it in a strong firm grip. 'I'll do anything for you, Rosha. You must know that.' She bowed her heard. 'Maybe you'll change your mind later on. It's early days.'

At that moment she admired Patrick for his understanding. If he had asked was there someone else she might have told him. Rosha was glad that he did not test her weakness because it would have distressed and certainly angered him if he knew about Edmund Catalong.

After he left she tidied the desk. All the unpaid bills were put on a wire spike. She checked through the large account book marked 'Land Lettings' and saw how many had not yet been paid. Nellie came in quietly with an uncertain look in her eyes.

'Don't worry about things, pet,' she said awkwardly.

'Nellie, I'm trying to sort out my father's affairs. Where does he keep his money for running the house ... wages and things?'

'In a big tin box under his bed. Locked − as if any one of us would look in or take a penny,' she added with a touch of annoyance.

Ha, Rosha thought, you'd look all right! 'It's not that, he has private papers in there ... his will. That sort of thing has to be kept under lock and key.'

A few days later Nellie and Rosha were standing outside the house talking over their plans for running Garton while Sean was away. They had grown close again. Only once did Nellie bring up Edmund's name.

'Have ye still got a notion of that boy Catalong?' she asked guardedly.

'He isn't a boy, Nellie. He's at Sandhurst training to be an army officer.'

'Huh! To bring more trouble on Ireland.'

'His father insisted on his going to Sandhurst. He's looking forward to the time when he can come back here and run the estate. There'll be big changes when he does, you'll see.' Rosha thought of the small estate called Horton, which Edmund had talked about. It was a warm secret that made their separation bearable.

'Under God, what's that comin' down the road?'

'A funeral?'

137

'Och, I know now. It's the Tolands from Iskaglen. They're emigrating.'

'Were they evicted?' Rosha asked quickly.

'Away back. For years they've been moving from one side of the family to the other, existing on the Poor Relief. The priest got up a collection.'

'Hello, there,' Nellie called as she and Rosha walked towards the gate.

The family and a crowd of mourning neighbours stopped when they heard the greeting. Rosha looked away, she couldn't bear the sight of the weeping women and clinging children. It was a heart-breaking scene and one which she did not intend to become involved in. Her father had taken this kind of burden on his shoulders far too often, and look at his plight now and the state of Garton.

Nellie embraced the woman. 'God bless ye and I hope there's happiness for ye in the new land.'

The woman looked shyly at Rosha, moved the child to her left arm and held out her hand with great dignity as though she were ashamed of her tears. Rosha bent over to kiss the little one's cheek; as she did so a smell of peat came from the woman's shawl. That's about all she has to take with her to a foreign country, she thought. The cottage, fields, all that their forefathers owned, was no longer theirs. Rosha drew back. 'Wait here.'

She tore up to the house to her father's box. The key which she had found the other day in Sean's room was in the lock. She put her hand into the bag containing some sovereigns and hurried down again. Patrick was there now shaking hands with the emigrants.

'Don't forget,' he was saying, 'send the young lads back when they're older to help us with the fight.'

'Take that.' Rosha pressed the money into the woman's hand. 'It'll help a bit in the new land.'

'Sweet God,' Nellie muttered in shock when she saw the amount.

It was plain to see by the woman's reluctant acceptance that her pride was trying to put up a fight. The carts moved on; the emigrating family in one, the other loaded with friends to see them off.

'I thought we hadn't a penny in the house,' Nellie said.

Rosha laughed. 'We haven't now.'

'Young eejit!'

'Rosha,' Patrick said, 'I'm going over by Togher Glen. I hear the castle has got away wi' another eviction o'er there. What about exercising your father's horse?'

'All right, I'll come with you.'

As they were approaching the rough road leading to the cottages they saw a group of people standing near a house down below. Also an official group: the bailiff in a new bowler hat, his helpers and the Constabulary. Such resistance as the family had offered had been of no avail; a battering ram had left gaping holes where the door and window had been. The walls on each side had tumbled to the ground.

Rosha looked at the neatly thatched roof and the strong chimney and knew that the occupants of this cottage had cared well for their home. Only recently whitewashed it stood stark against the clear blue sky, a poignant example of the eviction Cavalry. They tethered their horses, then approached the scene as inconspicuously as possible. The bailiff and the law hated witnesses when they were doing their day's work.

A cloud of feathers blinded Rosha as she came round the fuchsia hedge where the evicted family had taken shelter. Lying under the hedge was an old woman on a ruptured mattress. Sitting beside her was a young woman, wan and frail from childbirth, with a baby wrapped in her shawl. The husband, his face twisted with impotent anger, stood helplessly by. Perhaps it was the support of Patrick's presence that roused him for he made a sudden movement, fists clenched. Patrick gripped the man's arm.

'Ye can't do a thing, man. If ye touch one of them bastards, it's prison for ye. They're working fast because O'Neill's out of the way.'

'What are we goin' to do, Patrick Murphy?' he asked plaintively. 'The missus and the oul mother are helpless. The other two weans are playing down on the shore.' The infant began to cry. With shameful colour staining her cheeks, the mother unbuttoned her blouse and covered her breast with the shawl to feed the child.

Rosha had never experienced such a feeling of anger. She tossed back her hair and went up to the bailiff who was talking to the inspector. 'Well, gentlemen,' she said contemptuously, 'I hope you are pleased with your day's work? Where are those homeless people going to find shelter?'

''Tis their own fault,' the bailiff said surlily, 'they got notice long ago for not paying their rent and other matters.'

'*Damn you!*' She turned her back and walked away.

The inspector flushed with embarrassment at a young lady using such bad language. Without considering her words, she turned to the evicted man. 'We'll give you shelter at Garton until you can make some plan for the future. I'm going back home now to bring over the trap.'

Patrick looked startled at her suggestion. 'Rosha, I'll ride back to Garton. You'd better stay wi' the wimin.'

The man bowed his head in gratitude, then brought it up quickly. 'Patrick, I've a gun hidden in the loft of the cottage ...'

'We'll come back at dark and get it. There's work to be done here tonight.'

'M'back's hurting,' the old woman cried.

'Wid ye give me a hand, Pat, to sit her on the chair? She has to be moved like this all the time.'

They lifted the elderly woman into a low oak chair with curved arms and tucked pieces of bedding around her. When Patrick saw that the wreckers were about to move, he nodded to Rosha. They picked up the old feather mattress between them and set it out in the open. He took out his penknife and slit it right down the middle. The wind, which was blowing in the right direction, caught the feathers and sent them snowing all over the bailiff and members of the law. Patrick mounted his horse, then trotted over to have a last word with the evicted family.

'What the hell are you doing over there?' the bailiff shouted angrily, as they tried to pick white goose feathers off their clothes.

Laughing was the last thing Rosha expected to do at that moment; it spilled out of her, affecting the homeless family, and made the children, who had come up from the shore, roll over on the ground shrieking with laughter. Even the old woman cackled. Purple-faced with anger, the bailiff waved his stick threateningly.

'Sure 'tis only feathers in the wind, sir,' Patrick shouted and galloped away.

'Six of the O'Donnells, including the wee thing,' Nellie shrieked at Patrick. 'She's mad. Wi' no plan atal of their own, we could be stuck wi' them. Them O'Donnells are long-livers ... the oul wimin could be here for ever. Sacred Heart, what are we goin' to do? And where is O'Neill goin' to sleep when he gets out o'jail? Haven't they got any relations to take them in.'

'They have in Lisdare but they wont take the old woman,' Patrick said, standing awkwardly in the kitchen. 'It would be the workhouse for her. O'Donnell can't bear that ... it's his mother.'

Nellie's hand went on her hips and she said with asperity, 'Isin it time the Murphys put themselves out a bit o'er these evictions?'

Patrick had not thought of that because his home was now a different place. His stepmother in full control and not noticeably given to acts of charity.

'What about the wee place the Widda Flaherty was set up in for a few year before she caught yer father?' Nellie, like many others around Slievegar, still called Maria by that name.

'You're right, Nellie — you're quite right. That's where they could go.'

Nellie and Biddy prepared a huge meal for the homeless family and made them welcome. Though Nellie chatted away, prayers mixed with curses were flying from her heart. Please God let the Murphys take them in ... please God don't let that bitch of a widda stop it.

Patrick's plan was to speak to his father quietly and get him to agree. But Maria missed nothing and knew there was something afoot. She didn't trust Dan's second son. She came in and stood behind her husband's chair.

'It's the O'Donnells, Father.' He told Dan what had

happened. 'I'm thinking we could clear the wee stone house. It would suit them fine.'

'I see . . .' Dan said uncertainly, waiting for Maria to decide for him.

'And where are we to put the hay?' she demanded. 'The barn and other outhouses are full up.'

Patrick rose to his feet, all the dislike he felt for this woman showing on his face. 'Where we put it when you were homeless, ma'am, when *you* were evicted from your home.'

Maria was furious. 'O'Neill's got a big barn with a fireplace in it. It was part of the old house-building. It withstood the fire, I hear.'

'The Murphys didn't offer you shelter in their big barn, did they? My mother had the cottage cleared and cleaned for you.'

'That's enough, son,' Dan said feebly.

Ignoring Maria, Patrick said, 'We'll take the hay into the shelter, Father, it'll do well enough there.' He called to his elder brother who said immediately, 'Aye, we'll do that, Patrick.'

His young wife, who had the shyness of a servant and behaved like one because Maria treated her as one, said delightedly, 'Sure I know the O'Donnells well. I'll have the place spic and span in no time.'

'We could do with a woman's hand to sweep and clean,' Patrick told her gently.

When he went back to Garton, everyone looked hopefully at him.

'Your residence will be ready in a couple of hours' time, Mrs O'Donnell. Willie and I will drive the cart back to your old place and collect your bedding and furniture. He looked around him. 'Rosha, where's Paddy? I want him to put a flame on the hill. There's work to be done tonight.'

The plight of the O'Donnells had been resolved tonight but what about all the other families who were trying to find shelter around the countryside? Rosha wondered. Many were moving away, not prepared to wait and fight for their homesteads. Excitedly she told Nellie her plan.

'You know that bit of waste land at the foot of Iskaglen that

142

belongs to Garton? I think we could make use of it by putting up temporary homes for people who are homeless.'

'That's nearly opposite the castle across the bay.'

Rosha smiled. 'I know.'

Nellie gripped her arm excitedly. 'Oul Tom Cat will have a fit.' She felt relieved because there was always the frightening possibility that Garton might be landed with another family. The O'Neills were impulsive and generous; it was hard lines though that their generosity left the hired-hands with a cut in their wages.

'We could take away all the palings and stones from the empty cottages and start building straight away.'

'Wasin that what that Maud Gonne did o'er in Gweedore? The woman of the Sidhe, they call her.'

'She's got money, Nellie. We haven't any to spare.'

'Just don' ye forget that, my bold Rosha.'

Patrick was astounded that evening when Rosha turned up at the meeting, which was now held away in the hills of Slievegar. It was a secluded spot, beyond a gap where men were posted on the look-out. She spoke to Patrick about her plan.

'Stand up on that rock, Rosha,' he said, 'and tell them what ye have in mind.'

When Rosha told the surprised crowd she added, 'Catalong has acres of woodland. We could relieve him of some trees to help with the building.'

'Ah, careful now ...' Patrick interrupted.

'Go out at night in groups, three men to get on with the job and three on the look-out. If the castle men happen to come along, try to get away unseen. If not, attack them.'

'Begod she's got more power in her than Sean O'Neill,' a man whispered to his neighbour. 'Wasin he all for us workin' along wi' the Land League? And look where it's left some folk.'

'Aye, because they did in heed him and were secretly scraping up money and paying rents to avoid eviction. In the end Catalong had them out. Sure we're backward people in these parts. Hush now!'

Master Logue, who lived comfortably in the school house

belonging to Sir Thomas Catalong, said cautiously, 'Don't forget, Rosha O'Neill, the recent remedial Land Acts are gradually reducing the landlords to submission.'

'We know that tenants' rights are being slowly restored but it's not effective enough yet to put down all the landlords.'

'The Liberals are back in power and ...'

'And Catalong is still in power here,' she interrupted drily.

'Master ... Mr Logue,' Patrick began, 'what do you think about Rosha's suggestion to remove stones from old evicted cottages to start these buidlings?'

'Leave them,' he said with full authority in his voice that everyone remembered from their schooldays. 'The people will come back. Feudalism is nearly at an end in Ireland, thanks be to God.'

'God love ye, Master, for puttin' heart in us,' a man muttered.

# Chapter Thirteen

When Edmund came home from Sandhurst in April he found Alice Meckin and her parents about to dine with his father at Montan Square in London. A look of delight showed on the girl's face when he entered the drawing-room.

'Ah, Edmund,' his father said, 'what leave have you got?'

'Until the end of the month.'

'Good!' Lord Meckin slapped him on the back. 'You'll be able to join our house party in Scotland.'

'Do come, Edmund.' Alice spoke with an eagerness that was reflected in her eyes. Although Edmund liked her, he felt with some disquiet that their friendship was being misinterpreted by their parents and that Alice did not discourage this. He didn't know what to say now because he desperately wanted to go to Ireland, yet dare not broach the subject because his father was still violently angry about the destruction of Horton – as was Edmund himself. All the secret plans that he and Rosha had made about living there one day were no longer possible. 'I should be getting over to Merifield,' his father was saying to the Meckins. 'Damn' agent doesn't seem able to cope with some troublesome situation which has arisen.'

'Father ...' Edmund said tentatively, 'would you like me to go across to Ireland and see if I can handle it? Is it not time I became familiar with matters on the estate? In a year's time I'll have finished my course at Sandhurst and,' he added lightly, 'the world is at peace and seems likely to remain so. I'm told that few officers in the British army below field rank ever see active service on any battlefield.'

'Enough unrest in Ireland to keep any regiment busy,' Lord Meckin said gruffly. 'Damn' peasants need to be put in their place once and for all.'

Edmund bit his tongue on the quick retort that flew to his lips.

'Blasted Liberals had a crowd of the scoundrels released from Portlaoghise prison,' his father added sourly.

Edmund had not expected this mildness of weather on the way to Slievegar. There was a hum of bees on the fuchsias that grew along the road, a contented sound that fitted his mood. For once, he would occupy Merifield on his own apart from a few servants. At a cottage doorway a woman sat at her spinning wheel, a crown of snow-white hair glowing against the darkness of her shawl. He waved his hand. She had worked at the manor when his mother was alive.

After he had eaten a meal at the hotel in Dilford, Edmund went to the potter's yard. His longing to see Rosha was growing now that he was within minutes of seeing her. The yard was quiet and deserted. Though the storing shed had a reasonable stock and implements of the craft were in the workshop, there was a dead atmosphere about the place. Anxiously he went around to the street again and knocked at the front door of the house. Mr Sweeney opened it.

'Good afternoon, sir,' Edmund greeted him. 'We met sometimes ago when I called on Rosha O'Neill.'

'I remember, Mr Catalong. Rosha's back home. And I am ...' he held out his rheumatic hands ' ... not so fit anymore.'

'I am sorry, Mr Sweeney. What a terrible affliction for one of your talent.'

'God's will be done. Tell Rosha, if you see her, that I am easing off now and there may be a few things here she could make use of.'

'I will.' Edmund shook the potter's hand gently and walked away disappointed.

When they reached Merifield he asked the driver to drive on to the agent's house, situated on the boundary of the estate. He would be unknown to the new staff at the manor. Anyway, it would be polite to call on Captain Hurl first as his reason for coming to Ireland was to deal with matters in his father's absence.

Nellie saw the hired sidecar passing the house when she was cleaning Sean O'Neill's bedroom windows in preparation for his homecoming. 'The Lord save us,' she muttered, pushing the cleaning rag into her pinny pocket. 'There's young Catalong to add to m'troubles. Where's Rosha?' she yelled down the stairs to Biddy Coll.

'Widden I be the smart one to know that?'

Rosha was over in one of the storerooms helping Paddy to clear it. This would be part of her workshop one day when there was money to spare to buy equipment. She talked to him about her plans because the others were not interested. Gradually the financial situation at Garton was improving because she kept a strict record of all the expenses incurred in running the place. Tactfully, she had collected some outstanding bills and for the first time the dairy was showing a profit and meeting most of the household bills for provisions.

All this work gave her a feeling of deep satisfaction, as did the help and encouragement she offered to the people who had sought shelter in the settlement over on the peninsuia. Many were evicted years ago and since then had been seeking shelter where they could find it; one family had been living in a cave near the shore. They could dream now, not of a distant land, but of a good life in the land of their birth.

Captain Hurl was unable to hide his surprise when Edmund turned up on his doorstep. After tea, Hurl suggested that they walk down to the shore and take a look at the abominable constructions that were growing within sight of the manor windows.

'The beach below the house will no longer provide quietness and solitude for your father and his guests,' he complained. 'The silence is continually broken by the caterwauling of the children of those undesirable people who have settled across the water. This has all been brought about by that insolent young woman at Garton.'

Surprised, Edmund stared at him.

147

'The girl is as great a nuisance as her father,' he grumbled. 'She's been going around the countryside seeking help to enable her to build and furnish those shacks. We thought when O'Neill was safely in Lisdare jail ...'

'Mr O'Neill in jail? How long has he been there?' Edmund was horrified.

'Six months. Nearly time for him to come out again unfortunately.'

'Why was he put in prison?'

'For years he has been studiously usurping the authority of the English Courts with the backing of the Land League. While he confined his activities to his own district not much notice was taken, then he began to extend them to other parts of the county. The authorities decided to stop him once and for all.' The agent pulled at his chin. 'Indeed, I think that Miss O'Neill is worse than her father. She and her rabble meet in the hills, then go out and pillage the estate.'

'Pillage?'

'They're stealing our trees, sir, cutting them down at nightfall to build those huts over there. I've had to take on extra men to guard all the woodlands on the estate. That in itself is a problem because local men are afraid to work for us. Many of the men who go out have been attacked. I'm considering using firearms.'

'No!'

'I beg your pardon, sir?'

'Captain Hurl, I don't think it's a good idea to use firearms against a crowd of poor people who have been evicted from their homes over the years. When I was a boy I remember seeing people cowering under hedges, seeking shelter. Good luck to them if they steal a few of our trees. The woods needed thining anyway!'

The agent's face turned crimson. 'Really, sir, your attitude is quite incomprehensible. Have you no concern for your father's estate?'

'I don't want Merifield to end up like Horton.'

'I will discuss it with your father.'

'At the moment you are discussing it with me. Please, *no firearms* used against the people.' Edmund turned as he spoke and caught a glimpse of the little island around the bay. If Rosha found out he was at Merifield that's where she would go, he thought.

'Captain Hurl ... look, I think I'd like to stretch my legs across the shore. Would you mind telling the housekeeper that I have returned?'

'Very well,' the man replied stiffly.

Rosha walked over to the house to get two glasses of buttermilk. As she was passing the kitchen window on the way to the dairy she heard Nellie say to Biddy: 'I saw the hired car passing. Young Catalong's on his own this time. There's grand scallops down below the castle, but I widden venture if there was any danger of oul Tom Cat prowling around.'

'Did ye see the wee nebby wimin who's housekeeper at the castle now? Comes from the same part as m'self. Got her mother's backside and haughty carriage and ...'

'Hush! Is that Rosha running down the drive?' Nellie ran into the other room and glanced out through the window. 'Begod it is.' She plucked her shawl from the hook. 'I'll be away after the scallops now,' she said forgetting to pick up a bucket to put them in.

The girl darted in among the trees edging the castle woods, then suddenly disappeared. 'Be damn,' she muttered. Ah, well, I'll go and get the scallops and maybe land on the pair of them down on the shore. One good thing about the oul agent ... he dosin mind folk pickin' on the shore when that bugger Catalong isin in residence.

Bridie Boyce was finding the days long and tedious at Merifield. Her bulk and the movements of the child were wearisome. She had draped a towel across the mirror in her bedroom because she couldn't bear the sight of herself. Late every afternoon, when the workers went home for their tea, she stole out of the house and took the private path which went past Sir Thomas's rose garden. Lately, she ventured to the edge of the trees and watched the movement of the water and the reflections of the sky in its depth.

She was looking forward to getting into the place is Lisdare. The fact that it was part of the poorhouse for unfortunate girls did not bother her a bit. All she wanted was to get rid of this ugly burden. Then she would go home to Mam for a fine long stay, and afterwards, Mrs O'Sullivan promised, she would find her a good position. Indeed, a promise had already been given by the matron of the home that a place might be found for her there. The devil wi' that, Bridie thought spiritedly. I don' want to be kept reminded how unfortunate this girl was!

Edmund was on the island when Rosha arrived. They rushed towards each other, speechless in their joy at being reunited again. When they could bear to draw apart he searched her face and saw the change in her. She had a leaner look, the fullness gone from her cheeks, and her skin was a deeper colour. Her hair was drawn back unfashionably and knotted carelessly on the crown of her head. Somehow, the faded red skirt and blouse seemed a perfect foil for her colouring. Rosha had never looked so beautiful, he thought.

She noticed his scrutiny and held out her hands. He laughed at the signs of toil. 'Whatever have you been doing?'

'Helping to build those dwellings over on the point of Iskaglen. It was the only spare bit of ground I could find. Everyone gives a hand and when the work is completed we celebrate by having a bit of a hooly.'

'Oh lord,' Edmund said laughing, 'no wonder the agent's going mad!' His expression changed. 'Rosha, I have been worried about you. Were you ... all right?'

'Yes.' She blushed, then with a mischievous smile said, 'And I went to confession.'

Edmund winced, hating the humiliation she must have endured. 'No more woodland walks in the moonlight,' he said lightly. 'Wait until we're married.'

She studied their clasped hands. 'Do you think it's ever going to be?'

'One more year and my training at Sandhurst will be finished. Then we'll talk seriously and speak to everyone else concerned. All right, darling?' He drew her into his arms again. They were lost in their own world when a sudden noise drew them apart. 'The tide's coming in,' Edmund said.

'And I should be getting back to the house. I left Paddy waiting for a glass of buttermilk. We're clearing

150

one of the outhouses which I intend to use for my pottery.'

'Ah, that reminds me, Rosha. The potter ...' He told her about the man's disability.

'Poor Mr Sweeney, how terrible for a thing like that to happen to his hands. Wonder how much he'll want for the contents of his workshop?'

'You stop cutting down our trees and I'll buy them for you.'

She drew away, the words chilling her happiness. Alarmed at her expression, Edmund said quickly, 'Rosha, listen, I was to accompany my father to the Meckins' house in Scotland ... anyway, a letter came from Captain Hurl about the settlement across the water and the disappearing trees.' Rosha's hands fell to her side. Surely he's not going to change after everything he said in the past about his father's tyrannical ways? 'And this made it possible for me to come here and see you. I really am glad if our trees have helped to give those people shelter. But don't overdo it or kill one of our men!'

'Edmund, some of the people over there have been on the roads for years seeking shelter anywhere they could find it. My father is anxious that no more people will leave the land.' He looked so concerned that Rosha said in a lighter note, 'Is it a terrible sight from the manor?'

'Come and see for yourself.'

Bridie was feeling the benefit of a walk out of doors. This was a private part of the shore, only the very brazen would dare come over so far. A lonely place too, where once only seagulls disturbed the silence. Now the cries of the children across on the point of Iskaglen could be heard as far as the castle. The word made her smile. Devil a castle it was, and better it looked for her scrubbing and polishing. Sure aren't we the terrible race of people for thinking everything about the English is grand? A dirty house and a randy oul man.

Any thought of Catalong always brought a wave of black depression. She looked across at the point again, envying the happiness of the people who had gratefully found shelter there over the past winter. Now the men and women were

151

busy preparing the stony ground to grow a few crops for their survival. Begrudgingly, she conceded that it was a good deed Rosha O'Neill had done for them.

Bridie battled away at the depression that was now lying heavily on her mind. Life would never be the same again, she thought. She would have to live for the rest of her days with the dark secret that surely could destroy her. The thought of the birth had been growing more alarming since they visited the place where the baby was to be born. The inhuman cries coming from the labour wing were terrible; often she woke from her sleep with the sound in her ears. There were times now she wished she were dead.

Awkwardly she turned in alarm at the sound of footsteps coming around the curve of the land where bare roots of giant trees clawed the thin sandy soil. To her horror, she saw Edmund Catalong and Rosha O'Neill approaching. In confusion, she went to turn back to the shelter of the trees below the rose garden, when another sound came from the opposite direction. Nellie, with a bulging shawl flung across her back, came into sight.

The two girls stared at each other then Nellie began to scream — terrifying screams that froze the people across the water to stillness. Cornered between her sister, who had a look of sheer horror in her eyes, and the other two hurrying across the shore, Bridie felt an unbearable flood of shame and despair. She looked about her wildly and saw the calm blanket of water in the bay. In that moment of desperation it seemed to be the only place where she could hide herself. With head bent she stumbled to the water's edge and went forward, reaching out blindly.

'No, for God's sake, no!' was the last sound that reached her ears when Edmund Catalong leapt across the shore and plunged in after her.

Nellie's screams echoed again and again across the bay. The bundle of scallops on her back spilt around her like weird horns erupting from her body. She waded in, knee deep with flaying hands as Edmund tried to rescue her sister.

Rosha tore up the unfamiliar path to the manor. Nora and Barney were in the kitchen drinking tea. 'Get the doctor, quick. Bridie has fallen into the bay,' she shouted at them.

'God in heaven ... Jump on the horse, Barney. Pray God he's at home.'

Between them, Nellie and Edmund carried Bridie back to the house after they had tried to revive her. Rosha met them half-way. Nellie, her face grey and drawn, helped to get her sister undressed and wrapped in warm blankets. Mrs O'Sullivan put a light to the bedroom fire, then hurried downstairs for hot-water bottles. Rosha was at the kitchen door with two bottles wrapped in towels.

'Who did this to her?' Nellie whispered fiercely as the doctor examined her sister.

'Young Mr Catalong saved her,' Nora O'Sullivan told the doctor, ignoring Nellie's question.

After a while, he said, 'She's a strong girl. She'll be all right with care. Stay here with her, Mrs O'Sullivan.' And to Nellie, 'We'll have a chat down in the kitchen. Go and get some tea ready. I'll be down in a minute.'

When Nellie came into the kitchen, Rosha put her arms around her. 'Come on, Nellie dear, Bridie will be all right now.'

'All right?' she shouted. 'What is she doin' in this accursed house? I widden let me dog spend a night in it.'

Edmund tore off his soaking clothes, poured water from a china jug into the basin, washed and rubbed himself hard with a linen towel. He looked around for his trunk and found it was not in the room. He went to the wardrobe and took out the heavy dressing-gown he had left there on his last visit. Feeling warm again he lay down on top of the bed clothes. I'll have to wait until someone brings up the trunk, he decided wearily. Anyway he needed this moment of quietness to think over the dreadful thing that had happened. The faces of the three girls were before his eyes: Nellie's horror, Bridie's anguish and Rosha's distress.

Rosha and Nellie were sitting at the table when the doctor and Nora O'Sullivan came down to the kitchen. 'I'll kill the man who brought this to her,' Nellie was saying, 'a poor innocent wee girl.'

The doctor sat beside her and laid a hand on her shoulder. 'What happened to your sister mustn't pass any of our lips

153

for the sake of the young man upstairs. Is that understood?' he said sternly.

Rosha and Nellie looked at him, confused by his words.

'Dear Lord, there's his trunk,' Mrs O'Sullivan cried pointing to a corner. 'And him with not a stitch to put on his back.'

'Leave it,' the doctor said impatiently. 'He'll manage I'm sure. This young woman's need is greater.'

In carefully chosen words he told Nellie what the housekeeper had told him. He would rather not have repeated the story but it was unavoidable. This way he could give the necessary sympathy and understanding within the limits of his profession. He had his bread and butter to earn like the rest, but he knew what he'd like to do to men like Thomas Catalong. 'I have known Edmund since his childhood. He's a fine young man, not in any way like his ... parent.' He stumbled, a little flustered. Rosha and Mrs O'Sullivan glanced up quickly at his pause.

Nellie, soothed by the old doctor's compassion, said, 'Doctor, I hope he comes to a bad end.' He will, she vowed to herself, if I ever meet him again. The more practical aspect of the situation was discussed. Bridie must rest until the doctor thought her fit to travel to Lisdare.

'Your mother can be kept in the dark, dear,' Nora O'Sullivan said. 'Barney and I will take her in the black coach standing out there in the coach-house waiting for a job.'

'Mam must never know.'

'Don't fret, she'll never know.'

When Barney brought up the trunk with a gruff, embarrassed apology, Edmund dressed quickly. He took the passage to the back stairs that led down to the kitchen. As he was passing Bridie's door, which was ajar, it suddenly seemed of the greatest importance to go in and see the distressed girl who had tried to take her life. He remembered the expression on her face before she stumbled into the water – trapped, wild. Her dark hair was scattered across the pillow and her face looked pale and pinched. She opened her eyes.

'How are you?' he said softly.

'Only midlin' sir. I got ye wet.'

154

He shook his head to make little of it. 'Do you need anything?' Edmund glanced at the table where the doctor had left a draught in a dark blue bottle beside a mug of water.

She turned her head away and shutting her eyes murmured, 'No, thank ye.'

He bent down and said gently, 'Bridie, I'm sorry . . . very sorry for your unhappiness,' and left the room.

They'll have told him, she thought, weak tears rolling down her cheeks. It'll be hard on him to hear such a terrible thing about his own father.

It was three days before Rosha went back to the island. She and Edmund had spoken only briefly in the kitchen at the manor, after the doctor had gone away. Nellie told him bluntly that her sister had been raped and together they had left the house shortly afterwards. Rosha was sitting on a strong branch of the tree where they had built the little tree house when he came in slowly, hands in pockets, head bent, as if he had given up all hope of seeing her again. When she called, a look of gladness came to his face and he climbed up quickly beside her. They talked for a time, mostly about Bridie and the harshness of her life. After a while he said: 'Rosha, are we to meet here for the remainder of my stay in Slievegar? I would like to get away from this place.'

'Why don't you go to Dilford?'

'Will you come?'

'How can I?'

'You could stay for a few days with the Misses Houstons. I'll arrange it with Edith.'

'No, I can't do that. I must stay near Nellie until things are settled about Bridie. Perhaps, Edmund, it might be as well if you went back to England if you have attended to your father's affairs.'

He looked surprised. 'Rosha, you sound so different, almost bitter.'

At that moment she nearly broke her promise to the doctor and told him about his father. 'It's the unfortunate thing that has happened to Bridie and the effect it's having on Nellie.'

155

'Yes, I understand it must be difficult for you.' He paused thoughtfully. 'Rosha, please be very careful about cutting down trees, won't you? The agent has taken on another bailiff. A vicious-looking devil. They mean to stop it. When I'm gone they may well take more serious steps to protect the estate.'

'We'll take trees when we want them, Edmund. If they use firearms there are men around the country who are quite capable of doing the same.'

'You don't mean like the Fenians who burnt down Horton?' he asked angrily. 'Heavens, Rosha, you wouldn't have anything to do with those men?'

'Edmund, I grew up in a comfortable home, not caring about the events that were taking place before and after I was born. I remember children at school crying because they had been evicted and had nowhere to live. At that time the potato crop was threatened again with blight. Those people were on the Poor Relief and your father wanted more rent. Since my father was thrown into Lisdare jail I think about these things and feel different about everything.'

'I can't talk to you when you're in this mood.'

'Why should you care?' she said angrily. 'You'll walk away from Ireland again and forget what happens here — like the rest of them. Ireland and its problems are a nuisance to the people who made them.'

'That's not true as far as I'm concerned,' he said indignantly then reached over and took her hand. 'Don't let anything come between us, darling. I'll go to Dilford tomorrow. I think it would be easier for Mrs O'Sullivan at the present time if I was not in the house. Could you not manage just one day in Dilford? Remember the potter wanted to see you.'

'So he did. I'll try. If only Nellie would shout and scold, Edmund. It's the brooding quietness in her that bothers me. The story has to be kept from everyone in case Bridie's mother should get to hear of it, so she's not able to confide in Biddy Coll the way she used to. Biddy's a bit long in the tongue.'

He jumped down and held up his arms to assist her. They stood close together with the sound of the water in their ears.

In the silence it seemed to grow louder, dragging aggressively at the stones on the shore as though deliberately disturbing the peace of the island. Rosha rested her head against his shoulder.

He kissed her lightly on the cheek and said: 'I'll look out for you in Dilford. I'll be there until next Thursday, then I'll leave for England. Come to the hotel for your meal. Afterwards we'll go together and see the potter.'

Nellie went every day to Merifield to see Bridie. She couldn't get over the change that had gradually come over her sister. The look of death had left her face and instead of staying in bed resting, Bridie was now down in the kitchen every time she called.

'I told the doctor I was gettin' fed up with that oul bed and fidgeting to do something.'

'I can't do a thing with her, Nellie,' Nora O'Sullivan complained.

Doctor Friel was responsible for the change in her sister. He visited her frequently, talked and assured her that she had not committed a grievous sin by throwing herself into the bay. At the time, he said, her action was impulsive and not premeditated. 'We all feel like that occasionally,' he told her comfortingly.

'Well, never get the notion of goin' into the bay if it comes over ye, doctor. I'll never trust water again to end of m'days.'

Like Nellie, Edmund was delighted to see the change in the girl and the uninhibited way she spoke about her experience.

'Did I ruin yer suit, sir?'

'Shrunk a bit. It needed cleaning anyway.'

'As long as ye didin get yer death. The water was perishing cold.'

'It was,' he said gravely, 'and I'm glad it had no ill effects on you. Bridie,' he went on awkwardly, 'I'm sorry you were badly used. I hope your life will be happy again.' He held out his hand with a few sovereigns. 'It's a gift to spend when you're well again.'

She accepted the money gratefully and thanked him shyly.

Nellie's intention to keep Bridie's misfortune to herself never waivered until Rory Donavan arrived unexpectedly at Garton one day. It was a sullen afternoon with thunder storms threatening in the massed grey clouds. Rosha had business at the minister's house and Biddy was taking her afternoon's rest. She was just thinking that one day soon Bridie would be making the journey to Lisdare for the confinement, when the skies began to bark with a vengeance. Growls of thunder echoed through the hills and lightning darted across the peninsula. Suddenly the kitchen door flew open and Rory Donavan, with a fury of rain lashing behind him, staggered into the kitchen.

'Glory be to God,' Nellie cried, 'what are ye doin' out in this?'

Rory couldn't speak for a minute or two. She pulled a towel from the hot-press while he threw off his coat and boots, then he rubbed his hair and face and dried his feet.

'Git down to the room and I'll throw ye in some dry clothes. Yer wet to the skin.'

Socks and clothes belonging to the men went through the door after him. A few years ago Nellie might have slipped in coyly with them, but he was a changed man and she might suffer a rebuff on top of all her other troubles. When he came out she had a line tied across the fireplace on which he hung his things. On the table was a bowl of hot broth, slices of baked ham, pickle, bread and pats of butter. Tea was drawing on the hearth.

'Thank ye, Nellie. I got a lift to the crossroads, intending to go on up and see Patrick. It's about Sean O'Neill's home coming. A big fire will be lit on the hill to welcome him.' He looked at her and frowned. 'Is something the matter?' When she didn't reply he came over and put his arm around her shoulders. 'What is it, alannah?' His sudden warmth and sympathy made Nellie break down and cry. 'Surely it can't be that bad?'

For a moment it was Rory as he used to be; caring, showing tenderness towards her. She broke down completely and told him about Bridie.

White-faced and stricken, he went over to the table, sat down and covered his face as though he wanted to cry his heart out. After a minute he whispered, 'Dear Christ, the bastard! Catalong will not get away with this.' The look in his eyes frightened her.

Mother of God, why had she told him? 'Mam's never to know, Rory. No one knows except me, Rosha and the doctor. The O'Sullivans are caring for her and taking her to the home in Lisdare for the birth. The old Infirmary that used to be part of the workhouse.'

'The place for fallen girls,' he said bitterly and thought, That's how she'll be treated, like a fallen girl. 'If only I had stayed on the roads I wouldn't have lost touch with her all these months,' he said grimly.

Rosha told Nellie she was going to Dilford on Wednesday, that she had to see the solicitor and look in on the potter.

'Get a few messages,' Nellie suggested. 'Flour and meal need ordering.'

With a light heart, Rosha set off on Wednesday morning. She couldn't wait to see Edmund now. All the time they had wasted. But everything was against them. The trap was half-way down the drive when she saw Barney O'Sullivan coming towards her on horseback. 'Is Bridie all right, Mr O'Sullivan?' she enquired.

'Rightly, apart from a wee tumble on the bottom stair.'

'A tumble?'

'The missus is sure it will bring on her time so we're heading for Lisdare without delay.'

'What did the doctor say, or did you get him?'

'Get him? Begod, he's nearly taken up residence!' Barney gave crafty smile. 'Herself is makin' a note of every visit. At sixpence a time the agent will have a right wee bill! Divil a thing could the doctor find wrong. He thinks she may as well get on the road.'

'When?'

'As soon as the sister gets down to the manor and bids her farewell.'

'All right, I'll tell Nellie,' Rosha said flatly and turned the pony and trap in the drive.

Nellie dashed for her shawl and ran out of the house.

Resignedly, Rosha changed her clothes. She couldn't leave

159

Nellie this morning because she would be in a terrible state. About an hour later the girl returned to Garton and rushed upstairs, her eyes red with weeping.

''Tis that Rory Donavan,' Biddy hissed. 'He's done wi' her. I hope he hasin got her in trouble.'

Rosha did not reply. She followed Nellie upstairs and found her standing by a front bedroom window, her face pressed to the glass. She put an arm around her. At that moment the black coach from Merifield came stately along the road as though it were bearing a body on the way to the graveyard. Barney, looking quite unaccustomed to the lofty carriage, was dressed in his best suit and hat. The little curtain by the passenger window twitched and a hand appeared briefly. Nellie gave a howl of anguish.

'Come on up to your bed.' Rosha drew her out of the room. 'I'll tell Biddy you're not well.' Nellie threw herself across the bed and muffled her sobs against the pillow.

'What ails her?' Biddy snapped.

'It's her time of the month.'

'Well thank God for that, and us all behind wi' the eggs.'

'I'll give you a hand, Biddy.'

Rosha set of early next morning, glad to get away from the house. She was approaching the bridge at Togher Glen when there was a loud bellowing; it sounded like Skin-the-goat Duffy's bull and it was uncomfortably close. With horror she saw the gap in the field, which had been roughly filled with bits of broken bushes, beginning to move. She used the whip on the pony and prayed that she would reach the blacksmith's before the animal got free. His wife was searching for eggs along the hedge.

'Get in out of that,' she shouted, 'Skin-the-goat Duffy's bull is loose again.'

'Mother of God,' the woman said, whipping up her red flannel skirt and running, 'he'll destroy someone yet.'

It took four men to get the bull under control. Nearly an hour later, Rosha continued on her journey. At the hotel in Dilford she took the pony and cart around to the stables.

'Do you know if Mr Catalong is in the hotel?' she asked the boy.

'Went off on a conveyance about half an hour ago to catch the boat at Lisdare.'

In the dining-room the waitress slipped a letter out of her pocket and handed it to her. 'Yer to have a meal. Sit yerself o'er by the window and enjoy the view while I get it for ye.'

Dearest Rosha,

When you did not arrive yesterday I had little hope of seeing you before I left. My passage is booked on the boat and I cannot delay any longer before setting off on my journey. Yesterday someone here went to Merifield for a supply of vegetables and mentioned that the housekeeper and her husband were absent. The messenger was informed that they had gone to Lisdare, so I assumed it was time for Bridie to travel there and in the circumstances you would wish to remain home to comfort Nellie.

It is difficult for me to express my feelings in a letter. I love you deeply and hope it won't be long before we are together again.

With all my love
Yours, Edmund

Rosha ate her meal in a daze. She had just missed him but the letter was a comfort.

Afterwards she went around to see the potter. Mr Sweeney was in the drying-room wrapping tools in pieces of sacking; his greeting was not as friendly as she had expected.

'Young Mr Catalong has paid me well for all the things here that you wish to take away. A present,' he added drily.

'He shouldn't have done that,' Rosha said, embarrassed.

'It will not please Sean O'Neill if ever he finds out.'

Despite the potter's forbidding manner Rosha's spirits rose as she drove home. Now she had all the tools necessary to make a serious start on the pottery.

Captain Hurl wrote an indignant letter to Sir Thomas shortly after Edmund's visit. He was outraged by the indifferent attitude Catalong's son had shown towards important matters concerning the estate. The truth was, the agent's anger was

161

caused by his unsuccessful attempt to do anything about the unsightly settlement across the water. He had visited the place twice; on the second occasion the brazen daughter of O'Neill had asked him to leave. He was trespassing, she said. Unless, she added, to roars of unruly laughter by the riff-raff, he wanted to seek shelter. Now he had written fully about the matter to his employer.

When Sir Thomas received the agent's letter he was not pleased. After all, he would have to make the journey to Ireland instead of waiting until later. How dare the damn' peasants settle themselves in sight of his manor and cut down his trees to build their ramshackle huts? And damn it all, there was the added expense of having to hire another employee. It was not good enough!

# Chapter Fourteen

Bridie's first impression of the building called 'Kindly Light' was that whatever light it had it was not kindly. Nor was there any sign of benignity on the face of the woman who invited her to enter the home. She had a red nose and pointed chin; wore a blue and white striped apron with a cap to match. The woman led her down a long dim passage to a room crowded with girls who, Bridie thought with an unexpected fit of giggles, resembled seals flapping around on the shore. Do I move in the same way? she wondered, and sobered at the thought of sharing a room with so many.

'Boyce,' the nurse said, 'your bed is down there at the end by the window. The chamber pot is in the corner to be used by the four of you on that side of the room. Don't do your business in it, mind! For passing water only. The last one to fill it empties it down the wash-room.'

The crudity of the information made Bridie blush because everyone in the room was watching the new arrival. 'Nurse,' she said timidly, 'where is the wash-room?'

'Follow your nose,' the woman replied impatiently and hurried out the door.

The strong smell of Jeyes fluid guided Bridie to the wash-room where the girls had to strip every morning at six o'clock and wash themselves. The window, set high in the wall, had iron bars but no glass. Three cold water taps jutted from the wall like grey, accusing fingers; below, was a grating which ran the length of the bleak room. A water-closet was close to the door which let in a cruel draught. Beyond was a back yard where they exercised

163

themselves every morning and afternoon. A gate led to the outside world.

A young girl in the bed next to Bridie's prayed continuously on a rosary which she kept hidden in the pocket of her large grey smock.

'Are ye doin' a penance?' Bridie joked, wondering in the name of God when she was going to see a smile on her face or on the faces of any of the inhabitants in that long dreary room.

Tears rolled down the girl's face which she dried with her long plait of hair. 'I'm prayin' for me fella on his long journey across the ocean.'

'Why didin ye go with him?'

The tears rolled faster. 'He was transported for stealing ammunition from the Lisdare barracks. By the grace of God he escaped the rope − 'twas a near thing. If only m'father wid have let us wed. I was feared to tell him I was in the way ... expecting a wean.' The girl turned a grief-stricken face to the wall. 'Now I'll have to give it up after I've fed it and put some strength in it.'

Bridie's eyes widened in alarm, then her lips tightened determinedly. 'I'll have nothin' to do wi' that.' Imagine having to touch the ugly thing growin' in her body.

A few days later someone shouted down the long table where they all sat and sewed, 'Boyce, yer to go to the office, God wants to see you.' By now Bridie understood that was how they all referred to the matron. Feeling alarmed, she went along to the dark little office at the end of the hall.

'Sit down, Boyce. The housekeeper at Merifield Manor has given me some details about your background. In the circumstances, I have put forward a recommendation to the committee of the Kindly Light Foundation to employ you here afterwards until Mrs O'Sullivan can find suitable employment elsewhere.'

'Thank you, ma'am.'

Matron rustled some papers. 'I see that you have not been attending the bible class readings.'

'I'm a Catholic, ma'am. 'Twidden be right.'

'The word of God is always right, Boyce. In future see that you are present otherwise I'll have to reconsider the

164

special privileges allowed in your case. That will be all.'

Bridie lowered her eyes and bobbed a curtsey. 'Thank you, ma'am.'

Ye oul screw! I don' want to hear about oul Job's miseries, I've got enough of m'own.

Rory Donavan was not able to get to Slievegar so he had no news of Bridie apart from knowing roughly when the confinement was due. The farm belonging to his boss was in the process of being sold and they were stocktaking at the shop. He decided to call at the home and see her. When he knocked on the door of Kindly Light, he was told sharply that visitors were not allowed. He asked how Bridie was, but apparently even casual information about the inhabitants was forbidden. Furious, he walked on down the street wondering what to do.

'Were ye tryin' to see yer girl, son?' an old woman sitting on the doorstep enquired.

'No, my cousin,' he lied.

'Ah, well now, if ye have the patience ye might catch a sight of her. The poor unfortunate creatures often slip out to the shop there at the corner. Sure 'tis like a prison wi' the gates open. Them oul bodies of nurses are none too particular in the evenings.'

'Thanks, missus. I'll hang around and keep m'eyes open.'

The next evening he saw two girls coming out through the gate. There was a look of eagerness on their faces as they rushed across to the corner shop. On the second evening he was walking towards the building again when a girl, heavy with pregnancy, emerged. Her face was partially hidden by the shawl she wore. Rory drew back in shock when he realised it was Bridie. She moved slowly like an old woman, her slender body distorted by the bulk she was carrying. Before he could get across the street to reach her, she returned through the gate again. Little Bridie to come to this ... He crashed his hand against the wall. 'God help me to destroy that bastard Catalong,' he muttered.

A week later he was back again outside Kindly Light. Avoiding the old woman on the doorstep, he approached

165

a girl who was going into the shop. 'Excuse me,' he said, 'do you know Bridie Boyce? Would you mind giving her a message from me?'

'*That* wan. Message how are ye! I widden speak to her 'cause she widden feed her starving wean. No one will speak to her.'

Rory put his hand in his pocket and produced some money. 'Please tell her I'll be waiting outside every evening until she's well enough to come out. I'm her cousin.'

The girl grabbed the money and laughed. 'Cousin how are ye! I'll tell oul hard-heart.'

Three evenings later Bridie appeared at the gate. She had been shocked when Nellie confessed to telling Rory about her condition. Now she was very pleased to see him. 'I'm feeling great,' she said untruthfully, and wondered what he would say if she told him how depressed and unhappy she felt with everyone in that place against her.

He saw it in her eyes. 'Bridie, afterwards, it's a change you'll need away from the memory of everything.'

'I have to stay and work here until Mrs O'Sullivan finds me a job.'

'A job in another big house where some blaggard will abuse you?'

She looked at him, her eyes clear and hard. 'Rory, no one will ever abuse me again.'

He believed her and hated to see the change that had come over the happy young girl he had known all his life. 'How would ye like to go to Scotland for a bit? There should be plenty of jobs in Glasgow.'

'It would be great but I widden know where to turn in a big city.'

'Bridie, I want you to swear ye'll never tell a soul, but I'm goin' there m'self soon. See that woman sitting on the doorstep?' He waved and old Lily waved back. 'I'll tell her when I'm leaving and you must meet me down by the Glasgow boat. I'll get the tickets and see to things.'

'What about Mam? I was goin' to visit her before I got settled in another place. They won't let me out of here for two weeks.' She didn't add, 'because they're hoping I'm going to feed that thing'.

166

'Bridie, write to Nellie and let her break the news to your mother, mention Glasgow and say you're going with friends and will be back in the spring. Say nothing about me.'

She didn't know what to say. She felt too tired to argue. Why was it so important for him to leave that soon? Kindly Light has high ideals, Rory was thinking. If only they knew that the nurses don't bother to lock the gate and the girls could walk away any time. Ah well, maybe the girls didn't want to walk away either.

'Rory Donavan,' Bridie said with a spark of her old spirit, 'are ye goin' to rob your employer and make off wi' all the jewellery in the shop?'

He laughed. 'He's selling up. Thank goodness I've learnt something about the trade and saved a bit. Bridie, you'd better slip in through the gates again or else you'll be in trouble. It's getting dark.'

Later that evening she pulled her shawl around the big, coarse maternity nightdress and went down the passage to the wash-room. The back door was not locked yet, which was not surprising, because the two night nurses were old and indifferent. It was said that they drank gin to pass the time. Further along the passage in the opposite direction voices came from a room. She stood still and listened.

'Is that wee scrap whelping again? Did you give it the sugared water?' It was the voice of the red-nosed Clare woman.

There was a murmured reply. 'The mother ... huh! Wring its wee neck if she got a chance. Matron says it's to go to the children's home soon. They might be able to do something about it there. Boyce is not going to change her mind and the two cows in there with plenty of milk have refused to take it to their paps. You may as well go off now. 'Twill be a quiet night. No one in labour.'

Bridie drew back into the shadows when a short plump nurse came out of the room. The partly opened door revealed the other nurse stretched out on a settee, her eyes closed. Further along the passage a nightlight was burning in one of the rooms. Bridie paused. A sound like a cat mewing came from inside. She went in and saw a row of empty cradles. At the far end was a table with two tiny white coffins resting on it. Horrified, she went to hurry out when a faint snuffling came to her ears. She picked up the nightlight and holding it high crossed the room. The light fell on her own name – Bridie Boyce. It was printed in large letters on a white card pinned above one of the cradles. As she lowered the light and peered, there came a frail cry and a tiny hand fluttered across the thin piece of blanket. She touched it almost fearfully; it was icy cold. With a horrible fascination she pulled down the cover and saw the tiniest baby she had ever laid eyes on. Incredulously she looked at the little shrunken face and the mass of reddish-golden hair, the colour of her mother's. She felt frightened. Dear God, the child was dying. The place where unbaptised children were buried came to her mind. 'The Killeen' it was called; a tiny graveyard at the corner of a field or behind a ditch where white stones marked the graves. 'This poor wee mite is my baby,' she whispered. The pain that was constantly in her tightly bound breasts increased until it was agonising. She sobbed in fear, not knowing what to do. The child who looked like her mother was starving to death because she had abandoned it.

She put down the light and picked it up in her arms, then looked around wildly until she saw the chair behind the table where the coffins were. She rushed down, unbuttoned her nightdress and ripped off the grey breast-binders. It seemed unbelievable to Bridie that when she held the child to her breast the tiny mouth fastened on the nipple immediately. She held it closely with a feeling of overwhelming love. She tried to remember how the nurses had instructed the other girls about feeding equally from both sides. When it was replete the child fell asleep.

Without a thought to the future or how she was going to manage, Bridie Boyce knew that she must keep this child. As long as she lived it would never be hungry, cold or wet again. She pulled off the damp swaddling clothes from around its limbs and saw for the first time the sex of her baby. It was a little girl.

'Boyce, what are you doing in here?' The nurse's nose seemed redder and her temper worse than usual. Bridie, disliking the woman, realised that she must be very careful

168

to convince her or else the baby might be sent to that home straight away; or, anyway, after she had nursed it and given it a start in life, as they put it. A strict rule had been laid down by the Founder Fathers of Kindly Light that the future of all illegitimate children must be cared for by the charity. Under no circumstances could an unfortunate girl take it away, unless her parents were prepared to help rear it. All destitute children went to this other home in Lisdare where they remained until the age of fourteen.

'Nurse, I saw me baby by chance, it was hungry and I fed it,' she said hurriedly. 'Can I take it to the ward like the other girls after I've changed it?'

The woman glared at her, not quite trusting Bridie's change of mind. Still, there was something different about her, a glow as if she had come into a fortune. Next we'll have tantrums when she has to part with it, the nurse thought sourly. 'There are shelves with clean garments in the other ward. Next time, Boyce, don't unwrap your baby until a clean cloth's at hand. Do you understand?' she barked.

'Yes, nurse, thank you,' Bridie said meekly.

Down in the ward, where all the other girls and their babies were asleep, Bridie went to the shelves containing baby clothes and covers. Instead of taking one article from each shelf, which was the rule, she took two of everything. Nervously she undressed and cleansed her tiny daughter, gradually growing more confident in her movements. She placed her on the bed, crept over to the table, and taking a jug of water proceeded to baptise her Mary Anne. Mary for the mother of God and Anne, her blessed mother. They would protect her child.

She lay for hours making plans. Stealing extra clothes was the first step in her plan. Rory wanted her to go to Glasgow to get right away, start a new life. That's what she would do. He wouldn't be pleased about her baby but she didn't care. She fell asleep and almost immediately, it seemed, was awakened by a chorus of crying babies. Joyfully Bridie reached over and took Mary Anne in her arms.

The terrible news about Bridie Boyce took away some of the joy Sean O'Neill had been feeling since he arrived home from prison. Rosha had advised Nellie to tell him because the servant girl was still in a state of shock and behaving most peculiarly at times. He couldn't get over the changes Rosha had made to the house: all the rooms had been whitewashed and painted; the parlour was no longer a musty, neglected room but bright with new curtains and covers on the old furniture. He had to laugh when she said: 'They all sit around on their backsides half the winter; this year they were kept busy. Maybe,' she had added with a twinkle in her eyes, 'the next woman you bring along won't stick her nose up at the state of Garton!'

That, Sean thought wearily, will never happen again. All the fight and life has gone out of me. He had been dreading coming back to a mass of unpaid bills; not only were they all paid but there was a good balance in the bank. His daughter was a grand girl. If only she and Patrick would get married and have children, his contentment would be complete.

Rosha was standing by her bedroom window when she saw Nellie hurrying down the field towards the shore. There was no pail or bag in her hand. Strange, she never went that way for a walk.

This route was familiar to Nellie since her daily visits to see Bridie at Merifield. It led to the rose garden. She moved cautiously through the surrounding shrubs and saw with grim satisfaction that Catalong was in the glasshouse bending over boxes of tiny plants. She threw off her shawl, put a hand in her pocket and approached him stealthily. Though the door was open and she was swift, he half-turned at the sound behind him. Nellie lifted her arm and struck him with a knife between the shoulders: all her pent up hatred and anger gave her the courage to do the act. Nevertheless, it was a feeble thrust, for the knife covered with blood fell immediately to the ground as she sped away from the place.

Sean and Rosha were sitting talking at the table when she rushed in. Without a word, she pulled back her shawl and they saw the blood stains covering the front of her blouse and skirt. 'I've been to the castle grounds and attacked Catalong ... left him wi' blood pouring out o'him.'

Sean stumbled to his feet while Rosha sped to the back door and shot the bolt over. 'Quick, Nellie, get that blouse off.' When Nellie's movements became clumsy, Rosha tore it off her back and bundled it out of sight. Thank goodness Biddy was doing some shopping and the men away on the hill. 'Wash yourself quickly, there's blood on your hand and arm. Then get upstairs, put on clean clothes and settle in the back room with your sewing. Remember, you haven't been outside the house today. Did anyone see you?'

'I think he recognised me. I ... didin kill him.'

'It'll be bad for you anyway, Nellie,' Sean said quietly handing her a drop of whiskey. 'Do as Rosha says. It's going to be his word against ours.' They'll never believe us, he thought. The girl's done for. God help her, what a thing to do.

As Rosha was making some tea there was the sound of a horse out in the yard. 'Daddy, the minister. What a time for him to call.'

As usual, Mr Stewart tied his horse to the post and went around to the front door. Sean let him in. The minister shook his hand warmly.

'The good news has just reached me, Mr O'Neill. Thank God you're safely home again. You must take life easy now ...' He suddenly noticed Sean's colour and frowned. 'Are you well?'

'Come in and sit down, Mr Stewart. A terrible misfortune has taken place here today.' Briefly he told the clergyman the full story about Bridie and her sister Nellie who was mentally disturbed and had committed a terrible crime. As Sean spoke he suddenly thought, if this man could speak up for us, Nellie might be saved. 'Mr Stewart, could you possibly help us?'

'I would do anything to help you, Mr O'Neill, but how can I?'

'We're going to deny that she ever left the house today, that she's been busy up in the sewing room. What I'm going to suggest, Mr Stewart, is a difficult thing. I hate to ask you to dishonour your cloth or put a sin on your soul but unless someone like yourself speaks up for her the girl's done for. If you could say that you saw her here at the time the crime was committed ...'

The minister began to walk around the room in a state of

171

agitation. He stopped abruptly. 'You want me to say that I was present in this house at the time the deed was carried out, and that the girl was present?'

'Yes, that's what I'm asking you to do for a poor creature who was out of her mind.'

The minister pulled at his chin. 'Leave me for a while, Mr O'Neill. Let me pray and think about it. It's a great deal you ask of me.'

'It is, and I pray that God will guide you.'

It was the worst ten minutes of Sean's life. He was terrified the law would arrive before the minister could make up his mind. The door opened and Mr Stewart nodded to him. 'I have given it serious thought, Mr O'Neill. It seems to me that I must weigh good against evil. Sir Thomas Catalong is a man of low integrity as I myself know well. I am human enough to wish retribution on him — if he is still alive. However, if he has died because of the assault inflicted on him by your servant, I must withdraw my support. If he is merely injured, I will declare, and may God forgive me, that the girl did not leave the house. Now let us get some papers on the table and make a pretence of having been attending to other business affairs.'

'God bless you, sir.' Sean hurried upstairs to the sewing room. 'Rosha, some tea for the minister, and will the pair of you get on your knees and say the rosary? He's going to stand by us and say that he was in the house and Nellie never left it. Be calm now. Catalong will send the law but you've probably only scratched him anyway.'

Thomas Catalong was absolutely livid. First, with the doctor who made light of his injury and advised him to make no charge. And then with the Inspector of the Constabulary who could not make a charge because he had the word of his minister that the girl had not left Garton that afternoon.

172

# Chapter Fifteen

When word reached Edmund about the attack on his father he immediately applied for special leave. He knew that the injury was not serious but the intention was certainly grave. After a discussion with his commanding officer, he left for Ireland. Apart from the concern for his father, he desperately wanted to see Rosha again. To his surprise the doctor made light of the injury when he went to discuss it with him. A slight wound, he said. And though a young woman was thought to be involved, she had not been identified; there the matter had to rest. Edmund was puzzled for his father swore it was O'Neill's servant girl. Still, as Mr Stewart the minister had declared that the girl had not left the house during the time mentioned, it would seem his father was mistaken.

At first Edmund was dismayed when he heard that the Meckins were coming to Merifield, but now he realised their visit had some advantages because it had been arranged that his father would travel to Scotland with them afterwards. Rosha was in the paddock exercising a horse when he passed by on the morning after he arrived home.

'Let's walk up to the little coppice,' she suggested, catching hold of the reins. There, out of sight, he took her in his arms. He told her about calling in to see Edith Houston in Dilford, who was sending her an invitation. Rosha's eyes lit up. 'Edmund, it was kind of you to buy the things from the potter. Paddy and I have been busy arranging them. That day you left, last time. I just missed you —'

He looked at her without smiling and said quietly. 'We won't miss each other next time. Rosha ...'

'What is it?'

'Your father is coming up through the paddock.'

He saw the look of alarm in her eyes as she swung round. Edmund walked slowly from the coppice, Rosha followed. 'Good afternoon, sir.'

'Edmund came in to look at old Rill,' she said quietly, patting the horse's back.

Startled, Sean stared at her flushed cheeks. 'Good afternoon,' he said abruptly, and thought. My daughter is not telling the truth. 'Edmund' she called him, so naturally. He is certainly not a stranger to her, this son of Catalong's. Sean continued on up through the land and cut across to Garton again. Nellie was in the dairy. She jumped when he spoke because his voice was unusually curt.

'Rosha and young Catalong seem to know each other rather well.'

Nellie skimmed the thick custard of cream off the milk in the crock before replying, 'Sure they used to play together on the shore, Mr O'Neill, when they were younger.'

'Play on the shore? I didn't know that.'

'Och, many's a time we'd be down picking a few whelks and he'd come along. A lonely wee lad he was.'

Nellie thought, A year ago I might have said: 'There's something goin' on between them and you'd better put a stop to it.' After what happened at Merifield when she attacked Catalong, Nellie could not be disloyal to the girl. Rosha had stood by her.

The letter from Edith Houston arrived when they were all at the table taking tea. Delighted, Rosha read it and handed it to her father. He passed it to Nellie who read it aloud for the benefit of Biddy Coll and Paddy. It was a tactful, charming letter.

'We would be so pleased if you could spend a few days with us ...' and Edith went on to say that she had arranged some musical evenings. Sean was delighted that his daughter had kept in touch with the Misses Houston. Everyone knew and admired their efforts to revive an interest in Irish culture. There were some

174

fine people among the old English families, he had to admit.

'Certainly accept the invitation, my dear.'

'Yer new frock is nearly ready, Rosha. We'll have a fitting this evening and work on it all the 'morrow,' Nellie promised.

The silver leaves of the tall maple growing in the Houstons' front garden were fluttering in the warm summer breeze when Rosha arrived in the farm cart with Paddy and Willie, who were collecting a load of wood in Dilford. They placed her portmanteau in the porch and shuffled off in case the gentry saw the rough way their young mistress had travelled from Slievegar. Slipping her reticule and parasol on to her left arm, Rosha pulled the Houston's heavy door bell.

Annie, the maid, opened the door with a belligerent expression. ''Tis you, miss.' Before Rosha could greet her, the girl said in a rush of words. 'The news came this morning and they've taken off. The brother in Lisdare has passed away and amint I left wi' all the notes to deliver to the people who were coming the 'morrow evening for the music.'

'Their brother in Lisdare has died?' Rosha exclaimed. 'How awful for them.'

'Amint I just sayin' so? Miss Houston said you was to stay the night and wasin I being let home for our house Mass? Now I have to stay wi' you. Miss said ye'd better take the coach back to Slievegar in the morning.'

'There's no coach on Sunday,' Rosha said bleakly, wondering why everything she and Edmund planned was so ill-fated. 'Annie, deliver those messages Miss Houston left, then do as you originally planned. I don't mind staying in the house by myself.'

The girl looked at her, mouth wide open. 'You mean, miss, I can go home and help m'mam wi' the house Mass?'

'That's what I said. Miss Houston need not know.'

A dimple appeared on Annie's cheek and she rolled her eyes. 'And who's to tell her? Thanks, miss. I'll take the messages then cook the meal for you and Mr Catalong and be off home.'

Edmund arrived carrying a basket containing a large salmon. 'For the supper party tomorrow night. I hope Edith ...' He frowned. 'What is it, Rosha?' She told him. Though disappointment showed on his face he said, concerned, 'The death must have been sudden. How sad for them.'

'At least we won't have to put up with Bossy trying to spy on us! He looked at her for a moment then touched her face. 'That's better. You looked so dejected. Why don't you unpack your clothes? I'll carry your bag upstairs?'

'It seems hardly worthwhile unpacking.'

'Why, Of course, they won't be coming back for a few days.'

'Edith said I could stay tonight and take the coach home tomorrow, except she'd forgotten that it's Sunday and there is no coach. Edmund, could I hire a conveyance from the hotel after I've been to Mass in the morning?'

'Rosha, these few days together are all we've got. You mustn't leave so soon,' he protested. 'The Meckins are arriving later on in the week from London and I'm going to be tied to the house most of the time. There's no place we can meet in Slievegar.' He paused. 'Why can't you stay on here? Edith won't mind and you're not expected back.'

'How could I do such a thing when she's left me a message to return home?'

'Perhaps it would abuse her hospitality,' he said reluctantly.

'Miss O'Neill, when I clear the table and kitchen I'll be off,' Annie said, once the meal had been served. 'Ye'll lock up well when ye leave the 'morrow, won't ye? There's some gypsies camping just outside town. Them wans wid come into a body's house and help themselves. Hide the key under the big white stone at the bottom of the garden.'

Edmund was staring at her in amazement. 'She's not leaving you alone in this house tonight?' he asked when Annie went out.

'I said she could because her mother is expecting her home,' Rosha said bleakly.

He folded his arms on the table and smiled. 'Well, what

shall we do in this interesting town? Call on the disapproving potter or walk in the forbidden woods?'

Rosha had to laugh. After a while, Annie rushed in. 'Youse a'right?' and dashed out again, slamming the door.

'She's going to clear the table by picking up the cloth at both ends with everything on it and whisking it across her shoulder.' He rose. 'Come on, darling, let's go to the drawing room.'

'Would you like to see the schoolrooms, Edmund?'

'That would be very interesting. I can't wait!'

Hand in hand they went through all the dreary rooms until Annie left the house. In the drawing room they found that the fire was burning low and the maid had forgotten to bring up a supply of fuel. Down in the kitchen there was a scuttle full of coal and a basket of logs. As they were about to go upstairs again, a sound of footsteps fell outside. Edmund glanced through the window. Two men like vagabonds were in the yard. He opened the window and called out. The men ran away immediately.

'They must have seen the Houstons driving past their camp and think Annie's on her own,' he said when they went upstairs. 'Rosha, you can't be alone in this house tonight. I'll stay and sleep on the settee.'

Though she felt nervous, she was uncertain about his suggestion. 'Edmund, it would be terrible if the Houstons found out you were here all night.'

'I don't want to leave you,' he said gently.

She tugged at her handkerchief and suggested hesitantly: 'Shall we go for a walk then ... if it's not too late?'

'No!'

A faint blush rose in her cheeks at the tone of his voice. After a moment she ventured feebly, 'Maybe you're tired, you want to go to bed?'

'You're sitting on it,' he said, a glint of mischief in his eyes.

She rose awkwardly under his steady gaze and thrusting her fingers into a porcelain bowl of pot-pourri began to stir it as though it needed attention. As the scent of faded roses and myrtle filled the room, he put out his hand and drew her towards him.

177

'Rosha, do you not realise how much I love you? And,' he added teasingly, 'all you can think of is how to banish me!'

Losing her sudden shyness, she gripped his hand. 'Edmund, it's just that I am ...'

'I understand.' His lips moved over her face and hair. Perhaps,' he murmured, 'it's time for *you* to go to bed.'

She laughed. 'I don't know the way!'

'Ah, Rosha ...' He raised his hands and pulled the pins out of her hair until it tumbled down her back, then they were kissing with a longing and despair as though this was their last moment together. He fumbled with the fastenings of her bodice, until the silk gown slipped from her shoulders and lay in a shimmering pool by the fire. In her lace-trimmed cambric petticoat she lay beside him on the hearth, no longer shy or nervous with guilty thoughts, but freely and generously giving her love.

Later, when they settled down to sleep before the smouldering fire, he said, 'Darling, when I return to Merrifield, I'm going to talk to my father. I'll tell him I want to marry you, then I'll go and see your father.'

'There's going to be such awful problems.'

'I know, but,' he ran his hand through her hair, 'we can't go on as we were. Why don't we spend the next few days together? As you're not expected home, you could come to the hotel.'

Rosha shut her mind to the thought that she was doing wrong but the feeling in her heart and body was far stronger than the voice of her conscience. They were going to be married, she assured herself. Nothing could come between them now. Edmund tried not to think of the obstacles that would have to be overcome when he married Rosha. Of course it would end his career at Sandhurst. He was surprised to feel regret. Against all expectations, he was doing exceedingly well there and his father was actually very proud of his progress.

When Rosha went to Mass, he left by the garden entrance with her portmanteau. He told the maid at the hotel that he would like to reserve a room for Miss O'Neill who was waiting for the return of the Misses Houston. He also gave her a generous amount of money which was bound to seal her lips.

On Sunday afternoon, and again on Monday, the maid packed a basket of food for them. Edmund took two horses from the hotel stable and they rode far up into the hills where they rambled, talked, laughed and made love. At night he came to her room. A short, idyllic honeymoon, he said. He couldn't wait to put a wedding ring on her finger and ease away the stray guilty shadows that stole unbiddingly to her eyes sometimes.

They travelled separately to Slievegar on Tuesday morning. When Rosha walked up the drive to the house she saw immediately that something was wrong. The front door was shut and all the blinds were drawn. Nellie, with eyes red and swollen from weeping, met her in the kitchen.

'Sit down, pet, I'm afraid there's bad news. Did ye hear any word of what happened here, o'er at Dilford?'

Rosha shook her head guiltily. She and Edmund had lived in their own world entirely. 'What's happened? Daddy ...'

'He's had a knockin' but he'll be a'right, considerin' what he's been through.'

'For God's sake Nellie, what's the matter? Why are the curtains drawn?'

'Biddy Coll's dead. She died in the night.' Nellie began to cry.

'Oh, no!' Rosha ran to her father when he walked into the kitchen. There was a bruise on his forehead and he looked very pale.

'Sit down, my dear.' In a quiet voice he told her about the disaster that had struck the church during Mass on Monday. 'Heavy rain brought rubbish down in the mountain stream, blocking the culvert below the church which is partly over a ravine. He shook his head. 'But who would have thought it could have caused such a calamity? The pressure of the torrent weakened the masonry and the pent-up flood poured in with unbelievable force, slamming the church door shut. Up in the gallery we hung down shawls to the people below and hauled them to safety.'

'Biddy ...?'

'I saw Willie swimming towards her and decided I could help more people, too, by climbing down from the gallery.' He shrugged. 'The wooden railing broke and sent me crashing below.'

Speechless, Rosha thought, Monday was a Holy Day, a feast day and I'd forgotten to go to Mass.

'It was too much for old Biddy, the soul. God love her, she's at rest,' Nellie said pouring out cups of tea. 'Sure 'tis a good thing Paddy's a heathen or he'd have gone the same way. The old folk got the worst of it. Five dead and several injured.'

'Jayus, Nellie,' Paddy said coming in the door, 'is one wake not enough for ye?' he was stricken though. He couldn't believe that the bad-tempered old wman who had taken him in from the road and given him a home all those years ago was no longer with them. Pleaded wi' the mistress that he was starvin' and started him workin' as a scarecrow in the field to rid Garton of a plague of crows. Stood out there like an eejit, flapping his hands wi'out a care in the world. Paddy lowered his head to hide his blinding tears.

Biddy was laid out in the parlour. Rosha went down to see her and say a prayer for her soul. Though she had not felt a great affection for Biddy Coll, she wept because the housekeeper had been part of her life. The old woman lay in her coffin guarded by two large brass candle sticks, the flames of the candles searching into the dark corners of the room. Biddy had been cross with Rosha for spending money on the new covers and curtains; now she lay in dignity in the well-furnished room where mourners would come to pay their last respects and have a good look.

'Well, ye had a change at Dilford,' was the only comment Nellie made as they prepared food for the wake. In case she asked any questions, Rosha said quickly, 'Nellie, my father's had a bad fall.'

'He's mendin' fine. Guess who he pulled to safety? The widda Flaherty. Begod, 'tis a pity he didin drop her back again!'

'Is her husband all right?'

'He dosin go to Mass on Holy Days, nor has she been able

180

to make him. Rosha, there's a rumour that Rory Donavan is goin' to merica.'

'America?' She gave the girl a quick glance. Poor Nellie. All the plans she used to make about emigrating. Now Rory was going and leaving her behind. 'Do you mind?'

Nellie cut a slice of bread. 'Sure he lost the notion of me long ago.' And too quickly added: 'Bad news about the poor souls over at the point.'

'What is it?' Rosha asked in alarm.

'Tom Cat has got a bailiff patrollin' the beach and they're not allowed to pick any more. Sure the whelks and things, as well as the dulse, was keepin' them alive. Yer father's goin' to look into the matter. What can he do when the castle has always claimed mineral rights on the shore?'

Rosha was furious. What a despicable thing to do. When Biddy was buried she would go over and see what could be done to help. By then Thomas Catalong would know that his son wanted to marry her.

'Would ye hang up these tea towels, love? I'm up to my eyes.'

Rosha picked up the linen basket and made for the orchard. As she was hurrying up the path a bird with a damaged wing scurried out of her way into the bushes. She put down the basket and went after it, carefully pushing the branches aside. To her surprise, she saw sitting away down on the ground behind the old coach house, Rory Donavan, Patrick, and Neddie the boy. The expression on their faces alarmed her. Once again it occurred to Rosha that Neddie without his good-natured smile was unlike the crippled little fella that everyone liked.

What's Rory doing here? she wondered. He's supposed to be in Lisdare preparing to sail for America. As she watched, Rory drew a map on the dry earth with a piece of stick. They must be up to something. She frowned. What good was half a man like Neddie for the kind of activity she suspected the other two were involved in? Then she recalled the day he sprang on Catalong. Neddie might be capable of other surprising actions too. Thoughtfully she went on to the orchard and pegged the towels on the line, then went straight down and told Nellie who said fearfully: 'Rosha, don't mention what you've seen to anyone. God protect us, they're planning something.'

Edmund went to his father's study when he returned to the manor. He was nervous but determined. There were account books scattered across the desk.

'Sit down, Edmund,' Thomas Catalong said pleasantly, obviously pleased with the figures before him. He drew a line and sat back on the chair. 'Well, my boy?'

'What I have to say to you, Father, will come as a great surprise, but I must tell you that I have made up my mind. I wish to get married as soon as possible.'

'I don't think Alice Meckin or her parents would wish to rush into the occasion quite so fast.' Thomas Catalong smiled. 'You mustn't be so impatient, young man. Ah, is she *enceinte*?'

'Father, I'm not talking about Alice. We're friends, that's all. I want to marry Rosha O'Neill of Garton. We've known each other since we were children. We love each other and ...'

Catalong was completely stunned for a moment by Edmund's words, then he banged the desk with the flat of his hand as a dull angry red coloured his face. 'How dare you approach me with such a request. You will *not* marry that girl. I forbid it!'

'Can't we discuss this calmly, sir? I don't want to upset you.'

'Upset me?' roared Catalong in brutal anger, his face now white with rage and his hands clenched threateningly.

'Surely the choice of a wife must be my own?'

'*Those* people! Look out of that window. Just look what that girl whom you want to marry has done to Merifield.'

'She was trying to help the homeless people. It was the only suitable bit of land they had.'

'She did it deliberately,' his father roared again. 'And you expect me to accept such a person into our family. One of those people. You who will inherit this estate?'

Angry now, Edmund said heatedly, 'An inheritance begot by the suffering of other people.'

'You damn' young cad! I will have you know that I worked

182

hard to make Merifield prosperous. And what are *your* plans when you inherit this estate?'

'Give gack to the people what you have taken from them.' Afterwards Edmund realised that he should not have said that. It was tactless at that moment although it was true.

Catalong leapt to his feet, his face bruised with rage. 'By God, I've reared a cringing, good-for-nothing churl!'

By tomorrow morning he'll have quietened down, then I'll talk to him again, Edmund decided. Nevertheless, he said firmly, 'Nothing will change my mind about marrying Rosha O'Neill, Father.'

'Get out of my sight. I will deal with you later.'

When a sidecar from the manor passed a field in Slievegar early the following morning, the workers paused and looked at each other. One detached himself and walked slowly up to the hedge which had a wealth of growth shielding the field from the road. The others went on working. Some time later, Thomas Catalong and his driver were seen coming back along the road again. The look-out signalled. Rory Donavan went up and nodded to him to resume his work. The man took up a spade and began to dig close to the hedge; others moved towards him unhurriedly and laboured at the same task. The field, on the steep bit of land, was being trenched and drained; a slow arduous job but the task was important and had been planned for some time.

Rory tied a scarf around the lower part of his face and pulled down his cap. Making sure that no one was on this lonely part of the road, he suddenly appeared before the approaching horse and cart. 'Driver,' he ordered, 'jump down and get away into the woods. I've no wish to harm an innocent man. Fast!'

Thomas Catalong picked up the whip and slashed at the man in his path then brought it down on the horse, driving it away from the danger. Rory jumped out of the way then, aiming his pistol at Catalong's back, he pulled the trigger. 'That's for the destruction of my home.' He fired again. 'And that's for Bridie Boyce.' He dived into the hedge, pulled off the scarf and disposed of the gun in the place that had been prepared, where no one would find it. The leader of the work group came up and gripped his hand.

'Away now, man, as fast as you can. God go with you.'

Edmund and one of the workmen were walking along the drive when the frantic horse, foaming at the mouth, came tearing towards them dragging the cart precariously behind. Edmund sprang forward and grabbed the reins. Slumped down over the seat was the body of his murdered father.

When the estate employee was questioned by the Inspector of the Constabulary, he was unable to give a clear description of the man who had held up the sidecar. The gaffer in the field where the trenching was taking place said that none of his men had left during that time and, though they had rushed to the scene of the crime, there was no sign of anyone. It was customary for Sir Thomas to carry a pistol but the housekeeper reported that her employer had left in a great hurry. In fact, she'd go so far as to say he was not himself at all. The garrison at Ballymore were alerted and Her Majesty's navy brought into action in case the killer sought refuge on one of the small islands to the north side of the bay. Every house and cave in Slievegar and Iskaglen was searched. Suspects, all those who had spoken out against Catalong, were handcuffed in gangs like slaves and marched along the roads to the barracks at Lisdare.

The bailiff at the manor made a statement to the police. He said that if they found Rory Donavan they need look no further: he had on one occasion threatened Sir Thomas's life. The hunt went out for Rory then came statements from reliable people that Donavan had sailed for America. His former employer and his own mother told how they had bidden him farewell. Only Rosha and Nellie knew that Rory Donavan had not left the country. Not yet.

Neddie the boy was a familiar sight along the roads. With his short powerful legs he peddled his go-cart all over the countryside. Sometimes he took a notion to walk, but with the passing years he was seen more often now in the wooden vehicle with its four strong wheels. He was working with Patrick Murphy stacking turf when the constables came to the farm to ask questions of the men in the family. They were met by Maria who resented the way they entered her home. Murphy's wife made the sergeant in charge feel very uncomfortable.

184

'It's a known fact,' she said haughtily, 'that the menfolk of this family have never abused the law.'

After the constables had questioned Patrick in the kitchen, he and Neddie carried on stacking the turf. Some time later the members of the law left the farm. Patrick and Neddie saluted them respectfully as they passed by. When they were out of sight, Patrick checked the wheels of Neddie's carriage, as the locals called it, then padded the floor with sacks and thick rugs. Slowly and deliberately the two men began to unstack all the turf again.

Rory Donavan, his head and clothes covered in a thick layer of peat mould, emerged swiftly from the cavity they had made and shot into Neddie's go-cart, where he lay flat on the floor, his head pressed into the earth-smelling sacking. Patrick threw another armful of sacks on top of him then he and Neddie piled in turf.

'Safe journey, Rory,' Patrick whispered and began to reassemble the stack once again.

'Are ye a'right down there?' Neddie asked Rory, who's head rested a safe distance from the dwarf's strong feet working the peddles.

'Wid ye be, Neddie, wi' a load of peat on yer back?'

'Jabers, man, isin it better than a rope around yer neck? And arint ye the lucky man that Farmer Murphy always paye wee Neddie wi' a load of peat?'

Rory chuckled and tried to pretend he was up at the turf-cutting on the hill, sheltering from the rain with a sack over his head. The scent of the peat was in his nostrils, but the hard rocking go-cart reminded him that he was travelling in great danger to a place of safety. It was a long journey to the Red Barn and they did not dare to stop on the way. When finally Neddie arrived at their destination he drew into the far side of the yard by the hay shed.

'Rory,' he said, 'I'm away now to see Maggie to find out if the law has made a search yet.'

Maggie's eyes lit up when Neddie walked into the kitchen and whispered in her ear. She was prepared for these lodgers. Rory had called some time ago. 'Neddie,' she said loudly in her lisping voice as they walked across the yard, 'put yer vehicle inside the shed. There's rain in the wind and ye'll not be wantin' yer turf gettin' wet.'

'Ye honour me wi' yer attention, Maggie me heart, and 'tis meself that loves ye for it.' He peddled in through the wide doors and immediately the two of them began unpacking the load.

'My back's broken,' Rory moaned, trying to stand up straight. He was stiff and very sore. 'God bless ye, lass. I'll never forget your kindness.'

'Climb up quickly, Rory,' she ordered him. 'There's a wee loft and only meself that knows about it. I'll bring ye food and drink. Don't stir again till dark o'night.'

When Lord Meckin and his family arrived that afternoon at Merifield Manor they were unaware that their host had been murdered. They had seen some activity on the roads and assumed it concerned other matters. Ireland was an unsettled country. Edmund, shocked and distressed about his father's violent death, was after all very glad to see the Meckins. The quarrel on the previous day with his father had upset him because they had been getting on so well recently. He had gone early to the study that morning to talk to his father again and discovered he had left the house without a word.

Lord and Lady Meckin were very practical and helpful. Alice was kind and caring. When he told them what had happened on their arrival, she came over and put her arms around him and held him for a minute, not caring that her parents were standing there.

Lord and Lady Meckin went to bed early after dinner, tired from their long journey and disturbed by the terrible death of their friend. As they were undressing in their bedroom his lordship remarked to his wife, 'You know, my dear, that young man is going to inherit a vast fortune. Catalong had a pile under every finger, not to mention this vast estate.'

'Alice,' Edmund said as they stood by the drawing-room window, 'all this must be very distressing for your parents. They've been marvellous to me.'

She kissed him lightly on the cheek. 'Thank goodness we were here, Edmund. We'll do all we can to help you.'

186

While they were standing there, a light showed on the hill. 'I wonder,' he said, 'what is happening?' He longed to get out of doors and decided to walk up and see for himself. That day he had been meeting people continuously. The Inspector of the Constabulary, and Army and Navy commanders had all been to Merifield. The Meckins had constantly shown concern and Alice never left his side.

The light on the hill was not the flame that sometimes appeared but a large bonfire which lit up the countryside. A group of people were laughing and dancing while others strolled about talking. Edmund approached a woman who was sitting under a bush eating a piece of bread and an apple. 'What's happening?' he asked.

'Did ye not know?' she replied, bending down to pick up the apple that had fallen from her hand. 'Catalong is dead and we're free at last from his tyranny. Ten years ago he evicted us from our home. My husband died in the workhouse and me and the weans had to beg for shelter.'

He was turning away from the dreadful scene when he saw Rosha in a long black cloak. Nellie was beside her. He drew back in disbelief when Rosha thew a branch on the fire. In fact, though he was not to realise, a burning branch had fallen in Rosha's path and she tossed it back to the flames. How could she, he thought with anguish, take part in this barbarian celebration? Nellie saw him first, then Rosha turned her heard.

'Edmund ...' She went to run down the slope but drew back at the look on his face – anger, disgust.

'How *could* you?' he shouted. 'Coming to this devilish rejoicing ... from you I expected some compassion. A human being has been cruelly murdered. No matter what his faults, he did not deserve such a death. God, Rosha, he was *my father*.'

'Human being?' Nellie cried, her arms raised in outrage.

'Be quiet, Nellie! Edmund, I would not have wished such a death on anyone. I came here with Nellie because ...' She stopped, realising that she could not give any explanation without betraying Rory Donavan whom Nellie was convinced had murdered Edmund's father. Against her will she had accompanied the girl in a search for Rory who,

187

Nellie thought, might be hiding somewhere near, hungry and thirsty, waiting for the hunt to die down. He might even be injured. There were secret places, she said, where they used to go courting. He couldn't be far away. This was a short-cut otherwise Rosha would not have come to the hill. The people from the settlement, who were loud in their praises for the courageous man who had used his pistol against the one who had caused so much misery in their lives, had lit the fire.

Edmund turned away sharply into the crowd out of sight. Rosha went to go after him. Nellie caught her arm. She struggled to free herself but the servant girl was too strong. 'He dosin want to talk to you. Don' make a show of yerself, everyone's looking.'

Rosha's face crumbled in distress and tears filled her eyes. Nellie put an arm around her. 'Listen, pet, the minute lordie and his family leave the castle, get over there and see him. Sure yer his friend.' She paused. 'I suppose he was in Dilford?' When Rosha nodded her head, Nellie thought in alarm, Mary and Joseph, they were three whole days together.

Alice Meckin waited for Edmund to return. He came back nearly two hours later, his face pale and bleak. She went to the brandy decanter and poured him a large glassful. He gulped it down. Something must have happened when he was out. She did not ask. Instead she refilled his glass and poured a little for herself. Though the room was warm, Edmund shivered. She caught his hand.

'Come and sit down, Edmund.'

'I couldn't believe it, they've built a fire on the hill. A pagan custom, lit because my father was murdered.'

'Daddy says the Irish are a wild people.'

'I did not expect to see someone ... people I know and love to be there feeding the flames.'

Someone he loved? It was true then. Her brother, Roger, had always suspected that Edmund was attracted to a girl in Ireland. Alice remembered when he refused to accompany them to Scotland. How unhappy and hurt she had been at the time. How could he get involved with some ignorant, uneducated Irish girl from a thatched cabin? Alice had never

188

been to school. Mama did not approve of the establishments which had sprung up in recent years, though many of her friends attended them. A train of governesses, whom she realised now had a limited knowledge and ability to teach a spoilt little girl, had been responsible for her education.

'Edmund, why don't you go to bed?' She left her seat, went over and knelt beside him. Alice had been in love with Edmund for as long as she could remember. She knew he didn't love her. His perfunctory kisses after they spent an evening together made her aware of it. She was too sensible though not to realise that his unhappiness at this moment was partly caused by the action of someone he cared about.

He drank down the second glass of brandy with the speed of the first, as though determined to blot out the scene that had caused him distress. She sipped hers thoughtfully not liking the taste.

'May I come and say goodnight?' she asked gently.

'Of course.' He looked at her with a start as though he had forgotten her presence. The effect of the drink brought suitable words to his lips without conscious thought. When he was in his bedroom, he completely forgot about Alice Meckin and remembered Rosha with pain and anger.

Alice left her bedroom door slightly open, undressed and put on her night clothes. Edmund's room was opposite. When the rod of light under his door disappeared, she extinguished her lamp and went across the darkened passage. Confident by nature, she felt nervous now and appalled at her temerity in entering a man's bedroom in this manner.

'Edmund, I've come to say goodnight. I was worried about you.'

He put out his hand to light the bedside candle and accidently touched her arm. 'Alice, you're shivering with cold.' He pulled back the bedclothes and though the brandy was beginning to affect his head he realised in a vague way that his action was unwise.

Before he could retract, she completely disarmed him by whispering: 'Edmund, I'm so nervous, that's why I'm shivering. I've never done anything like this before but ... I love you.' She slipped into the bed and wrapped her arms around him tightly. Her lips covered his and silenced his surprised, muddled protest. Then, as the power of the brandy began to drug his sense and the comforting arms and body drew him closer, he realised this was the solace he needed to wipe out the memory of that dreadful day.

In the morning, Lady Meckin, who never rose early, went to her daughter's room. She wanted to talk to Alice about a plan she and Papa had discussed before they went to sleep last night. It was important to have a few words before Edmund was around. The bed was unslept in and there was no sign of her daughter. Edmund and Alice woke to hear Lady Meckin's high-pitched voice asking the housekeeper if her daughter had been moved to another room.

'No, my lady,' Mrs O'Sullivan replied. 'But,' she added tactfully, 'she may have moved herself.'

'Victoria,' Lord Meckin called, 'I think my dear we must spare the young couple some embarrassment. The situation is ... er ... delicate.'

Lady Meckin turned away her face to hide a gleam of satisfaction. In spite of all the plans she had made over the years to throw these two together nothing had come of it; now the situation seemed to have resolved itself.

'We feel asleep, Edmund. It was the brandy. I never meant to ... I only wanted to comfort you and go back to my own room. Mama always breakfasts in bed. Now they all know. What are we going to do?'

Alice sounded so distressed that he said quickly and with gentleness, 'It's all right, I'll speak to your parents.' With a feeble spark of humour he added, 'Mrs O'Sullivan was right – you did move to another room! Alice, thank you for being so generous and comforting last night.'

My God, he thought in panic, what have I done? How did Alice Meckin come to spend the night in his bed? She must have come in complete innocence and he had behaved like a cad becaused he was drunk. He had no head for brandy. It didn't matter now. One thing was certain, he had betrayed the trust of her parents who had been so kind to him; he was honour bound to make amends. They would expect that. Edmund tried not to think of Rosha: when he did, he saw her on the hill throwing fuel on the bonfire and rejoicing at the brutal death of his father. She went to that hill knowing the significance of the fire. God, how could she?

The day following the funeral, Sir Thomas's lawyer went to Merifield and read his will. Edmund Catalong, his son, had been disinherited apart from the few acres of land over in Inishowen on which the burnt out manor of Horton stood. He no longer had any claim to Merifield. The property, including the hotel at Dilford and a vast sum of money, had been left to Sir Thomas's sister's son, Colonel Henry Fulton.

Edmund was stunned.

'You must dispute the will on grounds of insanity,' Lord Meckin advised later.

'My father was not insane, sir,' Edmund told him. 'I have discussed it with the lawyer. He knows the circumstances which prompted him to change his will.'

'Edmund, I am greatly disturbed. You have asked for my daughter's hand in marriage and now we find that you are practically penniless. I think I have a right to know why you were disinherited.'

'Yes, Lord Meckin, I agree.' What a mess I have made of my life, he thought bitterly. At least when he hears what I have to say it will bring an end to my being considered a suitable son-in-law, apart from my losing a considerable fortune. He told him about Rosha and saw the cold, angry expression on the man's face.

'What about my daughter? The fact that you and she have become intimate made us assume that your intentions were serious. On the night of your father's death she spent the night in your room, didn't she? I must say I was deeply shocked.'

'Yes, she did. I would give anything to undo what happened that night, sir,' Edmund said candidly.

It was obvious to Lord Meckin what had happened. Alice had gone to his room. The girl was in love with him and his wife had been encouraging a match between them for years; indeed they had all expected them to get married one day. And all the time this damn' young devil was carrying on with a girl over here. Damn it, it was not good enough. He rose abruptly to his feet. 'I must speak to my wife.'

Lady Meckin was in the morning-room talking to their daughter. Alice had been crying.

'He is penniless,' Lord Meckin said tactlessly, 'she can't marry him.' He bent over his wife's chair and said a few quiet words to Lady Meckin who stared at him unbelievingly.

'I don't care about money,' Alice protested. 'He's the only person I have ever wanted to marry.'

'Darling,' her mother said firmly, 'Edmund has nothing, not even a roof over his head. We'll leave for Scotland immediately. You *must* get over this. I don't think, from what he has revealed to your father, that he wants to marry you anyway.'

Alice jumped to her feet. 'Go to Scotland immediately? You mean walk away and leave him when his father has only been buried?' She ran out of the room just as her father was about to tell her bluntly why Edmund Catalong had been disinherited. She must find Edmund. After what had happened between them he must ... he would want to marry her, she thought selfishly.

Edmund, who had been walking in the garden, came indoors feeling deeply relieved that this thing between he and Alice was about to come to an end. Just then she came out of the room, calling his name, with tears pouring down her face. She clutched his arm and drew him in before her outraged parents.

'I want you to know, Edmund, that it makes no difference to me about your father changing his will, and I *don't* want to know the reason either. I love you and want us to get married as soon as possible.'

He looked at the tight-lipped Meckins and felt trapped; at the same time he was aware how brutal it would be at that moment to repulse this unhappy, hysterical girl.

Henry Fulton, Edmund's cousin, who had just arrived from abroad, was appalled when he heard about his uncle's will. Though not a wealthy man, he felt that in all conscience he could not deprive the rightful owner of what he considered to be justifiably his. Indeed, when he considered the circumstances surrounding Edmund's birth, the injustice was even greater. Their lawyers discussed the unusual situation and in the end Henry Fulton agreed to hand over the Donegal estate of Merifield to Edmund Catalong. The rest of the inheritance would go to Henry Fulton and his descendants. If he died unmarried, to his brother.

Somewhat mollified, the Meckins decided that there should be a quiet wedding on their Highland estate. Desperately unhappy, Edmund wanted to get away from Slievegar. Not a day passed that he did not think about Rosha; the terrible scene of her joining in the celebrations on the mountain-side haunted him. He feltbitter about so many things. His father's unjust will and the man who had caused his death. Finally, the attitude the Meckins had shown when they discovered that he was penniless. Only Alice shone clearly through all the hate and bitterness: her determination, support and warmth had helped him, though he did not love her.

# Chapter Sixteen

Nellie Boyce was terribly shocked about her sister Bridie's decision to keep her baby and go to Glasgow. How was she going to tell Mam?

'Nellie,' Rosha suggested, 'go over to Iskaglen this afternoon and see your mother, but first call in at the manor and give Edmund my letter. I want him to get it as soon as possible.' Rosha knew that he had misunderstood her action on the hill. She had written him a long letter explaining. Much as she disliked his father, she could not have wished him to suffer such a death.

Nellie never thought she would go near the castle again but Rosha's letter had to be delivered. The housekeeper, who had not got over the confusion about the ownership of Merifield Manor, made Nellie welcome. Wide-eyed, she listened to the housekeeper's incomprehensible ramblings.

'So everything's all right then, Mrs O'Sullivan? Edmund Catalong has the estate? I've got my own bit of news for ye. It's about Bridie.'

'I wash my hands of her,' the woman retorted angrily when she heard what Nellie had to say. 'Glasgow? What will she find there to do? No servants needed in that dump. Potato picking is all she'll find to earn a penny. Never get a man to marry her with that encumbrance under her arm.'

'Isn't it dreadful, Mrs O'Sullivan? The wee thing got around her heart.'

'Huh!' Upset and angry, Mrs O'Sullivan said gruffly: 'How's your master, Nellie? I hear he's been ailing.'

'The heart's not behaving well.'

'It would be an honourable way to go and meet his maker. Not like my master,' she said bitterly.

'I've got a letter here for Mr Edmund. Miss O'Neill asked me to put it in his hands.'

'He's gone to Scotland with the Meckins. There's going to be a wedding up there. Quiet, because of Sir Thomas's death. The young master's going to marry their daughter Alice.'

'Edmund Catalong's going to marry the girl Meckin?' Nellie repeated increduously.

'Aye, quickly and quietly.' Nora O'Sullivan did not approve of Miss Meckin. Her behaviour in this house was disgusting. Spending a night in Mr Edmund's room. Hooking the poor young man in his sorrow, and him not himself. Now a hasty wedding. That's what the spoilt madam had set her mind on. 'There'll be a mistress in this house for the first time in twenty years,' she announced.

Thank God, Nellie thought, relieved, that'll stop Rosha's nonsence.

After her mother got over the terrible shock about Bridie, she wiped away her tears and said: ''Tis hard for a mother to give away a wee thing when it's wound its way around her heart. From the sound of it, Nellie, she's forgotten who fathered it.'

Sean O'Neill realised that his health was failing. What was to become of Garton? If only Rosha and Patrick Murphy would wed he would be a happy man. Some other girl would snap him up one of these days. The lad didn't come round the place as often now. In desperation, Sean took an action that made him feel embarrassed. He spoke to Patrick.

'She's the wife I want,' the young man replied with honesty, 'but I'm not going down on my knees to beg, Mr O'Neill. When I come to Garton now she's always over in that pottery and has more to say to Paddy than meself.' Patrick's life had broadened in many ways. He had become more sophisticated, more sure of himself.

Damn it, Sean thought impatiently, the lad doesn't know how to go about courting a lass. 'Come to tea next Sunday, Pat. Invite her for a walk, man. Pay her attention. Sure it takes time and care to catch a fish.' Sean sounded impatient and out of character.

'Rosha,' Nellie said, when she returned from Iskaglen, 'I want to have a word with ye. We'll walk away a bit from the house.'

'Come over to the workshed. I'm mixing clay this afternoon.'

'No, I want ye right away from the house.'

'Why are you being so mysterious? Did you give Edmund my letter?'

Impatiently Rosha followed Nellie towards the hill. 'Did you see Edmund?'

'He wasn't there. Mrs O'Sullivan told me he accompanied the Meckins to Scotland.'

'Oh.' Rosha's voice went flat with disappointment. She'd thought that when he had read her letter and understood, everything would be all right again. 'Perhaps he considered it wise to get away for a while, Nellie. Though he doesn't like going to Scotland. There's a daughter and he finds it embarrassing because the family are trying to make a match between them.'

This is much worse than I thought, Nellie decided. She didn't know how to break the news. Finally, she said bluntly: 'Rosha, he's marrying that girl. 'Tis all arranged. That's why he went to Scotland.'

Rosha stopped dead and stared at her. 'What are you saying? You're making it up. He wants to marry me. When he left Dilford he went straight home to tell his father.'

'Good God, that's why he was disinherited,' Nellie said flatly.

'Disinherited? What do you mean?'

Nellie repeated what the housekeeper had told her. It seemed the best thing to do. When she turned to Rosha again, the girl's face was chalk-white. 'Sit down, love,' she said quietly, 'sit down.'

Rosha pushed her away. 'What am I going to do?'

'Sure ye'll marry Patrick Murphy and forget all about him. It was only a bit of a romance. Nothing could have come of it.'

'I think I'm expecting his child ...'

196

'Jesus, Mary and Joseph, Rosha O'Neill, what are ye tellin' me?' Nellie shouted, her legs going weak with shock.

'Edmund said he would marry me straight away. First he was going to talk to his father then come to Garton to see Daddy.'

The witless pair! How could they have planned such a thing wi' an ocean of difference between them? 'When did ye last see yer monthly trouble?' Nellie asked sharply.

'Not last month. I was due after I came back from Dilford and it's past my time again. I was sick this morning.'

Nellie could have howled with anguish. 'We must think.'

'Go on home and leave me, Nellie. I want to be own my own.' Rosha couldn't bear the pain. Edmund had married that girl after he swore nothing could separate them. The night of the fire on the hill ... why had she listened to Nellie and not gone after him? She recalled his look of surprised disgust. He had misunderstood. But it couldn't be just that. There must be something else. Nellie's hand fell on her arm like a vice.

'Listen to me, Rosha O'Neill, ye can walk the feet off yerself later but it's talk we'll do now. Ye'll have to marry Patrick Murphy.'

'Patrick? Don't you think I've sinned enough? Marry Patrick when I'm expecting another man's child? It would be the blackest sin of all.'

'Arrah, give o'er about sin. A bit late to be talkin' about it now.' Nellie said brutally.

Rosha looked at her bleakly, needing her compassion. To marry Patrick was unthinkable.

'He's comin' to tea on Sunday. By then ye'll have told Sean O'Neill that you've made up your mind to wed the lad,' she insisted.

'No!' Rosha protested.

'What are ye goin' to do then? Tell yer father the truth of the story and put him in an early grave? May God forgive ye!'

Rosha began to feel she was in a nightmare. She would wake up and find Nellie sitting by the bed with soothing words. But the nightmare was real; she was in an irrevocable situation. She was not brave enough to tell her father the truth and perhaps to do so would, as Nellie said, bring him to an early grave.

In a voice free from anger, Nellie said gently, 'You see, love, 'tis the only way out. If Patrick's courtin' someone else then it'll be a black day for all of us.'

After a long pause, Rosha replied in a whisper, 'All right. Now go back to the house and leave me on my own.'

'There's mist on the hill, 'tis no day . . .'

Rosha turned abruptly and walked away. Nellie had no peace of mind until the girl walked into the kitchen an hour later. She handed her a drop of whiskey; it was accepted without protest.

When Rosha woke in the morning she was barely able to hold the cup of tea Nellie brought to her bedroom. Inertia seemed to have gripped her body: she was in a deep grey cloud of depression. 'There's a meeting the night in the hall,' Nellie chatted casually. 'Yer father is handin' over control to Patrick Murphy. With Catalong gone, folk can rest peacefully by their hearths now.'

'That's good,' Rosha replied without interest.

'I don' understand it, love,' Nellie chattered on, 'but it sounds great. Yer father was talkin' about it to Patrick the other day. Some new Act.'

Both English parties were doing their best to keep the Irish quiet. Now, in 1898, a Local Government Act was passed which took the administration of county affairs out of the hands of the old Grand Juries and gave them into the control of the County Councils elected by the people. Nellie had heard another piece of good news from Willie, who had been at the shebeen. Barney O'Sullivan, whose popularity was increasing nightly, told the eager ears of his listeners that the castle lawyer had been instructed by Edmund Catalong, before he left for Scotland, to dismiss the bailiff and his attendant. The agent was furious. There had been roars of joy in the drinking house. Barney's back was slapped continuously and his glass was never empty.

Patrick arrived on Sunday afternoon looking handsome in his best brown suit made of fine tweed. His thick sand-coloured hair was no longer unruly but smooth and well-cut. A fine figure of a man, Nellie thought. He had a

198

quiet humorous manner, spoke authoritatively on the land situation and the machinations of the landlords during these final years of 'piracy', as he put it. The men talked while Rosha sat quietly trying to pretend interest in her needlework. After a while Sean tapped out his pipe on the hearth.

'Well, you young people,' he said heartily, aware that his daughter was not as ease, 'if it's a walk you have in mind, make the most of the day.'

Rosha and Patrick went down the road to the paddock which led up to the heathland, where the heather still sparkled with colour. 'How's your stepmother, Patrick?' Rosha asked to break the silence.

'Less of the mother, Rosha.'

'What about your father?'

'Doing as he's told. It's a terrible job trying to have a private word with him these days. I'm thinking seriously of building myself a house on that land of ours above where the minister lives.'

'Building? Are you thinking of getting wed?'

He opened the gate and as she was passing through, he looked at her and said quietly, 'There's only one person I want to wed.'

Rosha glanced away, her heart thumping with anxiety. He put out his hand and turned her face towards him. 'Rosha, is there any hope for me atal? It's you I want and not the girl that Mrs Maria Murphy thinks she's chosen for me. Another simple girl who will become no better than a servant, like my brother's wife.'

'You wouldn't be able to build that house, Patrick, if you married me,' she said with a little smile. 'Apparently that was part of the marriage bargain struck by our parents years ago. The man who marries me will have to settle in Garton.'

Patrick couldn't believe his ears. His hand fell off the gate and his arms went around her. 'Are you saying you'll wed me?'

'I don't think I'm good enough for you, Patrick Murphy.'

'Sure I'll be the judge of that!' He bent his head and kissed her on the lips, a fresh clean kiss that didn't stir but warmed her.

'You're so nice,' she heard herself saying, and meant it. 'How are you going to put up with me?' Dear God, let me be worthy of this kind man, Rosha prayed. I believe if I told him the truth he might still want to marry me. She looked at him again and suddenly was not so sure. There was a hidden strength and depth to Patrick.

'Don't keep me waiting too long, Rosha. You might change your mind.'

'My mind's made up. Yes, there's no point in waiting or else you might start building that house and accept your step-mother's choice!'

He drew her into the shelter of the hedge; this time his kisses were more demanding.

My prayers have been answered, Nellie thought, when Rosha came home with her news, and I haven't even finished my novena yet. An early wedding before the winter sets in, they said. Poor Patrick, if only he knew there was no choice. Ah, she sighed, Garton's going to have a share of happiness at last, for it's been a terrible year.

Preparations for Rosha's wedding went racing ahead. Grace came over from Slievegar to help. The larder shelves began to groan with an abundance of food. Cakes, pies, baked hams, pork, beef and roasted poultry. A barrel of salted herrings and a string of dried ling were stored in the pottery. Sea-shell food was not included: that was ordinary fare and found free on the shores around Slievegar and Iskaglen. Since Catalong's death people could pick freely again. Sean had invited everyone. Paddy and Willie cleared and white-washed the barn. Rosha decorated it with greenery. Patrick built a little platform at one end for the musicians; there were three fiddlers and two melodian players.

'Nellie,' Grace whispered to her daughter, 'O'Neill's not goin' to have a penny to spare after this wedding. Did ye know there's firkins of whiskey and barrels of porter at the back of the dairy?'

'Mam, I'm not blind.'

The sudden announcement of the wedding had come as a shock to Grace. She had never seen the young couple out walking though she knew an agreement had been made in their youth. Rosha's eyes had shone for young Catalong

200

and now he himself had a sudden wedding. Nellie's lips were sealed and Grace was not one to pry. It was a mystery. She'd pray that the wee girl would be happy because she loved her like a daughter.

On the eve of the wedding Rosha dropped exhausted into bed after the last hurried fitting of her wedding gown. It was a deep rose-pink velvet with a short jacket trimmed with braid. Grace made a little hat to match of the same material. In the morning a stream of people made their way to church for the wedding-service. Maria Murphy, magnificiently dressed in purple velvet, seemed quite amicable.

Nellie was furious. 'She knew you were wearing velvet,' she complained to Rosha.

'The colours compliment each other,' Rosha said, laughing. She smiled and laughed a lot on her wedding day — Rosha the bride. The other Rosha, who wept at dawn, was banished for ever. Patrick was not getting a good bargain; he was being deceived. She must do everything to make up for that deception.

Nellie was determined to resolve another problem that might seriously disturb the union on the night of the wedding. She and Grace, with the help of the Murphy's servant girls, attended to the needs of the guests. Paddy was in charge of the porter and Willie poured whiskey. Nellie paid attention to Patrick's glass all the time, especially when the main part of the reception was over and the fun began. He was unsteady on his feet when he led Rosha out on the floor to start the dancing; soon the rousing music had everyone on their feet.

'You look very beautiful today, Rosha,' he said.

'And you look very handsome yourself, Patrick. It's a wonder I never noticed it before!'

He threw back his head and laughed. How strange, she thought, Edmund always did that. The unbidden thought was quickly cast aside.

'I am *very* happy, Rosha. I can't believe ...' They were jostled. He held her close.

It was Nellie who decided when it was time for them to slip away from the barn. If he drinks any more, she thought, he'll pass out and in the cold light of morn' the marriage will be consummated. God protect us against such a disaster! The lad was not used to drink. A hangover could take away his gentle nature and certainly make him aware that his bride was not a virgin.

A fire had been burning in Rosha's room since early morning. Sean wanted them to take over his large bedroom but she had refused. From the window it was possible to see part of the island where she and Edmund had built their tree-house. She undressed quickly, knelt down and said her prayers, then slipped into bed. Patrick threw his clothes everywhere, then extinguished the candle and climbed in beside her. That night he was rough and hurt her: he never behaved like that again in all the years of their marriage. The music in the barn went on through the night. Finally it stopped and guests who were staying in the house blundered up to bed. Dawn streaked the sky before Rosha fell asleep. Her dream was so real that she woke suddenly, troubled by its rashness. She was relieved to find herself still in bed.

In the world of her dreams she had risen, stole down through the silent house and ran to the shore. The sea breeze was fresh on her face and the air cleared her head, which ached slightly because she was not used to drinking so much port wine. Nellie had been insistent over in the barn that she drank a few glasses to relax her. A bride should be relaxed on her wedding night, she told Rosha. As she stood on the silent shore, a kite flew over head. She put her hands up eagerly to catch it, knowing it would lead her to Edmund. It was his kite and somewhere he was standing, holding the string in his hand. Her pink velvet gown was the problem; it was preventing her from reaching up. The kite sailed higher and higher. I must return to the house and change into my old clothes, then I can go back and find him she thought frantically and thrashed her arms around in the bed. Patrick, fast asleep, did not stir.

The entire countryside had heard the music streaming from Garton. There were shouts of laughter when couples began to dance outside in the cool air. A young man fell into the pond and had to be dragged out again. The sound could be heard at Merifield Manor. When Edmund and Alice

202

Catalong returned that day from Scotland and were told by the housekeeper that Sean O'Neill's daughter had been wed, Alice did not notice the startled look on her husband's face. She was pleased to find that the big bedroom overlooking the bay had been freshly decorated and also the dressing-room off it where they would perform their toilet. In time, and with the help of her father's money, this neglected mansion could be quite comfortable if not entirely gracious.

Edmund had to return to Merifield sooner than he cared to because confusion over the deeds had involved some complicated legal attention. Only letters of importance from his lawyer had reached him in Scotland. Now he had a pile on his desk to attend to, which he did after dinner. Letters of condolence were still arriving he saw with a grim expression. He couldn't wait to get back to Sandhurst and resume his army career. Alice said she would probably return to her parents' house in London and Edmund would be able to come there when he had leave. The house in Montan Square where he grew up was no longer his. It would seem strange to return to the one next door, where his lack of a fortune made him less welcome as a son-in-law to the Meckins.

He stared for a long time at the envelope addressed to him in a round careless hand, then ripped it open and read Rosha's letter, not once, but several times. He heard her speak the words, warmth in her voice when she wrote about his father's death. Her concern for his sorrow. He put the letter in the desk drawer and locked it. How could he have judged her so harshly? Edmund poured a glass of brandy, drank it quickly and left the manor. Above all, he wanted to be quite alone with his thoughts.

Without considering which direction to take, he found himself on the path to the shore. Here the sound of gaiety from Garton was tempered by the harsh rattle of pebbles being drawn into the water. He walked across to the bottom of the field and looked up in the direction of the brightly lit house, then went down to the rock where he had first seen her all those years ago. With the ghost of her laughter in his ears, he sat there remembering.

Alice Catalong was upset when she realised that her husband had left the house without saying a word. This was the kind of indifference he had showed before they were married. When she went to their bedroom the maid was building up the fire and replacing the copper warming-pan in the bed.

'What is your name?' she asked the girl abruptly.

'Annie, madam. I only arrived from Dilford yesterday.'

Not a local girl. Pity. She might have been prepared to chatter. Who was it in this place that Edmund had been attracted to?

'I had a grand reference from my last employers, madam, the Misses Houston. They ran a young ladies' school.'

'Why did you leave?'

'Their brother died in Lisdare and left them a lovely property. Sure, didin Miss Edith tell me herself it was time they thought of retiring, and wasin Lisdare the centre of culture wi' a theatre and all ...' She saw the disinterested look growing in her mistress's eyes and bobbing a curtsy went to leave the room.

'Please shut that window, Annie, before you go.'

''Tis lovely music, isin it? Miss O'Neill at Garton was wed today.'

'Oh, who is she?' Alice asked, pulling pins out of her hair.

'Her father is Sean O'Neill of Garton ...' Annie's voice trailed away, suddenly recalling how close this woman's husband had been to Rosha O'Neill. The pair of them courting and nothing came of it. As if anything ever could! Him one of the gentry and a Protestant.

Alice Catalong lifted her head and saw the girl's confused expression in the mirror and began to wonder.

# Chapter Seventeen

As each day passed at Kindly Night, Bridie's love for her child grew stronger. Soon they would decide that it was well nourished and fit to go to the home for destitute children. She witnessed the heart-breaking scenes when girls had to part with babies whom they had fed and cared for over the weeks since birth. Other girls were glad to be rid of the encumbrance. When a nurse was around, Bridie pretended indifference towards her child. A young mother who became too attached was considered to be a nuisance and nursing time was shortened if possible.

Mary Anne had had a bad start and though Bridie talked to the nurse about her skinny wee limbs, she knew her daughter was growing stronger every day. At night when everyone was asleep she held the child in her arms, marvelled at her perfection and made plans. Bridie had developed a sense of toughness and cunning. She ingratiated herself with the sour-faced nurses and never put a foot wrong. It was noticed how hard she worked while the others preferred to sit on their backsides. Boyce was the one who cleaned the ward, emptied the chamber pots when they rose to danger point and scrubbed the floor when accidents occurred. Every day she washed dozens of baby garments and managed to sneak a couple under her mattress, in various sizes; the largest size might fit Anne when she was about six months old. Later in the day she always slipped out of the institution and passed on a little bundle to old Lily.

Impatiently she waited for word from Rory to hear when

it would be time to make for the Glasgow boat. One day Matron sent for her.

'Sit down, Boyce. As you know there was an arrangement for you to continue working here when your child was ready to leave. Unfortunately it can't go yet because you failed to give it a good start.'

'I'm doin' my best now, matron,' Bridie said humbly. 'It was wicked of me but ... it was how it came to be.'

'Yes, well, we're not interested in how a child was conceived in this haven for unfortunate girls. Its immortal soul and its future welfare is our concern. However, I've decided that you can start your duties straight away. In future you will work in the kitchen, helping cook, but continue to sleep in the ward and care for your daughter. You may go, Boyce.'

Bridie's first day on duty made her aware of the advantages of working in the kitchen. The food in the home was dreadful, mainly because it was cooked carelessly. In the great dark kitchen, where cockroaches were no strangers and cook, like the night-nurses, was friendly with the bottle, Bridie prepared tasty meals for herself to enrich her milk. Every day she had to make a large batch of biscuits; by increasing the ingredients she was able to put some aside and hide them in a tin over in old Lily's room. God knows what was ahead of her when she left Ireland. One thing was certain, she was not going to be a burden on Rory Donavan.

'Boyce,' the nurse said to her one day, handing over some baby garments,' 'put these on your child tomorrow morning.'

Bridie grew cold with fear. These were the clothes children wore when they were due to leave Kindly Light. Somehow she found words. 'Am I goin' to get rid of her then? Thank the lord for that! I'm away now to do a bit of washing in the slop-room.'

Her apparent indifference made the nurse say to herself as she walked down the passage, 'That's a cold wee bitch.'

Scarcely taking the usual precaution of checking that the coast was clear, Bridie sped out through the slop-room door and across to Lily. The old woman was sitting by

206

the fire fast asleep. 'Lily, wake up.' The impatient shake made the old woman jump and complain, 'Is the house on fire, daughter?'

'Lily, can I come and lodge wi' you in secret until me friend comes? I'll pay you. I must get away from that place.'

'Surely, if ye don' mind throwin' yerself down in the corner there. Yer man has paid me well enough. Maybe a wee penny for baccy if you can spare it.'

Before nightfall Bridie made another trip to Lily's. She packed her clothes in the old valise that Mrs O'Sullivan had given her before she left Slievegar. Also some food from the kitchen. When the nurses were at tea she took it across the street and hurried back again to prepare for her escape with the baby. As a member of the kitchen staff, she could dress up and go out openly for messages at the shops without being stopped. Bridie waited until all the girls in the ward had settled down for the night and only one lamp was burning on the table. She gave Mary Anne a good feed, then tied the shawl around her waist and cradled the baby inside it. The large cape which Mrs O'Sullivan had given her years ago was now a perfect fit. She slipped it on. Her full bosoms pushed the material outwards and hid the bump below. With her heart in her mouth, she walked out of the ward and hoped oul red-nose was at the gin bottle.

'Boyce, come here!' It was the voice of the short fat night nurse. Carefully, Bridie turned round. The woman was standing half-way down the hall. 'Come to the office at once, Boyce. There's papers to be signed and matron wants them done before she comes on duty in the morning.'

Mother of God help me, Bridie prayed, trying not to show her alarm. 'Sure I'll just relieve m'self and be there right away,' she called.

'Come *now*.'

'I'm nearly burstin', nurse. You don' want an accident in the passage, do ye?'

'Don't be long then,' the woman said bad-temperedly.

Bridie walked out of Kindly Light for the last time. When she was inside Lily's place, she shot the bolt across the door, sat down on a chair and said a prayer of thanks as she tore her cape open to look at the baby who was sleeping like an angel.

Old Lily laughed until tears ran down her cheeks when she saw it.

'I don' know what yer fella's goin' to say to that, daughter. Ye've just missed him. Yer to be at the docks tomorrow morning at seven o'clock.'

Bridie could have wept for joy. Nothing could stop her now.

Though she arrived early at the docks the following morning there was already a crowd before her. A miserable-looking lot of creatures, she thought. Mostly men going to Scotland to pick potatoes. Her valise was heavy and she felt tired after the long walk to the quay. She found a sheltered spot, put down the bag and sat on it, then waited anxiously for Rory to put in an appearance. She gazed at her daughter, warmly wrapped against the chill of the early morning. The tiny cheeks had filled out and she looked healthy.

Rory, with his cap pulled well down and a muffler around his neck, walked over cautiously to the crowd of men waiting to board the boat. No constables in sight. The story that he had gone to America had gained him some freedom; still, he was not taking any chances. He had no regrets about killing Catalong. His only regret was in deceiving his mother and Mr McGowan, the pawnbroker. McGowan had been good to Rory, letting him buy a quantity of jewellery at a low price before the business was sold. For years he had been saving hard, planning for the future. He had learnt a lot about the trade – gold and silver, the various stones. He knew where to go for bargains. Pawn shops. He heard there were plenty of them in Glasgow. Jewellery was often stolen from employers then pawned for a good price and never collected again. That's how Mr McGowan made his pile. Rory's dream was to start up a business one day; he was going to work towards that aim. In the meantime he would turn his hand to anything, earn money and keep his eyes open in the back streets of Glasgow where such shops were to be found.

'Rory ...' Bridie stood up and waved her hand.

He turned, then paused when he noticed the child in her

208

arms. 'Are you holding someone's wean?' he asked, coming over to her.

'No. I'm holdin' m'own wean.'

His expression hardened. 'Christ Almighty, yer not serious? Are you mad, Bridie Boyce? Get that thing back where it came from. I'm not taking you and that bastard to Scotland.'

Bridie's hand flew out and slapped him hard on the face. It was the ugliest word she had ever heard. 'Look at her, Rory Donavan.' She pulled back the shawl and the child's large blue eyes gazed up at them. 'That's *my* baby!' she screamed.

The crowd behind them became silent. Husbands and wives fighting on the quay was not an unusual sight and it was great entertainment. Passed the time until they were allowed to get on the boat.

'Hush, will ye!' Rory looked across his shoulder. The last thing he wanted to do was draw attention to himself. In a quiet voice he said, 'Take it back, Bridie. How can ye start a new life with that encumbrance?'

'She's my baby, Rory Donavan, and no one's goin' to take her from me.'

In a last effort he said, 'In that case I won't buy ye a ticket so you can't go to Glasgow.' It was untrue for he had already bought their tickets.

'I'll buy me own ticket,' she snapped. 'I don' need anyone to bother about me.' She pushed him aside. 'Bugger off, Rory Donavan.'

Speechless, he stared at her. Little Bridie, so gentle, full of fun, had come to this. Then he saw the tears in her eyes. 'Catalong did his vilest act when he abused you,' he said slowly.

'I hope he'll rot in hell one day.' Bridie no longer regarded her child as having anything to do with the man who had used her.

'That's where he is at the moment, Bridie.' He put his arm around her. 'Come on, alannah, they're boarding the ship.'

Meekly she went with him, knowing in her heart she would be lost without him. It was much later when she

209

happened to overhear a conversation on the boat that she understood what Rory meant about Catalong. The man had been murdered.

Bridie managed to get a corner seat on a wooden bench down in the steerage on the Glasgow boat. Rory stored their luggage under it and went up on deck. In his absence, she fed the baby and made it comfortable, then ate a biscuit and drank from her bottle of water. After a while Rory returned. He had someone with him. A big fella who looked vaguely familiar. Then she remembered.

'I mind you,' she said. 'Didin' ye cod us out of our places in the Red Barn years ago?'

Kevin O'Hara threw his head back and laughed. 'I'm honoured you remember. And who have you got there?' He looked curiously at the baby and at the girl's ringless finger. 'Yer wee sister?'

Bridie glanced at Rory then at Kevin O'Hara and said calmly, 'that's right, my wee sister. Only the two of us left in the world. Me mam passed away at the birth, and I'm the only one to care for her.' God forgive me for them lying words and take great care of m'mam, she prayed.

'Bridie, Kevin here says he knows of cheap lodgings in Glasgow, and there's employment around in the clothes merchants' establishment.'

'That's grand, Kevin.' She felt suspicious of this boyo, but with that welcome news she offered him some food with Rory.

'The place is called the Cat Pit because it's for women only. Rough, I expect, but it'll cost ye only a few pennies for a bed.'

When the boat crept up the Clyde the following morning, a white ghostly mist fell around it. They waited a long time before it finally docked. Bridie's first glimpse of Glasgow was a mass of dingy looking buildings, then a glow of sunlight rose and spilt across the city. Excited, she watched the transformation. Wasn't it the great beautiful place? That was the first and last time she was to consider Glasgow beautiful.

The lodging house for women was in a dark close off a main road. When Kevin walked in boldly ahead of Bridie and Rory, a big woman with a dark moustache who was standing behind a counter waved her arms and shouted, 'Nae men allowed in here. Hae ye no eyes in yer heed? There's a notice on the door.'

'I beg yer pardon, ma'am.' Kevin tipped his cap politely. 'We're anxious to get our sisters settled for the night.'

Bridie hurried up to the woman. 'Have you got a bed, ma'am?'

Without replying, Mrs Brogan, who owned the lodging house, took a key off the hook and threw it across the counter. 'That'll be threepence. If ye want to stay longer book again in the morning. Breakfast down in the kitchen will be another three if ye want it.'

Sixpence a day, Bridie thought. Rory saw the anxious look cross her face.

'Bridie,' he said, 'will you take a bit of money to see you through?'

'No thanks, Rory. I've got enough until I start earning.'

'They say Glasgow is full of thieves. Where d'you keep it?'

'In a strong purse next to me skin ... what are ye doin', Rory?' He was pressing a half-sovereign into the baby's hand.

'An old custom. You can't object to that. Bridie, why don' ye say yer a widda? It's a more likely story.'

She flinched as if he had struck her. 'I'll be no widda nor will I ever be a wife.' She couldn't bear to think of her body being used in that way again.

He saw the anger and fear in her eyes and understood. Kevin, who had been trying to pour charm on the fierce big woman, gave up and said they must go or there'd be no potato digging job for them. 'Good-day to ye, Mrs Brogan. 'Tis a fine establishment ye've got here.'

'Don't forget, Bridie, I'll be by again soon to see you,' Rory said.

'That ye won't man,' Kevin laughed. 'Ye'll dig all day and drop down dead every evening.'

'Watch that cod O'Hara,' she whispered to Rory. 'He'd steal the shirt off yer back.'

And I thought Kindly Light was bad, Bridie thought as

she climbed the bare staircase with its dirty walls. At least there was a clean smell in the other place; here it was stale, fetid with a sharpness she couldn't identify. At the top of the stairs there was a big square room with twelve beds. Luck was with her again as regards position. She had the bed down next to the wall.

There was no pillow on the bed, only a rough bit of sheeting covering the mattress. She pushed her bag underneath and sat down wearily on the bed. It had been a long walk from the docks. The baby began to whimper. Turning her back on the room, she undid her clothing and began to feed the child with a feeling of protective love. This tiny wee mite who was so dependent on her.

'What have ye got there, hen?' a voice asked from the next bed. 'A wee dollie?'

Bridie buttoned up her blouse and turned. ''Tis m'wee sister.'

'Hasn't nature been generous providing ye so well!'

Bridie blushed and laid the baby on the sheet.

''Tis a'right, hen. Mollie Duncan can keep her gob shut. Hae ye just arrived in Glasga?'

'I came over in the boat from Ireland.'

'Ye'd be as well to tak' a look at yer bedding in case any wee beasties plan to keep ye company the night. Lice like the Cat Pit.' Mollie held out her arms. 'I'll hold the wean for ye.'

Alarmed, Bride began to inspect the mattress. When she rolled back the bottom of the sheet and blanket she saw printed across them, THIS WAS STOLEN FROM THE BROGANS. She gave a peal of laughter. 'Who would want to steal them rags?'

'The ould wifies tak' them to the market and try to sell them for a few pennies to buy Red Biddy. They'd cut the hair off ye while yer sleeping. I've seen a girlie like you losing a mop in the night.'

'How long have ye been lodging here, Mollie?'

Mollie Duncan's black eyes danced in her long pale face. 'I dinna ken rightly.' She slapped the side of her head. 'Och, aye, since I've been working at Pillars doon the road.'

'What kind of a job have ye got?'

'Sewing buttons on men's britches.'

'Any chance of me finding work there? I'm desperate for a job.'

'Can ye sew?'

'Surely.'

'I'll speak for ye. What a lovely wee bairn. Not a bit like you.'

'She's the image of m'mother.' Bridie felt a little spring of happiness. What a lucky chance meeting someone like Mollie and to hear of a possible job. She opened her bag and shared the food. Only scraps left now but it tasted good. Her companion wolfed it down. 'Yer hungry, Mollie?'

'Aye, love, haven't had a bite since breakfast. They dinna pay much at Pillars. I get eight shillings a week and it costs me three and six pence to live here. By the end of the week I havena much left.'

'I'd need more than that,' Bridie said worriedly. 'Are there other jobs besides sewing on buttons?'

'Och, aye, I'm one of the lowest paid.'

Mollie told her where the kitchen was. They were allowed to cook a bite and boil a kettle but not allowed to take anything upstairs, she was told. Down in the dungeon of a kitchen Bridie filled a battered tin kettle and put it on the greasy stove to boil. Someone had left a pot of hot water; she poured it into a bath and washed all the baby's soiled clothing, then hung it to dry on the line above the fire. She made a pot of tea, poured it into her big bottle and hid it in her shawl.

The kitchen began to fill with women starting to prepare food. The smell of bacon frying nearly drove her mad. Tomorrow, she promised herself, I'll buy some bacon. Two women began to scream and tear at each other; another came in covered with a blanket with its glaring warning. When Mrs Brogan arrived she pulled the fighters apart and snatched at the blanket. The woman was wearing nothing underneath. Bridie looked in horror at the dirty withered body; it was the first time in her life she had seen a naked woman.

'Are ye trying to make off wi' me blanket? Get upstairs or I'll ha'ye oot in the street. Who owns them clouts on the line?'

213

Scared by the violence around her, Bridie said, ''Tis me, ma'am. They're the baby's.'

Mrs Brogan grunted. 'See that none of youse wans touch them rags or her wean will be messing the bed.'

Scarlet with embarrassment, Bridie retorted, 'You needin' worry, Mrs Brogan, I'm a clean body and that's more than can be said for this place.'

There was hush in the kitchen. No one ever stood up to Big Brogan. She'd have you on the street and it was the best value in Glasga. The woman held up a threatening hand at Bridie.

'Watch yer mouth, Paddy, or I'll hae you and yer effin bastard out too.'

Bridie gathered her things together and hurried from the kitchen. Please God, she prayed, don't let me have to stay here too long. Let me get a good job so that I can keep the wee hoard under me shift in case my baby ever takes ill. Mollie was delighted to get a drink of hot black tea. When she heard what had happened in the kitchen, she said, 'I'll go down and get yer things later. Big Brogan will hae it in for ye now. Bite ye tongue, hen, that's what oul Mollie does.'

There was not much sleep for anyone in the Cat Pit that night. A woman with long grey straggly hair, wearing only a shift, went raging up and down the floor, threatening everyone. Mollie sat on Bridie's bed to protect her and the baby. Finally Mrs Brogan came in with a man. He caught hold of the woman, who dragged her long nails across his face; he rammed her against the wall until Mrs Brogan collected her clothes.

'Thank God,' Bridie said when they bundled her out of the room.

'They'll throw her out on the street wi' the clothes after her and bar the door.'

They were no sooner settled down when screaming and crying could be heard from the room above. Mollie, who was back in her own bed, put a hand over and touched Bridie's shoulder. 'Don' worry, hen, thems the drunks up there. They'll all be locked in for the night so they can smash each other as much as they want.'

'How do they relieve themselves?'

214

'Same as us, 'cept the piss pots are in the room and ours are out in the wee lobby by the door.'

As the cacophony went on into the night, Bridie again prayed that she would not have to spend too long in the Cat Pit.

The room was airless and dirty. She and Mollie kept themselves as clean as possible but fleas and lice had a way of seeking out the two clean occupants. They had decided to find a room together where they could share rent and food.

On the day that the forewoman at Pillars said there was a vacancy for Bridie, one of the workers told Mollie that her husband had left her. The woman was prepared to rent a room and take her two weans into her own bed. Bridie was overjoyed at all this good fortune. The room in Dare Street was spotless and cost three and sixpence a week. There were two beds, a pot for cooking and a tin for making tea. The tiny grate which heated the room as well as their pots burnt sticks and coal which they bought at the corner shop in small quantities. No drunken prostitutes to shout at them or landlady to beat them into submission before granting the smallest request. Just a nice little sad woman struggling to bring up her two children on a pittance.

They moved into Dare Street one evening and the following morning Bridie rose at six, dressed and fed Mary Anne and accompanied Mollie and their landlady, Morag Dobie, to work. The baby was accepted as long as it kept quiet. A pile of rough tweed trousers and jackets were placed before her to be buttonholed. For six days' work, from seven o'clock in the morning to six-thirty in the evening, she was paid the same as Mollie, eight shillings a week. This was the lowest rate because they were supposed to be learning the trade.

Now Bridie was able to write home again letting Mam know how she fared. She waited anxiously for a letter in return as home-sickness wrenched at her heart. Though she liked the rough friendly Glasgow people, she disliked the crowded streets and the grubby tenement buildings which swarmed with people. Every day she thought of the green fields and hills of Iskaglen and the quiet bay.

The days were growing shorter and colder. Every evening

they lit a fire in their tiny grate and boiled a pot of soup made with bones and cheap vegetables from the market. Sometimes Bridie made Irish stew with scraps of bacon bought at the shop for two pennies a pound. There was always a loaf of bread and a scrap of lard in their food box. Fuel for the fire was heavy on their little budget. Not a coal was wasted. At night, before they went to bed, they filled the can with water, sat it on the fire and used it for making tea and washing themselves in the morning.

One day the woman in charge on the next floor sent for Bridie. 'There's a vacancy up here,' she said, 'where we do fine work for ladies of quality. Your stitching is no bad.'

'Am I gettin' promotion, ma'am?'

'I canna promise 'til you prove it with your work. You'll earn another shilling a week.' The Irish were considered to be cheap labour and the boss liked a low wage-list.

'That's grand. I'll try to do the job well. There's a box downstairs I keep the baba in. It'll fit o'er on that ledge in the corner.' And I'll go behind the bales of cloth to feed it, she planned.

The next morning a petticoat of fine white lawn was placed before her on the work table. She was instructed to work a row of small buttonholes then sew on tiny pearl buttons. The surprised look in the forewoman's eyes told her that her work was satisfactory. Next day she was given a length of ruching to work around the necks of ladies' silk bodices; she was also asked to sew narrow hems on two camisoles. The variety of work pleased her.

Mollie was furious because she was being paid a lower rate than the other workers on that floor. Bridie found it difficult to explain to her friend that she was now learning a trade. The basic skills she knew because her mother was a highly skilled needlewoman and had taught her. It was the variety of work passing through this upper workroom that had opened her eyes. She had seen beautiful garments in the shop windows, which she had gazed at every Sunday when she went out walking with Mary Anne and often wondered where they came from and who made them.

'Bridie Boyce,' the forewoman called to her one evening when the others were preparing to leave, 'come and tidy the cutters' work-table and empty the basket down in the boiler room. That Miss Pillar,' she groused, 'we always have to go tidying after her. I just canna understand how she manages to fill that basket everyday.'

Just the sort of job I want, Bridie thought with delight. Often she wondered where all the snippets of material went to. If she could find enough, there was the possibility of starting to make a patchwork quilt. This part of the workroom was unfamiliar to her because the mighty, bad-tempered Miss Pillar of Pillars was avoided by all the staff. She was known to have got workers the sack when they displeased her. She took the bisom and swept all the bits together.

'Would it be all right if I took some of the wee scraps?' she asked the forewoman.

'Aye, as long as the Pillar dinna catch you at it. I'll be away now, lassie.'

Bridie giggled at this apt description of the boss's daughter, a tall, thin woman who dressed in unbecoming shades of beige. Bridie fell on her knees before the bits of coloured silks, crepe-de-Chine and organdie, as though they were precious gems. At that moment they had the same importance for her. She sorted through them before throwing away the useless bits and discovered the reason for Miss Pillar's frequent outbursts of bad temper. There were several badly cut garments hidden at the bottom. It was obvious that the owner's daughter was not good at the job and her unsuccessful work fuelled the boiler every evening. Bridie trembled at the importance of her find. It would never do if Miss Pillar found out she had taken away her wasted efforts. She smoothed them out, ran down to the make-shift cot, picked up the baby and placed all the bits of material inside the shawl.

In the evening, after supper, Bridie reshaped a bodice of shell pink crepe-de-Chine, then stretched down to the bottom of the portmanteau where she found her precious roll of lace. When the bodice was sewn and trimmed with the exquisite lace, Mollie's eyes widened in astonishment. 'Sure them things sell for pounds in the shops,' she told Bridie.

There was one badly mutilated length of lawn cloth. Bridie

inserted another piece, sewed it neatly and handed it to Mollie, who possessed only a few grey tatters of underwear.

'Och, hen,' Mollie crowed in delight, ''tis yoursel' should be doing the cutting at Pillars.' What a clever lass she was and the way she rigged up the old piece of curtain over the corner of the room for them to wash in private. Mollie had never been so happy. She lived all the week for her free day on Sunday which she spent mostly in bed, sleeping or gazing at the fire while Bridie took the bairn out for a walk around the streets. They bought cheap stale bread on Saturday and toasted it before the fire for tea; spread with dripping it was a feast.

'Leave the wee thing behind today, Bridie,' Mollie suggested one Sunday. 'There's a cauld wind out there. I'll mind her.'

Gladly Bridie accepted the offer. The bitter wind was sending papers and dust flying along the streets. Sometimes she grabbed a sheet of newspaper and read it, then walked along, briskly, glad to be free of Mary Anne's increasing weight.

Two people were coming slowly up the street towards her. The man looked vaguely familiar. Who would she know in this city dressed like a gent? The girl was wearing a smart brown coat trimmed with fur, her bonnet and muff matched exactly. As they drew nearer, Bridie exclaimed, 'Why, it's Kevin!'

Kevin O'Hara gave her a quick look, raised his hat and walked on beside his companion. Bridie coloured with embarrassment, realising how shabby she must look in her old-fashioned clothes. He was ashamed to know her. How did that cod O'Hara manage to rig himself up like that? Sure he and Rory could hardly be finished with the potato digging yet. He must have robbed a bank, the sly twister.

'Bridie . . .' She was about half-mile down the road when she heard her name called. Kevin came panting after her on his flat feet, all dignity lost in the ungainly stride.

With hands on her hips, she demanded, 'Are ye sure I won't show you up?'

He laughed. 'Ach, woman. That was the boss's daughter. I was walking her to the stables.'

'Begod, you've come up in the world, Kevin O'Hara.'

A wicked grin covered his face. He slapped her shoulder as though she were an oul cow. 'Aye, girl, that I have. Let no man stop me!'

'Where'd ye get the clothes? Steal them?'

'Is it abuse I'm to get after breakin' m'neck to catch up with you? Rory Donavan's been searching this city for weeks trying to find you. When did you leave Brogan's Lodging House? He went there.'

'The fleas and lice drove me out. I'm sharing a room with another woman in a nice clean place and I've got a job at Pillars.'

'Pillars? That place belongs to Mabel's uncle, the girl you saw me with just now. Her father has a clothing factory and a warehouse where I got m'self a job. I'm a clerk,' he added proudly.

'You look a dandy.'

'Bought m'clothes in a pawn shop. God, Bridie, I'm glad you didn't come wi' us to the pratie fields.'

'Was it rough?'

'We're a down-trodden race to come over here to do such work. Rory and meself dug out the tatties and the weemin followed with sacks tied around their waists. The poor creatures had to lug along two wicker baskets, one for good praties, the other for brock – pig food. Sure it would break yer heart to see them squelching along in their bare feet, mud to their thighs.'

He's not too bad, she thought. There's a soft spot in his nature. 'Kevin, what's Rory doing now?'

'Got a wee stall in a market. Thon boyo knows a thing or two about jewellery. He took me with him when he decided to leave the farm. Jayus, Bridie, we were sleeping head to boot in thon farm on oul wet straw. The lassies at one end and the gasairs at the other. Now tell me how you're making out with the wee one.'

'Great altogether. I'm going now to look in the windows of some of the posh shops,' she said excitedly, and told him about the scraps of material and the use she was making of them. He nodded thoughtfully.

'Maybe I can do better than that, alannah. If you get a

219

wheen of things together ye could peddle them around the big stores. Come on, I'll show you a quality shop for the gentry.'

'Do they have gentry in this country, Kevin? The people on the streets of Glasgow all seem to speak with the same accents.'

'Gentry? Didin ye know girleen that the English paid a long call on this country too?'

The following day Bridie heard the landlady calling, 'There's a fella down here called Donavan wanting to see ye.'

'Rory!' Bridie tore downstairs calling, 'Come on up.' He stood at the bottom of the stairs. 'Rory, it's great to see you.'

'And yerself, Bridie. How're ye doin'?'

'Fine.' He followed her up to the room.

'Mollie, this is our next-door neighbour from home.'

'I'm pleased to meet ye. I'm just goin' down to see the landlady,' she said tactfully.

Bridie poured a cup of tea and gave him a slice of the fried bacon and batter on the pan. She noticed the good suit he was wearing and the nice clean collar. He handed her a parcel. 'Whatever is it?' She opened it excitedly and saw a length of dark blue woollen material.

'I thought it'd make you a frock.'

'It's lovely.' She could see it in her mind's eye. Full skirt, plain bodice with a little lace collar. 'Thanks, Rory. I'm never out of yer debt. What's the story about you settin' up in the market?'

'A fine wee business, Bridie. I'm buying and selling jewellery and bits of silver. M'dream is to have a shop one day. The market's cold in the winter, they tell me, and already there's a cranky wind gettin' at me through the open door.'

'God save us, ye'll have to buy yerself some red flannel!' They talked about home and then he said cautiously, 'Remember, Bridie, I asked you not to mention about my going to Scotland?'

'I didin, Rory. And I never will.'

'My story is this. I went to America, didn't like it and

220

came back to Glasgow. Keep it to yerself for a while. It's too soon for the story to go home.'

She touched his arm. 'I won't mention yer name 'til ye tell me. And one day I'm payin' every penny of that fare. Now, another drop of tea?'

'I'm glad you've got settled. How's the wee thing?'

'Look at her,' she said proudly, 'takin' notice of everything.'

'Bridie,' he said anxiously, 'there's a long way ahead. If ever you need help or move away again, will ye let me know? Goodness, I'm nearly forgetting the parcel Kevin O'Hara sent. It's bits from his warehouse that are no good, he says.'

She had been wondering about the other parcel that Rory had placed beside him. When it was opened she sat back on her heels, unable to believe what she saw. About a dozen pieces of satin and other fine materials, all in pastel shades. 'Rory, d'ye think he stole them? Look at the length of them pieces.'

He shrugged. 'O'Hara said they're no use for makin' things. See, there's a thread pulled and a mark on that piece.'

'The marks are all at the edge,' she said thoughtfully. 'I can cut them away.'

'Well, good luck to you.' He rose. 'Come and see me one day at the market. My name's over the stall,' he added proudly.

'Surely I'll see a look of ye first,' Bridie said laughing happily.

Over the next few weeks Bridie worked harder than she had ever done before. She rose an hour earlier in the morning and often worked far into the night, sewing away by candlelight. She dipped into her precious savings to buy some layers of wadding to make the design she had worked out for some handkerchiefs and nightdress cases. Rosha O'Neill had a pretty one, otherwise she would not have known such things existed. The pieces she picked from Miss Pillar's basket made most of the cases. During these weeks Mollie helped her by shopping, cooking and washing the baby's clothes. When they were paid their wages, Bridie insisted on giving her friend a small sum. Though she had nothing left over and occasionally had to take from her secret hoard, she felt instinctively that she was investing part of her security money for the future.

It was fortunate, Bridie thought, when Mollie's accident occurred, that she was so well ahead with her sewing because suddenly she had to do everything herself. They were walking home from work one day when a bare-footed boy ran out before a horse and cart. Mollie rushed after him and slipped on a piece of rotten fruit, twisting her right arm. The rule at Pillars was that if you didn't work you were not entitled to wages. And if you stayed away too long, you lost your job. Now Mollie had to remain at home, unable to contribute to food or rent.

When she wept at her misfortune, Bridie soothed her by saying, 'Sure we can cut out all the luxuries and eat simple food!' which made poor Mollie laugh. Though she was worried about their limited resources, it increased her determination to succeed in selling what she had worked so hard to make. She missed a whole night's sleep to cut and sew a dress from the material Rory had given her. If she was going to call at grand shops she must look her best. Kevin had hinted that the day they met in the street. 'Ye don't want them to think yer a gypsy, alannah,' he said, glancing at her shabby clothes.

Mollie's accident made it possible for Bridie to go without the child in her arms. The next problem was getting time off work.

'They'll no let ye off, hen. Tak' the time and bedam to them. Dinna go in one mornin'. Pretend ye had a belly ache.'

Kevin O'Hara had suggested her trying Macduffs first. They had a select clientele and a reputation for treating their staff fairly. She was not to mention where she got her material, Rory had suggested tactfully when he brought the parcel. Though Kevin was allowed off-cuts and end bits at a low rate, it would not do if he was known to be passing them on to someone in the trade. Bridie wondered how Kevin had really acquired the pieces but was too desperate to let it bother her.

222

In the large entrance hall of Macduffs, she removed her shabby cape and folded it over her arm. ''Dinna slink into the shop, hen,' Mollie said before she left the house. 'You look a right bonnie wee lady in that rig.' The dress and tiny bonnet-styled hat, which she had made from the same material, gave Bridie a lot of confidence.

Agnes Logan, the manageress, didn't give Bridie time to feel ill at ease. She noticed the shabby bag in the girl's hand and the neat fitting frock. The lace collar and the girl's hair and eyes told her a lot. Irish, of course. She smiled.

'Good-day, ma'am. I wonder if you would be interested in some work which I have done in my spare time?'

'Let me see.'

She unfolded the parcel and square of linen protecting the work and displayed everything on the counter: a pair of cambric pillowcases edged with lace and several other articles, including a child's cot cover, lightly padded, with a pillow to match. Agnes Logan picked up a handkerchief case beautifully made in ribbed silk and covered on one side with a square of lace. Just what I want for the Christmas stock, she thought. These things were becoming so fashionable.

'This is fine work. The lace design is most unusual. How did you come by it?'

'I made it, ma'am.'

Miss Logan looked curiously at Bridie. The only Irish girls she had seen around Glasgow were the riff-raff off the boats. Poor creatures in ragged clothes and black shawls, hoping to get work picking potatoes on the farms outside town.

'What is your name, dear?'

'Bridie Boyce.'

'Bridie, I like your work. Bring me anything you do and ...'

At that moment the door behind them swung open. 'Good morning, Mrs McFadden,' the manageress said. 'Ah, I see your son has accompanied you today.'

The woman laughed. 'Reluctantly, Miss Logan. He's condescended to carry my parcels.'

Ronald McFadden looked at Bridie, then to her confusion his head came back quickly again. She turned to the counter and clumsily knocked something to the floor; he moved to her side and picked it up. Bridie had never seen such a good-looking man; fair, with eyes a strange shade of blue.

'Oh, my,' his mother exclaimed, 'what pretty things. Are they for sale, Miss Logan?'

'Indeed they are, Mrs McFadden.' She nodded to Bridie. 'Would you wait in my office over there?' Agnes couldn't believe her luck in finding such an efficient seamstress. Customers like Mrs McFadden demanded hand-sewn garments and would not accept any work done by the new-fangled machines, as she called them, though God knows they had been around long enough. The machines were a blessing. She'd heard that the first ones to arrive over in Donegal had been wrecked during the night by tailors and garment workers. There were ugly moods here, too, because it was the only way poor women with children could make a spare penny.

Ronald McFadden couldn't take his eyes off Bridie as she walked across the floor. he had never been so instantly attracted to any girl.

Agnes Logan walked briskly into the office. 'Bridie Boyce, I would like you to bring work in on a regular basis. We can supply material and deduct it from your wages. Now I'll settle your account. As you see I've noted the items where lace has been used. Those articles are on a different rate.'

Bridie lowered her eyes to hide her delight. It was far more money than she expected. She felt like dancing out of the shop. In the entrance hall she stopped to put on her old cape. Before she could slip it across her shoulders, a hand touched her arm.

'Can I help you?' Ronald McFadden was beside her, his hand outstretched. 'It's rather heavy for such slender shoulders,' he said, unaware that its weight had been keeping Bridie warm on cold nights for years.

'It's the oldest thing in my wardrobe,' she said, laughing because, apart from her old black shawl, it was the only thing in her wardrobe! He laughed too, with delight, watching the changing expression in her eyes. Bridie felt a little spring of happiness, an indefinable joy that she had never experienced before. Ronald knew what was happening to him. He was falling in love with this unusual girl who spoke with a soft

224

musical accent. He glanced at the watch in his waistcoat pocket.

'Drat it,' he said regretfully, 'I've got to go and meet my mother.'

She went to move away, suddenly feeling confused. He put his hand out to detain her. 'Please ... Miss Boyce, may I call on you one day? I'd like to see you again.'

Alarmed now, Bridie said quickly, 'It's not possible.'

'Don't say that.' Agnes Logan called him. When he turned, Bridie had darted away. 'Will she be coming back again?' he asked Agnes, his voice flat with disappointment.

'I hope so, Mr McFadden. She's going to do some work for Macduffs.' Agnes felt sorry for the handsome spoilt son of the wealthy McFaddens, nursery gardeners with a vast estate who were planning a suitable marriage for their son.

On her way home, Bridie made a decision. She would work afternoons only at Pillars: that way she wouldn't miss out on the basket containing Miss Pillar's flops which never failed to surprise and reward her.

# Chapter Eighteen

Rosha had no idea that Patrick was seriously involved in any political movement. He had been to Dublin in the summer to take part in the celebrations to commemorate the 1798 rebellion when the Society of United Irishmen attempted to overthrow the government, but this was normal for any conscientious young Irishman. But as the months of her pregnancy slowly passed, she began to suspect that her husband's frequent absence from Garton had some serious significance. Around the country he was now regarded as Sean O'Neill's successor, a leader of the community.

Patrick went to Merifield Manor to see Edmund Catalong to find out what his intentions were towards the people whom his father had evicted. Edmund told him that he wished above all to act towards them with perfect justice, and indicated how he planned to carry out the improvements on the estate. It was soon known that many of the evicted tenants were being allowed to return to their holdings. Though Edmund gave them gifts of fir poles for the roofs which his father had pulled down, he had not the money to help them with proper reconstruction. Joyfully, people patched up their old cabins and tried to work the land which had fallen out of cultivation.

In the early days of their marriage Patrick suggested to Rosha that they might make more use of the parlour because he wanted a place for his books and papers where he could work undisturbed by Nellie Boyce. With her advancing pregnancy Rosha found she needed to rest in the afternoons. Now she dozed on the settee in there, or sometimes sewed or read a book. She missed going to the pottery but they all fussed about her catching colds or getting overtired, Sean more than anyone. Already he had brought the doctor to see her and made arrangements for him to be present at the confinement.

Patrick was always thoughtful and kind to her except when he went off on one of his missions without forewarning. His frequent absences made it easier for Rosha to bear her guilt over his delight at her pregnancy. One day she was rearranging a drawer in their bedroom for the tiny garments which she had knitted and sewn when her hand touched the box containing the ring Edmund had given to her. She opened it and looked at the opal. All the joy and hope they had shared together, she thought sadly. Clutching the ring, she went down to the parlour and lay on the settee before the blazing fire. For the first time since she married Patrick, Rosha wept bitterly.

She was in a deep sleep when a hand touched her shoulder. Thinking it was Nellie with a cup of tea, she struggled to sit up. The box containing the ring rolled to the floor.

'Patrick,' she said, startled, 'I didn't know you had returned home.'

'Why, Rosha ... you've been crying.' He sat on the edge of the settee and put his arm around her.

'I was dreaming.' She tried to smile. 'I think it must be one of the things women in my condition go through.'

He bent down and picked up the box which had fallen to the floor. She wanted to snatch it from his hand. When he opened it, she saw the puzzled expression on his face. 'How strange,' he said, 'Maud Gonne wore one like that when I saw her in Dublin at the '98 centenary. It must be valuable. She's a very rich woman.'

Rosha felt caught, stricken to silence, unable to offer an excuse for having such a valuable ring in her possession. A strange look came to his eyes and he glanced at the cushion, damp with her tears. The door opened and Nellie came in carrying a cup of tea. She closed it slowly, alarmed at the scene before her. Placing the cup beside Rosha she took the ring out of Patrick's hand and said: 'Ye've been through yer mother's trinket box again,' as though Rosha was a child

227

and inquisitiveness was forbidden. 'Sure that wee ring dosin hold a candle to the ruby one you gave her, Patrick.'

Rosha put out her hand to pick up the cup. It was trembling. 'Patrick says, Nellie, that Maud Gonne wears one like that.'

'Aye, wi' her money there's not much she need go without.'

'Maud Gonne is not like that,' he protested. 'She's a fine, selfless woman. Always spending her money on other people. She brought an end to the famine down in County Mayo last year.'

'My father says the poet Yeats is devoted to her.'

'Mam says she saw her over at Iskaglen when the worst of the evictions were takin' place, a great wolfhound by her side. The beauty of her makin' even the bailiffs stare,' Nellie told them hurriedly, glad that the conversation had taken a safe turn.

'The clergy listen to her because they know she has the good of the people at heart.'

'Begod, she must have some power in her, Patrick, to keep those boyos in their place.'

'Nellie!' Relieved, Rosha began to laugh.

'Patrick, the men are having their tea in the kitchen. Wid ye like to have yours here with Rosha?'

'I'll join the men.'

The incident of the ring was cast out of Nellie's mind. As far as she was concerned now, Patrick *was* the father of Rosha's child. Edmund Catalong was no longer a threat to the happiness of Garton. He and his ring must be forgotten. She tossed it into her pocket. Rosha lowered her eyes to hide their protest. Everything was going well for both her families, Nellie thought contentedly. Letters were arriving frequently from Bridie. Money in the one for Mam, and a request for as much lace as she could send. Bridie was getting on in the world. Mary Anne was a wee dote, she wrote.

Bridie hurried home from Macduffs with a large parcel under her arm. Miss Logan had asked her to work on a special order. A trousseau, she called it. Bridie sketched

228

a few designs, inserting panels of lace in the bodices and underskirts.

'This has not been done before, dear,' Miss Logan said. 'That lassie will have to pay a hefty price. The McFaddens can afford it!'

Bridie couldn't wait to get started on the work. On a previous visit, over a cup of tea in Miss Logan's office, the manageress had persuaded her to give up her part-time job at Pillars. Slave labour, she called their rates for workers. 'Don't worry, dear, with your standard of work you'll never be short of a penny.'

She missed the basketful of disasters Miss Pillar left behind her every day; unfortunately the supply of free material had ceased since Kevin O'Hara ran off with his boss's daughter to Gretna Green. She was now buying cheap cuts in the market and more expensive lengths from Macduffs at a special rate. At least she no longer had to suffer the guilty feeling that Kevin might have been helping himself. After all, he had helped himself to his employer's daughter, the handsome rascal!

She was turning into Harper Street to visit the market when someone called her name. Her heart thumped with a confused feeling of alarm and delight. Ronald McFadden overtook her and raised his hat.

'May I carry your parcel, Miss Boyce?' He eased it from under her arm. 'You have been avoiding me,' he said. 'I called several times when you were due at Macduffs and waited at the entrance but you didn't appear again.'

Embarrassed, Bridie replied hurriedly, 'It's quicker if I leave by the back entrance. I need to go to the market to buy spools of thread and things.'

'Surely Macduffs can supply them?'

'Too expensive. I get bargains in the market.'

He laughed. 'Miss Boyce ... Bridie. I want very much to see you again. Not just in the street. May I take you out to dinner one evening?'

'Oh, no,' she said in alarm, 'I never go out. I have to work hard for a living. Others are dependent on me.'

'Your parents?'

'My wee sister and a friend who helps to look after her.'

She saw the puzzled expression on his face. Then he said pleadingly, 'Surely a cup of tea and cakes in Lobban's wouldn't take too long? Let's go to the market first, then tea. Please?'

She paused before replying, though longing to accept his offer. Why not? Mollie was looking after Mary Anne. Smiling excitedly she said, 'Yes, all right.'

He called a cab. 'To the market and then Lobban's restaurant.'

Bridie had never driven in a street cab before. She rested her head against the padded back, enjoying the wonderful extravagance as the horse trotted along the busy street. Ronald put up his hand and turned her face towards him. Startled at the contact, she drew back.

'What is it?' he asked gently. 'I just want to look at you.'

She blushed and turned away. His hand dropped. 'I'm only paying you a compliment, Bridie. I think you are the most unusual girl I have ever met in my life. Why are you always avoiding me?'

'I don't think your mother would approve of your being friendly with me.'

He was silent, acknowledging the fact. Then said spiritedly, 'I don't care what she thinks.'

With more bluntness she told him, 'The manageress at Macduffs has been aware that you've been waiting for me at times. She has pointed out that your mother would not be pleased. Mrs McFadden is one of their best customers. I dare not lose my work. I'm just a seamstress, a sewing woman. I live in one room with my sister and a friend in a poor street not far from the market.'

'Why do you say you're just a seamstress? You're making my sister's wedding trousseau because she and my mother are so impressed by your work. Apparently your designs are quite unusual. You are designing, Bridie.' He took her hand and she scarcely noticed. 'Why do you think so little of yourself?'

'That's what the English have done to us over there,' she said, laughing. 'Sure, we think we're nobodies! But say all that again, Ronald. It sounds great!'

They were both laughing when the driver shouted down, 'Market, sir.' Bridie climbed out of the cab.

'Wait here,' Ronald told him, 'we'll be back in a minute.'

'If it's all the same wi' you, sir, I'll be paid now. The last man who told me to wait didna remember, and went in one door of the market and out the other.'

Impatiently Ronald searched for money while Bridie went over and gazed in the window of the bookshop next to the market. She did this every time she came here, wishing she could afford to buy a copy of the *Ladies' Dress Journal*. Lost in thought, she turned to find him by her side holding out a copy in his hand.

'You bought it for me?' she said incredulously.

He smiled. 'It's only a magazine and one which you might find useful for your work.'

As they were going through the entrance Rory Donavan came out of the market. He was gripping the bag in which he carried his valuable stock to and from the stall. Bridie had planned to avoid the side where it was situated, but here he was looking disapprovingly at her companion. She introduced them and after a few words, Rory walked on.

'I don't think your Irish friend approves of me,' Ronald said, smiling, and watched with enjoyment while Bridie made her purchases. Everything was carefully inspected and he noticed her delight when a small discount was given. In the carriage again, she felt her happiness was unreal, as though she was not entitled to such a feeling. Ronald McFadden was so kind, so thoughtful.

'Look what I found in there while you were paying for your purchases.' He unfolded a large, richly embroidered canvas bag.

'Is it a present for your mother?'

'No, it's for you. See how well it holds your shopping.'

How badly she needed a bag like this to carry her work to Macduffs. He thinks of everything, she thought, and turned to thank him. His eyes sent an unfamiliar feeling through her body. It startled her. The minute they set foot in the restaurant, Bridie pulled off her old shabby cape, then was horrified when Ronald hung it up among the mass of beautiful wraps and expensive furs. The silver tea service did not alarm her because she had been well trained by Mrs O'Sullivan. Her mouth watered to see a three-tier cake stand piled with delicious cakes, and a basket of hot scones and mounds of cream in a glass dish.

Ronald couldn't take his eyes off her. The dark blue frock and lace collar showed up her clear skin. 'If you don't eat, Ronald McFadden, I won't put a bite in m'mouth either, and I'm dying to try the scones and cakes.'

He kept turning the knife over on his plate. 'Bridie, am I to hang around several months before I can find an opportunity to speak to you again?'

She offered him a scone. 'I'm sorry ... I can't think of anything but my work, my responsibilities.' She said it firmly and he knew she meant it and would have to accept her decision.

When they left the restaurant, she would not accept a drive home. 'I've eaten too much. I need exercise.'

'Let me walk a part of the way.'

At the corner, where she turned to go off in the direction of Dare Street, she held out her hand. 'Thank you, Ronald, for everything.' He held on to it for a moment. She withdrew it gently from his grasp and walked away quickly. Her heart was beating fast.

At the bottom of Dare Street, Bridie heard a child screaming. Uneasily she hurried on towards the house. Though Mary Anne was a happy little thing and rarely cried or screamed, there was a familiar ring to the sound. She began to run, the heavy bag banging against her legs. Morag, her landlady, and her daughter were coming in the opposite direction. The girl, who had just started working at Pillars, had a bandage around one of her hands.

'That's your wean, Bridie,' Morag called. 'Och, surely that Mollie's no' on the batter again.'

'Batter? What d'ye mean ... you don't mean drink? Mollie never drinks.'

As they hurried through the door, Morag said, 'Is tha' all ye know? Even the Cat Pit threw her out one time. I wouldna had her here if it wasna for you, and me desperate for a penny. The silly oul bisom. Drink's ruined her life.'

Bridie ran up the stairs. The smell in the room was awful.

Mary Anne was standing up in the old cast iron crib with one arm caught between the bars. The child's face was scarlet and she was very dirty. So was the bedding. Bridie eased the child's arm free. 'There, pet.' She wiped her face, cuddled her for a moment, then tore over to Mollie who was lying in a drunken stupor. She lifted her hand and began to beat the woman over the head. 'Get up and out of this room,' she screamed. 'I've kept you since Pillars wouldn't have you back, I've even given you a bit of money, and all the time you've been secretly drinking.'

'Ah, buck off.' Mollie pulled a pillow over her head.

Bridie pulled it off again, picked up the pail of cold water and tipped it over her friend.

Furious, and with glazed eyes, Mollie sprang to life, a vitriolic flow pouring from her lips. 'Ye wee bisom. If it wasna for the bairn I'd beat the daylights out of ye. Irish upstart, that's wha' ye are! Trying to speak swanky, trying to be a lady, and you just an oul thieving Paddy.'

Morag came into the room and tugged at Bridie's sleeve. 'She's like that when she's on the batter. Dinna tak' any notice. She'll no remember a word when she sleeps it off.'

Bridie began piling Mollie's clothes together. 'She's getting out of my room. She's fouled the air. *Get out!*' she screamed at Mollie, and pulling her by the arm sent her reeling towards the door. Morag took the woman downstairs and came straight up again.

'You see to the wean. I'll light the fire. The wee thing must be frozen.'

As soon as the room was warm enough Bridie bathed Mary Anne and sat her on the rug while she stripped and washed the dirty cot, then bundled up all the soiled clothes, including Mollie's bedding, and put them outside the door to take down later to the wash house. Where did Mollie get the money to drink? she was wondering when her eyes fell on the tin where the food and fuel money was kept. She knew before she rattled it that the tin was empty; every penny of the week's housekeeping money had gone on drink.

Rory was right, she thought. He'd warned her not to trust anyone. One day he had pointed to a Savings Bank where he kept his money and some valuable stock and suggested she put her spare cash in there too. Nervously, she had gone in later and placed her 'emergency money' in an account. Every time she was paid by Macduffs she added to it. It gave her a feeling of security.

Her landlady came up again with a cup of tea. 'Bridie, there was an accident today at Pillars where the glove workers are. A spike broke and went through my Sally's hand. I was let out to take her to hospital.'

'Oh, I'm sorry, Morag. Is it bad?'

'Could have been worse. The thing is, she hates making gloves. Would you teach her to sew? She could keep an eye on the wean for you.'

'She can watch me working until her hand has healed.' Bridie thought regretfully about Mollie who had been helping with a little order for a stall in the market which sold bed linen. Cotton pillow cases with a trimming of cheap machine-made lace.

'We canna throw Mollie out, Bridie, or she'll land in prison again.'

'I know that, Morga. She was a good friend to me and I won't forget it. I lost my temper. Would you let her sleep on the settle in the kitchen providing she doesn't drink again?'

'Aye, the bairns are wild fond of her.'

If only Ronald McFadden could have seen what she came home to, Bridie thought miserably. One thing she was determined about: she would never again share a room with anyone. She needed time and silence to think out the ideas that were teeming through her head. Mollie never stopped talking.

Bridie felt she had to get out of the house again after the terrible scene with Mollie. She was coming downstairs carrying Mary Anne when Morag's son, Donald, came from the kitchen with a piece in his hand. The boy seemed older than his years because he worked so hard. Every morning before school he carried eighteen cans of milk up four flights of tenement stairs for a wage of one and sixpence a week. Later in the afternoon he went to work in the brickyard where his father and grandfather before him had been employed.

'Is the wean no' heavy for ye, Bridie?' he asked, his sharp little face full of concern.

'The shawl is well knotted, Donald. It supports her, but m'back aches after a while.'

'Why don' ye borrow ma's pram?' He opened the door of a room which Bridie had often wondered about.

'M'da used to sit in here 'cause he couldna abide weans. Ma's gan to let it when she can afford to buy another bed.'

Inside the room was a pram standing beside a sideboard. Two chairs and a table stood in the centre. Highly polished lino covered the floor. 'Donald, go and ask your mother to come out,' Bridie said excitedly.

'I hear ye nearly kilt oul Mollie!' he said, laughing across his shoulder as left the room

Morag was delighted to sell the pram for a few shillings. 'My man was gan' t'tak' it back to the market to sell. I wasna sure in case ... He's awa now and divil tak' him!'

Bridie took down a pillow and a blanket from her bed and sat Mary Anne in the pram, who looked alarmed after the security of her mother's arms. They all took turns to wheel her around the room; soon the child was jumping up and down excitedly. Rory was surprised and delighted to see her when she wheeled the pram into the market.

'Where'd ye get that perambulator?' he enquired. For the first time he really looked at Mary Anne and saw what Bridie had always maintained: that the child was the image of her mother. She told him about Mollie. He looked grave. Bridie was so easily taken in by people.

'Anyway, Rory, I'll have to stand on me own two feet now. I'm away to the linen stall to see if I can pick up some bargains. How'd ye like a piece of pork pie for tea? I'll bring some back and fetch two mugs of tea afterwards.'

'I'd enjoy that.' Stand on her own two feet ... God love her, sure what had she been doing since the age of fourteen? Still, when he saw the life of young people here in Glasgow, he considered that after all Donegal children were not so badly off.

Bridie managed to get the best part of a bolt of damaged

material. It was patterned with bright colours which immediately sent an idea for a dozen or more pairs of cushions dancing through her head. They ate their pork pie in companionable silence and while they were sipping their tea he talked about his business. The stall was doing well. One of his customers, a Jew, was sending others to him because Rory was beginning to get a reputation for being an honest man.

'That's great.' She was delighted for him.

'By the way, Bridie, I wrote to my mother some time back and told her I didn't like America and had settled in Glasgow, so you're now free to mention me when you like.'

'All right, Rory,' she said hurriedly, not wishing to know why the tale was necessary but more than certain that she knew the reason.

'Bridie,' he said hesitantly, 'that McFadden is a playboy.'

'I like him, Rory,' she replied quietly, noticing his frown.

'He's got a reputation around Glasgow,' he said bluntly.

'Have you been taking the trouble to find out about him?' she asked crossly.

'I feel concerned about you.'

She brushed some crumbs off her skirt. 'I don't need your concern,' she said unfairly. 'Miss Logan at Macduffs is concerned too, but for a different reason. She's frightened his mother might find out that her son is taking an interest in me.'

'So it's gone that far?'

'It'll go where I want to take it, Rory, and no further.'

He wiped his hands on a cloth and began to wrap some jewellery in tissue paper. He felt so angry he could scarcely look at her. 'Better move off now, Bridie. The market will be shutting soon.' I'll have a word with that damn young cur, he thought angrily.

Next morning Mollie opened the door and walked into the room.

'Hello, love. I just came to say I was sorry.'

'Don't walk in here, Mollie, unless you're invited,' Bridie said briskly. 'It's no longer your room. You stole my money and neglected Mary Anne. I have arranged with Morag to let you sleep on the settle-bed in the kitchen where you were last night. If you don't like it, find somewhere else.'

Mollie flinched as if Bridie had struck her. ''Twill be the Cat Pit for me, hen, if I canna stay here wi' m'friends. If I dinna earn some money I canna go there either. Could I no' earn a penny wi' you? You said m'work was good.'

Bridie couldn't bear her humility and look of desolation. 'Your work is very good, Mollie. I've got a lot on hand at the moment and could use some help. But touch the bottle again and you're out. Morag is a poor woman. You'll have to earn enough to pay her for a bed and a bite to eat.'

Mollie's face fell. She'd thought the previous arrangement of eating together and doing the shopping wouldn't change.

'That's the last word I have to say, Mollie. Just don't forget that I hate and detest drunks.'

''Twas the oul arm, Bridie, and me losing the job at Pillars. I won't touch a drop again. It gives me a bad nature. 'Tis the devil's water.'

'Well, we won't mention it again. Ah, there's Rory.' He smiled at Mollie who scuttled down the stairs. 'Thank goodness you came just now.' Bridie told him what had happened. 'What are you doing here at this time of the day?'

'Come downstairs to see this.'

A horse and cart were drawn up outside the house. On the cart was a large bulky object. Rory and the driver began to ease it down on to the road. 'What have you got there, Rory? A piece of furniture?'

He looked a little unsure. 'No, a sewing machine to help you get through some of the work faster. A man I know gave it to me at a bargain price. It's second-hand. I'll come back this evening and show you how to work it.'

'It'll no' go up the stairs, Rory,' the owner of the cart said. ''Twould bugger it up to try. Can ye no' leave it down here somewhere?' he added, anxious to be off again.

'Put it in the room beside the pram for now,' Bridie suggested. 'Unfortunately the room's going to be let later on. Wonder where I'll keep the pram then?'

'This room's for letting? For heaven's sake, Bridie, take it.'

She looked at him as though he was losing his senses.

237

'You've got to invest to get a business going,' he insisted. 'With this space you'll be able to do twice as much work.'

And because she always trusted him, she nodded her head and tried not to think about all the debt she was running up that morning. He touched her arm. 'When have I ever let you down, Bridie? You and I are going to do what the Irish seldom do in Glasgow — make good. Oh, by the way, Kevin O'Hara is back, walking around in great style with the heiress on his arm!'

'Sure, I knew that cod would land on his feet.'

'Landed on his backside with a soft cushion underneath. O'Hara likes the easy life and he's gone the right way to achieve it. Mabel, his wife, is expecting a wean. Ah, he enquired about you and says he will resume your business arrangements when his affairs are settled. The newly weds are looking for a house. A wedding present from his father-in-law. So.'

Bridie stood on her toes and kissed him on the cheek and wished with all her heart that this good man hadn't lost his notion of her sister. Poor Nellie, a skivvy to the end of her days likely, looking after that spoilt Rosha O'Neill. Rosha Murphy now. Just think of it, that nice Patrick dancing to Rosha's tune too.

# Chapter Nineteen

Doctor Friel was fast asleep when Willie from Garton came banging on the door. 'It's Mr O'Neill's daughter, Doctor,' the housekeeper said, coming into his room with a lighted lamp. 'Before it's time, it sounds like.'

Resignedly the doctor shook himself awake. O'Neill was probably prancing up and down the drive awaiting his arrival. 'Make me a strong cup of tea, Mrs Nolan.'

'Will there be time, Doctor? The man's in a panic. It's one of the hands.'

'Send him away. Tell him I'll be up in a while.' The birth's right on time, the doctor thought wearily. Twelve o'clock and the labour probably just beginning. I'll be there 'til morn'.

'The child is arriving before its time, Doctor,' Sean said, worry edging his words when the doctor arrived at Garton. 'Remember my wife ...'

Doctor Friel patted his shoulder. 'Don't worry, I'll take care of everything. Has the midwife arrived?'

'It's Grace Boyce. She's been here for a few days.'

A few days? Huh, that was well planned. 'A good sensible woman, none better. And she learned a lot from helping the old midwife.'

Grace and Nellie were in the room with Rosha. A fire burnt in the grate and the air was scented with a huge bowl of spring flowers. He sent the two women out and began his examination. 'How long have you been feeling discomfort, Rosha?'

'Not long.' She lowered her voice. 'Doctor, my father and Grace are making a terrible fuss.'

'I know. Everything seems normal here.' He tucked the bedclothes around her and sat on the edge of the bed. 'Look, my dear, it will be some time before your child is born.' He explained about the long labour for a first confinement. 'I'm going to give you something to make you feel sleepy. I'll settle down in that comfortable chair by the fire. The minute you need me, I'll be here.' He lowered the lamp and went out of the room. Grace, with a worried expression, was outside the door.

'Everything's ready, Doctor.'

'Good. Tell Nellie to leave an armful of peat in Rosha's room then take yourselves off to bed. I'll call you when I need you,' he said firmly. 'Now off you go.'

When he noticed her glance at the comfortable chair where he hoped to have a few hours sleep, he added, 'Rosha will be yelling her head off before a son or daughter puts in an appearance. For God's sake, woman, she's got a tongue in her head if she needs me.' *She thinks I'm too old for all this and begod she's right. It's in my comfortable bed I should be.*

Rosha didn't yell her head off when the birth pains increased. She moaned and lamented; no other sound escaped her lips. 'Where's the husband?' Doctor Friel asked Grace.

'Away on business.'

Damian Murphy was born at six o'clock in the morning. Grace wiped Rosha's brow and murmured, 'Yer a brave wee lass. There, pet, ye've a fine wee boy.' Sean, who was sleeping by the fire downstairs, was aroused and told that he had a handsome, dark-haired grandson. He wept with joy.

Doctor Friel left the house, refusing Nellie's offer of breakfast. *The birth adulation would go on for hours he expected. Never in his long years of experience had he been less needed at a confinement; Grace Boyce had been quite capable of delivering Rosha's son as she did many another girl's. Well, Sean O'Neill, you'll pay handsomely for my night's discomfort, and for the burden of a secret which, were it known, would shock the entire countryside. My God, the way history repeats itself!*

Damien was a few months old when Rosha realised with a

terrible shock that Patrick wanted to go and fight in the Boer War against England. She knew what they said – England's difficulty is Ireland's opportunity. A vigorous campaign had been started by the Nationalists to prevent Irishmen from enlisting in the British army. It was taken up by the *Inghinidhe ne hEireann* – Daughters of Ireland – a revolutionary organisation founded by Maud Gonne for the complete independence of Ireland. They walked O'Connell Street in Dublin handing out leaflets to Irish girls who kept company with the English Red Coats, trying to shame them. They followed recruiting sergeants into public houses and distributed to the customers thousands of leaflets which said it was an act of murder to kill anyone in an unjust war.

'The enlistment of Irishmen in the British Army has slowed down throughout the country,' Patrick told Rosha with delight. 'They're sending over Queen Victoria, the Famine Queen, to try and boost things.'

'I suppose Maud Gonne is encouraging Irishmen to go and fight for the Boers?'

'I didn't say that she – '

'Look, Patrick,' Rosha said angrily, 'we've had our war here, a land war, that should be enough for you and everyone else. We've fought the landlords – at least one very powerful and ruthless one in Slievegar. I just can't go wild with excitement over your interest in their Boer War.'

'I don't understand your or your father's lack of interest when an Irish Brigade is preparing to go out to the Transvaal to fight against the English.'

'Long before you thought of it my father and eventually myself were fighting evictions,' she said unfairly. 'Please don't go around here trying to rouse feelings for the Boers. There are men in Slievegar and Iskaglen who for the first time in years are beginning to enjoy the comfort of their own firesides again. Leave them in peace. Don't try to influence them. That's all I ask of you.'

'That was not my intention.'

'It's yourself then?' she said flatly.

He looked uncomfortable. Rosha jumped to her feet, scattering all the papers on the desk and knocking over a vase which crashed to the floor with a loud splintering noise. 'How could you even think of it? My father has become a semi-invalid. Garton is your responsibility now — and you're going to walk off to war. Much as I sympathise with the Boers, I think your place is here in Slievegar, apart from your numerous trips around the country.'

'You know, Rosha,' he said quietly, 'I would have given anything to have been here for the birth of our son. It grieved me that I was not at home.' She looked away, guilt, pain and anger driving her finger nails into the wood of the table. 'The Boers,' he went on, 'are confident of defeating the English. There are manoeuvres that will outwit them in the end. Help from our Irish Brigades now will make ...'

'I *don't* want you out in the Transvaal, Patrick. I want you in my bed. I want another son — soon. Then a daughter, two of them. I want a houseful of children. I grew up an only child. So did my father. There's been far too many lonely children at Garton.'

'Begod, if that dosin settle ye, Patrick Murphy, I don't know what will,' Nellie said, coming in with a bisom and shovel to sweep up the broken vase.

'Nellie, I dislike your habit of listening to conversations.'

'I dislike the way you're drying up that girl's milk. Didin ye know, ye thick skull, that a nursing mother shouldn't be disturbed?'

Without taking his eyes off Rosha, he said, 'Go out, Nellie Boyce, and mind your own business.' She shut the door gently behind her. Patrick walked around the table and took Rosha in his arms. 'I love my country, and I love you very much, too.'

Begod, he's got that the wrong way round, Nellie grumbled to herself at the keyhole. Irishmen must be the worst lovers in the world. She felt tired and grumpy these days; what with helping Rosha with the baby, extra housework, and carrying trays upstairs to Sean O'Neill because the doctor had ordered him to spend more time in bed. O'Neill had longed for a grandson. Now that a fine wee lad had arrived, he seemed to be fading.

The arrival of the sewing machine made all the difference to the work in Bridie's workshop, for that's what

242

Morag's front room had become. From those first lessons given by Rory some months ago, she had taught herself how to use the machine confidently and efficiently. As before, all her work was hand-finished in the beautiful feathery stitching that had brought recognition and eventually promotion at Pillars.

Everyone worked hard, including Mollie who seemed to be keeping off the bottle. When her breath smelt of cloves they all kept a tight watch on her in case she went on the batter again. Sally was a natural needlewoman; as well as sewing, the girl looked after Mary Anne who loved and trusted her. Morag also worked for Bridie. She had been dismissed from Pillars for throwing a tin of pins at Miss Pillar who had refused to pay the few shillings compensation which had been promised for the injury to Sally's hand.

With all this extra help Bridie realised she would have more time to develop her own designs and increase output. Macduffs were delighted with the work she supplied and gave her another big order for Christmas.

'We'll do a window, Bridie, with your special designs — no trouble about your supply of lace, dear?' Agnes Logan asked quickly.

'No, my mother can keep me supplied because she's got a little group of neighbours working together. They need the money, Miss Logan,' she said pointedly, 'and as long as I can give them a fair price, Mam can badger them to get on with it.'

'My, our window display garments are not going to come cheaply! Husbands with money will have to dig deep in their pockets this Christmas. We'll do special presentation boxes too. That'll put the price up.'

The mention of Christmas made Bridie think. Morag had made animals and dolls for her children when they were younger, which she had passed on to Mary Anne. Another entry went into her notebook. Toys. The set of cushions they made for the market stall was a great success. Why not invest in velvet and offer a range to Macduffs and some of the other big shops? There was one in Argyll Street she might try. Though Bridie had a fair turn-over now, there were four wages to be paid every week, including her own. Somehow there wasn't all that much left to put in her special account at the bank. Rory said Macduffs were taking advantage of her and she should be paid more by this time.

The following week she took along a sample cushion cover to Macduffs; it was worked in panels of velvet and satin. She made a point of telling Miss Logan that she had done a different design for a shop in Argyll Street. The manageress's head shot up.

'My, Bridie,' she said sharply, 'you're becoming very businesslike. I thought we had exclusive rights to all your work for the high class market?'

With equal sharpness, Bridie said: 'I didn't know we had that arrangement, Miss Logan.'

The woman laughed uncomfortably. She was receiving a special commission through this lassie's work; every sale to the nobs gave her a bigger pay package. Miss McFadden's trousseau had allowed her to put a tidy bit of money aside. If Agnes Logan's conscience reproached her for being a little greedy she dismissed the thought quickly. After all, talented though the lassie was, she was no more than an outworker and lucky to have a market in Macduffs.

'Bridie . . .' Her heart leapt at the sound of Ronald McFadden's voice as she walked away from Macduffs. She no longer slipped out the back way as Miss Logan had suggested but left by the front entrance, half-hoping she would see him again, yet not sure that she wanted to. She had heard that he and his mother had been abroad. Thank goodness she was wearing her new blue suit, a bargain from the second-hand clothes stall at the market. 'I was hoping I'd meet you. Would you take tea with me?'

'Yes, thank you.' He went to hold up his cane for a cab. 'Could we not walk, Ronald? It's such a lovely day.'

Coming towards them was a couple who had just alighted from a carriage. It was Kevin O'Hara, wearing a pale grey suit, and his wife Mabel. Bridie saw the surprised look in Kevin's eyes for Ronald had placed her hand in the crook of his arm. Proudly Kevin introduced his wife who clung to his arm tightly as if she was frightened he would run away. Ronald and Mabel apparently knew each other and they began to chat about their families.

244

'Kevin,' Bridie said quickly, making the most of this opportunity, 'I have a little workshop now. Could you supply me with some material? Trade reductions?'

'A workshop? Isn't that grand.' He reached in his pocket and handed her a card. 'That's my business address, Bridie,' he said, trying to sound casual.

'Thanks, Kevin. It will make all the difference if I can have a wholesale supplier.'

He winked. 'Leave it to me.'

He may be a bit of a trickster, Bridie thought warmly, but he's loyal to old friends. To think how they had landed in Glasgow to work in menial jobs. Now they were behaving like their betters. When they parted, Ronald said, laughing, 'I hear your friend swept Mabel off her feet!'

'All the way to Gretna Green and into a cushy job for the rest of his life.'

He laughed. 'Have you known him long?'

'We met many years ago.' She thought of the Red Barn and the rough stone floor where they had all lain. How shocked Ronald would be if he knew she had been on her way to a hiring fair. He treated her as if she were somebody and was giving her great confidence.

'What are you thinking about?'

Guilelessly she said, 'You ...'

'I think of you all the time.' His hand tightened on her arm. 'I was longing to see you again.'

Her heart began to race at his words. She wanted their friendship to go on for ever, just like this, walking out and taking tea. She was terrified to think of it going any further, yet longed to feel his arms around her. There was the dark secret in her life: her illegitimate child. If he ever found out, he would probably turn away in disgust.

While they were taking tea he pleaded to be allowed to call for her one evening. 'We could go to the theatre or anywhere you like.' When he got no response, he said firmly, 'Bridie, I must see you soon. Will you walk with me in the park tomorrow afternoon? Surely you can spare a half-hour from your work?' He was desperate to take her in his arms.

'Yes, all right,' she said, her eyes shining with happiness.

Ronald knew a quiet place where, under a willow tree, he kissed her for the first time. Over the next few weeks they met frequently. Once the branches of the willow fell around them, Bridie flew into his arms. Ronald was tortured by his increasing love and desire for her. He knew his mother would be outraged but he was determined to marry her. He had never made love so gently; and though it drove him mad at times, he was reluctant to visit one of the many 'ladies' in Glasgow. After Bridie it would seem distasteful. Lord, no one would believe he was such a reformed character!

It was a wet afternoon with a grey haze hanging over Glasgow. Bridie was thinking nostalgically of the clear blue skies at Iskaglen when a cab drew up outside the house. She pushed aside her needlework and rushed downstairs. Rory and Kevin were standing on the doorstep, each with a large parcel under their arm. She invited them upstairs where the kettle was simmering by the fire.

'Isn't it great to see the pair of ye?' she said happily, heating the pot for tea.

Kevin tipped the hat to the back of his head and walked restlessly around the room. 'Arrah, Bridie, it does m'heart good to have two friends from home to talk with and know that yer both doin' well and earnin' an honest penny.'

She gave a peal of laughter. That Kevin! 'I suppose you're a manager in your wife's family business by now?' she said, her eyes on Rory struggling with the string on one of the parcels.

'Getting there, alannah, getting there.'

She looked again at Rory who was wearing a new suit. Taller and better built than Kevin, she suddenly thought what a handsome man he was. He lifted his head and smiled. 'Rory, I'm just thinking what a fine figure of a man ye are, but don't be too long about getting that parcel open. Kevin, come on, do the other one.'

She buttered slices of the soda bread she had baked that morning. Kevin picked up one and began to eat it. 'God love ye, Bridie, sure I haven't tasted a piece of scone since I left home.

'Teach Mabel how to make it.'

'Thon girleen couldn't boil an egg,' he said quickly, and for the first time Bridie wondered if Kevin felt uncomfortable among the wealthy Glasgow family. Ah, well, there could be worse burdens! 'Did yer man here tell ye about his good fortune?' he asked her.

'What's happened, Rory?'

'I signed a contract with my Jewish friend this week and I'm taking o'er a business premises in Argyll Street.'

'Opening a shop? Oh, I'm so pleased, Rory.' Impulsively she went over and for the first time in years, put her arms around him and kissed his cheek. He bent over the parcel quickly and pulled it free of the thick cord. Again, Bridie exclaimed in pleasure. It was a bolt of white satin. Kevin ripped the cord carelessly off the other parcel and tossed a mass of coloured lengths across her bed: crepe-de-Chine, voile, organdie, silks and satin.

'Pay for the bolt of satin, Bridie,' he said. 'There's a bill in there somewhere. This other parcel is just odd bits. Not a penny for them.'

'You're a darlin', Kevin, and thank God still a bit of a crook,' she said, glancing at the low figure on the bill.

The two men roared with laughter and sat down to their tea, finishing off the entire scone of bread with great enjoyment. They laughed and talked about Ireland, sometimes breaking into Gaelic or, forgetting how anxiously they were trying to improve their speech, lapsing into dialect.

'Do you mind, Bridie, if I stay a while?' Rory asked when Kevin left. 'Glasgow is a lonely place on a Sunday. I'd love a wee house just outside the town and a bit of ground where I could get my hands into the soil again. God, how I miss turning over the good clean earth.'

'Stay, Rory and welcome. It's my day to take Mary Anne to the park. Would you like to come with us? The rain has ceased and with luck that blade of sunshine lurking up behind the clouds might put in an appearance.'

Mary Anne jumped with excitement when she realised they were going for a walk.

'She's a lovely wee thing,' Rory said as they pushed the pram down the street. How he longed to take care of them both. He loved Bridie but was well aware she regarded him only as a friend. The dream of a little house with a garden grew stronger each day though it was touched with bleakness at the thought of there being no one to share it with. He couldn't help worrying about Bridie, especially since Kevin told him he saw her walking out with Ronald McFadden.

'Rory, are ye thinking about your shop?' Bridie asked. 'You've got an anxious look on your face.'

There was a time when he would have said, I'm worrying about you. Now he realised how unwise it would be to say anything. She was rapidly growing into an independent young woman. He must not do anything to spoil the happy relationship between them. They walked along briskly, enjoying the clean pure air in the park and the scent from the few blossoms on the shrubs. Mary Anne laughed and chattered with excitement. Rory held out his arms and she immediately reached towards him. Bridie wheeled the empty pram, watching in amazement at the way Rory had taken to her child. He paused to let Mary Anne have time to notice the birds and grasp the branches waving above their heads, then walked along slowly holding her hand. When rain threatened to fall again, he put her back in the pram and pulled up the hood.

Back at Morag's front door, he said reluctantly, thinking of the dreary room at his digs, 'Well, I'll be away now Bridie and let you get on with your work.'

'Come on up and have a cup of tea before you go, Rory.'

The kettle sitting on the tiny hob of the fireplace was singing away. Bridie wet the tea and sat Mary Anne on a blanket spread across the floor, where she chewed on a crust of bread.

'Rory, there's something I want to show you. No, don't spoil her,' she protested as the child held up her arms to him.

'She's lovely, Bridie. I mind you at that age, always tottering after Nellie.'

She glanced up at the mention of her sister's name. 'Is it all over between you?'

'Years ago. We're the best of friends. That's the way it is now.'

'Look at this journal, Rory.' She flicked over the pages and pointed to a page displaying ladies' petticoats and other garments. 'That's the kind of work I do except my designs are different. I insert panels of lace or add touches of it to the material. Miss Logan at Macduffs was very excited when I first showed her my work. Now it has become popular with her customers. They're doing a full window display in December and selling garments in special presentation boxes.'

'Have you been offered a higher rate for your work yet?' he asked quickly.

'No, I haven't, though I have hinted several times. What I was wondering about, Rory, do ye think I should send my designs to the editor of this journal? Wouldn't it be great to see them printed? I might even get a free copy. Do you think they would be interested?'

His frown was deepening. 'Wait a minute, Bridie, let me get this right. You do the designs, all the work, and Macduffs are still paying you at the same rate?'

'Here's my little account book, see how it works. The market business is very good and Mollie and Sally like doing that kind of plain sewing.'

He glanced through the book and put it down. 'Bridie, have you taken note of Macduff's prices in their windows?'

'They don't put prices on articles in that department. The ladies who buy delicate underwear are not bothered about cost.'

'Hah! Hand made silk underwear and the finest Irish lace. Mark my words, the customers are paying through the nose.'

'Hand finished since I got the machine.'

'You need another machine,' he said thoughtfully.

Wouldn't that be great altogether? thought Bridie. No need to keep changing from tough cotton thread to silk all the time. And one worker getting impatient waiting for the other to finish.

'This is what I suggest,' Rory said thoughtfully. 'Write out something for this editor and include copies of your sketches. Tell them that you work for Macduffs and about the special window display in December.'

'Wouldn't I need to mention it to Miss Logan first?'

'Hold your patience! When the letter is written and acknowledged, then tell Miss Logan.'

'Rory, she'll be furious.'

He rose to his feet and looked down at her. 'Bridie, do you not realise that this could be the chance of a lifetime? A chance to make it on your own. You won't need Macduffs if this fasion editor is interested. You'll have private clients, who'll pay top prices, and demands from other shops.' He thought of the empty premises next door to the shop he was renting from his Jewish friend. Just right for Bridie. A good address in town for wealthy clients. Begod, she'd be made!

As Rory walked away he thought, This has been my happiest day since I arrived in Glasgow.

# Chapter Twenty

The surprised look on Nellie's face told Rosha there was something of importance in the letter she was reading.

'Bridie wants Mam to go and visit her in Glasgow. Did ye ever hear the like? She suggests we put her on the Glasgow boat at Lisdare and they'll meet it at the other end.' Nellie shook her head impatiently. 'As if m'mother would ever face a journey like that! Sure that boat leaves at eight o'clock in the morning.'

Rosha thought for a moment. 'If we set out a five o'clock or earlier ... You could look after Damien and Father and I'll take Paddy.'

Nellie folded the letter. 'We'll not get into a fuss about it for divil a boat will Mam take,' she said dismissively. 'Sure she's never even been as far as Lisdare.'

Rosha was inclined to agree. They were both wrong. Grace was delighted at the idea. 'If ye stick me on the Glasgow boat I've got nothin' to worry about. I'll find another oul body like meself and sit beside her and yarn. Anyway,' she said in a brisker tone, 'there's a load of lace t'go over. The weemin are working day and night gettin' it done. Bridie's needin it.'

On the morning she was due to leave, Grace, who had spent the night at Garton, rose at four o'clock, went down to the warm kitchen where she washed and dressed, then made a pot of porridge and filled the big iron pan with slices of ham and eggs. The smell got Paddy out of bed. Damien, a sturdy little boy of nine months, spent the night in Nellie's room so that he would not be disturbed by his mother's early rising.

As they were turning out of the drive, Rosha noticed her father standing at his window. They all waved vigorously. Sean opened the window and called out, 'God speed your journey, Grace.'

'Isin he about early, Rosha?' Grace commented.

'Sometimes he feels easier if he gets up and walks around the room. His breathing is so difficult,' she said worriedly.

'Bejay, that oul jail in Lisdare was the ruination of the man,' Paddy grumbled.

''Twas, Paddy,' Grace agreed. ''Tis not the best of mornin's, is it, Rosha?' she said, deliberately changing the conversation. 'I feel like a lady in this grand outfit ye gave me, pet.'

'Better on your back, Grace, than hanging away up there in the wardrobe,' Rosha replied, looking at the runnels of mist lying on the fields. The coat, which had belonged to Rosha's mother, was made of grogram with braid down the front and around the collar. The hat, neat and perky, had a feather adorning the back. The rig took years off Grace's age.

They made good time and arrived in Lisdare ready to exercise their legs and have something to eat. Rosha had packed two separate baskets of food, one for the journey and another for Grace to eat on the boat. She saw Grace on board where she found her a comfortable seat near two elderly women.

'Paddy,' she said when she joined him again, 'I'll go and do some shopping and we'll meet in the town square about an hour's time.' he nodded happily and went off to enjoy this unexpected trip to the big town.

As Rosha was passing the Catholic church she decided to go in and say a prayer for her father's health. She had been here twice before for confession. The last time was a week before her marriage when the young priest of the previous occasion had become more matured, she recalled. If he was shocked by her confession that day she was not aware of it. He was strict and forbidding and stern about her sin of deception. She left the church again and took a lane that led to the centre of the town where the shops were situated. Coming towards her was an army officer. He moved out on the road to allow her the use of the narrow pavement, then stopped dead.

252

'Rosha ...'

The colour drained from her face. They approached each other slowly, their eyes filled with shocked surprise. Sometimes she had wondered what they would say when they met again. Enquire about each other's children, work ...? It was not going to be easy or casual like that at all. How could it ever be so? she wondered now, her eyes widening in distress.

'God, Rosha!' He held out his hand and taking hers led her to the little park nearby which, like the lane, was deserted.

'After all this time,' he said, his eyes searching her face. 'There's no time to say all the things I have said to you so often in my thoughts. I've got to be at the barracks soon.'

'There's nothing we can say now, Edmund. It's too late,' she said sadly.

'On your wedding day,' he went on with bitterness, 'I returned to Slievegar and read your letter. Afterwards, I stood on the shore below the field where we played as children.'

And on my wedding night I dreamt that I went down there. 'It wasn't just the fire on the hill, Edmund, was it? There was something else? I've always told myself so. *That* made it bearable, your marrying ...'

'Yes,' he said with increasing bitterness, 'there was something else.' She stepped aside to avoid a cluster of daisies as they walked slowly around the park. She was empty of thoughts and words just aware that he was there by her side and of the joy rising in her heart.

'I'm sailing today for the Transvaal. It was postponed once before.'

'The Boer War? Edmund, take great care, won't you?' She gripped his hand tightly then suddenly smiled. 'Thank God I've had this chance to meet you.'

He turned to her. 'Rosha, I'll always feel the same about you. Nothing will ever alter that.'

'Take great care,' she repeated, pain beginning to ache in her throat.

He released her hand and kissed her cheek, then smiled and walked away. It was only then that she realised a soldier was waiting for him at the top of the lane.

Emotionally exhausted after the brief meeting, she went

into the hotel and ordered tea. She was two months pregnant and anxious not to overstrain herself.

On the journey back to Slievegar, Paddy asked occasionally, 'How far across the ocean will Grace be now, Rosha?' The distance of this far off country across the sea was incomprehensible to him.

Nellie came hurrying out to the yard when they drove in. 'Thank God yer back, Rosha. Yer father is poorly. The doctor's been. I'm afraid ...' she muttered brokenly and turned her head away.

Rosha raced into the house and up the stairs. Patrick was kneeling beside the bed with a rosary in his hands. He rose and put his arm around her.

'Daddy ...' She fell on her knees beside the bed.

'My child,' Sean said faintly.

She kissed his forehead and took his hand, tears streaming down her face. She heard the door opening and shutting. Father Gibson and Nellie came into the room. The priest had been in the house for some time and had already given the sacrament of Extreme Unction.

The funeral of Sean O'Neill who had fought so valiantly for tenants' rights was attended by hundreds of people from all over Donegal. He had endeared himself to everyone. Damien was confused at first with all the people who called at Garton but then began to enjoy the attention. Patrick was very protective towards Rosha. He insisted that the doctor gave her a potion to make her sleep at night. Meeting Edmund again and the death of her father had exhausted her mentally and physically.

Bridie and Rory waited anxiously for the Glasgow boat to dock. People were beginning to wave but she couldn't see her mother. 'She's missed the boat, Rory. She's changed her mind at the last minute, or that Rosha O'Neill has talked her out of coming.' Passengers began to flood towards them. Grace Boyce, concerned about holding on tightly to her luggage and keeping a sure footing, kept her head down. Not once did she look in the direction of the well-dressed couple who were scrutinising everyone who came down the gangway.

She recognised Rory Donavan first; he stood head and

254

shoulders above all around him. Grace drew in her breath when she realised it was Bridie by his side. 'Sorrow a welcome from the pair of ye!' she laughed. 'Are ye goin' to let an oul woman make her own way around this strange city.' She was beside them before they realised who this smart woman was.

'Mam!' Bridie screamed in delight, and threw her arms around her mother. 'Sure 'tis yourself that's been misleading us. Weren't we looking for a wee woman in a shawl?'

Grace found Rory very changed. Gone was the look of wild bitterness. He now looked prosperous though somehow not altogether content. At Dare Street, Sally came to the door holding Mary Anne by the hand. The little girl was dressed in a blue frock with a white sash. Though she was only two years old, she had a mass of auburn-coloured hair which Sally had tied back with a blue ribbon.

Grace held out her arms, tears starting in her eyes. 'Arrah, she's beautiful.'

The child held tightly to Sally's skirt. Bridie knelt beside her. 'Remember I told you Granny was coming to see you?'

'Give her time, Bridie love. We'll be the best of friends after while.' And so they were. For the two weeks of Grace's visit her grandchild never left her side.

Bridie was delighted by the amount of lace her mother had brought over from Ireland. She explained about the new rate she had now established for work trimmed with lace, which meant there would be more money for Grace and her workers. 'There's a lot of cheap machine lace coming up from England, Mam. I use that for some markets. When I add your lace to garments, the price is greatly increased.' This was pleasing news, as well as the obvious success of Bridie's and Rory Donavan's businesses.

Going around the big shops in Glasgow was a great treat for Grace, but one she thought she could quite easily live without. Her weekly trip to Tin Lizzie's was more fun. Now that the gentry were in residence again at the castle, it gave them all something to gossip about.

'Bridie,' she asked one day, 'is that Mollie downstairs all there?'

'Not when she hits the bottle!'

'Get rid of her, love, if she's fond of a drop.'

'She's got no one but me and Morag and she works well ... usually.' What would her mother say if she knew how Mollie had rescued her from the Cat Pit? All that part of her life Bridie had kept to herself. After nearly two weeks in Glasgow, Grace was beginning to miss the good clean air of Iskaglen, the green hills and plucks of white clouds moving across the high blue skies. The poverty here, that stung you at every corner of the tenement buildings, was different from that in Donegal and contrasted harshly with the careless wealth of the ladies and gents in town. Though she was sad to leave Bridie and Mary Anne, she was looking forward to going home again.

Though Ronald McFadden had not been encouraged to call at Dare Street, he came quite often to Argyll Street, where Rory had obtained the two rooms next-door for Bridie from his landlord. The place was large and spacious with a work and fitting room. She worked here with Morag, while Mollie and young Sally remained in Dare Street. As Rory had predicted, her work was becoming well known and her bank balance increasing at an astonishing rate. Bridie had never in her life felt so happy. She saw Ronald nearly every day. She loved being with him. He made her laugh and was full of flattery.

Ronald had not spoken yet to his mother about Bridie. He was hoping that her increasing achievements in the world of ladies' fashion would make her acceptable as a suitable wife. His mother was a terrible snob. He had always dreaded the thought of getting married and settling down, but Bridie had changed all that. She was sweet, modest and full of fun, everything that a man could wish for in a wife. His mother would be charmed when she got to know her.

On the weekend before his parents made their monthly trip to Edinburgh to visit his grandparents, he said impulsively, 'Bridie, would you like to come out to the country on Sunday to visit my home?'

She flushed with pleasure, thinking he wanted her to meet his family. Eagerly she accepted his invitation and for the first time suggested he call for her at Dare Street. Better for him to see where she lived if they were going to be married one day. Attractively dressed in a cream and white frock with a matching jacket and hat, she was waiting on the doorstep when he arrived. Every curtain in the street twitched at the sight of the electric driven car with the coachman sitting behind the seat.

'It's quite safe,' Ronald laughed at Bridie's startled expression, and helped her into the richly upholstered vehicle with its folding hood.

Angus Sinclair the coachman, who had worked twenty years for the McFadden family, looked dourly at the poor place where the young master's friend lived. A respectable enough looking wee body, he thought, but the mistress would nae be pleased if she knew where the lassie came from. A passing fancy nae doubt. The laddie was none too particular at times.

Ronald eased down Bridie's glove and kissed her wrist. She felt her blood racing, and blushed. If he asks me to marry him this day, I'll say yes, she decided. They drove along very fast on a straight country road. Ronald told her that the Electric Victoria could do twelve miles an hour and could manage nearly forty miles on one charge. She didn't know what he meant, but it was lovely sitting beside him in this unusual conveyance.

A short driveway led to a fine house built of Aberdeen stone. Though it looked large on the outside, Bridie thought it was quite compact inside. Leading from the hall was a library, dining-room and morning-room. Ronald took her upstairs to the drawing-room. Two large sofas on each side of the fireplace were upholstered in dark brown velvet; there were several matching chairs and small tables covered with velour cloths fringed with bobbles. Several silver-framed photographs were arranged on them. There was no one in the room.

'Ronald, where's your mother and father?'

'Next time you come they'll be looking forward to meeting you,' he said evasively. A maid wearing a black frock, white pinny and cap tapped at the door and came in.

'Will ye be wantin some tea now, sir?' she enquired. Her

257

eyes went to Bridie and she noted jealously how beautiful she was. He'll no' be groping me today, she thought. I wouldna be sure she's a lady though, gawping there at everything.

'No, thank you, Sheila,' Ronald said hurriedly. 'We'll take a walk in the garden first. I'll ring when we require tea.'

'Right, sir.'

When the door closed behind the maid, he took Bridie in his arms and began to kiss her. She responded eagerly, feeling safe in his lovely home and knowing now that his intentions were serious. He took her hand and led her to the alcove at the end of the room where a small desk stood by the window. Against the wall, out of sight of the drawing-room door, was a chaise-longue. He removed her hat and jacket and drew her down on the seat. Gradually his gentle kisses became increasingly demanding. His lips caressed her neck but when they moved further down into the curve of her breasts, she said half-protestingly, 'You shouldn't ...' But the blissful sensation was different, exciting, and she drew him closer. Suddenly his gentle touch changed and he was pressing her right down into the seat with increasing weight. When she opened her eyes and saw the expression in his, she was immediately reminded of the man who had raped her.

'Ronald McFadden, what are you doing?' she screamed, and freeing her hand, smacked him hard across the face.

Frustrated, he muttered, 'Bridie, don't do that. I love you.'

'Take me home!' she shouted. 'I'll kill you, Ronald McFadden, if you ever touch me again.' She pushed him away and stormed down through the drawing-room.

'Bridie!' He hurried after her and caught her hand. 'Bridie, I'm sorry. I lost my head.' Damn, how could he have been so stupid ... an innocent girl not used to men. After all the weeks of constraint he had gone and spoilt everything. 'Darling, forgive me.'

She turned at the sound of remorse in his voice. He looked so young, and very unhappy. 'Let me ring for tea and afterwards we'll take a stroll in the garden.'

'No, Ronald, I don't want any tea.' She began to feel ashamed at her outburst but he had startled and frightened her. They had never lain down like that before. It was lovely . . . if only she hadn't opened her eyes. 'I'd as soon go home.'

'All right.' He took her hand. 'Will you marry me?'

She stretched out for her hat and placed it on her head. 'I do love you but – '

'Say you'll marry me. Please?'

She smiled happily. 'Yes, I'll marry you. Ronald, I'm sorry I hit you.' There was a red mark across his face. She put up her hand and touched it gently.

He kissed her fingers then her cheek. 'Come on, darling, I'll take you home then. I'll call tomorrow at Argyll Street.'

Rory Donavan was just turning away from the house in Dare Street when the car drew up. He glanced at Bridie and thought she didn't look herself: very pale and excited. He felt anxious. 'I just called when passing, Bridie. I must get back.'

'Can I offer you a lift, Mr Donavan?' Ronald asked politely, hoping his offer would not be accepted. He had nothing to say to this big red-haired Irishman.

Rory had plenty to say to him. 'Thank you, Mr McFadden.' He told the driver where he lived. When they drove away Rory said, 'I would like to have a word with you, Mr McFadden. It's about Bridie. I am several years older than her and have known her since she was a child.'

'Yes, Bridie mentioned that.'

'And in the circumstances, Mr McFadden, though Bridie would be annoyed if she heard me saying this, I feel responsible for her welfare.'

'Yes?' Ronald snapped impatiently.

'I'm wondering what's going on between you and what your intentions are? Because,' Rory said bluntly, 'you've a certain reputation in this town.'

'Isn't Bridie old enough to look after herself?' Ronald replied, his face colouring in anger at the implication.

'Frankly,' Rory said, 'the girl is unpredictable. She can be quite simple about some matters and amazingly sharp in other ways.'

'You can set your mind at rest, Mr Donavan, about her welfare. I have asked Bridie to be my wife.'

Astonished, Rory turned in the seat. 'You have?'

259

'For the moment I don't want it spoken about because I haven't yet told my parents.'

Rory held out his hand, trying to show a delight which he did not honestly feel. 'I'm sorry. I misjudged the situation. If your intentions are to make her your wife, that is different.'

The following morning Bridie ran in next door to tell Rory her news. Her eyes were shining with happiness. 'So,' he said, trying to look pleased, 'you're going to be wed? I'm glad,' he added untruthfully, turning away from the brightness of her face.

'Ye don't look all that glad,' she said bluntly.

'I am,' he insisted. 'You love him and he's asked for your hand. You'll never want again, married into that family.'

'We'll always be friends, Rory, won't we? I don't know what I would have done without you all these years.'

'Ah, well, now Ronald will look after ye.' He paused then added hurriedly, 'I think I'll be going back to Ireland soon.'

'Back to Ireland? Away from Glasgow?' Her face clouded with dismay.

'To tell the truth, Bridie, I don't like it here all that much. I've got a fine business and built up some capital but money isn't everything. I want to get back to Ireland. Patrick Murphy has written and said there's an opening for my type of shop in Lisdare. He's urging me to come back again, join the movement and fight for the Cause.'

''Tis trouble you'll bring on your back, Rory Donavan. I thought you were going to buy a nice wee house with a garden.'

He tried to speak lightly. 'With no one to share it, Bridie, it would be a lonely house.' He placed a brooch of garnet stones on a pad of black velvet. 'So, Ronald's accepted the situation about Mary Anne? I misjudged him entirely. He's a stronger character than I gave him credit for,' he added half-apologetically.

She turned. 'Accepted?'

'Your child.'

'My sister, Rory.'

260

'Your ... God almighty, you're not going to marry the man with that lie between you?'

'He's not going to be told that story ... not yet. He might not want to marry me,' she said, her voice dropping.

'Bridie Boyce, how could you do such a thing?' he retorted angrily.

'I'll do it. If I was able to get m'self out of the Cat Pit to where I am now and her accepted as m'sister ...'

'That's different. It would be morally wrong to marry a man with that lie between you. *Tell him*. He's in love with you. It won't make any difference. Whether he tells his family or not is another matter.'

She looked at him obstinately.

Rory banged his hand on the counter. 'He *must* be told.'

Bridie her face flaming with anger, shouted, 'Mind your own business, Rory Donavan.'

He picked up a tray of rings from the counter. 'Very well. I wash my hands of you. You've become very hard, Bridie. I rejoiced at the God-given talent that raised ye up in the world. To think you've come to this, casting aside all sense of decency.'

'You've made a good job of pushing some things out of your life too, Rory,' she said, her eyes hard with anger. 'You murdered Catalong, didn't you?'

He flinched at the ugliness of the word. That she should be the one to accuse him.

'I did not murder him, Bridie,' he said quietly. 'The man condemned himself to death by his actions. I was his executioner.' He walked quickly around the counter and through the door of the storeroom which he closed behind him.

Bridie's achievements did not make up for her lack of background as far as Ronald McFadden's mother was concerned. The girl, she thought, had pleasing manners and a good appearance, but her son could marry anyone. On her next visit to Macduffs Mrs McFadden mentioned some of her misgivings to Miss Logan while the manageress was pinning up the hem of a new gown. Agnes Logan

261

had never forgiven Bridie for stealing a march on her over the designs in the Fashion Journal which had taken away customers from Macduffs. Now the young madam was advertising her own work with fittings supervised by the designer. Huh! What had made Miss Logan's blood boil was the effrontery of the wee bisom going to the boss over Agnes' head and requesting a contract to supply a certain amount of work to the store at a special rate. And an address in Argyll Street, no less! But the same lassie had cooked her goose when she made a delivery man out of oul Mollie from the workshop. Mollie with booze on her breath wasna very discreet. With a little encouragement she gave away a few things about Bridie Boyce.

'It's not for me to say, Mrs McFadden, but Miss Boyce is not all that she seems to be.'

'What do you mean?' Mrs McFadden swirled around, the pinned up hem dragging through Agnes' fingers tearing at her skin.

'As far as I know she came over from Ireland in a shawl with her bundle in one arm and a wee bairn in the other.'

'A child?' Mrs McFadden repeated horrified.

'The woman who delivers garments from her workshop had a drop on her one day and blabbed a bit.'

Mrs McFadden was too put out to notice the common words from the usually polite manageress. With tight lips she left the shop to seek out her son.

When Ronald McFadden arrived in Argyll Street one day unexpectedly, Bridie looked up eagerly. Previously there had been mention of a family party to which Bridie had been invited. His intention was to announce their engagement. Ronald's expression puzzled her because his easy-going smile was missing.

'What's the matter, Ronald?'

'That's for you to tell me.' It was then that Bridie heard the quiet anger in his voice and became alarmed. 'What kind of game have you been playing with me over the last few years when all the time you've been mothering an illegitimate child? Pretending to be a modest virgin, making certain I would wed you.' His anger grew when he remembered the day at his home when she had repulsed him. How he had suffered and reproached himself afterwards. After that incident he had been almost frightened to take her in his arms. He grabbed her arm as his bitterness increased. 'Your sister? *Your bastard*, isn't she?'

Bridie went very pale. 'Ronald, I can explain. I must tell you what happened to me. It was wrong of me to deceive you about Mary Anne but ...'

'Wrong?' he shouted. 'You've played your game very carefully over the past few years. Bridie, the good Catholic, when all the time you're no better than a whore.'

She stiffened at the ugly insulting word. At that moment she smelt the whiskey on his breath. This was a different Ronald altogether. She stamped her foot and tried to wrench her arm free from his grip.

'Shut up, Ronald McFadden,' she shouted. 'You listen to me. I was raped by an English nobleman.'

His hand slid up her arm and he felt the soft warm skin underneath the silk material and thought of the times it had tortured him. And after all, she had lain with another man while he had burned with desire because she had planned to keep him that way until the ring was on her finger.

He pulled her towards the inner room, the excitement of desire lighting up his eyes. Terrified, Bridie fought and screamed. She put out a hand trying to catch the edge of the sewing machine to stop him. Her fingers grasped one of the drawers which came flying out, scattering reels of cotton, pins and needles all over the floor. The unexpected clatter stopped Ronald for a second. His grip slackened and Bridie sprang away. Mother of God help me, she prayed, dashing for the door. He came after her. Just as his hand tightened on her arm again, his foot landed on a spool and he went sprawling across the floor.

She was out and into Rory's like a flash, forgetting their quarrel and the coolness that had lain between them since they had words. Rory took one look at Bridie's dishevelled appearance and obvious distress. He tore round the corner and through the door. He had seen McFadden getting out of a cab sometime ago.

Ronald, with strands of thread clinging to his clothes like

263

spidery tentacles, was picking himself up off the floor when Rory came in.

'Don't bother to get up McFadden,' he said threateningly and catching him by the neck of his coat pitched him out through the door to the road where he landed in the filthy gutter. 'Now ye buck,' Rory shouted at him, 'learn some manners to go wi' yer fine clothes. If I catch you around here again I'll break every bone in your body.'

'A gan' awa and fight yer own size,' an old crone shouted at the big raging Irishman. 'A'll git the polis on ye.'

A gang of ragged, barefooted boys appeared from nowhere, the mud and dirt from the wet streets clinging to their legs. They crowded around Ronald McFadden and tried to help him to his feet, all eagerly making suggestions.

'Git up mistah and gae him wan in the gob ... wid ye like a cab, mistah? ... come o'er to ma's mistah and she'll tidy ye.' They all had their eyes on Ronald's pocket and watched the stealthy hand that crept towards it. 'I'm just clearin' awa the horse shit, mistah,' the culprit whined. 'Come awa and git into a cab afore that big loon comes oot again.'

'He didn't give me a chance to explain,' Bridie said tearfully to Rory. 'He just went for me. He was going to ...' She covered her face with her hands and began to cry.

'Ah, he's had a drop on him, Bridie ... more than a drop, I should think. When he hears the truth of the story it'll be all right again.'

She shook her head, remembering Ronald's outrage because he thought she was not the virtuous girl that he had imagined. Not a chance to explain because she had committed the unforgiveable sin of bearing an illegitimate child. It was my own fault she accused herself. I should have told him. I should have listened to you Rory. 'Maybe I'll be no good to any man as a wife,' she sobbed. 'After what happened in Ireland, my body freezes when there's more than kissing. God help me.'

Rory wondered how he could comfort her after that terrible scene. 'It was foolish to think I could wed and be happy, Rory. Sure I'd be cheating any man who took me to the altar.' She caught his arm. 'Would you do something for me? Will ye go and see him, Rory, tell him the truth of the

264

story. I can't bear him to think ... he's been good to me.'

'All right, Bridie. I'll have to apologise anyway. At least I should have picked him up from the street and thrown him into a cab. I doubt if he had any money left in his pocket after thon wee fellas had a go at him. I'll tell him exactly how Catalong treated you.' She's still in love with him, he thought bleakly.

She rose, went over and laid her head against his shoulder. He stood stiffly, longing to put his arms tightly around her, to comfort her. Instead he patted her shoulder.

'I'm glad we're friends again, Rory,' she whispered, and thought, what am I going to do when he leaves Glasgow.

# Chapter Twenty One

'Patrick,' Rosha said frowning, 'you're not going away before Damien's birthday? It seems to me,' she added slowly, 'whenever anything of importance is happening at Garton, you take off.'

Patrick placed his daughter, Deirdre, in the cradle and gently tucked the blanket around her. 'I don't think that's fair, Rosha,' he remarked quietly. 'I explained to you before how important it is that I attend the party meetings. Since the Parnell Split which nearly ruined the Cause, John Redmond needs all the support he can get now he's been given the leadership and has united both sides of the party.'

'My father always maintained that no one could replace Parnell's leadership,' she said indifferently, wondering when he would face up to the fact that his involvement with politics was seriously undermining the welfare of Garton.

'After the O'Shea divorce, little more than one quarter stood by him. I reckon that was what killed him,' Patrick retorted.

'Travelling across the country in damp clothes did more to hasten his death,' Rosha told him impatiently. 'And you'll do the same yourself, Patrick. You often arrive home soaked to the skin.'

'There are some of us who are prepared to suffer in the struggle for Ireland's freedom,' he said defiantly. 'Unfortunately many have lost their enthusiasm to fight against England. It must be aroused again.'

'I wish you'd arouse the same enthusiasm for Garton,'

she replied resentfully. 'I have the children and the pottery to look after.'

It was the main point of friction between them and one that caused many a row.

'I am never absent during the harvest or at other ...'

'We take in casual farmhands,' she interrupted, 'and some of them are good for nothing. Why don't you go to the fair at Lisdare and hire a lad? We could take one on for a year and train him.'

'I won't belittle any man to hire him at one of them rabbles.'

'That's Rory Donavan's tune you're playing.'

'Rory suffered that indignity more than once.'

'He should complain! Look how well he's doing.'

'I wish to goodness he'd come back. We need men like Rory in Ireland. He could do well setting up business in Lisdare.'

'And the rest of the time fighting for the Cause.' Why am I so disinterested in politics? Rosha wondered. The hours she spent in the pottery gave her the greatest satisfaction and contentment. Thank goodness Paddy was able to give a helping hand while Nellie, with the help of Patrick's younger sister, Una, helped to run the house. Without Paddy it would have been impossible to continue the work. In summer the marl had to be dug out of the pit in the field, then treated and left over the winter for the frost to break down the particles and make it mouldable. Keeping it covered with wet sacks was a big job in itself. After all that, the clay had to be treated in the field before it was ready for use.

At first, after they were married, Patrick used to help Paddy. Now he spent increasingly more time down at his desk in the parlour writing articles for the United Irishman. When he broke his silence at meal times it was to talk about Griffiths' Sinn Fein policy. Griffiths had suggested the withdrawal of Irish members from Westminster and the setting up of an Irish Council to be responsible only to the Irish Nation.

'Sean O'Neill must be turning in his grave, Patrick Murphy,' Nellie scolded at times, which annoyed him. 'Wid ye think about getting the men up the hill and

267

seeing to the turf instead of sitting down there writing a lot of oul nonsense?' Nellie was troubled about Willie, too. Always slipping off in the direction of Merifield. The sly bugger was up to something.

To prevent quarrels between herself and Patrick, Rosha often let Nellie do the scolding. Still yer tongue, love, Nellie warned her, and just accept the fact that yer man is married to politics. But nothing compensated Rosha for the emptiness of their marriage.

Late one evening, she saw Paddy carefully moulding a piece of clay over in the barn. Sometimes when she came on him playing with a lump, he would give a guilty grin and toss it away. Now, standing outside in the dark, she was aware how sensitively his hands worked on what appeared to be the small bowl of a pipe. She moved away thoughtfully and walked towards the hill. Rain had pounded the earth for days, making the peaty ground on the way up feel like mulch under her feet. This weather was disastrous for the crops; an ill-boding for the harvest. High winds had ripped through the bay sending up plumes of water. On the hills, rain sent white ropes cascading down, flooding the moorland. There was silence around her. All the small creatures had crept into the comfort of their nests. She loved being alone up here in the evening, away from her noisy household. Every time Patrick was absent from home she took this walk to the hill.

The sudden appearance of a man standing further along the path surprised rather than alarmed her. She knew everyone in Slievegar but this was not a path used late at night. It led to a little plateau where a flat stone, called the hermit's rock, made a convenient place to rest. The figure turned in her direction and said, 'Rosha?'

She walked towards him slowly, noting the cane in his hand as he limped down to meet her. Unable to believe that it was Edmund, she hurried to his side. He laid down the cane and enfolded her in his arms. They stood there silently, her face pressed against his shoulder, then they sat down close together.

'Edmund, we heard rumours that you'd been taken prisoner.'

'It's a long story but I managed to escape.' For the first

time he found himself talking freely about his experiences in South Africa. 'The War Office and the military commanders misjudged the strength of the enemy,' he said. 'They were certain the Boers would be defeated easily.'

'Did you see anything of the Irish Brigades out there?'

'My jailer at the prisoner-of-war camp in Pretoria told me that the Irish Commando were doing fine work — for the Boers!'

'Patrick tells me there are thousands of Irishmen wanting to get out to fight for them.'

'There are Irishmen fighting on both sides, for and against England. It's a guerilla war now. Only those who know the country and speak the language would be of use to the Boers. I heard that some of the Brigade were returning to Ireland again.'

The rain that had held off for a few hours began to fall steadily.

'Edmund, you're a long way from Merifield.'

'My horse is tethered down the lane by the woods.'

Impulsively she said, 'Come down to Garton to the old barn it's now part of the pottery. I'll be able to give you a hot drink.'

He struck a match and held it to the face of his watch. Smiling, he said, 'Rosha, do you realise it's eleven-thirty?'

'Of course, you should be getting back home.'

'Alice and I sleep in different rooms since my return. My restless movements disturb her. The pain in my leg seems to worsen when I rest so I get up and walk about a bit.'

They made their way slowly down the hill. When they reached the barn Rosha lit the lamp and placed bits of kindling on the fire which Paddy had carefully raked and covered with ash. The kettle was hot and didn't take long to boil.

He looked around him with interest. 'That door over there leads to the drying room,' she told him. 'When the barn was built up again after the fire, we put two large windows in here.'

'Why is there such a large fireplace?'

'This was the original old house, built about three hundred years ago. In here would have been the kitchen.'

269

While the tea was drawing she went over and joined him. It was then that she saw the pipe Paddy had been working on. Not hidden away but proudly displayed for her inspection.

'Edmund, look at that. Paddy made it. He must have been practising every time he was over here on his own.'

He nodded thoughtfully and examined it. 'Seems quite perfect,' he commented.

'I should have taken more notice of what he was doing. All the time I'm trying to keep up with orders. Repetitious work can be very boring. I long to make beautiful objects.' She poured out all the frustration she felt about trying to run a pottery on her own and the problems with the neglected land. He listened quietly and sympathetically, never taking his eyes off her face.

When tea was poured into two tin mugs he sat on the wooden stool by the fire and she on one of the big logs. He laughed. 'I still remember how good the tea tasted in a tin mug that day in the corn field when we were children. Remember Nellie disapproved of your companion!'

They chatted and laughed about those times, then sat quietly reflecting on the happiness they had shared.

'You know, Edmund, about Paddy ... he's never been to school and can't read or write. He's always been considered only fit for cleaning out the byre and the stable. Yet he does everything around the pottery, apart from making things. And now I've discovered that, with some encouragement, he'll be able to do that too.'

'Where's he from originally?'

'Nobody knows. He came off the roads.' When she told him the story about Paddy's job as a scarecrow, he didn't laugh like everyone else who heard the story.

'The poor man,' he said sadly. 'Wasn't he lucky to call at Garton? And luckier still to spend the rest of his life helping you.'

The easy companionship they had shared over the past hour, talking freely as they used to, became charged with feeling. They raised their eyes and looked at each other, the pain of their loss naked for both to see. Rosha scrambled to her feet. 'We mustn't become serious.'

'Don't be unhappy, Rosha,' he said, rising slowly. She

270

turned her head away. 'I have two beautiful children.'

The sound of footsteps came across the yard. She knew it was Paddy's shuffling step and went to the door.

'Jayus, Rosha, what are ye doin' out here at this time o'night?' He saw Edmund, drew back startled and mumbled, 'Yer honour – '

Edmund went forward and held out his hand. 'Paddy, I've just been admiring that fine piece of work you did.'

Paddy's head shot up like a child's and he looked at Rosha for confirmation. Clumsily, the old man took Edmund's hand. He couldn't believe that one of the gentry was lowering himself to shake hands wi' the likes of him. He didn't even stop to wonder what one of them was doing so late in the old barn with his young mistress. But everything Rosha did was right. He had built his life around her. He even agreed to go to Mass at Christmas and Easter, providing he could stand near the door in case the priest came after him and he'd be able to make a quick escape.

'I must be on my way,' Edmund said.

'I'll walk as far as the lane with you. Paddy, there's hot tea in the pot. Put the fire down again before you leave.'

'A'right, Rosha.'

They walked slowly towards the lane, until they were near the post where his horse was tethered. 'Paddy must have got out of bed again to take another look at his pipe,' she said laughing.

'Keep him at it. Maybe he'll soon be able to turn his hand to a chamberpot and spare you for greater things!'

As they laughed again, she noticed how his limp had increased. He stopped. 'No further, Rosha.' In the stillness the horse heard his master's voice and neighed. His arms went around her tightly and their lips met, aching with longing and a frustrated joy.

When Rosha knelt down to say her prayers before slipping into bed, she thanked God for the two gifts he had sent her that day: the few precious hours with Edmund, and the discovery of Paddy's talent.

Bridie, in her unhappiness over Ronald McFadden, worked harder, not even taking an hour off to visit the market which

271

she had always enjoyed. Mollie had confessed, not to Bridie but to Morag Dobie, that she had let the cat out of the bag one day when she did a delivery at Macduffs. Morag thought it was her duty to tell Bridie because her unhappiness was plain to see after the courtship with the dandy, McFadden, had ended. Mollie, burdened with guilt, looked old and dejected for a few weeks until Bridie said to her one day: 'I know what happened Mollie. Logan's a crafty article. She got it out of you, didn't she?'

'She put two and two together, hen,' Mollie said eagerly.

'If you hadn't been oiling yer tongue wi' booze and trying to hide it with mint drops, I'd be a happier person this day, Mollie Duncan.'

When the woman flushed painfully, Bridie added hurriedly: 'It was stupid of me taking Mary Anne to the shop when my mother was visiting us. Anyway, Mollie, I'm warning you that I can't afford to have anyone on the bottle working here. Maybe it's sew your fingers into a seam you'll do one day!'

Rory's visit to Ronald brought her no hope. 'He was drinking,' he told her, 'and it was early in the afternoon. He made no sense.'

'What did he say?' she begged.

Rory shrugged. 'Forget him, Bridie,' he advised.

'Forget him,' Kevin O'Hara advised her also. 'He's weak and spoilt, alannah, and tied to his mother's apron strings.'

For the first time in weeks Bridie giggled. 'Kevin, I don't think his mother wears aprons.'

He slapped her on the back. 'That's the girl.' Then with the same reluctance as Rory, he went on, 'He's got another colleen on his arm these days, Bridie. The daughter of an eminent Dublin doctor who's taken on a practice in the best part of Glasgow.'

Kevin's words stabbed her. Was he codding? If doubt showed on her face, Kevin was ready to wipe it off again. 'There was a swanky ball in the town hall last night. Mabel showed me a picture of the pair of them in the paper. They were arm in arm wi' McFadden wearing a wee tartan skirt. God bless the mark, 'twas a pity he couldna buy himself a new pair o' legs to go wi' it!'

'Ah, well,' Bridie said with asperity, 'that girl's not likely to have come off the boat wi' a shawl around her shoulders.' That was the last time Ronald's name was mentioned between the three of them. She did not have long to dwell on her personal problems because the next morning Morag came upstairs in a terrible state. 'It's wee Donald. He hasna come back from delivering milk up at the tenements. I'm worried, Bridie, for there's a wild gang o' laddies around there. I hope they didna go for him.'

'He's quick and smart, Morag. Why don't you go and look?'

'There's that big order for the market. We promised to hae it o'er by ten o'clock.'

'I'll go then. I'll surely meet him coming back.'

'Dinna go wi' them fine clothes on ye, hen,' Mollie croaked. 'That lot wid hae them off yer back.'

'I'll risk it, Mollie.' She kissed Mary Anne who was hanging on to her skirt and called for Sally to take care of her.

Bridie knew roughly the area where Donald did his milk delivery for a pitiful wage. A few years ago, with a shawl around her shoulders and the baby wrapped in her arms, she had explored that part of the town. She remembered well the blackened walls of the buildings where families crowded into one room. She had been worried then about the Penny Mob gang, but doubted if they would have given her a second glance. Now it was the San Toy boys who roamed the streets. She tightened her grip on the umbrella and moved quickly down a close off the High Street. Women were standing about or sitting on the pavement gossiping with young babies clutched in their arms. Older children played around them, most of them barefooted, their legs bent with rickets. The boys wore caps large enough to belong to their fathers. It dwarfed their appearance and gave their childish faces a menacing look. The women eyed Bridie with suspicion and envy and the children's eyes fastened on her tight-fitting waist jacket which had a row of pearl and silver buttons.

She went over to the women and smiled. 'I'm looking for the wee boy who delivers the milk,

Donald Dobie he's called. Would you have seen him?'

'Bin and gan' hours ago,' one muttered.

Bridie hurried away. One of the boys came after her. 'He's haed a beefin' up the alley, miss.'

'Oh no!' she exclaimed in alarm.

'Aye, the big loons haed a go at him. He had a braw penny on him and they nabbed it.'

'Show me where he is.' Bridie opened her hand and revealed some money she had been clasping. He went to snatch it. She held her arm up high. 'Show me, love, then you can have sixpence. Why didn't you tell your mother down the close there what happened to the boy?'

'Aw, them oul wimin dinna belong t'me. I dinna ken them.'

At the end of the alley, sitting on a pile of garbage, was Donald. Surrounding him was a circle of stones in readiness in case the enemy attacked him again. Rosha could not understand why he was sitting there so still, even though his right eye was cut and swollen. As she came nearer she noticed that his left leg was jutting out at an unnatural angle.

'Gie's the money,' the barefooted urchin demanded.

'Just a minute.' She ran up to Donald. 'They bate me up, Bridie, and when I wouldna part wi' the money they shoved me down the stone stairs. Then they got it off me.'

'Can you stand on your leg?'

'Naw. I crawled up here.'

'Don't worry, Donald, I'll get you home safely.' She turned to the boy. 'You know Argyll Street?'

'Aye,' he said sullenly, his eyes fastened on her hand.

'Go to the jeweller's shop with Rory Donavan printed over the door. Tell him I'm in trouble and to come here quickly. There's the sixpence promised. When you bring him back here, I'll give you a shilling.'

He snatched the sixpence out of her hand and ran down the alley. Bridie wiped Donald's face and could have wept for the pain he must be suffering. For the second time within a few weeks, she was greatly relieved to see Rory's tall figure striding down the alley. Heavens, she thought, what would I do without him.

274

'Good God,' he exclaimed looking at the boy's leg. 'We'll have to get him to the hospital.' He touched Donald's shoulder. 'Don't worry, lad, we'll look after you.'

Bridie turned to the little boy and held out the money she promised. He snatched it, grabbed her umbrella and disappeared in a flash down the alley. Rory carried Donald to the Infirmary where it was confirmed that the boy's leg was broken. After they had set it, a cab took the three of them back to Dare Street where Donald, pale and silent, was fussed over by all the women. 'Twa wages gan', the milk round and the brickfield money,' his mother said tearfully.

'Morag,' Rory touched her arm, 'I could do with a lad about the place for a few hours every day. Cut out that milk round and let him come to me in the afternoons after school.'

'We need a messenger boy to deliver work on Saturdays,' Bridie added. 'I'll give you ten shillings, Morag, to get him fitted up in the market. He'll need to look smart delivering parcels to our customers.'

''Twas God sent you to m'hoose, Bridie Boyce, for I've never wanted since ye put a foot across m'door.'

Bridie thought Rory ought to share some of the glory too!

When they arrived back in Argyll Street, she invited Rory into her workroom for a cup of tea. 'There's something I have to tell you,' he said, stirring sugar in his cup.

Her heart sank. The time has come for him to tell me he's thinking of selling up and going back to Ireland. He hadn't mentioned the possibility since the trouble over Ronald McFadden. For weeks she had noticed how kind and thoughtful he was towards her.

'You're going then?'

'It's not that.' He paused for a moment. 'Remember you asked me to enquire about renting the rooms upstairs where my landlord lived before they bought their new house?'

She looked at him eagerly. 'What did Mr Cohen say?' Bridie was very anxious to move out of the small bedroom in Dare Street. Morag had agreed that she could take Sally with her when she found a suitable place. The flat above her workroom was big enough to accommodate them comfortably and also space for a store room.

When Rory didn't reply immediately she asked, 'Is something wrong?'

'It's Mr Cohen's mother. She doesn't want you to have the place upstairs. She's a strict, religious woman and ...'

'It's Mary Anne, isn't it? And me not married? They all think I was living in sin and maybe still am, don't they?'

'I'm sorry, Bridie. The flat belongs to his mother and there's not a thing Cohen can do about it.'

Bridie knew that the story about Mary Anne had got around. The child called her 'Mama', in spite of Mollie's efforts to teach her another name. And there was Ronald McFadden. How many people knew that he had jilted her because he had discovered that she had an illigitimate child? Glasgow was a big city but the people in the clothing trade were a close community.

'I should have taken your advice years ago, Rory, and called myself a widow.'

'Wish to heavens I could have spare you this.'

She tried to smile. 'It's the first time since I was a child that you haven't been able to help me,' she said lightly. 'It's not your fault.'

Ah, but I could help you, he thought despairingly. I could make you my wife and no one would dare cast a condemning eye or speak ill of you again. He had thought a lot about Bridie in recent weeks. She didn't love him. He couldn't hang around and wait until she fell in love with some other man and suffer all that pain again. So far he'd planned his life carefully. Hiring himself to farmers to bring home money to pay the landlord his rent. His work in Lisdare and planning the execution of Catalong and giving some people in Donegal hope for a better life. What was he going to do about Bridie? Time was running out. A business was going up for sale in Lisdare and Patrick wrote that a decision would have to be made soon. Part of his nature disliked the thought of becoming involved again in the political situation over there. All he wanted now was a little house with a bit of ground and, above all, the woman he loved to share it with him. Every other prospect seemed bleak.

Bridie was certain that Rory was making plans to return to Ireland soon. She couldn't imagine what life in Glasgow would be like without him. Even when she was planning to marry Ronald McFadden, she had not liked the thought of Rory not living there too. Strange how life was. Once, she thought that having enough money to live comfortably on was all she would need to make her happy. She considered the other more serious aspects of her life: the stigma of illigitimacy that might seriously affect Mary Anne later on. Agnes Logan had thrown the first stone; now Rory's friends had rejected her as well. Where would it end? When he left Glasgow she might even have to leave these rooms in Argyll Street; in fact that was a probability.

Rory saw her unhappiness. At that moment he could not offer comfort or a solution because his own life was in a state of turmoil too.

'Bridie,' he said, brushing crumbs off his jacket, 'I must get next door. What about the pair of us taking a day out in the country next Sunday? It'll do Mary Anne good.'

'All right,' she agreed, but her reply lacked enthusiasm.

On Sunday, Rory arrived at Dare Street in a pony trap loaned by Kevin O'Hara. Mary Anne, dressed in a green print dress and white pinafore, was jumping up and down on the doorstep with excitement. Bridie had no idea where they were going. Though still feeling unhappy by the unpleasant turn of events over the past months, she was determined to enjoy this day in the country.

Rory, looking happy and relaxed in a Norfolk jacket and breeches, came early. Bridie pulled on her straw hat and laughed. 'That's a grand rig, Rory. It makes you look prosperous.'

He tugged at the high collar on his shirt. 'To tell ye the truth, I feel over-dressed. Kevin talked me into buying it yesterday.' He looked at them with open-faced admiration. 'A bonny picture the pair of ye make.'

'Where are we going?'

'Where we can get some good fresh air.' She followed the direction of his eyes. Fat flies staggered somnolently across the cobble-stones after feasting on the remains of the food

277

left lying around on the ground by Saturday night revellers. The skeleton of a pig's foot clawed at the iron grating at the end of the alleyway as though trying to escape the colony of flies that had descended on it. A haze hung over the city, trapping the dust and stifling the air.

There were few vehicles on the main road. Soon the trap turned right and went down a lane where hawthorn, wild roses and honeysuckle bushes netted the view on each side. The road began to widen, leaving the hedges behind. Through the trees on the right Bridie could see the shimmer of water, like flashes of light darting through the branches. Another turn and they were at a loch surrounded by a sandy beach. Beyond lay an expanse of land peaceful and serene. Hedges of gorse and broom made a ribbon of bright colour towards the hill where patches of harebells grew in clusters near a belt of purple heather.

Mary Anne ran down to the sandy beach while Rory attended to the pony. Bridie just stood there and gazed at the beauty around her. The air was fragrant with the scent of broom and sharpened by wild mint and thyme growing on the grassy bit that lay along the verge of sand. She fetched the rug and spread it on the beach in preparation for their picnic. Rory, who had brought a bucket and spade for Mary Anne, helped her to build a sandcastle. After a while he let the child continue by herself and brought the basket which Bridie had prepared from the trap.

She laid out the food then sat back on her heels and laughed. 'I can't believe it! 'Tis like a different world out here, and not all that far from town.' Her eyes had brightened and her cheeks glowed with colour. 'Rory, have you ever seen broom so lush on the stem and so vibrant in colour?'

'There's great soil in this country for growing things. They say there's parts of the Highlands where strawberries grow to the size of small apples.'

'You tell me? It must be a warm place then. Look how contended Mary Anne is.' They watched the little girl's tiny fingers patting and moulding the sand.

'Though she looks like your mother, Bridie, every movement is yours.'

Bridie shrugged. 'She'll have a better life than I did, Rory.

Her future makes me feel very ambitious.' A frown crossed her brow as she thought of the obstacles that could hinder her. There would be the schooling, the little convent where Bridie thought she would start her child's education. The nuns were mostly Irish from the sound of their voices at Mass. How understanding would they be? All the explanations that would be necessary about her illegitimate daughter. She tossed a pebble across the sand. I can't go through life seeking sympathy by explaining to everyone that I was raped by an English landlord. Who's going to believe the story anyway?

Rory, who had noticed the fleeting, disturbed expressions on her face, jumped to his feet and held out his hand. 'Come on, Bridie, let's go for a stroll. Mary Anne?'

About an hour later, he said, 'I think it's time to make a move.'

'So soon? I wish the day could go on for ever,' she said regretfully.

'We'll have another day like this.'

He's only saying that to comfort me, she thought. He's longing to get back to Ireland.

'Bridie, we're going on somewhere else.' She packed the things hurriedly into the basket, scarcely hearing what he was saying. The pony headed in the direction of Glasgow again. We'll soon be home, she thought disappointed.

'Whoa ...' Rory pulled on the reins, jumped down off the trap and led the animal down a wide lane where he turned into a drive. Rowan trees grew along the way, their red berries sparkling in the sunlight.

'This place is called Rowan Cottage.'

'Are we visiting someone?' she asked anxiously.

'There's no one in the house. It belongs to Kevin's wife, Mabel. He asked me to call in and take a look around. Mabel had just inherited it from an old uncle.'

Roses grew all around the front of the building; richly scented creamy blossoms that crept up the walls and framed the windows. Rory unlocked the door and they stepped into a wide hall with a curving staircase. The old oak chest standing near the door had a brass candlestick and snuffer on it, which Bridie noticed were in need of a polish. Light streamed from the rooms on each side: a dinging-room and a large living-room, where a chintz-covered settee and two armchairs stood near a wide stone fireplace. The fireplace was filled with unused logs sprinkled liberally with soot from the chimney. That fire hasn't been lit for some time, she thought. Elegantly designed furniture, from another age, was arranged around the room, not overcrowded as Bridie had seen in some of the houses where she visited clients. Here, there was good taste and reserve; from the look of the bookcase with its variety of books, it must have been the home of a scholar. She noticed the interest Rory showed in the books.

'Look out that back window at the view, Bridie,' he urged her as though he had just created it. There was a lawn surrounded by a flower garden, beyond an orchard. 'There's two acres of land behind that. Good fertile land needin' digging, so Kevin tells me.' He caught her arm. 'See the hill in the distance? The loch – Loch Mor, where we've just been – lies in its lap. Come upstairs. Kevin says there are four rooms and a wee one off the main room.'

Some cottage, Bridie thought when they made their way down to the kitchen again. Here she felt a pang of envy for the woman who would run this fine place. Everything was well planned apart from the maid's bedroom off the kitchen which was damp and darkened by a tree growing close to the window. The brass bedstead was dingy, dangerously broken in parts and a sagging mattress had pushed the bed-springs right down to the floor. Back in the kitchen, Rory took a doll off the dresser which was crowded with colourful delft. He handed it to Mary Anne who immediately sat down on the rug and began to nurse it. The doll had a pretty china face and light blue eyes, reminding Bridie of some of her customers.

'Rest your feet, too, woman,' he said smiling, pointing at a comfortable old couch in the corner. Bridie was thinking of the lovely bathroom upstairs and the comfortable lavatory. No hen-roost privies in this house with splinters on the seat!

'Isin't it a grand property, Rory? Will they be keeping it for their holidays or weekends? Some of my customers have places like that.'

'No, Mabel and Kevin are expected to join her parents at a big place they've got further up the country. There's fishing and shooting apparently. Kevin's good with a rod and a gun; that made him very popular with Mabel's father. Mabel doesn't want to be bothered with this house. Kevin said it'll either be sold or let out on a long lease.' He rose abruptly and began moving restlessly up and down the floor.

'Well,' Bridie, said stretching out on the settee. ''tis a pity they won't keep it. I like it better than their big place in Glasgow. I'd give m'right hand to live in a place like this.'

Rory stopped by the settee and looked down at her. 'You wouldn't need to do anything as drastic as that, Bridie.' He took his hands out of his pockets and sat on the edge of the settee beside her. 'You could marry me.' He saw the look of shock on her face and flinched inwardly. Determined to say what he had planned, he hurried on, 'I know you don't love me and I know how you feel about marriage. But because you were in love with Ronald McFadden you thought you could face it.'

White-faced, Bridie said hurriedly in a low voice, 'Rory, I couldn't marry you. It wouldn't be fair. At the same time, I can't bear the thought of you leaving Glasgow. I have always loved you as a dear, dear friend.'

He took her hand. 'I want you to understand this. I would make no demands on you. I want to look after you and Mary Anne. I think life is going to be very difficult for you otherwise. I can give you both my name and protection.' He stood up. 'Come upstairs again. I want to show you something.'

In the main bedroom, overlooking the garden he said, 'This could be your room, and the wee one off it Mary Anne's. Remember this, I would never come into this room unless you wished it.' When she looked doubtful, he said lightly, 'Sure all this wouldn't be half as bad as parting with your right hand, now would it?'

She didn't respond to his humour. With more seriousness, he went on, 'I'm heading towards thirty, Bridie. I want to get my life settled.'

'What about Ireland?'

'I've come to realise that I've not got that kind of patriotic fervour any more. I don't want to hide in ditches with red coats searching for me. For mark my words, things will come to that over there.'

'I'm glad for your sake, Rory. The last time I went to see Mabel to do a fitting, she told me Kevin doesn't want you to go either.'

He smiled. 'I know. Kevin O'Hara is a sentimental old divil. Ah, well, if I decide to buy this house maybe they'll give me a bargain!'

'You'd *buy* it?'

'If the bank will give me a loan. I've had my fill of landlords,' he said drily.

'Rory, with my business growing all the time, I could help you. Perhaps the bank would be more agreeable with two flourishing business behind the loan.'

Though he was impressed by her shrewdness, he couldn't believe that she was actually agreeing to his proposition. 'You'll marry me then?'

Bridie saw the light of gladness in his eyes, then the uncertainty. Rory who had never been uncertain about anything.

'Maybe you'd like to think about it? I'd understand,' he added hurriedly.

# Chapter Twenty Two

'Patrick, where's Willie?' Nellie asked. 'The cows are out behind in the field and the fence needs mending.'

'Hasn't he fixed it yet?'

'Not unless you told him. That man's got to the stage that he'd have to be told to chase a fox away from the hen-house door,' she complained.

Patrick was rising from his seat when Rosha laid a hand on his arm. 'Finish you breakfast first. There were times when she felt heartily discouraged. Her father had always maintained that when Patrick took over he would make the estate prosperous again. As it was turning out, Patrick was worse than Sean for getting involved in outside interests and putting only the minimum effort into Garton. Sean had been concerned about the tyranny of unjust evictions, whereas Patrick was bothered about the fate of the entire country. Ireland was a demanding mistress of those who tried to serve her; Patrick one of her most dedicated servants.

Rosha's gaze went to Nellie. She was the most enduring of them all. 'Nellie, you look tired. Why don't you take tomorrow off? I'm not too busy at the pottery.'

'Maybe I'll go over and visit Mam.'

Patrick rose, came around the table and rested his hands on Rosha's shoulders. 'What about yourself taking a bit of time off?'

She looked up and smiled. Nellie beamed at this rare show of affection between them. He pulled out the chair that Damian had just vacated and sat down beside her. 'You know there's a train running from Lisdare to Dublin now?

What about coming to Dublin with me next week for a couple of days? I think Yeats and George Moore are putting on a double bill at the Gaiety.'

Rosha's eyes lit up. 'I'd love that.'

'You go, Rosha,' Nellie urged. 'Mam will come over and give a hand. Paddy's al'right over in the pottery on his own, isn't he?' Paddy was one of the miracles that Nellie believed in firmly. Only God could have unleashed such talent in an ignorant oul man like that.

'I'm afraid I've got bad news for ye,' Grace announced to Nellie when she arrived at Iskaglen the following day.

'Bridie?' she said in alarm.

'Keeping well, as far as I know. Haven't heard from her for a while. It's Willie Doherty, yer Willie at Garton. I hear he's bin walkin' out big Madge from up the mountain.'

'Mam, he's bin walkin' her out for ten years now. Give him another ten and maybe he'll wed her.'

Grace hung the kettle on the iron hook and moved the crane. 'From what I heard at Tin Lizzie's, 'tis a case of havin' to wed her.'

'No! The sly devil. She'll lose her place at the castle.'

'She'll be all right on that score for that's where the bad news comes in. Her Ladyship has offered Willie a job, and when they're wed they'll get one of them new cottages they've built on the estate.'

Nellie jumped to her feet, scattering the hens who had slipped in for a sly pick under the table. 'He can't do it, Mam. What wid we do wi'out him at Garton?' She gulped down a cup of tea and went straight back again.

Willie was in the stable attending to Rosha's horse when she returned. The farmhand thought she was going to strike him when she pounced through the door.

'Well, Willie Doherty,' she shrieked at him, 'what have ye got to say for yerself? Has yer treachery struck ye dumb, ye sly bugger? Is it true yer leaving Garton after all these years wi' no experienced man to take yer place?'

Willie kept turning the cap rapidly in his hand as though preparing to send it spinning out to the midden. 'Ah, jay, Nellie,' he said at last, 'a man has to make up his own mind sometime.'

'I don' know why ye want to bother at yer age when up t'now someone's done it for ye! A bomb under yer arse widden move ye at times.'

Willie began to slink through the doorway. 'Me and Madge is going to wed 'cause the priest has ordered it. I was approached wi' a job at the castle and a cottage to go wi' it. Jay, Nellie, a man's gotta end his days under his own roof.'

'Yer own roof? Oh, no, Willie Doherty, the cottage belongs to the Catalong estate. Put a foot wrong and ye'll be out on yer backside again. The castle agents are not known for their compassion.'

'I promised to marry Madge and there's no cottage at Garton and that's a end to it.' He slammed the cap on his head giving finality to his words.

'What about the bit of land Sean O'Neill left you in his will?' Nellie threw at him. 'If ye were any good ye could've built a place.' What was going to become of Garton with only half of Patrick's attention on it? she thought unhappily. Though she often scolded about Willie's slackness, he did understand the land and he trained the casual workers.

Nellie, who hadn't been near the castle for years, went straight down to see Mrs O'Sullivan. With a nervous glance at the inner door the housekeeper said: 'We've been short of experienced workers, dear. Apparently the idea came from the mistress. She got the agent to approach Willie.'

'Didin she know that sort of thing isin done here? Going after a man who's worked on another farm for thirty years.'

'She's English, dear,' Mrs O'Sullivan whispered. 'Over there it's every man for himself. Mind you, I don't know what the master will say. A very considerate young gentleman.'

By the time Nellie returned to Garton, Willie had spoken to Rosha. Patrick was annoyed because he had passed him on the drive earlier on and the man had not indicated there was a matter of importance to be discussed. Nellie looked at him obliquely and had to bite her tongue on the words that were in her mouth – the responsibility of running Garton was still on Rosha's shoulders. However, she had rarely seen Patrick looking so cross. Of course, she thought, he knows

285

that in future he won't be able to take himself off anytime he fancies without a reliable man here.

The three of them sat at the table drinking tea in miserable silence. After a while Patrick turned to Rosha and said thoughtfully: 'Wasn't there a proviso in your father's will? Something about Willie having the land as long as he worked at Garton?'

Rosha stared at him. He jumped to his feet. 'I'll ride over to Dilford and see the lawyer.'

'There's a copy of the will upstairs in the tin trunk.'

The two women didn't speak a word until he came down again and announced: 'Willie forfeits the land if he leaves Garton. It was to allow him some independence in case he wanted to get married or just build his own place.'

'So,' Nellie said triumphantly, 'O'Neill saw the slyness in Willie Doherty's nature and didin just hand o'er that bit of land.' She looked at Patrick. 'He'll be up in the willow field mending that dam. Go and bring the gombeen down and put the situation to him in Rosha's presence.'

'Yes, do that,' she said quickly, knowing that her husband resented and often ignored the orders that Nellie threw at him occasionally.

'Gombeen is not the name I'd give him, Nellie. I'll speak to the man where he is so as not to take him away from a job of work.'

With the disturbance over Willie, who, when presented with the conditions of Sean O'Neill's will, wavered like a bull before a storm, Rosha thought that the promised trip to Dublin would have to be cancelled. Willie, however, unlike the intemperate bull, hesitated about taking the final plunge before claiming his partner and hung around Garton undecided, putting up with the lash of Nellie's tongue.

Rosha realised that the offer of higher wages and the cosy cottage on the Merifield estate would be a great temptation to any man, especially one who wanted to get married. Illogically, Willie seemed upset because Sean O'Neill had doubted his loyalty.

For her journey to Dublin Rosha wore a suit of fine Donegal tweed woven in a mixture of blue and gold wool. She also packed a frock for the visit to the theatre. They stayed in a small hotel near Phoenix Park which seemed to be crowded with people Patrick knew. After a meal they went to a social gathering at someone's house. Everyone there, like Patrick, had political interests; with surprise she realised that he was considered of some importance by these people. The hesitant farmer from Slievegar had a new identity in Dublin. With an assured manner, he spoke authoritatively on subjects that arose in the course of the discussions.

It was assumed by the clever young women in the party that his wife shared the same interests and enthusiasm, though as a mother of young children, running a home and a pottery, she had not the time to become politically active. Rosha was aware that, because she had fought a landlord over evictions (Patrick never failed to mention this), it gave her some standing among these people. She felt diminished by Patrick's friends and not at ease among the well-dressed, intellectual Dublin women who talked continuously about Griffiths, Gonne, Connolly and many others. Tomorrow she would go her own way, browse and shop until it was time to attend the theatre.

Dublin was like a foreign city. Black-shawled women rubbed shoulders in the street; they spoke rapidly, excitedly, to each other as though they were revealing the threat of an imminent disaster. And other women, elegant, aloof, paused to greet friends, then continued unhurriedly on their way. She wandered through the shops, making small purchases; gifts for the children, Nellie and others.

It was in the main shopping area that she found a shop selling pottery and porcelain. She was about to go inside when a shadow fell across her shoulder and a voice she had not expected to hear said: 'If I had known you were in Dublin, this is where I would have come to find you.'

Rosha turned slowly, unable to hide the rising joy that showed plainly in her eyes. In the crowded street their hands met involuntarily, tightened, then instantly fell apart. 'Edmund —'

He glanced along the street. There was a restaurant frequented by his fellow officers and their ladies. 'Come and take some tea.'

She followed him, her eyes on the pavement. What would Patrick's friends think if they saw his wife in the company of an English army officer? The people whose one dream was to rid Ireland for ever of the English army. She was safe in this restaurant; from the murmur of conversation she knew that all the customers were English.

'You're looking well,' Rosha said conventionally.

'Life is very leisurely here. The wives love it. We are lavishly entertained by some of the townspeople and there's a constant round of Castle parties.'

She moved aside for the waitress to lay the table. 'Is your wife here?' she asked when the girl went away.

'She was for a time. Did you come to Dublin for any special reason?'

'Patrick's got some business here and tonight we're going to the theatre.'

'There's a lot of activity going on at the moment by the Nationalist party.' And, he thought, the authorities are keeping a close watch on Patrick Murphy and his friends.

She raised her eyebrows. 'What do you expect? The English are not welcomed by everyone here. Foreign soldiers in our land!'

He smiled. 'How many times we've had this discussion in the past.' With a more serious expression he added, 'I think you know, Rosha, how I really feel about our presence in this country.'

'Do you still feel the same, Edmund? With that uniform on, I need to be convinced.'

He looked steadily at her for a moment, then his hand went down under the table and reached for hers. The unexpected touch made her heart leap wildly and her face blazed with love and longing to be close to him.

'Remember Dilford, my darling,' he said in a low voice. 'Riding in the silent hills, our long days together.'

'Edmund, sometimes down through the years when my life was difficult, I took out those memories. Like precious jewels hidden in a box, I poured over them; full of guilt, pushed them away again.'

'Rosha,' he withdrew his hand and leaned across the table, 'come with me now. Let's take a cab and get out to the country for a few hours, away from Dublin and everyone. Oh God, how I've longed for you at times.'

'Yes ... oh, yes. How, where?'

They finished their tea quickly and he asked for the bill. As the girl made it out laboriously, he enquired how things were at Garton. With some hesitation she told him about the offer his agent at Merifield had made to Willie Doherty.

'How dare the agent do such an underhand thing?' he said angrily. After all the trouble there was on the Catalong estate in my father's day, he thought, and all my efforts to improve relations with the people.

They left the restaurant and walked around the corner to where a few sidecars were waiting. 'Straight down this road and we'll soon be out of town,' Edmund said, helping her on the vehicle. And to the driver, 'Drive out to the country, please. I'll direct you later.'

'Right, sor.' Ha! The driver thought. By the look of this pair they can't get away fast enough.

'Rosha ...' The surprised voice of her husband fell like a whiplash on her ears. 'Good day, Captain Catalong,' he said coldly.

Rosha stepped down again, eyes lowered in case Patrick should see her unbearable disappointment. She dusted her skirt, raised her head and smiled.

'Hello, Patrick. Edmund has just offered me a lift back to the hotel.'

'Ah, well,' her husband said, 'it won't be necessary now. I've arranged to meet someone back there.'

She held out her hand to Edmund. 'Thank you so much for the kind offer. It was convenient that Patrick came along. Now you won't have to go out of your way.'

The driver kept staring up at the sky with a surprised expression as though he had just discovered it.

'How could you,' Patrick said, flushed with anger as they walked away. 'Driving in broad daylight in the company of an English officer. What would people think if they saw you?' She shrugged and turned her head to hide the tears that were threatening to spill down her face.

Lady Alice Catalong was annoyed and confused when

the agent brought Edmund's letter, demanding that their arrangement about the employment of Willie Doherty should be cancelled immediately. When Annie the maid came into the room she said casually: 'Did you go to the shop yesterday?'

'I did, madam, and it was packed with the hens laying so well and everyone buying their groceries and oil. Nellie from Garton was saying that the eggless customers should be allowed down first because Tin Lizzie counts every egg before she hands o'er the groceries. Nellie was in a wild hurry because her mistress had taken off for Dublin.'

So, Alice Catalong thought, they must have met. How else could Edmund have found out about their attempt to take the farmhand from Garton? Alice would never forget the letter she found in Edmund's drawer one day when her husband went away, forgetting to lock it. That letter left her in no doubt that Rosha Murphy was the woman whom Edmund had loved and wanted to marry.

A week later, an abject Willie walked into the kitchen at Garton and announced that the castle did not want his services after all. Would he still be entitled to that bit of land?

'Ye widden if I had anything to do wi' it,' Nellie said belligerently. When he went down to the room she raised her voice so that he could hear. 'Patrick, get that man out of this house and give him a pile of stones so that he can build a place of his own, for I refuse to make his bed or feed him for any longer than I can help it.'

# Chapter Twenty Three

'Mother of God!' Nellie exclaimed.

Rosha entered some figures in the ledger. 'What is it?'

Nellie, looking shocked, was holding a letter in her hand. 'Ye'll never believe it, Rosha, our Bridie is marrying Rory Donavan.' She looked around her frantically. 'Where's the calendar? What's the date?'

'It's the twenty-seventh of September,' Rosha told her glancing at the wall.

'She's soon to be wed,' Nellie said flatly, then added bewilderedly, 'she told me she'd never want to marry anyone. That what had happened to her with Catalong made that sort of thing impossible. You know, Rosha!' There was a silence between them for a moment. 'That Rory Donavan is a lusty thing,' she blurted out indignantly. 'How's she goin' to manage him?'

'Nellie, she's no longer the person you knew. She sounds a sensible young woman the way she writes about her business,' Rosha said gently, wondering if Nellie really minded. 'It must have been difficult making her way in a strange town with a child. Now she's got Rory to look after her.'

'Aye,' Nellie replied in a sad voice which made Rosha wonder if her feelings for Rory were indeed a thing of the past as she had always maintained. Rosha went to pick up her pen again when Patrick walked in and threw down a letter with a gesture of disgust.

'Rory's marrying Bridie Boyce.'

'I know, Nellie's just told me.'

'A marriage of convenience,' he complained in a disgruntled voice. 'He's stuck with Bridie Boyce and her daughter.'

'That's unkind, Patrick. He's probably fallen in love with her.'

'Huh! He's been stuck with her for years. How could a level-headed man like Rory Donavan get himself involved in such a situation when he knows he's needed here in Ireland?'

Perhaps, thought Rosha, he wants to forget what happened in Ireland. The death of Thomas Catalong might be on his conscience, in spite of the trial by secret 'court' that decided Catalong had to die before he destroyed any more lives.

'This marriage will bring him no happiness,' Patrick insisted. 'Rory is a born patriot. He's turning his back on his own nature.'

Rory had never felt so happy in his life. The financial agreement over Rowan Cottage had been settled sooner than he had expected. His friend Kevin had wangled a bargain for them and the bank had given them the necessary loan. The other part of the bargain which came as a delightful surprise was Mabel's lack of interest in the contents of the cottage, even though Rory pointed out that the shelves contained some valuable books.

He and Bridie, with Mary Anne, went out to Rowan Cottage every moment they could spare. Sally accompanied them on Sundays and while they cleared and dug over the ground, she cleaned the house and emptied the linen cupboard to air all the sheets and blankets. Bridie began to see a change in Rory. During the years they had been together in Glasgow, he had seemed like a much older man; serious, without humour. Now he laughed and talked away, seeming younger and more carefree.

As the day of their wedding grew nearer, she tried not to think about it too much. It was just as well that all the work kept her busy. Too busy, Rory said. She should take on another experienced worker to give her more free time. She was also occupied making her wedding dress and an outfit for Mary Anne. the dress of peach-coloured silk had ribs of gold braid around the lower part of the skirt with a short jacket to match. What, she wondered sometimes, was Sally going to make of her and Rory getting married and sleeping in different rooms at Rowan Cottage?

Kevin and Mabel had insisted on holding the wedding reception in their spacious home. The only guests invited were Morag, Sally and Mollie; also Rory's friends, the Cohens. He had explained to them about the tragedy in Bridie's life. Now they treated her with great affection and kindness. Bridie also loved Kevin's fat, complacent wife, who had borne him a child every year since they were wed.

They were married on a chilly, wet day at the beginning of October. Kevin was best man and Mabel, Matron of Honour. After the service, the house in Branton Avenue where Kevin and Mabel lived was warm and welcoming. When they were going through the hall, Mollie nudged Morag and whispered, 'I used to work in a house like this in Glasga. Where'd all the lovely flowers come from at this time o'year?'

'McFadden's hot-houses,' Morag whispered back, and they both rolled their eyes and glanced at Bridie.

The two women huddled together, alarmed and shy to be part of all this rich hospitality. They were also embarrassed to be served by maids in uniform who addressed them as 'Madam'. Morag had been surprised at their being invited to the wedding; Bridie had warned her, though, to keep an eye on Mollie. They all knew that with too much drink in her, oul Mollie was fit to bawl everyone out of the house. It was a risk Bridie was prepared to take because she had been her best friend in the big lonely city.

'Drink up, woman,' Kevin urged Bridie, pouring a clear sparkling wine into her glass. 'Didn't I open this special one for yourself?'

Rory, in a navy serge suit and white shirt, smiled at her. Bridie thought he looked very handsome. They seemed like different people today in their grand clothes, being entertained in this cluttered but fine house.

'Don't force her,' he said. 'Bridie's not fond of drink.'

'Sure don't I know that, and haven't I served her a mild, gentle drop?' The bottle was wrapped in a white linen napkin. 'The best stuff doesn't do any damage,' Kevin added reasonably.

The meal was sumptuous and leisurely. Still at the table, Kevin told them some funny Irish yarns, then Rory's friend Mr Cohen followed with a few Jewish stories. When Mollie staggered to her feet and shouted, 'Bridie, hen, will I telt the one aboot the Cat Pit?' Bridie's foot gave Kevin a warning kick.

He jumped to his feet. 'Now we'll hear that in a minute, Mollie m'dear. I think it's time we let the girls clear the table.'

Tea and wedding cake were served in the drawing-room, then it was time for the coach to take the two women and Sally back to Dare Street. On its return, it would drive out to Rowan Cottage with Bridie, Mary Anne and Rory. The rain had not stopped all day. In fact, Kevin said, it was getting worse and wouldn't they be eejits traipsing away out there to a damp unwelcoming cottage when there were spare bedrooms in this very house?

'Everything is ready,' Bridie told him. 'The cottage had fires burning in it all day yesterday, Kevin. It couldn't possibly be damp.'

'Woman, dear, the rain's been pumping down all day and isn't it under the doors it'll be by now? Do ye want to go down on yer knees mopping up in them fine clothes? Hould yer wish, woman, and sit down,' he ordered. 'If ye spend the night with us, we can have a jar for another hour or so. Ye can't take the wean out in this weather.'

'Ach, stay, Bridie,' Mabel pleaded too. 'We'll feel right flat if you go now. Didn't Rory promise to sing?' She moved over to the piano. Kevin pulled the bell and when the maid arrived he told her their guests were staying the night. He left the room and returned with a tray of drinks.

'Is this the same one I had before?' Bridie asked him.

'It is, alannah, it is. And you'd better finish the bottle because 'tis only yourself that fancies that one. It won't keep.'

Bridie thought it was a very pleasant drink, not even going to her head. Rory sang Irish and Scots songs. She remembered now what a fine voice he'd had when he was on the hill herding. They all joined in, then the three of them danced a jig on the expensive carpet while Mabel deftly picked out a tune on the piano. Mary Anne slept soundly on the red velvet settee by the fire. An hour later they were ready for bed.

When Rory had told his friend a few days previously the truth about their marriage, Kevin was horrified. He wondered how Rory could accept such an arrangement, though he realised that the daft cratur' was in love with the girl. Well, he had done his bit with the 'best champagne', as his mother-in-law called it. He just hoped that Bridie's heart would soften towards his friend. Begod, it was hardly a heart matter; something of a far more serious nature indeed!

'Mrs Donavan,' the maid said, 'I'll show ye to your room.'

Rory carried Mary Anne upstairs. Bridie followed, her head spinning. She went into the bedroom and sat on a low easy-chair by the fire. She didn't know for how long until Rory came in and bent over her.

'Bridie, Mary Anne is tucked up in bed in a wee room through that door down there. Come along,' he said gently, 'I'll help you to undo some of those buttons.'

When the tight-fitting dress was over her head and she stood in her white cambric petticoat, she said, unashamed and uncaring about her scant attire, 'Rory, I'll kill that Kevin. The drink's gone to m'head suddenly and I feel marvellous.'

He laughed. 'Step out of your gown. It's around your ankles. Can you manage the rest while I go to the bathroom next-door? There's a nightdress laid out on the bed there.'

With clenched hands Rory went to get undressed. 'Christ, this is much worse than I imagined,' he muttered to himself.

She was lying in bed with a copper warming pan beside her when he returned to the room. He bent down and kissed her cheek, took the warming pan away and tucked in the bedclothes. 'Goodnight, Bridie.'

'Rory, where are you sleeping?'

'On the chair down over there by the fire.'

The room will grow cold during the night, she thought lucidly. In a few moments the fear that had recently occupied her mind was being replaced by the side of her nature that often made sure, positive decisions when an opportunity arose. Now, feeling in a relaxed state, she realised that this chance to give herself in marriage might not come so easily living in a cottage with separate bedrooms. There might not again be a flow of expensive wine to mellow her mood and release the tensions in her body.

'Rory, I think I'm almost drunk. I don't want to sleep alone in this great big bed,' she said, not knowing what she wanted, but prompted by an age old wisdom that warned her that no marriage could survive under the conditions that Rory had offered.

He hesitate for a second then extinguished the lamp, threw off his dressing-gown and came in beside her. His arms went around her and he kissed her gently. She was aware of his uncertainty, his fear of alarming her.

'Rory,' she whispered, then giggled, 'I think I feel ... wanton.'

Then he understood.

In the morning Mary Anne stumbled into the room rubbing her eyes. 'Rory, are you in the wrong bed?'

He stretched out his arms, picked her up and placed her between them. 'No, 'avoureen, I think I'm in the right one.'


Bridie felt quite contented over the weeks following her wedding. Rory was a devoted husband and she tried to be a good wife. Every time she felt herself longing for a little magic, a spark of romance, she prayed to be forgiven for being disloyal. If that letter had not come from Ronald McFadden shortly after she was married, she would have been left with the unpleasant memory of their last meeting and cured forever of the feeling she'd had for him.

Ronald, apparently, was about to leave Glasgow to travel south and had written the letter before departing, unaware that Bridie was already married. He mentioned Rory's visit and apologised for his abominable behaviour that day in Argyll Street. Beside himself with anger and disappointment, he had written, he did not realise that she was still the same lovely girl he had fallen in love with. If only she had told him at the beginning of their friendship about this unhappiness in her life, his only desire then would have been to protect her. He loved her still and hoped she would allow him to come and see her on his return to Glasgow.

Rory, who had been present when the letter arrived, read it too. Without a word he threw it on the fire, turned and left the room. It was never mentioned again between them. As the flames devoured the paper Bridie winced with pain, and remembered Ronald's laughter, his impulsive generosity, and the sheer joy she felt when they were together.

She walked to the window and saw touches of gold and amber lighting the hills. Soon the entire land would be burnished with glowing colours which would eventually fade to the bleak, bareness of winter. As she went to move away, a letter that had arrived from Ireland that morning fell down and scattered its pages around her feet. Rory always left her Patrick Murphy's letters to read but they seldom had the kind of news she wanted to hear. They had one purpose only, Bridie felt, and that was to get Rory back to Ireland to join the party. She glanced through it briefly, then gripped the pages with excitement. George Wyndham, the Irish Chief Secretary, was going to bring about sweeping measures in land reform, he wrote. The power of the landlords was going to end in Ireland forever.

Recommendations had been made to Wyndham by a group of Members of Parliament, tenant representatives and other landlords, after a serious incident on a Lord Treyne's estate where paraffin had been poured on the thatched roof of a cottage, causing serious injury to the occupants. Come home next year, he added, and help us build the biggest bonfire ever seen in Donegal. We're going to celebrate the end of the landlords power in our land.

When Rory drove up to the house later on, she rushed out to greet him. His face lit up at her welcome. Since Ronald McFadden wrote that letter he had been feeling uneasy. He had asked Kevin O'Hara to pass on the news about their marriage and hoped that would be an end to it. Bridie never mentioned McFadden's name again. He hoped she had forgotten him entirely.

# Chapter Twenty Four

'He's coming over, Rosha.' Patrick came into the room and held up a letter. 'Rory's coming over in July for the celebration with Bridie and the daughter. Do you think we could put them up here? Grace hasn't got room over at Iskaglen.'

'Of course we can. Mary Anne will be company for Damian.'

'I'll write and invite him so. We'll make a great party of it. And thank God there'll be something to celebrate.'

Nellie carried the good news to her mother. Sunshine warmed her back as she crossed the glen, and the air was drenched with the sweet scent of wallflowers growing around the crumbling walls which had once been part of someone's home. Never had she seen such spring weather, as if God was bestowing every grace on them this year. Soon, Patrick said, this land would belong to the people again – the curse of the English landlord gone forever. It was unbelievable.

Three neighbours who had returned to their homes in Iskaglen sat on stools crocheting under the fuchsia hedge outside her mother's cottage. The spoke softly in Gaelic as their fingers weaved intricate patterns in lace.

'Where's Mam?' she called to them.

'Killin' herself because Bridie's comin' home at last.'

'Oh, she's heard then?'

Grace walked briskly out of the house with a bucket of whitewash in her hand. ''Tis yerself, Nellie. I'll wet the tea so.'

298

'Aye, do that, and give me the bucket if yer planning to whitewash.'

'If yer going to give me a hand, get out of them clothes.'

Nellie followed her mother indoors. The walls were gleaming white. Some of Bridie's prosperity had brought extra comforts to the little home. Two easy-chairs stood before the hearth and a thick woolly rug (a present last Christmas) lay before the fire. A bit of a nuisance to Grace because she had to remember to whip it up every time she left the cottage in case sparks fell from the fire. The hens, who stepped in daintily every morning to remind her it was near their feeding time, were terrified of the alien spectacle lying on the stone floor and shrieked furiously at each other if they were accidently pushed near it in the hustle to claim fallen crumbs from the table.

'I'll sleep in the loft with Mary Anne. Bridie and Rory can have my bed,' Grace told Nellie.

'Rosha's invited them to stay at Garton, Mam.'

Knowing Bridie's feelings about Rosha, Grace said shortly, 'No, Nellie, she won't go there. Bridie will come to her own home. You'll see.'

She was right. Bridie would not hear of staying at Garton.

Patrick and Grace travelled to Lisdare to meet the boat and they all returned to Garton for a meal. Rosha's children, Damian and Deirdre, were shy of the visitors. Mary Anne, who had recently started attending school, was forward, Rosha thought.

'Show Mary Anne your toys,' she suggested to her son.

When Damian drew back, Mary Anne put out her hand and with a smile and said, 'Show me.'

Deirdre, frightened that she was going to lose her brother to this girl with dancing ringlets, grabbed Damian's other hand and the three children left the room.

Nellie glowed with happiness. Not a bit of change in our Bridie, she thought. Rory was different. He spoke well and dressed like a gentleman. He treated her sister as if she were a piece of china. Bridie, who had fought her way from Mrs O'Sullivan's kitchen to great heights, God love her.

'Would you like to see the pottery?' Rosha suggested to Bridie when Patrick began to explain to Rory how the new Land Act was going to work out.

'The landlords are raising no objections to the proposed bill because the government is giving them a free gift of twelve per cent for every property they sell to the tenants on their estates. For instance, if Grace's little place was valued at one hundred pounds, Catalong would get a bonus of twelve pounds.'

'That's one man who deserves it, I suppose, for he's surely given back to the people more than he could afford.'

'That's a fact, Rory.'

'So you tell me that the landlords will have to sell the land to their tenants? And the government will advance the money to the tenants who will repay the loan by annual instalments?'

'That's right, over a number of years. Some of the people might be paying even less than the landlords were demanding for rent.'

'God bless George Wyndham,' Rory said fervently. 'It's the most sweeping measure of land reform ever introduced.'

Patrick paused and looked at his friend. 'Now that we're getting the ownership of the land, the next step will be our country. It'll be an uphill struggle.'

'I'm not coming back, Patrick,' Rory said quietly, wanting once and for all to make his intentions clear.

'You're needed, man. Men like you are few and far between. Glasgow sounds a terrible place. You'll change your mind, surely?'

But Rory knew in his heart that his work for Ireland was over.

As the sun sank beneath the western hills, Patrick Murphy ceremoniously lit the massive bonfire which had been building up for days on the hill of Slievegar. He had intended making a long speech but he got no further then reminding the people that the year 1903 would go down in history as the year

Landlordism had been abolished in Ireland. At that point someome thrust a flaming torch into his hand and he had no choice but to light the fire.

When the flames leapt joyfully through the dry wood, the crowds gave a tumultuous cheer. Then the music-makers gathered, prepared to play long into the night. Later, the wine of the mountain − poteen − would be passed around among the older men, while the younger ones danced and sang. Having chosen their partners, some would slip away into the shadows. Friends greeted each other joyfully. Everyone looked happy. Some felt bewildered, almost unbelieving that such good fortune was coming their way. Mary Anne, standing beside her mother, was silenced by the spectacle and shy in the presence of the people who welcomed her parents back to Ireland. When Rosha and Damian joined them, Mary Anne took Damian's hand and asked her mother if they could go for a little walk.

'Not too far, pet,' Bridie warned.

'I'll go with them,' Patrick offered.

When he returned with the two children, he was accompanied by Edmund Catalong and his daughter, Victoria. Everyone looked at them in surprised silence until Rosha said as naturally as she could: 'Hello, Edmund. How nice to see you on the hill.' She bent down to the little girl. 'Victoria, I used to play with your daddy when I was a bit older than you are now.'

Ah, she managed that well, Nellie thought, her face stiff with alarm.

'Come down to the house and have a drink, Mr Catalong,' Patrick invited. 'It's a special day. And may I say I know of no other landlord who has the right to be here this day.'

'Thank you for saying so and for your invitation which I would like to accept.' Edmund smiled. 'Victoria saw the fire from Merifield and insisted on coming to see it.'

'Edmund, you've met Bridie,' Rosha said casually. 'This is her husband, Rory Donavan.'

Rory and Bridie felt very uneasy meeting Edmund Catalong. She remembered the day he had pulled her out of the bay, half-drowned. Rory's memories were darker. He had shot this man's father. The enormity of the act − though at the time he felt it was justified in defence of the people – stuck him more forcibly than ever before. He had no wish to drink with the son of the man whom he had executed.

'Nellie,' Bridie said hurriedly to her sister, 'would you take Mary Anne down to the house? There are some people here we haven't greeted yet.'

Damian caught Victoria's hand. She was like the little princess, with the long golden hair in the story that Mummy read to him. Mary Anne pulled away from Nellie and caught Damien's other hand. As they all walked down the hill, Nellie thought, Dear God protect these children and let them take different paths in life. They must never become too close.

Back at Garton, Nellie and Grace went into the kitchen and began to cut slices of cake to serve with the drinks. Rosha left the two men in the dining-room discussing what the new Land Act would mean to the farmers and went to join the children in the parlour where they were taking turns to sit on the rocking-horse which Patrick had made for Deirdre. A half-hour later she was laughing, enjoying their play, when the men came into the room. It was time for Victoria to go home, Edmund said. Damian looked at him curiously.

'Victoria says you're a soldier. My daddy's a farmer.'

Nellie came to the door. 'Patrick, the priest's called about the dance in the hall tomorrow night. He wonders if ye could spare him a minute.'

'Well, Damian,' Edmund said when Patrick went out, 'I wish I was a farmer too. But I am a soldier and have to leave for India in a few weeks' time.'

He looked at Rosha and she knew that the words were meant for her.

'Where's that?' the little boy asked.

'It's a country a long way away. But I'll come back to Slievegar again, for this is where I want to be.'

When Patrick returned to the room, Rosha caught the swift fleeting, but vulnerable glance that seemed to search between her and Edmund, as though seeking some truth. Though she felt alarmed, she knew that the scene before him could not reveal anything. Edmund's arm was around Deirdre who, with great excitement, showed off her ability to speed the movement of the rocking-horse. She herself was tightening the ribbon on Victoria's hair. When Rosha glanced again at her husband he was smiling at Deirdre, then at her, sharing their love for the child who was recklessly showing off on the wooden horse.

The following evening Patrick took Nellie and his sister to the celebration dance at the hall. Only Rosha and Paddy were left at home. She felt restless and unhappy because Edmund was leaving for India; it would be years before he returned. If only they could have a short time on their own to say goodbye.

'Paddy,' she said impulsively, 'will you stay indoors and mind the children? I want to go for a walk.'

'Surely, Rosha. 'Tis a fine night and maybe I'll take a dander m'self when you get back.'

A warm wind tossed strands of hair across her face as she climbed to the hermit's stone where she sat and wished with all her heart that Edmund would come. Never in her life had she longed for anything so much. She could bear the thought of the long lonely years if only she could see him just once more.

Rosha had no idea how long she had been sitting there when the sound of a horse came from down below. She dropped her face in her hands and made the old childhood wish – if you don't look you will get your wish. Then he was beside her.

'I hoped,' he said, slipping off the animal's back, 'but did not think it could possibly happen this time. Where's your husband?'

'Everyone but Paddy has gone to the parish hall for the dance.'

They stood close together on the flat rock, then he took her hand and they walked slowly up into the blue mist stealing down the hill.

The years following the Wyndham Land Act completely changed the lives of people living in Iskaglen and Slievegar and throughout Ireland. Men no longer in fear of the landlord or bully bailiff, tilled their own land and prospered. On the hills the shepherd boys herded their fathers' sheep and sang melodious tunes or played on their bamboo whistles.

Sometimes Grace Boyce thought of the lonely shepherd and said a prayer for his soul, but sadness in her life was a thing of the past. All over the glen cabins were rising from the ground again like the flowers in spring. Down the road on the spot where their old home was, Rory Donavan had a fine house built for their summer holidays. His mother came back from Dilford after falling out with her brother so she and Grace went back to their old neighbourly ways.

The only shadow in Grace's life was the enmity that existed between Bridie and Rosha; it had always been there but now it seemed to be ten times worse. It was a mystery to Grace why Rosha objected to Damian and Mary Anne playing together. Every summer when Rory and Bridie returned to Iskaglen, Mary Anne ran across to Garton and always returned complaining. As Grace was thinking about these things, Rosha, with Nellie sitting beside her in the trap, drove into the yard.

'Mam,' Nellie called out, 'me and Rosha are doing some shopping in Dilford. Wid ye like to come?'

'Indeed no, for I have a pile of work to do.'

'Told ye so,' Nellie murmured to Rosha. 'Ye canna prise her away from the place these days.'

'She's content.'

When they arrived back in Slievegar later that afternoon, they saw some people running down the shore road. Damian, who had just got back from his college in Lisdare, where he was a weekly boarder, ran out of the paddock. Rosha stopped the trap.

'Mother, something must have happened down by the bay. I'll go and see.'

Just then the coach from Merifield Manor came along the road but was unable to pass. Alice Catalong looked out through the window with an impatient expression. Damian took the reins from his mother's hand and led the pony and trap close to the hedge.

'Sorry, m'lady,' Nellie called down. Her ladyship did not acknowledge the apology. She was frowning and staring hard at Damian.

'This is Damian Murphy,' Nellie said hurriedly, 'my

mistress's son.' Nellie gestured towards Rosha but Alice Catalong went on staring at the youth.

Shocked, she withdrew her head and thought, My God, he must be Edmund's son ... the same colour eyes and expression. She tapped on the panel of the carriage and said curtly, 'Drive on.'

Furious, Damian said: 'How could Victoria Catalong have such a terrible mother?' He looked at Rosha. 'She just ignored you.'

'I didn't realise you knew the girl.' Rosha spoke slowly, alarmed at the little scene that had just taken place. She wondered what Edmund's wife was thinking. Though Damian's hair was dark he had in recent years looked increasingly like his father.

'Her father's cousin, Colonel Fulton, lives in that big house next to our college,' Damian told her. 'When we're allowed out to shop in town we sometimes meet Victoria and her friends in the tearooms.'

Sweet God, Nellie thought clutching her bag, his half-sister – and Rosha's worried sick about Mary Anne. A frightened shout came from the beach then a man called: 'They can't get the boat out of the whirlpool. Not enough power behind the oars.'

Damian leapt up on the hedge. 'It's the castle boat,' he said over his shoulder. 'Victoria's cousins keep taking it out and they don't understand about the whirlpool. I warned them ...' He tore down the field.

'My son's been making friends that I did not know about,' Rosha said slowly.

'Like yerself, pet, if ye remember!'

At the Garton gates, she said to Nellie: 'Take the trap on to the house. I must go down there and see what's happened.'

The sight that met Rosha's eyes on the shore was confusing and harrowing. Two strong swimmers waded up from the bay, one carrying a girl, the other a boy; at the same time Damian struggled out of the water and rushed over to the man who laid the body of Victoria Catalong gently on the sand. The boy was revived but his companion was not. Rosha saw the anguish on her son's face. At that moment people from

305

Merifield rushed across the shore and Damian was pushed aside. She put her arm around him and led him home. He was shivering, frightened and shocked.

The only words he spoke while a hot bath was being prepared were: 'Victora was a good sport.'

It had been three years since Rosha had seen Edmund. Now she heard he was coming home from India on compassionate leave. He did not get back to Slievegar until weeks after the funeral; he was coming to take his wife to London to stay with her elderly parents. As Patrick was away from home that week, Rosha took her customary stroll up the hill. By the time she reached the hermit's stone the sky was darkening and the first stars appearing; then the moon came sliding in and out between the clouds, as though playing a game. A single sweet piercing birdsong was followed by a twittering of contentment as birds snuggled into their nests.

Footsteps fell on the path below. She jumped to her feet and waited. Edmund approached slowly. She held out her arms. 'Oh, my love, I'm so sorry.' He didn't speak but she could feel his tears on her face.

'Victoria,' he said at last, 'was unlike ... she was a spirited girl.'

'I know, my son said.'

'Your son tried to save her.'

At that moment Rosha wanted with all her heart to break the vow she had made at Damian's birth and shock him out of his grief by saying, 'our son' but he went on talking about his dead daughter.

'There is so little left,' he said with bitterness. 'The child made our marriage work.'

'Edmund, your hands are cold, it's getting chilly. Come on down to Garton and I'll make you a hot punch. Patrick's at a meeting in Lisdare.'

'No, I'd better get back to Merifield. God, Rosha, it's good to talk to you again. Can you manage to come tomorrow evening? We leave the next day.'

Rosha did not see Edmund again because on the following day Dan Murphy dropped dead while he was spraying wash on the potato crop. Willie fetched Patrick back from Lisdare.

After the will was read Patrick's grief was somewhat assuaged because Dan, despite all his promises to Maria, his wife, left her just enough to live on comfortably, and her son, Ruairi, only a small holding, instead of inheriting everything as Maria had always assumed.

'Patrick, why did he leave you so much money as well as part of the land? After all, you have Garton.'

He walked over to the window and pulled back the curtain as though what he had to say was revealed in a tableau out on the lawn. 'I think I'm beginning to understand. Remember, it was your father that Maria wanted to marry and not Dan Murphy. When Sean O'Neill did not seem in a hurry to make her mistress of Garton she, getting desperate, accepted Dan and built up a hatred against Sean. Rosha, I know this will shock you ... my father suspected that Maria had something to do with the fire at Garton all those years ago.'

'Oh, no —'

'I have no reason to believe or disbelieve his suspicions but I certainly had proof that she informed the barracks at Lisdare on the night Sean was arrested. Everyone was of the opinion that all those months in prison was the cause of his early death. My father grieved for him but he felt guilt as well — guilt for Maria's actions. I believe' he said slowly, 'that my father wanted to return something to Garton which would eventually benefit his grandchildren, Deirdre and Damian. So, Rosha,' he came over and put his arm around her shoulder, 'now we have a much larger estate.'

'Too big, with the master seldom at home!'

He gave one of his rare smiles. 'Perhaps I'd better go to the hiring fair and find a lad to train to help run the farm. Someone near Damian's age.' Patrick was delighted at Damian's increasing interest in the land.

Feeling a warm affection for this quiet strong man who truly only loved the country he was prepared to die for, she said anxiously: 'Patrick, when you're away from home, take care, won't you? Ireland is unsettled again. I don't think any country is worth a man's life.'

'Ah, Rosha —'

# Chapter Twenty Five

With the outbreak of the 1914 war Patrick's party split when his friend Redmond pledged to support England in the war for the defence of small nations. This resulted in a large number of Irishmen joining the British army, which outraged Patrick who was helping to plan an insurrection. Every time he returned to Garton over the next couple of years he spent his time organising groups of volunteers in preparation for an uprising. On one of his last visits he told Rosha that he was going to make a will.

'Apart from yourself,' he said, 'I'm leaving the bulk of my money to Deirdre. Damian will inherit the land.' Then he went on to say with complete frankness that he was also investing a certain amount of money in Ireland. When the rebellion eventually took place in Dublin in 1916, Rosha realised that her husband's investment was for buying arms.

A few weeks before the rebellion, word reached Slievegar that Edmund Catalong had been killed in France. Nellie would never forget how they heard that tragic news. It was one Sunday at Mass when the priest got up and startled the congregation by offering prayers for the soul of Major Catalong who had been reported killed in action in France. Old Father Gibson would have broken the news in another way but this younger man who replaced him was cool and businesslike about everything. But then maybe Father Gibson would have thought twice about praying for the soul of a Protestant!

When they arrived back at the house that Sunday Rosha

went straight up to her room, changed her clothes and went riding in the hills, her face stricken and colourless. Up there, Nellie suspected, she made a grave of her sorrow and every day since took her grieving heart to it and maybe shed silent tears.

The sound of footsteps going around the house made Rosha lift her head from the ledger she was working on. Usually Deirdre assisted her with the accounts but she and Damien had been invited to Edith Houston's to spend part of the Easter holiday in Lisdare. Though her sister had died years ago, Edith still lived in the large house surrounded by several young relations. Rosha hoped fervently that Damien would be attracted to one of the girls and weaken his attachment to Bridie Donavan's daughter.

She went over to the window, moved the large bowl of primroses and looked out. These were troubled times in the country and, since the unsuccessful rebellion in Dublin on Easter day, men were fleeing from the capital. No word from Patrick. Every night they all knelt down in the kitchen and said the rosary for his safe return. The knock on the front door startled her. Only strangers or the Protestant minister came to that door.

Nellie hurried down the hall and pulled back the heavy bolts. Two men stood outside.

'I would like to speak to Mrs Patrick Murphy,' one said.

'Come down to the kitchen and I'll fetch her, sir.'

'I wish to speak to her alone,' he replied. 'My friend will wait in the kitchen.' He turned to his companion and began to make sign language to which the other grunted a reply.

Wide-eyed, Nellie made for the room. 'Rosha, love, there's a quare pair outside. A fine-lookin' man in a green uniform and a deaf and dumb mute, God bless the mark.'

'Send in the man in uniform,' Rosha said slowly, a coldness spreading through her body. A man of medium height with dark hair heavily streaked with grey came into the room and shut the door behind him. Without introducing himself he held out his hand.

'No, I won't sit down, Mrs Murphy, my companion and I have a long way to travel before dawn. I'm afraid I'm the bearer of bad news. It should have reached you sooner but I wanted to come personally to see you.'

Rosha clutched the back of her chair. 'Patrick?'

'Yes,' he said gently. 'He was killed on Easter Day, may God rest his soul. Many of my friends were killed too but ...' He swallowed with emotion and she saw the grief on his face, 'Patrick, though many years younger than myself, was the friend I valued most. He was a courageous man, Mrs Murphy. Tell his children that they have reason to be very proud of their father.' He then gave her information about the arrangements for the burial and left the house.

Rosha and Nellie wept together in the kitchen until Paddy, Willie and Dinny, the new farm hand, came in from a ceildhe.

'Rosha,' Willie said immediately, 'I'll go o'er and tell the wife that I'm goin' to Lisdare to fetch the youngsters. I'll have the pair of them back wi' you as soon as possible.'

'It's too late, Willie,' Rosha said gratefully, 'tomorrow morning will do. The roads are being patrolled after dark and it's not safe with the trouble in the country.'

'I'll be off at dawn so. The children should know wi'out delay that their father was kilt.'

The two women looked at each other and shared the same thought: Damien's father was killed in the battlefields of France weeks ago.

Months passed before Rosha went riding in the hills again. She felt it would be a betrayal of Patrick's memory. In the hills, she sometimes felt that she was trying to find the spirit of Edmund; the hermit's rest was his memorial stone, the place where they sat and talked. Deep in her heart she could not accept Edmund's death, but realised she was foolishly denying the evidence that surely must have been there for the War Office to announce it officially.

Life at Garton changed in many ways after Patrick's death. Damian, with the responsibility of owning so much land, told Rosha that he wanted to leave college and take a course in farm management at the new place in Lisdare. She was delighted at his enthusiasm. Dinny, he suggested, should be hired on a permanent arrangement and paid a higher salary. Also, with a view to the chap getting married one day, a cottage should be built on a half-acre of ground. A young wife would be a help to Nellie.

'Are you sure about Dinny?' Rosha asked Damian. She thought he was a handsome-looking rascal, his dark flashing eyes always teasing Deirdre.

'I'm sure,' he said confidently. 'Dinny does every job thoroughly. Father noticed that last time he was home. 'And,' he smiled, 'Dinny is very funny, he makes me laugh. We need some laughter around Garton after all the sadness.'

'Aye,' Nellie agreed, 'that lad has a way wi' him.'

'Another thing, Mother, I think your workshop should be extended. You need more space.'

Rosha laughed. 'You'll be running through your inheritance, darling.'

'No, I'm going to increase it. And Nellie's going to invest the money Father left her in Garton!'

That made them all laugh. Nellie had never in her life been so surprised and delighted as when Patrick's will was read and it was revealed that he had left her twenty pounds. Paddy and Willie received ten pounds each. All the resentment she had felt about Patrick's neglect of Garton was forgotten and now she only recalled the good-natured boy of long ago. When Damian left the kitchen, she said thoughtfully to Rosha: 'He'll be landing a wife on us one of these days before we know!' And Rosha, thinking of his attraction to Mary Anne Donavan, turned away, her eyes filled with fear.

The stream behind the workshop brought a coolness to the hot summer's day. Rosha loved this place where the water ran through the land to the river. As she sat down under a bush of dogwood, which was starred with a mass of white flowers, a fragrance rose from the bruised clover on the ground. By the edge of the stream a blue butterfly fluttered around, then lighted close to the forget-me-nots. She thought of the story Nellie had told her that afternoon about Alice Catalong marrying Edmund's cousin, Colonel Fulton, who had inherited the vast Catalong estate.

Sitting there peacefully by the stream, Rosha thought, too, of the dream that came frequently in her sleep these days, haunting her with memories, stirring her heart with remembered love and pain. Always the same dream: Edmund laughing and pulling her through the meadow.

'Damian . . .' A voice broke the silence, shattering her. It was Mary Anne. The Donavans had returned from Scotland again.

About an hour later, Rosha was standing at the workshop door, comparing two shades of colour, when the two young people came into the yard. They both looked flushed and happy. Damian quickly dropped his arm from around Mary Anne's waist and gave his mother a challenging look. Mary Anne looked uncomfortable at the expression of disapproval on Rosha's face.

'I hope,' Rosha said to her icily, 'you realise that Damian isn't free to run off somewhere every day when you come here on holiday?' She turned to her son. 'This is a busy time on the farm.'

'Mother,' he said protestingly, 'I am aware of my duties.'

Mary Anne turned and ran off towards the kitchen. Damian went to the stable, his face dark with anger. Feeling defeated, Rosha was about to turn away when she heard Bridie calling her.

'Just a minute, Rosha, I want to talk with you.'

How confident she has become, Rosha thought. Grace had told her that Bridie had a successful fashion show in Glasgow and Edinburgh and her designs in linen were becoming very popular for summer wear.

'Why,' Bridie asked bluntly, 'do you object to the friendship between our children? Every time Mary Anne comes to Slievegar you find an excuse to separate them.'

'I think they spend too much time together,' Rosha said lamely.

'You think my daughter isn't good enough for your son, don't you?' Bridie's eyes sparkled with anger. 'She has a lot of friends in Glasgow. Mary Annie is very popular. But your son is the one she seems to prefer.'

'Isn't she rather young to have so much freedom?'

'No younger than you when you trailed after Edmund

312

Catalong. Then,' Bridie added spitefully, and out of character, 'you married Patrick Murphy who you couldn't be
bothered with.'

Nellie, who had heard the raised voices, came over to them.
She lifted her hand and slapped her sister's bare arm. 'Will
ye *shut* up!'

Rosha went into the workshop, sat down, and covering her
face with her hands, began to weep. What was she going to
do? The situation was hopeless, impossible. Mary Anne was
Thomas Catalong's daughter and Damian his grandson.

'All the success is going to her head. Dry yer eyes, love,
I want to talk to you.'

'Nellie, I should have handled it better. Lord, I'm so
worried.'

'Rosha, now listen to me. Edmund and Patrick are both
dead. ''Tis time a serious situation was faced for that's what
it's developing into. Tell Bridie the truth and let her handle
Mary Anne. Poor weans, I feel sorry for them for they can
never be wed. Something *must* be done soon.'

'What about Damian? All these years he's believed Patrick
was his father. He would be so shocked.'

'Shocked that his mother lay with another man ... a
man whose father nearly destroyed the people,' Nellie said
bluntly.

'Nellie!' Rosha protested.

'Begod, if I don't do something to shock ye, the situation
will get worse. Do you think Damian will keep away from
Mary Anne because you disapprove? He's a strong-minded
young man.'

'He's going to Lisdare for a wedding, and afterwards for
an interview at the agricultural college. They won't have all
that much time together. He's staying with Miss Houston.
I'm hoping he'll meet someone there and this thing with
Bridie's daughter will end.'

Nellie walked to the door. 'There's no talkin' to ye, is
there?' she said impatiently. 'The thing between you and
Edmund Catalong didin end, did it? Maybe your son has
the same kind of feeling for my niece.'

Over the following months Nellie nagged Rosha to tell

313

Damian about his father. 'The boy will have to be told soon. Prepare him before Mary Anne returns in the summer.'

And each time Rosha replied with a feeling of panic. 'Nellie, I must chose the right time.'

'If yer hoping he'll meet someone, ye can forget it.'

'Yes, that's what I am hoping.' The thought of telling Damian the truth about his birth filled Rosha with dread. Perhaps he would turn against her, hate her for the deception.

'Letters are passing between them.'

'Letters?' Rosha said in alarm. 'When? How?'

'Mary Anne sends them to m'mother, who's heartily sorry for the youngsters.'

'Grace hasn't mentioned it.'

'Huh! Is she likely to?'

At Christmas, Rosha did not receive the usual greetings card from Bridie and Rory. A letter was enclosed in Nellie's.

'They're takin' an Easter holiday this year, Rosha.' She put out her hand. 'There's less time than you think.'

They looked at each other for a few minutes, then Rosha said with a feeling of anxiety and, strangely, relief, 'I'll speak to him in the new year ... at the right moment.'

'Aye, do that, love. I'm getting too old to be burdened with this thing any longer.'

A cold silence lay across the woods; the hard frost held the ground captive and beneath its icy web indistinguishable plants lay curled and bruised. Rosha pulled the fur collar of her coat around her neck and approached the stream where the water shivered in the cold. To her delight she saw clustered under the protection of the ditch, a clump of delicate trefoil leaves of wood sorrel – a promise of spring. What, she wondered, her pleasure suddenly diminishing, would spring hold for her?

She returned to the workshop where Paddy was piling wood and peat on the fire. When the kettle began to sing he wet the tea and handed her a mug. Clasping the hot drink, she sat down beside him and in a companionable silence they watched the flames rollicking up the chimney. Then

314

they spoke about their work and an order to be delivered to Dilford.

'I must get it ready, Paddy. Hope the weather will improve so that you'll be able to travel safely on the road.'

Paddy spent most of his waking hours in the workshop. At this time of year the fires, oil stoves and lamps needed a lot of attention. Frequently he spent the night on a pile of rugs before the fire. When Rosha finished her work and went over to the house he took a walk around the farmyard and checked on the livestock, all snug and well fed in their stalls. He looked up at the sky bright with a million stars. Aye, 'tis goin' to be a dang cold night, he thought, knocking icicles off the drinking trough. He stamped his feet on the cobble stones and hobbled over to the comfort of the workshop again. Just as he was about to pull the door behind him, a short burst of light appeared away down the drive. The wee folk lighting their fire, he chuckled, but hurriedly shut the door.

A sound of footsteps fell outside, followed by a knock. Too startled to move Paddy stood there, his mouth wide open. The door was pushed, not aggressively, almost apologetically. A man came inside with a hesitant movement, yet not with the servility of a tramp.

'Forgive me if I've startled you,' he said, in a voice that had a faraway familiar ring.

Paddy immediately noticed the long warm coat and the fine leather boots. He sighed. Ah, me, a gent who's horse has become unshod and I'll be expected to do something about it.

'Paddy,' the man said, 'I don't wish to alarm you ... it's me, Edmund Catalong.'

Frightened, the old man stumbled backwards. 'Ah, Jayus, sir, sure yer dead ... ye went down in battle.' Trembling, he stretched his arm and turned up the lamp.

'No, I'm not a ghost, Paddy.' Edmund smiled. 'Here, take my hand.'

The hand that clasped Paddy's was cold but not from the grave. 'May I sit down? I've been walking for hours.'

Still shaking, though aware that it was indeed a flesh and blood man that stood before him, Paddy pushed the stool over the floor. 'Ye'll need a hot drink, sir.'

'I'd be most grateful. Then if you'd go across to the house and tell Nellie to come here? It would be best if I spoke to her first. Rosha ... is she well?'

'Aye, she's well.' Paddy handed him a mug of hot tea and scuttled out of the door across to the kitchen where Nellie was washing dishes.

'Nellie Boyce, will ye get o'er the yard quick? Major Catalong, Rosha's friend, has just appeared.'

Nellie gave a shriek of nervous laughter. 'Begod, ye've been at the bottle, ye oul scoundrel!'

'God strike me dead, Nellie Boyce, 'tis himself that's in it. He wants to talk t'ye afore he sees Rosha.'

She stared at him. 'As God's yer honour?'

He nodded. ''Tis himself.'

Nellie went slowly through the workshop door. Edmund rose to his feet and held out his hand. 'Surely you don't think I'm a ghost, too, Nellie, do you?' He picked up the tin mug. 'Remember? You gave me tea in it that first time we met in the corn field.'

'Sir, what's the meaning of it? I'm shocked to death.'

'Nellie, listen, my death was wrongly reported. I want you to speak to Rosha. Tell her I'm here then take me to her.'

'She's down in the parlour. Come over to the kitchen.'

Rosha was on the floor packing all Patrick's papers into a trunk, a job she had put off doing for months. Nellie knelt down beside her and in a few words told her about Edmund. Rosha didn't move. She remained on her knees, stunned with shock.

Edmund paused by the door, said her name, then rushed across the room and took her in his arms. Speechless, she allowed herself to be led to the settee. When she turned to him she saw the harsh scar across his forehead and signs of the illness that had nearly killed him.

'I'm sorry not to have given you some warning, Rosha. I'll explain later.'

'How did you get here?'

'I travelled yesterday from England with my Aunt Madeline. She's staying in Dilford. I took a sidecar from the hotel. When the horse slipped on the road I told the driver to return.'

'You must be tired out.'

He smiled. 'I am rather. Just give me a moment to rest then I'll tell you everything.'

The sudden shock of seeing him began to ease. 'First, you must have some hot soup and food.' She rose, took a bottle of whiskey and a glass from the cupboard and moved a table beside him. 'I'll be back in a minute.'

Edmund poured himself a drink, then for the first time in months let his thoughts drift back to that terrible day in the trenches when he removed his jacket and wrapped it around an injured fellow officer who was shivering with fever. It was an impulsive action but when the bombardment suddenly came again, he lost his identity and almost his senses. Afterwards, he vaguely remembered trying to dig himself out of a sea of mud to a waste land where men and animals' limbs were scattered on the putrefying earth. His one lucid thought at that moment was to get away from the brutality of this inhuman war, this perversion of life. Edmund held the glass of whiskey to his lips and drank deeply, recalling his desperate fear when he dragged himself past skeletal trees, away from the man-made hell.

He felt the touch of Rosha's hand and smelt the bowl of rich soup.

'Did you fall asleep, Edmund?'

He opened his eyes and let words follow the stream of his thoughts. 'After I stumbled half-blinded from the battlefield, Rosha, two monks found me and carried me to their monastry where they nursed me back to health. Physically I became stronger but mentally I was a wreck. When they got in touch with my unit I was sent back to England to an officers' home in Surrey. Afterwards I went to my aunt's house in London.'

Nellie came in, spread a white cloth on the table and placed some food on it. 'Thank you, Nellie.' He turned to Rosha. 'Could I possibly beg your hospitality for the night?'

She covered his hand with hers. 'Of course, Edmund. Nellie has already lit a fire in one of the spare rooms and the bed's being aired. You can stay here as

317

long as you like. When do you have to return to your unit?'

'I hope,' he said with some bitterness but not conviction, 'that they forget all about me.' He gave a little smile. 'Perhaps they will find a cosy job for me in the War Office!' He gripped her hand. 'Rosha, the reason I returned here was because I read of Patrick's death in London. I was helping my aunt in a centre for destitute men when I came on a pile of old newspapers and read about the uprising in Dublin. It was an Irish paper with a list of the men who had been killed and those condemned to death. I am very sorry. Patrick was too young to die.'

They were silent for a moment, then he spoke about his wife. 'As you probably know she married my cousin, Henry Fulton, after my death was reported. According to my aunt they went to India where he is working on a major recruiting campaign with the Indian army. Alice is expecting a child in five months' time. God knows how she took the news when the War Office informed her that I was alive. I wish I could have spared her that unhappiness. After Victoria's death we were not happy together.'

Rosha was about to ask him how the War Office could have made such a serious mistake in reporting his death when he put down his fork and knife and covered his face with his hands. 'My God, what a mess I've made of my life.'

She put her arms around him. 'Don't Edmund – '

'You know, I will die and no one will bear my name. Though God knows,' he said contemptuously, 'I'm not even entitled to that.'

'What do you mean?'

'I was not Catalong's son. According to my aunt my mother fell in love with her father's agent, a young Irishman of humble background. Though she was expecting his child they were forbidden to marry and a bargain was struck with Catalong who was a friend of the family.'

'Bargain?' Rosha repeated, his words releasing her of the burden she had carried for years.

'He was offered the Merifield estate if he married my mother and fathered her child. No wonder he didn't like me!'

318

There was a knock at the door and Damian came in. 'Mother, I'm back.'

'Come in, Damian. Do you remember Captain Catalong? He was reported killed.'

The youth gave a wide grin. 'Goodness, sir, I've heard lots of stories like that but didn't believe them. Did you ...'

'Edmund's very tired, darling. Tomorrow.'

'Of course. Can I do anything to help?'

She smiled. 'Help Nellie to keep a good fire burning in his room, your grandfather's old bedroom.'

When Damian closed the door behind him, Rosha pushed the table aside and sat beside Edmund. 'A little while ago you said that when you die ...' She paused, trying to find the right words. 'Edmund, you have a son. Damian is your son. Patrick,' she added sadly, 'didn't know. Only Nellie and I will carry this secret to our grave. Now you. Damian loved Patrick.' When she raised her head and looked at him, his eyes were filled with joy.

Three days later Edmund's aunt drove up to Garton. Rosha recognised Madeline at once; the same friendly expression, but with the advancing years she had put on a lot of weight. Madeline held up her hand and laughed.

'Don't look so alarmed, dear Edmund. No letter has arrived from London yet. Your leave is still safe! I simply came to see if Rosha wants to get rid of you.'

Edmund put his arm around her. 'Aunt Madeline, she's not going to get rid of me this time.'

'Well, my dears, I do hope everything will work out for you.'

The three of them spent a happy day together. When it was time for the elderly woman to leave, she said to Rosha: 'He's looking so much better. I think he wants to stay with you until he's called back to London. Is that all right?' she asked anxiously. 'Your family — '

Rosha said simply: 'I wish he could stay here forever.'

Two days later she and Edmund were eating a late breakfast with Damian when there was an urgent knocking at the front door. To their surprise they heard his aunt's voice.

Edmund winced. 'Word must have come that I've got to

leave immediately. Why didn't she send one of the staff at the hotel with the letter?'

Madeline came into the room looking very pale. 'Edmund, my dear, I'm afraid there's some very sad news. I've had a letter from Henry Fulton. Alice ... Alice is dead. She caught some kind of virus in India.' Her eyes filled with tears. 'Poor girl ... He's now back in Lisdare and has asked me to go and see him.'

Edmund said immediately 'I'll go with you.'

She held up her hand. 'No, my dear, I don't think that would be a good idea just now.'

'Your aunt's right, Edmund,' Rosha said quietly.

'It would please me best if you stayed here with Rosha and fully recovered your health. Heaven knows how much longer you've got anyway.'

A few days later when Edmund and Damian went out riding, Rosha said to Nellie: 'Would you like to go down by the shore for a walk?'

'Aye, I could do with a breath of fresh air.'

The field by the shore, where crops of corn had been reaped in the past, was now lying fallow; next harvest it would be brightened again by a sea of waving corn and, later, stooks where children would come and play tig, following the custom of generations. As they walked along the beach, Rosha said, 'Nellie, I've got something important to tell you.'

'Aye,' Nellie said cautiously.

'It's about Damian and Mary Anne.' She paused. 'They're not related because Thomas Catalong was not Edmund's father.'

Nellie stood shock still, tears filling her eyes. 'I've been praying for a miracle.'

'I'll tell you the full story in a minute but there's something else I want you to know. Edmund and I are getting married when the time for mourning is over.'

'Better late than never, pet,' Nellie said briskly, but the tears were now streaming down her face.

'What do you think Damian will say?' Rosha asked anxiously.

'Huh!' Nellie dashed a hand across her face. 'I can tell ye what he *has* said, "I think my mother and Edmund Catalong

320

are falling in love. She always seemed so lonely, now she's different. Maybe she'll begin to understand how I feel about Mary Anne.'

The two women smiled, linked arms and walked over the shore.

You have been reading a novel published by Piatkus Books. We hope you have enjoyed it and that you would like to read more of our titles. Please ask for them in your local library or bookshop.

If you would like to be put on our mailing list to receive details of new publications, please send a large stamped addressed envelope (UK only) to:

Piatkus Books: Windmill Street
London W1P 1HF

PIATKUS

The sign of a good book